"AN

# HELLIONS OF HALSTEAD HALL

The "captivating" (*Booklist*) and "essential"
(*Library Journal*) new series from *New York Times*
and *USA Today* bestselling author

## SABRINA JEFFRIES

### Praise for
### *THE TRUTH ABOUT LORD STONEVILLE*

"Jeffries pulls out all the stops with a story combining her hallmark humor, poignancy and sensuality to perfection."
—*Romantic Times*

"The first in a captivating new Regency-set series by the always entertaining Jeffries, this tale has all of the author's signature elements: delectably witty dialogue, subtly named characters, and scorching sexual chemistry between two perfectly matched protagonists."
—*Booklist*

"Lively repartee, fast action, luscious sensuality, and an abundance of humor make the first installment of the Hellions of Halstead Hall essential for libraries."
—*Library Journal*

**This title is also available as an eBook**

"*The Truth About Lord Stoneville* has the special brand of wit and passion for which Sabrina Jeffries is recognized, where each enthralling scene will thoroughly capture your imagination."

—singletitles.com

"Sabrina Jeffries excels in the historical romance genre, and *The Truth About Lord Stoneville* is no exception. . . . Starts another excellent series of books which will alternatively have you laughing, crying and running the gamut of emotions. . . . Enjoy Oliver's transformation from unreformed rake to devoted husband, and I guarantee you will have a tear in your eye."

—Romance Reviews Today

**More acclaim for Sabrina Jeffries and the "warm, wickedly witty" (*Romantic Times*) novels in her national bestselling series**

**THE SCHOOL FOR HEIRESSES**

*WED HIM BEFORE YOU BED HIM*

"Includes all the sweet, sexy charm and lively action readers have come to expect, and true love triumphs over all obstacles. . . . Bravo to Jeffries."

—*Library Journal*

"An enchanting story brimming with touchingly sincere emotions and compelling scenarios. . . . An outstanding love story of emotional discoveries and soaring passions, with a delightful touch of humor plus suspense."

—singletitles.com

## DON'T BARGAIN WITH THE DEVIL

"The sexual tension crackles across the pages of this witty, deliciously sensual, secret-laden story. . . . Teases readers with hints of the long-awaited final chapter, *Wed Him Before You Bed Him*."

—*Library Journal*

## LET SLEEPING ROGUES LIE

"Consummate storyteller Jeffries pens another title in the School for Heiresses series that is destined to captivate readers with its sensuality and wonderfully enchanting plot."

—*Romantic Times* (4½ stars)

"Scandal, gossip, greed, and old enmities spice up the pot in this fast-paced sexy romp that bubbles over with Jeffries's trademark humor and spirit. . . . Sparkling dialogue, stirring sexual chemistry, and an engrossing story."

—*Library Journal*

## BEWARE A SCOT'S REVENGE

"Irresistible. . . . Larger-than-life characters, sprightly dialogue, and a steamy romance will draw you into this delicious captive/captor tale."

—*Romantic Times* (Top Pick)

"Exceptionally entertaining and splendidly sexy."

—*Booklist*

# Sabrina Jeffries

# A Hellion in Her Bed

POCKET STAR BOOKS

New York   London   Toronto   Sydney

Pocket Star Books
A Division of Simon & Schuster, Inc.
1230 Avenue of the Americas
New York, NY 10020

This book is a work of fiction. Names, characters, places, and incidents either are products of the author's imagination or are used fictitiously. Any resemblance to actual events or locales or persons, living or dead, is entirely coincidental.

First Pocket Star Books paperback edition October 2010

POCKET and colophon are registered trademarks of Simon & Schuster, Inc.

For information about special discounts for bulk purchases, please contact Simon & Schuster Special Sales at 1-866-506-1949 or business@simonandschuster.com.

The Simon & Schuster Speakers Bureau can bring authors to your live event. For more information or to book an event contact the Simon & Schuster Speakers Bureau at 1-866-248-3049 or visit our website at www.simonspeakers.com.

Illustration by Alan Ayers; handlettering by Iskra Johnson.

Manufactured in the United States of America

10  9  8  7  6  5  4  3  2  1

ISBN 978-1-4391-6754-0
ISBN 978-1-4391-6757-1 (ebook)

*To the two women who've been essential to my career from the beginning: Micki Nuding, otherwise known as Super Editor, and Pamela Gray Ahearn, aka Super Agent. I greatly appreciate your using your superpowers on my behalf!*

*And to Claudia Dain, Deb Marlowe, Liz Carlyle, Caren Crane Helms, and Rexanne Becnel—ya'll are the best friends an author could ever wish for. Thanks for always talking me off the ledge!*

# A
# Hellion in
# Her Bed

# *Prologue*

*Eton College*
*1806*

hirteen-year-old Lord Jarret Sharpe didn't want to spend the night in hell. He glanced out the coach window at the moon and shuddered. It must be nearly eight—they would arrive at Eton just when the boys were being locked into the Long Chamber. And hell would begin.

Tugging at his black cravat, he looked over at his grandmother. What could he say to make her change her mind? Six months ago, she'd carried them off to live with her in London—away from Halstead Hall, the best place in the whole world. She wouldn't take him to the brewery with her anymore. And she made him go to horrible school. All because of how Mother and Father had died.

A chill froze his soul and he felt like something had died in him, too. He couldn't eat, couldn't sleep . . . he couldn't even cry.

What kind of monster was he? Even his older brother Oliver had cried at the funeral. Jarret *wanted* to cry, but the tears wouldn't come. Not even late at night, during his nightmares about Father in the coffin.

He'd read the newspaper accounts of how the bullet had "shattered his lordship's face," and he couldn't forget that image. Bad enough that he was still haunted by seeing Mother, stiff and pale, lying in the casket with her snowy gown covering her bullet wound. Every time he thought of what Father's closed casket must mean, he could hardly breathe.

"Tell Oliver I expect him to write me every week, do you hear?" Gran said.

"Yes, ma'am." A sharp pain seized his chest. He'd always secretly believed he was Gran's favorite. But not anymore.

"And you, too, of course," she added, her voice softening.

"I don't want to go to school!" he burst out. When her eyebrows lifted, he added hastily, "I want to stay home. I want to go to the brewery every day with you."

"Jarret, my boy—"

"No, listen!" He mangled the mourning gloves in his lap as his words came out in a rush. "Grandfather said I'll inherit the brewery, and I already know everything about it. I know how the mash is made and how long to roast the barley. And I'm good at math—you said so yourself. I could learn to manage the books."

"I'm sorry, lad, but that's just not wise. It was wrong of me and your grandfather to encourage your interest in the brewery. Your mother didn't want that for you, and she was right. She married a marquess precisely because she wanted greater things for her children than mucking around some brewery."

"*You* muck around it," he protested.

"Because I have to. Because it's the primary support for you children until your parents' estate is settled."

"But I could help!" He yearned to be of some use to his family. Plumtree Brewery was far better than learning about who crossed the Nile and how to conjugate Latin; what good were those to him?

"You can help more by taking up a respectable profession, the kind you can only get at Eton. You were born to be someone far greater—a barrister or a bishop. I could even bear your being in the army or the navy, if that's what you wanted."

"I don't want to be a *soldier*," he said, appalled. The very thought of holding a pistol made his stomach roil. Mother had accidentally shot Father with a pistol. Then she had shot herself.

That part was confusing. Gran had told the newspaper that when Mother had seen Father dead by her hand, she got so sad that she shot herself. It didn't make sense to him, but Gran had ordered them not to speak of it again, so he didn't. Not even to ask questions.

It hurt something awful to think of Mother shooting herself. How could she have left the five of them alone? If she had lived, she might have let him have tutors at home, and he could have kept going to the brewery with Gran.

His throat tightened. It wasn't fair!

"Not a soldier, then," Gran said kindly. "Perhaps a barrister. With your sharp mind, you could be a fine barrister."

"I don't want to be a barrister! I want to run the brewery with you!"

Nobody at the brewery ever said nasty things to him. The brewers treated him like a man. They would never call Mother "the Halstead Hall Murderess." They wouldn't tell vile lies about Oliver.

When he realized Gran was watching him, he smoothed the frown from his face.

"Does this have to do with the fights you got into at

school?" Gran asked with worry in her voice. "Your headmaster said he's had to punish you nearly every week for fighting. Why is that?"

"I don't know," he mumbled.

A look of extreme discomfort crossed her face. "If the other boys are saying nasty things about your parents, I can speak to the headmaster—"

"No, damn it!" he cried, panicked that she could read him so well. She mustn't speak to the headmaster—that would only make everything worse!

"Do not curse at me. Come now, you can tell Gran. Is that why you don't want to go back to school?"

He stuck out his lower lip. "I just don't like studying, is all."

Her sharp gaze searched his face. "So you're lazy?"

He said nothing. Better to be branded a laggard than a tattletale.

She gave a heavy sigh. "Well, not liking to study is no reason to come home. Boys never like to study. But it *is* good for them. If you apply yourself and work hard, you will do well in life. Don't you want to do well?"

"Yes, ma'am," he muttered.

"Then I am sure you will." She glanced out the coach window. "Ah, here we are."

Jarret's throat closed up. He wanted to beg her not to make him go, but once Gran made up her mind, no one could change it. And she didn't want him at the brewery. No one wanted him anywhere, anymore.

They left the coach and walked to the headmaster's office. She signed him in while a servant brought his trunk upstairs to the Long Chamber.

"Promise me you won't get into any more fights," Gran said.

"I promise," he said dully. What did it matter if it was a lie? What did anything matter?

"That's a good lad. Oliver arrives tomorrow. You'll feel better once he is here."

He bit back a hot retort. Oliver tried to look out for him, but he couldn't be everywhere at once. Besides, at sixteen, Oliver spent all his time brooding and drinking with his older friends. Tonight he wouldn't be here at all.

Another shudder wracked Jarret.

"Now give Gran a kiss and tell me good-bye," she said softly.

Dutifully, he did as she bade before trudging up the stairs. He'd scarcely entered the Long Chamber and heard the doors being locked behind him when that beast, John Platt, sauntered up to paw through his bags.

"What have you brought for us this time, Babyface?"

Jarret hated the nickname that Platt and his friends had given him because of his hairless chin and short stature. But at seventeen, Platt was a foot taller than him and a whole lot meaner.

Platt found the paper-wrapped apple cake Gran had given him and took a big bite out of the middle while Jarret watched, gritting his teeth.

"What, aren't you going to take a swing at me?" Platt asked as he waved the cake in front of Jarret's face.

What was the point? Platt and his friends would beat him up, and he'd just get in trouble again.

Every time he cared about something, it got taken from him. Showing that he cared only made it worse.

"I hate apple cake," Jarret lied. "Our cook puts dog piss in it."

He had the satisfaction of watching Platt glance skeptically at the cake before tossing it to one of his stupid friends. He hoped they choked on it.

Platt turned to searching his bag again. "What have we here?" he said as he found the gilded box of playing cards Jarret had received from his father as a birthday present.

Jarret's blood stilled. He thought he'd hidden it so well. He'd brought the cards to school on impulse, wanting something to remind him of his parents.

This time it was harder to stay calm. "I don't know what you plan to do with those," he said, attempting to sound bored. "You can't play worth a damn."

"Why, you little weasel!" Grabbing Jarret by his cravat, Platt jerked him up so hard it cut off his air.

Jarret was clawing at Platt's fingers, fighting for breath, when Giles Masters, a viscount's son and the brother of Oliver's best friend, wrenched Platt's hand from his cravat.

"Leave the lad be," Masters warned as Jarret stood there gasping. Masters was eighteen, very tall, and had a wicked left punch.

"Or what?" Platt drawled. "He'll shoot me? Like his brother shot their father to gain his inheritance?"

"That's a damned lie!" Jarret cried, balling up his fists.

Masters put a hand on his shoulder to stay him. "Stop provoking him, Platt. And give him back his cards or I'll make a hash of your face."

"You won't risk getting into trouble this close to matriculation," Platt said uneasily. Then he glanced at Jarret. "But I tell you what. If Babyface wants his cards back, he can play piquet for them. Got any money to wager with, Babyface?"

"His brother doesn't want him gambling," Masters answered.

"Aw, isn't that sweet," Platt said with a smirk. "Babyface does whatever his big brother tells him."

"For God's sake, Platt—" Masters began.

"I've got money," Jarret cut in. He'd learned to play cards at Father's knee and he was pretty good at it. He thrust out his chest. "I'll play you."

With a raise of his eyebrows, Platt sat down on the floor and sorted out the cards to make the thirty-two-card piquet deck.

"Are you sure about this?" Masters asked as Jarret sat down across from his archenemy.

"Trust me," Jarret replied.

An hour later, he'd won his deck back. Two hours later, he'd won fifteen shillings off Platt. By morning he'd won five pounds, much to the dismay of Platt's thickheaded friends.

After that, no one called him Babyface again.

# Chapter One

*London*
*March 1825*

In the nineteen years since that fateful night, Jarret had grown a foot taller and had learned how to fight, and he was still gambling. Now, for a living.

Today, however, the cards were meant to be only a distraction. Sitting at a table in the study in Gran's town house, he laid out another seven rows.

"How can you play cards at a time like this?" his sister Celia asked from the settee.

"I'm not playing cards," he said calmly. "I'm playing solitaire."

"You know Jarret," his brother Gabe put in. "Never comfortable without a deck in his hand."

"You mean, never comfortable unless he's winning," his other sister, Minerva, remarked.

"Then he must be pretty uncomfortable right now," Gabe said. "Lately, all he does is lose."

Jarret stiffened. That was true. And considering that he supported his lavish lifestyle with his winnings, it was a problem.

So of course Gabe was plaguing him about it. At twenty-six, Gabe was six years Jarret's junior and annoying as hell. Like Minerva, he had gold-streaked brown hair and green eyes the exact shade of their mother's. But that was the only trait Gabe shared with their straitlaced mother.

"You can't consistently win at solitaire unless you cheat," Minerva said.

"I never cheat at cards." It was true, if one ignored his uncanny ability to keep track of every card in a deck. Some people didn't.

"Didn't you just say that solitaire isn't 'cards'?" Gabe quipped.

Bloody arse. And to add insult to injury, Gabe was cracking his knuckles and getting on Jarret's nerves.

"For God's sake, stop that noise," Jarret snapped.

"This, you mean?" Gabe said and deliberately cracked his knuckles again.

"If you don't watch it, little brother, I'll crack my knuckles against your jaw," Jarret warned.

"Stop fighting!" Celia's hazel eyes filled with tears as she glanced at the connecting door to Gran's bedchamber. "How can you fight when Gran might be dying?"

"Gran isn't dying," said the eminently practical Minerva. Four years younger than Jarret, she lacked Celia's flair for the dramatic . . . except in the Gothic fiction she penned.

Besides, like Jarret, Minerva knew their grandmother better than their baby sister did. Hester Plumtree was indestructible. This "illness" was undoubtedly another ploy to make them toe her line.

Gran had already given them an ultimatum—they had to marry within the year or the whole lot of them would be disinherited. Jarret would have thrown the threat back in her face, but he couldn't sentence his siblings to a life with no money.

Oliver had tried to fight her edict, then had surprised them by getting himself leg-shackled to an American woman. But that hadn't satisfied Gran. She still wanted her pound of flesh from the rest of them. And now there were fewer than ten months left.

That was what had put Jarret off his game lately—Gran's attempt to force him into marrying the first female who didn't balk at the Sharpe family reputation for scandal and licentiousness. It made him desperate to win a large score, so he could support his siblings on his winnings and they could all tell her to go to hell.

But desperation was disaster at the gaming tables. His success depended on keeping a cool head and not caring about the outcome. Only then could he play to the cards he was dealt. Desperation made a man take risks based on emotion instead of skill. And that happened to him too much, lately.

What on earth did Gran think she would accomplish by forcing them to marry? She'd merely spawn more miserable marriages to match that of their parents.

*But Oliver isn't miserable.*

Oliver had been lucky. He'd found the one woman who would put up with his nonsense and notoriety. The chance of that happening twice in their family was small. And four more times? Abysmally small. Lady Fortune was as fickle in life as in cards.

With a curse, Jarret rose to pace. Unlike the study at Halstead Hall, Gran's was airy and light, with furnishings of the latest fashion and a large scale model of Plumtree Brewery prominently displayed atop a rosewood table.

He gritted his teeth. That damned brewery—she'd run it

successfully for so long that she thought she could run their lives as well. She always had to be in control. One look at the papers stacked high on her desk made it clear that the brewery was becoming too much for her to handle at seventy-one. Yet the obstinate woman refused to hire a manager, no matter how Oliver pressed her.

"Jarret, did you write that letter to Oliver?" Minerva asked.

"Yes, while you were at the apothecary's. The footman has taken it to the post." Although Oliver and his new wife had already left for America to meet her relations, Jarret and Minerva wanted him to know of Gran's illness in case it *was* serious.

"I hope he and Maria are enjoying themselves in Massachusetts," Minerva said. "He seemed very upset that day in the library."

"You'd be upset, too, if you thought you'd caused our parents' deaths," Gabe pointed out.

That had been Oliver's other surprise—his revelation that he and Mother had quarreled the day of the tragedy, which had led to her going off in a rage in search of Father.

"Do you think Oliver was right?" Celia asked. "*Was* it his fault that Mama shot Papa?" Celia had been only four when it happened, so she had little recollection of it.

That wasn't the case for Jarret. "No."

"Why not?" Minerva asked.

How much should he say? He had a strong memory of . . .

No, he shouldn't make baseless accusations, no matter *who* they concerned. But he should tell them his other concern. "I well remember Father at the picnic, muttering, 'Where the devil is *she* going?' I looked across the field and saw Mother on a horse, headed in the direction of the hunting lodge. That memory has been gnawing at me."

Gabe took up Jarret's line of reasoning. "So if she'd left in search of Father, as Oliver seems certain that she did, she would have found him at the picnic. She wouldn't have gone elsewhere looking for him."

"Precisely," Jarret said.

Minerva pursed her lips. "Which means that Gran's version of events might be correct. Mother rode to the hunting lodge because she was upset and wanted to be away from everyone. Then she fell asleep, was startled by Father, shot him—"

"—and shot herself when she saw him dead?" Celia finished. "I don't believe it. It makes no sense."

Gabe cast her an indulgent glance. "Only because you don't want to believe that any woman would be so reckless as to shoot a man without thinking."

"I would certainly never do such a fool thing myself," Celia retorted.

"But you have a passion for shooting and a healthy respect for guns," Minerva pointed out. "Mother had neither."

"Exactly," Celia said. "So she picked up a gun without forethought and shot it for the first time that day? That's ridiculous. For one thing, how did she load it?"

They all stared at her.

"None of you ever thought about that, did you?"

"She could have learned," Gabe put in. "Gran knows how to shoot. Just because Mother never shot a gun around us doesn't mean Gran didn't teach her."

Celia frowned. "On the other hand, if Mother set out to shoot Father deliberately as Oliver claims, someone could have helped her load the pistol—a groom, perhaps. Then she could have lain in wait for Father near the picnic and followed him to the hunting lodge. That makes more sense."

"It's interesting that you should mention the grooms,"

Jarret said. "They would have had to saddle her horse—they might have known where she was going and when she left. She might even have said why she was riding out. If we could talk to them—"

"Most of them left service at Halstead Hall when Oliver closed the place down," Minerva pointed out.

"That's why I'm thinking of hiring Jackson Pinter to find them."

Celia snorted.

"You may not like him," Jarret told her, "but he's one of the most respected Bow Street Runners in London." Although Pinter was supposed to be helping them explore the backgrounds of potential mates, there was no reason the man couldn't take on another mission.

The door to Gran's bedchamber opened, and Dr. Wright entered the study.

"Well?" Jarret asked sharply. "What's the verdict?"

"Can we see her?" Minerva added.

"Actually, she's been asking for Lord Jarret," Dr. Wright said.

Jarret tensed. With Oliver gone, he was the eldest. No telling what Gran had cooked up for him to do, now that she was "ill."

"Is she all right?" Celia asked, alarm plain on her face.

"At the moment, she's only suffering some chest pain. It may come to nothing." Dr. Wright met Jarret's gaze. "But she needs to keep quiet and rest until she feels better. And she refuses to do that until she can speak to you, my lord." When the others rose, he added, "Alone."

With a terse nod, Jarret followed him into Gran's room.

"Don't say anything to upset her," Dr. Wright murmured, then left and closed the door.

At the sight of his grandmother, Jarret caught his breath. He had to admit that Gran didn't look her usual self. She was propped up against the bed pillows, so she wasn't dying, but her color certainly wasn't good.

He ignored the clutch of fear in his chest. Gran was merely a little under the weather. This was just another attempt to control their lives. But she was in for a surprise if she thought that the tactics that had worked on Oliver would work on *him*.

She gestured to a chair by the bed, and Jarret warily took a seat.

"That fool Wright tells me I cannot leave my bed for a month at the very least," she grumbled. "A month! I cannot be away from the brewery for that long."

"You must take as long as necessary to get well," Jarret said, keeping his voice noncommittal until he was sure what she was up to.

"The only way I shall loll about in this bed for a month is if I have someone reliable looking after things at the brewery. Someone I trust. Someone with a vested interest in making sure it runs smoothly."

When her gaze sharpened on him, he froze. So that's what she was plotting.

"Not a chance," he said, jumping to his feet. "Don't even think it." He wasn't about to put himself under Gran's thumb. Bad enough that she was trying to dictate when he married—she wasn't going to run his whole life, too.

She took a labored breath. "You once begged me for this very opportunity."

"That was a long time ago." When he'd been desperate to find a place for himself. Then he'd learned that no matter what place you found, Fate could snatch it from you at a moment's notice. Your hopes for the future could be dashed with a word, your parents taken in the blink of an eye, and your family's good name ruined for spite.

Nothing in life was certain. So a man was better off traveling light, with no attachments and no dreams. It was the only way to prevent disappointment.

"You're going to inherit the brewery one day," she pointed out.

"Only if we all manage to marry within the year," he countered. "But assuming that I inherit, I'll hire a manager. Which you should have done years ago."

That made her frown. "I do not want some stranger running my brewery."

The perennial argument was getting old.

"If you don't want to do it, I'll have to put Desmond in charge," she added.

His temper flared. Desmond Plumtree was Mother's first cousin, a man they all despised—especially him. Gran had threatened before to leave the brewery to the bastard and she *knew* how Jarret felt about that, so she was using his feelings against him.

"Go ahead, put Desmond in charge," he said, though it took every ounce of his will not to fall prey to her manipulation.

"He knows even less about it than you do," she said peevishly. "Besides, he's busy with his latest enterprise."

He hid his relief. "There has to be someone else who knows the business well enough to take over."

She coughed into her handkerchief. "No one I trust."

"And you trust *me* to run it?" He uttered a cynical laugh. "I seem to recall your telling me a few years ago that gamblers are parasites on society. Aren't you worried I'll suck the life out of your precious brewery?"

She had the good grace to color. "I only said that because I couldn't stand watching you waste your keen mind at the gaming tables. That is not a suitable life for a clever man like yourself, especially when I know you are capable of more. You have had some success with your investments. It wouldn't take you long to get your bearings at the brewery. And I will be here for you to consult if you need advice."

The plaintive note in her voice gave him pause. She sounded almost . . . desperate. His eyes narrowed. He might be able to make this work to his advantage, after all.

He sat down once more. "If you really want me to run the brewery for a month, then I want something in return."

"You will have a salary, and I am sure we could come to terms on—"

"Not money. I want you to rescind your ultimatum." He leaned forward to stare her down. "No more threats to disinherit us if we don't marry according to your dictate. Things will return to how they were before."

She glared at him. "That is not going to happen."

"Then I suppose you'll be hiring a manager." He rose and headed for the door.

"Wait!" she cried.

He paused to glance back at her with eyebrows raised.

"What if I rescind it just for *you*?"

He fought a smile. She must be desperate indeed if she was willing to bargain. "I'm listening."

"I will have Mr. Bogg change the will so that you inherit the brewery no matter what." Her voice turned bitter. "You can stay a bachelor until you die."

It was worth considering. If he owned the brewery, he could help his brother and sisters if they couldn't meet Gran's terms by the end of the year. They'd be on their own until Gran died, of course, but then Jarret could support them. It was a better situation than their present one. "I could live with that."

She dragged in a rasping breath. "But you'll have to agree to stay on at the brewery until the year is up."

He tensed. "Why?"

"Too many people depend on it for their livelihood. If I am to leave the place to you, I must be sure you can keep it afloat, even if you hire a manager to run it once I am gone. You need to know enough to be able to hire the right person, and I need assurance that you will not let it rot."

"God forbid you should trust your own grandson to keep it safe." But she did have a point. He hadn't set foot in the place in nineteen years. What did he know about the brewing business anymore?

He could learn. And he would, too, if that's what it took to stop Gran from meddling in their lives for good. But he would do it on his own terms.

"Fine," he said. "I'll stay on until the year is up." When she broke into a smile, he added, "But I want complete control. I'll keep you informed about the business, and you may express your opinions, but my decisions will be final."

That wiped the smile from her face.

"I'll run Plumtree Brewery as I see fit without any interference from you," he went on. "And you will put that in writing."

The steel in her blue eyes told him she wasn't as ill as she pretended. "You can do a great deal of damage in a year."

"Exactly. If you'll recall, this wasn't my idea."

"Then you must promise not to institute any major changes."

He crossed his arms over his chest. "No."

Alarm flared in her features. "At least promise not to make risky investments."

"No. You either let me have full control or find yourself a manager."

It felt good to have the upper hand. He refused to have her coming behind him, second-guessing every decision. If he was going to run the place, he would run it his way. And once the year was up, he'd be free to live his life as he pleased . . . and ensure that his siblings could do so as well.

Not that Gran would accept his terms. She'd never given up control of anything, for even a day. She certainly wouldn't give it to her "parasite" of a grandson for a year.

So it was with some surprise that he heard her say, "Very well, I will meet your demands. I will have it put into writing for you by tomorrow."

The gleam in her eyes gave him pause, but it was gone so fast, he was sure he'd imagined it.

"I do have one caveat," she continued. "You must keep Mr. Croft on as your secretary."

Jarret groaned. Gran's secretary at the brewery was one of the strangest men he'd ever met. "Must I?"

"I know he seems odd, but I promise that in a week or so you will find yourself glad that you kept him on. He's indispensable to the brewery."

Well, it was a small price to pay for gaining his life back. He'd definitely gotten the better end of their bargain.

# Chapter Two

Plumtree Brewery was nothing like Annabel Lake had expected. Breweries in her town of Burton were small, cozy places that smelled of hops and roasting barley. Plumtree Brewery smelled primarily of the coal that fired the massive steam engine she was gaping at. It powered long rakes that moved in eerie silence to stir the malt in the twelve-foot-high boilers. Her brother's brewery, Lake Ale, had nothing on this scale. Perhaps if it had . . .

No, the equipment wasn't causing Lake Ale's present crisis. Hugh's drinking was the cause of *that*.

"You there, what are you doing?" asked a workman with arms the width of tree trunks, who was loading a barrel onto a wagon.

She picked up her box, careful not to jar the contents. "I'm looking for Mrs. Hester Plumtree."

"That way." He tipped his head toward a staircase leading up to a second-floor gallery.

As she mounted the stairs, she drank in her surroundings.

The place was a brewer's dream. The iron floors and brick walls made it nearly fireproof, and the gleaming coppers were two stories high. Imagine measuring hops into *that*. It boggled the mind!

After she, her sister-in-law Sissy, and Geordie had arrived in the city early this afternoon, she'd sampled Plumtree's porter in the inn. She had to admit it was impressive, nearly rivaling her own recipe.

A smug smile touched her lips. Nearly.

With some maneuvering, she opened the door at the top of the stairs and stepped into another world. A woman clearly ran this brewery. The outer office had fashionably striped settees, walnut chairs, and beautiful but sturdy rugs. Annabel couldn't imagine a man caring about such things.

Sitting at a neat walnut desk in the center of the room was a slender blond clerk, so absorbed in his work that he didn't notice she'd entered. She approached the desk, but he continued to excise clippings from a newspaper with a razor, making precise cuts along lines that appeared to be ruled in.

She cleared her throat.

He jumped up so dramatically that his chair fell over. "Who . . . what . . ." As he spotted her, he fixed a smile to his face that made it look like a skull in repose. "May I help you?"

"I'm sorry, I didn't mean to startle you. My name is Annabel Lake. I'd like to see Mrs. Hester Plumtree, if you please."

Alarm spread over his features. "Dear me, you mustn't. That is, you *can't*. It's impossible. She's unavailable."

"How could she be unavailable?" Annabel knew a dodge when she saw one. Beyond him was only one door. It had to be Mrs. Plumtree's, and since the clerk hadn't said she was out, the woman must be closeted in there, avoiding visitors.

"I heard she's here from dawn to dusk every day, and it's not quite three."

He blinked, clearly thrown off guard. "Well, yes . . . that is true, but not today. You must leave. No one is allowed in. No one. Leave your name and where you can be reached, and when she becomes available once more—"

"How long will that be?"

Sheer panic crossed his face. "How should I know?" He wrung his hands, casting a nervous glance at the door. What a strange little man.

She softened her tone, attempting to put him at his ease. "Please, it's very important that I speak with her."

"No, no, no, no, no . . . It's out of the question. Quite entirely out of the question. Not allowed. She is . . . I mean . . . You simply must go!" He came around the desk as if to escort her out.

Annabel hadn't come all this way just to be tossed from the office by some odd clerk. Before the man could react, she darted around the desk the other way and rushed through the door into the office beyond.

The person behind the massive mahogany desk was decidedly not an aging woman. A *man* sat there, a young man about her age or slightly older, with raven hair and handsome features.

"Who the devil are you?" she burst out.

Leaning back in his chair, he laughed. "I rather think that should be *my* line."

The clerk rushed in to grab her arm. "My lord, forgive me." He tried to tug her toward the door. "Beg pardon, but I don't know why the young lady—"

"Let her go, Croft." The man stood, his eyes still glinting with amusement. "I'll take it from here."

"But my lord, you said no one is to know that your grandmother—"

"It's all right. I'll handle it."

"Oh." Two spots of color deepened in the clerk's cheeks. "Of course. Well then. If you think it's safe."

The man chuckled. "If she bites or sets fire to my desk, Croft, you'll be the first person I call."

Croft released her arm. "There you go, miss. Talk to his lordship. He'll take care of you." Then he slid from the room, leaving her alone with what could only be one of Hester Plumtree's grandsons.

Oh, dear. Annabel had heard about the outrageous Sharpe men from Sissy, who'd never met a gossip rag she didn't like. When the man strode for the door, shutting it firmly behind her, she felt a moment's panic—especially when he returned to give her a thorough once-over.

She wished her day gown didn't shriek of last year's fashions, but it couldn't be helped. Times were lean in the Lake family. She'd rather not waste her funds on clothes when she could save toward a good school for Geordie, since Sissy and Hugh clearly couldn't afford one.

Which of the infamous Sharpes was he? The madcap youngest grandson, Lord Gabriel, whom people called the Angel of Death for his reckless horse racing and all-black attire? No, for this man wore a waistcoat of buff velvet beneath his dark blue coat.

Might he be the eldest, the notorious rakehell? Not him, either—Sissy had just this morning read to her the news that the Marquess of Stoneville was honeymooning in America with his new wife.

That left only the middle grandson, whose name she couldn't recall. He was a gambler and probably a devilish rogue like his brothers. No man could have the features of Michelangelo's David without attracting a great many women. And those unearthly eyes—they seemed to change from a gorgeous blue to an equally gorgeous green with every trick of the light. Men as handsome as that quickly learned that they could take advantage of their good looks whenever they wished. Hence the roguery.

"You'll have to forgive Mr. Croft," he said in a low rumble, leaning against the desk's cluttered surface. "Gran has trained him to hold off intrusions at all costs, Mrs. . . . ."

"Miss," she corrected him automatically. When a wolfish smile tugged at his full lips, she fought the sudden shiver coursing down her spine. "Miss Annabel Lake. I'm a brewster, Lord . . ."

"Jarret. Jarret Sharpe." His face had stiffened.

That wasn't unusual, she thought cynically. The men running the large breweries seemed to have nothing but contempt for female brewers. That was why she'd come to Mrs. Plumtree in the first place—so she wouldn't be brushed off.

"I suppose you're here looking for a position," he said coldly. "My grandmother must have sent you."

"What? No! Why would she send me? I don't even know her."

He eyed her warily. "Forgive me. Brewsters are rare enough these days, but young, unmarried, and pretty ones . . . Well, I just assumed that Gran was up to her tricks again."

"Tricks?"

"Never mind. Not important."

"I beg your pardon, sir, but if I might speak to Mrs. Plumtree—"

"That's not possible. At present, she's . . . unavailable."

Annabel was rapidly growing to hate that word. "But surely she'll return soon?"

At the hopeful note in her voice, he gentled his expression. "Not for some time. She's spending the next year dealing with family concerns."

A year! By the time a year had passed, the creditors could be hauling away Lake Ale piece by piece.

He must have sensed her distress, for he added, "But she left me in charge, so perhaps I can help you."

*Him?* What was his grandmother thinking? How could a woman whose business acumen was legendary hand over her business to a scapegrace?

Annabel surveyed him, trying to determine his reliability. For a gentleman given to sedentary pursuits, he filled out his coat and trousers very well. But what man wore superfine to a brewery?

A man who knew nothing about the business, that's who. A man who probably dabbled in it to amuse himself, which meant he was of little use to her. Still, what choice did she have? He was in charge. And she and Sissy had come all this way.

Steadying her nerves, she held up her box. "I'm here on behalf of my ill brother to propose a business venture."

He arched one finely groomed black eyebrow. "What sort of business venture? And who is your brother?"

"Hugh Lake. He owns Lake Ale in—"

"Burton-upon-Trent. Yes, I've heard of it."

She blinked. "You have?"

Leaning back, he thumbed through a stack of papers until he found one with scribbled notes. "Your father, Aloysius Lake, founded it in 1794, and your brother inherited it a few years ago when your father died. Your specialties are brown ale, porter, and small beer." When he glanced up to find her gaping at him, he said, "I do try to know something about our competition."

So he wasn't just a pretty face, after all. "Actually, I'm here because Lake Ale would rather be your business associate than your competitor."

With a dubious expression, he crossed his arms over his rather impressive chest. "According to my information, Lake Ale only produces fifty thousand barrels a year to Plumtree's two hundred fifty thousand. I fail to see what you can do for us."

She wasn't sure which shocked her more—that he knew Lake Ale's level of production, or that he spoke to her like an equal. It was gratifying not to have him suggest that she trot on home and get her brother. Then again, given his grandmother, he was probably used to women knowing such matters.

"Before I explain, I wish for you to sample something." Setting the box on his desk, she withdrew its precious cargo—a bottle of ale and a glass. She uncorked the ale and filled the glass halfway, careful not to put too much head on it.

When she offered it to him, he eyed her askance. "Thinking of poisoning the competition?"

She laughed. "Hardly. But if it makes you feel better, I'll drink some first." She sipped, and his gaze dropped to her mouth. There was no mistaking the glint in his eyes when he followed her tongue as it swept the foam off her lips.

"Your turn," she said coldly. She thrust the glass at him, half expecting him to make some naughty comment about her mouth before progressing toward suggestions that had nothing to do with brewing.

Instead, he held up the glass to scrutinize the amber liquid. "It's a pale ale?"

"Yes, an October brew."

"Ah. Nice orange-gold color." He swirled it in the glass, then thrust his nose into the scent, breathing deeply. "Aggressive aroma of hops. Some fruity notes."

While he sipped it, she twisted her mother's ring on her finger. It had always brought her good luck, which was why she never took it off, even at the brewery.

His eyes deepened to a cobalt blue as he let the ale lie in his mouth a brief second before swallowing. He sipped again, as if to confirm his impressions.

Then he drained the glass. "It's quite good. Full-bodied, with a nice bitter finish. Not too much malt, either. Some of Lake Ale's stock?"

She let out a relieved breath. "Yes. I brewed it myself."

He straightened to his full height, which was considerable compared to her own five foot one. "I still don't see how this concerns Plumtree."

"I want you to help me sell it."

With his manner all business again, he handed the glass to her. "I'll be perfectly frank with you, Miss Lake. This isn't the time for new ventures in the ale business. With the Russian market going soft—"

"That's precisely why I'm here. With my brother ill, we, too, have been having difficulties. But I can help both our companies make up for the loss of the Russians." She packed the glass in her box, leaving the ale bottle on the desk. "You've heard of Hodgson's Brewery?"

"Of course. He dominates the India trade."

"Not since he joined up with Thomas Drane. They decided to cut out the East India Company by shipping it directly there themselves."

His eyes widened. "Idiots."

"Exactly. No one takes on the Company and wins." Though the Company profited from the Indian goods brought to England, it allowed its captains to profit from goods they brought out to India and sold to Englishmen there. Ale had become the captains' primary private cargo, specifically the October ale brewed by Hodgson's. The brewery had thought to cut out the captains and was now suffering for it.

"Hodgson's has also stopped giving credit and raised its prices," she went on. "So the East India Company captains decided to cut out *Hodgson's* by finding a brewer to brew his sort of ale for them. They fixed on Allsopp's in Burton. His first shipment went out two years ago, and they've received nothing but glowing reports. It's a huge market that Lake Ale wants to get into. But we need help."

"My grandmother tried to compete in the India market years ago unsuccessfully."

"She was trying to sell *Plumtree's* October brew, right?"

He hesitated, then nodded.

"We've discovered that Burton water produces a better October brew than London water. Allsopp is putting half his export production into India pale ale. I could do the same if the East India Company captains would deal with Lake Ale, but they won't, because of my brother's"—she stopped just short of saying "unreliability"—"illness. And because I'm a woman. They don't trust us to come through, and I don't dare put it into production if they don't buy it. That's why I need you."

His eyes narrowed. "You want me to sell your ale to the Company captains."

She beamed at him. "Exactly. It could be advantageous for us both, compensating us for the losses we've both suffered ever since the Russians raised the tariffs on English ale."

"What makes you think *we've* suffered losses?" he drawled.

"Every brewery has suffered losses, and you know it."

Glancing away, he rubbed his hand over his chin. "It's an intriguing proposal."

"Then you'll consider it?"

His gaze met hers, full of regret. "No."

Her heart sank. Plumtree Brewery had been her only hope! "Why not?"

"For one thing, I've only been here a week, and I'm still assessing the situation. So I'm not going to launch into some foolhardy experiment, and certainly not just because a young brewster has a harebrained scheme—"

"It's not a harebrained scheme!" And at nearly thirty, she wasn't all that young. That was the trouble with being short—it misled people about one's age. "Ask anyone about Allsopp's success. I'm sure other London brewers have noticed. And I brew an excellent October beer—you admitted as much yourself!"

"There's more to it than that," he said in that patronizing tone she'd become so familiar with in dealing with the male brewery owners in Burton.

She thrust out her chin. "You mean, because I'm a woman."

"Because you're a *brewer*. Brewers look no further than their noses. They create a superior brew, and they think that's all it requires. But there are factors beyond the ale's quality. I'm sure your brother realizes that, which is why he didn't come himself."

"He didn't come because he's ill!" she cried.

"Then surely he sent a letter of introduction, putting you forward as his representative."

She swallowed. Of course he hadn't. Hugh thought that

she and Sissy were in London to look at schools for Geordie. "He was too ill for that."

Lord Jarret merely arched an eyebrow.

Exasperated, she tried another tack. "For a man who gambles a great deal, you're certainly cautious about investing."

The corners of his lips twitched. "I see that my reputation precedes me."

"When you spend your time scandalizing society, you must expect people to talk about you. Though I can't imagine why. If you balk at a sure investment like this, you can't be too reckless or brave a gambler."

To her vast annoyance, a smile broke over his face, exposing not one, but two dimples in his cheeks. "My dear Miss Lake, such tactics may work on your hapless brother, but I have two sisters of my own. I can't be goaded quite so easily. Sticks and stones and all that."

Curse him for being such a . . . a *man*. "Your *grandmother* would see the profit to be made from this plan. Your grandmother would understand."

The smile vanished. He stepped closer to loom over her, all six feet of him. "My grandmother isn't running this company at present. But even so, I doubt she'd approve."

She fought not to be intimidated by his sheer size. "How do you know, if you don't ask her?"

"I don't need to ask her."

"You just said you've only been here a week, and you're still sorting through things." She tried to stare him down, but his height made it more like staring him *up*. "You could be wrong about this, you know. I'd at least like to hear from *her* that Plumtree Brewery isn't interested."

"That's impossible. At the moment, she is—"

"Unavailable. I know. How convenient." She glared at

him. "You ignore a perfectly good opportunity to make money because you can't be bothered. I wonder what your grandmother would think if she heard of it."

"Threats don't work on me either, Miss Lake. Now if you'll excuse me . . ."

When he headed for the door, panic seized her. "Lake Ale is in a precarious position," she called out, "and all I ask is that you present my proposal to your grandmother. Why is that so difficult? If Lake Ale fails, forty men will lose their employment. My family will suffer, and—"

"Oh, for God's sake." He whirled to face her. "Will you be satisfied if I speak to my grandmother about your proposal?"

Hope sprang within her. "Yes. Though it might be better if *I*—"

"Not a chance. I'll present the idea tonight. But when she refuses to pursue it—as I'm sure she will—you'll accept that answer as final. Is that understood?"

She hesitated, then nodded. Really, he gave her little choice.

He swung the door open. "Come back tomorrow morning, and I'll tell you what she said. Good day, Miss Lake."

She bit down on her lip to keep from protesting his cursory dismissal. This was the best she would get from him; now she simply had to hope that he did as he promised.

As she descended the stairs, however, she wasn't at all sure that he would. He seemed determined to dismiss her plan. Why, he hadn't even heard about the disastrous situation with Hodgson's! He probably thought she was exaggerating the whole thing.

But if he spoke to his grandmother, he would learn . . .

She sighed. That was a very great *if.*

Outside the brewery, she found Sissy and Geordie waiting

on the steps for her. Sissy leaped up the moment Annabel approached, the hood of her cloak falling down to expose her pretty blond curls.

"Well?" she asked hopefully. "What did Mrs. Plumtree say?"

Annabel sighed. "She wasn't there. I spoke to her grandson."

"You *met* one of the famous Hellions of Halstead Hall?" Sissy's blue eyes lit with excitement. "Which one?"

"Lord Jarret."

"The gambler? Is he as handsome as they say? Did he have a look of dissipation about him?"

"Come to think of it, no." That was odd, given the scandalous stories told about him—how he'd once gambled for two days straight without sleeping, how he'd lost a thousand pounds in a single hour . . . how he changed women as often as he changed his drawers.

That wasn't surprising, when he had eyes the color of the ocean and a lazy smile meant to make a woman shiver. Not that it did that to *her*. No indeed.

"Lord Jarret had a look of roguery about him," Annabel said stoutly.

"Then why on earth is his grandmother letting him run her brewery?"

"Because he's a man, of course. He gave me little hope of her being interested in my proposal, though he did promise to speak to her about it."

"Do you think he will?"

"I don't know. He's an annoying, arrogant fellow. I doubt he can be trusted to do anything. He acted as if I were imposing on him simply by suggesting a perfect way for his company to make money."

"That's because you shouldn't have been telling him what to do, Aunt Annabel," Geordie put in. "It's like Father always says, women—"

"I know what your father always says." That women didn't belong in breweries. That if she'd stop going to the brewery, some man might actually marry her.

She heartily wished Hugh wouldn't say such things in front of Geordie. Now the lad was taking up that cry himself, and Hugh *knew* why she didn't wish to marry. Because she'd have to leave Geordie behind. And how could she ever do that?

He was her son.

Of course, Geordie didn't know that. He didn't know that Annabel's fiancé, Rupert, had sired him or that Annabel had borne him shortly after Rupert had died in battle. Geordie had been raised believing she was his aunt. And there was nothing Annabel could do about that—not if he were to have a life free of the stigma of bastardy.

But she could certainly make sure he was loved and cared for, even if the woman he called Mother wasn't her.

A sob clogged her throat, and she choked it down as always. Her son was growing up so quickly. One day, she and Sissy and Hugh would have to tell him the truth. When he was young, the three of them had thought it best to keep the secret quiet, for fear he would let it slip to someone. But lately Sissy had been saying they should tell him. That it was time.

It *was* time—she just couldn't bear to do it. He would be so hurt when he realized that his whole life had been a lie, that his real father was dead and his real mother was a wanton. And then he would blame her, and she might lose him forever. She just couldn't risk it. Not yet. Not until things were settled with Hugh.

A scowl touched her brow. What were they to do about

Hugh? He got more hopeless by the day. The more melancholy he became, the more he drank and the less he cared what happened to the brewery. They'd hidden it so far, but eventually people would figure out that he missed so many days in the office and appointments with important vendors because he was drinking himself into a stupor in his study at home.

"You ought to listen to Father," Geordie said in the pompous tone he'd adopted after turning twelve. "He's only trying to help you get a husband before you get too old, you know."

"Geordie!" Sissy chided. "Don't be rude."

"I don't want a husband anyway, Geordie," Annabel said wearily.

That was a bald-faced lie. She wanted a husband and children and a home of her own, like any other woman. But what man would have her once he knew she was no longer chaste? And even if some fellow were understanding about her youthful love for Rupert, he wouldn't wish to take on her bastard. She'd have to leave Geordie behind, if only to spare him the cruelties of being branded illegitimate.

She couldn't bear that.

And she had no desire to bring scandal down upon Sissy and Hugh; they'd been good to her. Some families would have abandoned her entirely for her . . . mistake.

"So what do we do now?" Sissy asked.

"We have no choice but to wait until tomorrow and see if Lord Jarret does as promised. Though I'd feel much better if I could speak to Mrs. Plumtree myself."

"Why can't you? Surely we could find out where she lives."

"If only we could." She thought through what Lord Jarret had said. "I'm not sure she's at home, anyway. He said something about her dealing with family concerns. She might be anywhere."

"Well, if he's going to consult with her, he has to go to where she is, doesn't he? We could just follow him."

Annabel gaped at Sissy, then caught her up in a hug. "You're brilliant! Yes, that's what we must do. Or rather, what *I* must do. He'd surely notice three of us following him. He won't notice one woman."

"You should let *me* do it," Geordie said, puffing out his chest.

"Absolutely not!" Sissy and Annabel said in unison. Then they laughed.

They'd always been in perfect accord when it came to Geordie. Annabel couldn't have asked for a better mother for her son. Sissy and Hugh had their own children, too— who were currently with Sissy's mother in Burton—but Sissy never treated Geordie any differently than she did the others.

Another woman might have resented having her sister-in-law's by-blow foisted upon her a year after her wedding, but not Sissy. She'd dreamed up the ruse of telling everyone that she and Annabel were going north to help a cousin cope with a long-term illness. Sissy had even gone so far as to write letters back to town about the child she bore. Then she had embraced the babe with utter joy, welcoming the grieving Annabel into their family, too.

In return, Annabel had adopted the role of doting aunt, helping to look after the children when she wasn't at the brewery trying to fill Hugh's soggy shoes.

"Geordie," Sissy said, ruffling the boy's straight brown hair, "let's leave this endeavor to Annabel, shall we?"

"Aww, Mother, stop that!" He shrugged off Sissy's hand with a scowl. "I'm not a boy anymore, you know."

"Oh, a big man now, is he?" Annabel teased.

"I *am* a man." He scowled at them both. He had Rupert's scowl. "Father says so."

"Well then," Annabel said, "you can take good care of your mother on the way back to the inn." They were staying close by, thank heavens. "I'm remaining here."

"Alone? Until after dark?" Sissy said, a hint of alarm in her voice.

"I'll be fine. Lord Jarret will surely leave in a couple of hours—he isn't exactly the diligent sort. There's plenty of shops across the street that give me a good view of the brewery. I'll dally in them until I see him come out." When Sissy still looked worried, she added, "I'll be careful, I promise."

"At least wear my cloak." Sissy stripped it off and handed it to her. "Perhaps if you keep it buttoned, with the hood up over your head, no one will realize you're a woman. You're so short, it even covers the bottom of your skirts."

At the very least, it would afford her some protection from the nippy air once the sun went down. "This may take me a while, you know," she said as she removed her bonnet and gave it to Sissy, then donned the cloak. "Once I find out where Mrs. Plumtree is, I'll have to get in to speak to her."

"After you're done, take a hackney back." Sissy pressed some money into her hand, along with the extra key to the inn room. "Don't even think about returning to the inn on foot."

Annabel stared at the coins, a lump forming in her throat. "I'm sorry I dragged you into this, Sissy. I'm sorry that my brother—"

"Shh," Sissy said softly. "It's not your fault. Anyway, Hugh is a good man when he isn't . . . in the doldrums." She cast a furtive glance at Geordie, who was listening avidly as usual. "I'm sure you'll be able to convince Mrs. Plumtree to help us. And if you can give a new purpose to Lake Ale, it may even jog Hugh out of his melancholy state."

"We can only hope," Annabel said as she slid the money and key into the cloak pocket.

That was their plan, meager as it was. Hugh had seemed interested in entering the India market every time she'd mentioned it, but he was too sunk in drink to pursue it. So she and Sissy hoped to present him with a fait accompli wherein Plumtree Brewery agreed to do the marketing. Perhaps then he'd rouse himself to carry the scheme to fruition. It ought to be enough to turn Lake Ale around, which could do nothing but raise Hugh's spirits further.

They had the brewery manager's blessing, and she still hoped to gain Mrs. Plumtree's help, no matter what the woman's arrogant grandson said.

She set her shoulders. She *would* gain the woman's help, with or without Lord Jarret's approval. Because it might be the only way to ensure her family's survival.

# Chapter Three

Jarret stared at the half-empty bottle of ale Miss Lake had left behind. Brewsters generally produced ale for their own taverns or families. To his knowledge, no woman other than Gran actually worked in the rough-and-ready atmosphere of a major brewery.

Was that why he'd let the chit's talk of an ill brother get under his skin? He should have tossed her out the minute she mentioned involving Plumtree Brewery in her plans. Because damn if it didn't tempt him. It was just the sort of high-risk venture that sparked his interest . . . and just the sort of high-risk venture he must avoid if he were to save the company from certain ruin.

With a heavy sigh, Jarret stared down at the numbers that had been plaguing him when Miss Lake first entered. Plumtree Brewery was in trouble. The Russian situation had lowered its profits dramatically, which explained why Gran had been desperate for someone to run the place.

This was no time for taking great risks with the company. While Miss Lake's plan could stanch the loss of profits from the gaping wound dealt by the Russians, it could also provide the killing blow. He couldn't chance it.

Still, assuming that Miss Lake hadn't lied about brewing the ale herself, he had to admit she was good. He didn't profess to be an expert, though—it had been a long time since he'd looked at ale as anything other than a drink to accompany his meal.

Grandfather had been the expert. Jarret flashed on an image of the old man setting piles of malt before him to teach Jarret how to know which roast produced which sort of ale. Grandfather used to let him add the yeast to the fermentation vats, saying that one day the whole place would be his. As a boy, that had made him swell with pride and yearning . . . until Gran had snatched it all away.

He scowled. Now he was here again, smelling the wort and tasting the green beer. Thanks to her, it was as if nineteen years had melted away to nothing. Except that he no longer wanted to sacrifice his life to the brewery.

"Croft!" he barked.

The clerk appeared instantly in the doorway. Gran had been right: Croft might be awkward with strangers and possess an odd manner, but he knew Plumtree Brewery inside and out.

"Would you send Mr. Harper up here?"

"Of course, my lord. And may I say again how sorry I am that I allowed that woman to get past me. I didn't know what to tell her. You said not to let anyone know that Mrs. Plumtree is ill, and the woman kept asking questions—"

"It's fine, Croft. Everything is well." Gran had insisted that her illness be kept secret from all but her closest intimates. She didn't want her competitors swarming over the company like vultures if they thought it was in a weakened state.

"And how is your grandmother doing, if I may ask?"

"She was holding her own when I left her last night," Jarret evaded. But her color wasn't good, and she coughed a great deal.

As Croft hurried off to fetch Harper, Jarret worried. He'd expected Gran to revert to her usual self after their agreement. Instead, she'd worsened over the past week. Dr. Wright said she suffered from something called edema of the lungs and might never recover.

The thought of Gran dying made something twist in his belly. She'd always been there, her energy and passion for the brewery making her larger than life. Even when she was fighting with them, she was the glue that held them together. If she died . . .

She *mustn't* die. It was unthinkable.

"My lord? Mr. Croft said you wished to see me?"

He looked up to find Mr. Harper, the company's finest brewer, standing there with hat in hand. Jarret gestured to the bottle of ale. "I'd like your opinion on that October brew, Harper. There's a glass in the sideboard."

Gran kept her store of brandy in there. A faint smile touched his lips. Mother had always been mortified by the fact that her mother drank brandy, a very unladylike thing to do. But Gran was unlike most women.

Except, perhaps, for Miss Lake.

He scowled. Miss Lake was *not* like Gran, else he wouldn't have spent half their encounter wondering what lay beneath her outmoded gown of green wool. Short though she was, like a pixie venturing out from the forest, she had a woman's shapely figure—all soft curves and cunning temptations. And the one time she'd smiled at him . . .

God, it had transformed her whole face, making her brown

eyes sparkle and her lightly freckled cheeks flush. The dark curls that framed her face had hinted at the lush waves of shimmering mahogany that undoubtedly lay beneath her jaunty bonnet.

She had the look of a well-fed country lass untouched by the city's foul stink. He liked earthy women, always had; he far preferred them to the elegant, gossipy bitches who populated society. Miss Lake was the sort of female he could imagine dancing around maypoles and walking with her beau on the village green. The sort who considered any flirtation a prelude to marriage.

That's why he'd assumed that Gran had sent her. It was exactly something Gran would do—try to get him to hire some pretty female brewer in hopes that the woman would tempt him into marriage, so Gran could still get her way.

Miss Lake would certainly have been a good choice for such a plot. The minute she'd tipped up her pixie's nose at him, he'd wanted to go exploring beneath that bonnet and gown. Confound it all.

"Well?" he snapped as Harper sipped the ale, then sipped again.

"It's good. Better than most October brews I've tasted."

"Damn," he muttered.

"I beg your pardon, my lord?" Harper asked.

He didn't want to have his opinion about the ale confirmed. He didn't want to hear that Miss Lake had a viable brew to sell, that she could make a go of her scheme if only he would cooperate.

"Are you considering the India market?" Harper said, startling him.

"Why do you ask?"

Harper shrugged. "With Hodgson's on the ropes and the

Russians not buying, I've been thinking we should try our hand at a pale ale for the East India Company." When Jarret just stared at him, annoyed that everyone in creation seemed to know about Hodgson's but him, Harper added hastily, "I realize Mrs. Plumtree has been against it, but times are hard. It's worth another look."

"Tell me exactly what happened to Hodgson's that made the East India Company unhappy."

Harper explained a series of what sounded like unwise business practices to him, though he hadn't been around long enough to be sure. Much as he hated to admit it, Miss Lake's proposal sounded as if it had merit . . . *if* he could trust her company to produce what she promised, which was by no means certain.

"Could you produce an October ale as good as that?" Jarret asked, flicking one hand toward the nearly empty bottle Harper had placed on the desk.

Harper colored. "Don't know as I could. That's a damned fine brew. I'd have to know the recipe. But Hodgson's wasn't any better than ours. We'd still have a chance of competing, if they're on the outs."

*Burton water produces a better October brew than London water.*

Jarret stared at the few ounces left in the bottom. "Thank you for your opinion, Harper. That will be all."

What did it matter if Miss Lake had produced an excellent ale for the India market? Just because she was moving to take advantage of Hodgson's foolish mistakes didn't mean he should risk all on her scheme.

*If Lake Ale fails, forty men will lose their employment.*

He scowled. That wasn't his concern. It wasn't his job to

save every ailing brewery in the country. He'd have enough trouble saving this one.

This was precisely what he'd wanted to avoid—being drawn in to caring about something. He didn't want to end up like Gran. She'd struggled to gain her daughter a fine marriage, and instead her son-in-law had made her daughter miserable. She'd worked for years to put Plumtree Brewery at the top, and in one moment, a decision made by Russians halfway around the world had thrust her and the family company into difficulty.

That's what came of putting your heart into something. A man could do everything right, and Fate could still jerk the rug out from under him.

Now he had no choice. Though he'd been dealt a bad hand, he had to make the most of it. Plumtree must survive if his family was to survive, and it looked as if he was the only one who could make sure that it did.

No, it had to do more than survive—he had to make it stronger than before, so he could walk away at the end of the year without any guilt. So he could return to his life as a gambler, where his only risk was monetary, where he wasn't tempted to care. Where he understood that life was unpredictable and nothing could be counted on.

Miss Lake would have to find another fool to back her and her brother's risky scheme.

*All I ask is that you present my proposal to your grandmother.*

He snorted. Gran was even less likely to embrace the plan than he. But he'd promised the chit he would present it, so he would.

A knock came at his door, and he looked up to find his friend Giles Masters standing there.

With a smile, he jumped to his feet. "What the devil are you doing here?"

As a barrister of some renown, Masters spent his days arguing cases halfway across town.

"I've come to drag you away from all this," Masters said with a sweep of his hand. "Your brother told me that you weren't joining us for our whist game tonight, and that's unacceptable."

"You say that only because I've been losing lately, and you want to make some money off me for a change."

Masters struck his chest in mock horror. "Can't your oldest and dearest friend merely want you to join him in an evening of scintillating conversation and manly pursuits?"

"Is that what you call it?" Jarret eyed him askance. "The last time we gambled at one of Plumtree Brewery's taverns, you and Gabe got drunk and competed to see who could fart the loudest. You won, as I recall. To the detriment of everyone in the room."

"Ah, but I did it while being brilliantly witty. So there you have it—scintillating conversation and manly pursuits." He waved his hand toward the door. "Now come along. Those of us who actually *need* to slave away during the daytime hours desire entertainment, and we won't tolerate refusals from those like you who only dabble in a profession."

For some reason, Jarret didn't like being regarded as a dabbler. "Why play whist when we lack a fourth?" he said sourly. "And I hate to upset your apple cart, but even after Oliver returns from America, he may not join us at the tables very often. He's turned into a sober married man, more's the pity."

Masters sighed. "Your brother and mine both. A good bachelor is hard to find. That's why the rest of us must stick together." He grinned. "Besides, we *have* a fourth. Gabe convinced Pinter to join us."

"Pinter! You mean the bloody fellow didn't scowl and protest that cards are a frivolous pastime?"

"He's not so bad, you know. He's a good sport, and once in a while he even has a sense of humor. Come along, and you'll see that for yourself."

Jarret glanced at the piles of papers on the desk. He'd been poring over the books for days, and no great solution to the brewery's problems had presented itself. Perhaps he could think better if he cleared his head. And how better than with a good game of cards, a few tankards of Plumtree's best porter, and a tumble with a tavern maid?

Miss Lake swam into his mind, her pretty eyes beseeching him for help, and he cursed under his breath. He could talk to Gran in the morning.

Besides, he'd been planning to speak to the Bow Street Runner about tracking down the former Halstead Hall grooms. Might as well do it tonight. "All right. Lead on."

ANNABEL FOLLOWED LORD Jarret and his dark-haired companion from the brewery. Was the other fellow Lord Jarret's brother, joining him to visit their grandmother? She was having a hard time keeping up with their long-legged strides without breaking into a run. Sometimes being short could be terribly inconvenient.

It didn't help that there were men and boys with advertising boards everywhere, blocking her view. And she kept having to resist the urge to gaze at the wonders she was rushing past—the enticing millineries filled with the latest fashions in bonnets, the print shops with their outrageous and colorful displays, and the vendors hawking mouthwatering sausages or ornaments for fire stoves or even cures for syphilis.

She blushed as she passed the latter. *That* wasn't something she saw on the streets of Burton.

It took the gentlemen fifteen minutes to reach their destination. When it turned out to be a tavern, she halted in front of it, incensed. So much for Lord Jarret's promise! She should have known a man like that wouldn't do as he said.

Unless they were just stopping in for a drink before they visited their grandmother? That was possible. The tavern bore a sign that read, "We sell Plumtree Brewery's best," and a company tavern would be a logical choice for the grandsons of the owner to have a drink, would it not?

Now she had to decide: Wait out here until they came back out? Or go in?

Waiting wasn't a good plan. Night was falling, and London was notorious for its footpads. But she couldn't give up her chance to learn Mrs. Plumtree's whereabouts.

Fortunately, it was early enough that the people entering the tavern tended to be workmen and couples seeking a quick supper. She'd be less noticeable now than at any other time. So she walked in and took a table near Lord Jarret's. She kept her head down and ordered a meal, figuring that would allow her more time to linger.

But before the food came, two more gentlemen joined Lord Jarret's party. Clearly this wasn't a casual drink between brothers. When they called for a pitcher and broke out the cards, she knew precisely what it was. A night on the town.

God rot Lord Jarret! He clearly had no intention whatsoever of speaking to his grandmother about her proposal. Now what should she do?

An hour, a kidney pie, and a pint later, she still hadn't

decided what to do. But she'd gleaned some information.

The dark-haired man wasn't Lord Jarret's brother, but an old friend named Masters, who was apparently also a man of rank. Lord Jarret's actual brother was the man with the golden-brown hair, Lord Gabriel, who enjoyed tormenting the other two with frequent allusions to their advanced age.

The fourth man, whom they called Pinter, was a black-haired, raspy-voiced fellow with a quiet, almost somber manner. Though he didn't share their joviality, he occasionally made a dry remark that appeared to startle them. She couldn't tell if he was their friend or just along for the ride. He didn't seem to have any sort of rank. He was also the only one who didn't flirt outrageously with the tavern maids.

As best she could tell, Lord Jarret and his brother had been winning fairly steadily. The other two men were grumbling about it.

Curious to see what their game was, she rose and passed as close to the table as she dared. They were playing whist. She lingered near Lord Jarret long enough to see that he was quite good, which was probably why he and his brother were winning.

The man named Masters called for another pitcher of ale. "What happened to your losing streak, Jarret?" he complained as he threw down his cards.

A smug smile touched the lord's lips. "You and Pinter don't present much of a contest."

"I beg your pardon," Pinter said, "but I've had the devil's worst hands. Even skill can't trump bad luck."

"That's as good an excuse as any," Lord Jarret taunted him. "What's yours, Masters? Shall we up the stakes, give you a chance to win your money back? I need a good challenge."

"Oh, yes, let's up the stakes, big brother," Lord Gabriel said cheerily. "Seeing as how you've regained your touch and all."

Too bad she couldn't join them. She knew exactly what stakes *she'd* ask for. She'd been playing cards with her family all her life, starting with her parents and Hugh, then adding Geordie and Sissy after she'd left home and Geordie had grown old enough to grasp the rules. Although they hadn't played much recently because of Hugh's . . .

Tears stung her eyes. Curse Hugh for his weakness. She missed her sweet big brother. He hadn't been himself in some time. Though she suspected she knew why he'd begun drinking so heavily, it didn't make it any better.

Pinter tossed down his cards. "If you up the stakes, I'm out. The magistrate's office doesn't pay me enough to gamble like you lords."

"Do you think we barristers have money to burn?" Masters grumbled. "I assure you, we do not."

"But you have a rich brother to cover your losses," Pinter pointed out.

"Stop being a stick in the mud," Masters said. "I told Jarret you were a good sport. Are you going to make a liar out of me? If you quit, I'll have to quit, too, and I'll have no chance to win my money back."

"Not my problem." Pinter drained his tankard and set it down with every appearance of being done.

Annabel quickly stepped forward and lowered the hood of the cloak. "I'm happy to take his place."

Did she imagine it, or had the entire room gone completely still?

Lord Jarret's eyes narrowed on her. "Miss Lake. Fancy seeing *you* here."

She hid her trembling hands in the pockets of her cloak.

"I'd even be willing to up the stakes, if Lord Jarret would play for something that really matters."

Lord Gabriel glanced from her to his brother, then broke into a grin. "Do enlighten us, madam. What is it you'd like to play for?"

With a scrape of his chair, Lord Jarret stood. "If you'll excuse us for a moment, gentlemen . . ." Grabbing her by the arm, he hustled her out into the hall.

As she jerked free of him, he said, "What in the hell do you think you're up to now, Miss Lake?"

She met his furious gaze steadily. "The same thing as earlier. I want your help. I'm willing to play cards to get it."

"Women like you don't belong in a tavern."

"You know nothing about women like me. All you know is this frivolous life of gambling and drinking and wenching." He was just like Hugh had become, selfish and irresponsible. "You couldn't even stay away from it long enough to speak to your grandmother on Lake Ale's behalf!"

"You were *following me*?" he said, his voice incredulous. "Have you lost your mind? This part of London is a dangerous place for—"

"Oh, spare me your concern. It's as insincere as your promises."

His expression grew stony as he crossed his arms over his chest. "For your information, I plan to speak to Gran in the morning."

"You told *me* to return in the morning, remember? And I daresay that after drinking with your friends all night, you'd have forgotten your promise. If you haven't already."

A muscle ticked in his jaw. "So you decided to gain my compliance by gambling with me?"

"Why not? I play cards very well. Your friend Pinter seems determined to leave, and you did say you wanted a challenge."

"I suppose you want to play for something having to do with your scheme regarding Lake Ale."

"Yes. I want your agreement that Plumtree Brewery will help us. That's all."

He glared at her. "All? You have no idea what you're asking."

"I'm asking you to help me save my brother's brewery. Of course, you would probably rather see a competitor fail."

"Don't be absurd. I don't care about some half-pint brewery in Burton. Plumtree is five times the size of Lake Ale."

"Which means you have no reason to refuse us your help."

A grim smile crossed his lips. "What if I win? What do *I* get out of this little high-stakes game?"

She slowly slipped her mother's ring off her finger, fighting not to show how much it meant to her. "This. It's solid gold with rubies and diamonds. It's worth at least two hundred pounds. That should make it worth your while."

He uttered a mirthless laugh. "A ring. You think that's equivalent."

"It's a lucky ring," she said, desperate to make him agree to the game. "Whatever brew I make while wearing it comes out splendid."

"I'm sure that adds to the ring's value tenfold," he said sarcastically.

He was *so* annoying. "Fine, if you're afraid to play whist with me . . ."

His eyes turned the same cobalt blue that she'd noticed earlier when he was tasting her ale. "So you think you can best me at whist, do you?"

"Absolutely," she said, though she wasn't at all sure. But she had to try.

He stepped closer, until he loomed over her like some giant in a circus. "The only way I'll agree to your wager is if we make it more personal."

She swallowed. "Personal?"

"The match will be between us—two-handed whist. The first one to win two out of three games wins the match and the wager."

"Very well."

"I'm not finished. If you win, Plumtree Brewery will join Lake Ale in getting into the India market." A sinful smile curved up his lips. "But if *I* win, you warm my bed tonight."

# Chapter Four

Jarret could tell he'd shocked her. Good. The woman needed some sense knocked into her. If his sisters had attempted something like this, he would have locked them up and thrown away the key.

Follow him through the streets of London alone at night? Sit in a tavern with no protection? Challenge him to cards? The woman was too reckless for her own good. Fetching and desirable, but reckless as the very devil.

She wouldn't be insane enough to accept his wager, though. And when he escorted her back to wherever she was staying, he'd tell her companions to keep a better eye on her.

She tipped up her chin. "I accept your offer."

"The hell you do!"

Her lips thinned into a stubborn line. "So you were lying *again*? You weren't serious about the wager?"

"I wasn't lying the *first* time!" he practically shouted.

"But you were just now?"

The prim tilt of her head set her curls bouncing. For some reason, that maddened him even further. He had to stop letting her get under his skin, damn it. "*You*, madam, need a keeper."

"And I suppose you're volunteering for the position," she said archly. "But you don't own a cage large enough to hold *me,* my lord."

He thrust his face into hers. "You're willing to risk ruin, the loss of your reputation and virtue, the hope of ever marrying, on the off chance that you'll beat me at cards and win my help with Lake Ale?"

An odd look came over her face. "Desperate times call for desperate measures."

Sucking in a heavy breath, he glanced away from her. He understood desperation. He'd felt it quite a bit as a boy. And he'd spent many a long night playing cards with men who, down to their last sixpence, prayed that the next turn of the card would recoup their fortunes.

But he'd never seen desperation in any woman but his mother. It unsettled him.

"Besides," she added, "I happen to think it's not an 'off chance.' I'm quite a good whist player, if I do say so myself."

He snorted. Right. Some provincial brewster was going to best him at cards. That would be the day.

Still, he shouldn't risk it, not with Plumtree in its present state. He would never even have suggested the wager if he'd thought she would accept. He had no right to wager the brewery's very future.

"Of course," she went on, "if you're afraid you'll lose—"

"There's no chance in hell you'll beat me," he retorted.

Why was he even worrying? He could win a game of two-handed whist blindfolded. Then Miss Lake would trot back home to Burton a wiser woman.

A ruined woman.

He ignored the twinge of his conscience. If she wanted to throw everything away for this, what did he care? It would serve her right. Then she wouldn't continue to do foolish things like accost men in their offices or follow them to taverns.

And God knows *he* would enjoy it.

"Very well," he said. "We'll play for the stakes agreed upon."

To his surprise, relief crossed her pretty features. "Thank you." Sudden mischief glinted in her eyes. "I promise not to beat you too badly. I wouldn't wish to embarrass you before your friends."

A laugh erupted from him despite everything. God, she was a piece of work.

When they reentered the tavern main room, it was to find Masters taking money from other fellows, while Pinter lounged against a post, scowling at the proceedings. Word must have already traveled down the street that a woman had challenged Hetty Plumtree's grandson to a card game, for the place was busier now.

"What's all this?" Jarret asked as he held out Pinter's empty chair for Miss Lake, then took Masters's seat across from her.

"Masters bet that you would agree to let Miss Lake play," Gabe remarked. "Pinter and I said you wouldn't. Odds are five to one against."

"Well," Jarret said dryly, "for once Masters is right."

Several men around the tavern groaned. Masters pulled up another chair and began to count his winnings.

"Do I get a cut of your profits, Masters, since they depended on me?"

"Actually, they depended on my knowledge of you, and clearly I know you very well." Masters cut a sly glance at Miss Lake. "You can't turn down the chance to spend time with a pretty woman, no matter what the reason. Aren't you going to introduce us?"

With a sigh, Jarret performed introductions all around.

"Enchanted to meet you, Miss Lake." Masters flashed her a seductive smile. "We're delighted to have such a fetching addition to our gaming table."

Miss Lake rolled her eyes. "I see that you possess the same manners as Lord Jarret. It must make your mother so proud."

"He doesn't practice them on his mother," Jarret drawled, fighting a laugh. Women were usually easy prey for Masters. Nice to find one who wasn't. "She'd give him the sharp side of her tongue."

"Mother's tongue doesn't have any other side," Masters grumbled. "And now that my brother is happily married, she's been sharpening it on me much too often."

"Enough chitchat," Gabe said. "What are we playing?"

"I suspect that Jarret wants to play Irish whist," Masters drawled, using a vulgar euphemism for swiving.

"What's that?" Miss Lake asked.

Jarret glared at Masters. "Nothing. My friend is merely being an idiot." He shifted his gaze to Gabe. "And *we* aren't playing anything." Jarret shuffled the cards. "Miss Lake and I are playing two-handed whist."

"With what stakes?" Gabe asked.

"That's private," Jarret answered.

"Ah, a *private* wager." Masters smirked as he leaned back in his chair. "The best kind."

"Get your mind out of the gutter," Jarret snapped. "Miss Lake is a lady."

"And sitting right in the room—fancy that," Miss Lake said. "If you have an insinuation to make, Mr. Masters, perhaps you should say it to my face."

Jarret glanced at her, surprised by her unruffled tone. Then he noticed that her hands, clasped together on the table, were trembling ever so slightly.

Good. She wasn't as self-composed as she seemed. Perhaps next time she'd think twice before agreeing to something as mad as this.

"No insinuation." Masters's gaze flicked between her and Jarret. "Just an observation."

"Perhaps you should take your observations off elsewhere," Jarret said. "Since it's private, there's really no reason for you lot to hang about."

Gabe laughed. "I'm not leaving, old boy. The night is young."

"And I wouldn't miss this for the world," Masters said.

"Suit yourself." At least he'd tried to get rid of their audience.

Jarret laid out the deck for her to cut. Then they both drew. When he lost, he handed her the deck to deal.

"Masters leaned back to address the men crowding round the table. "I'll offer five-to-one odds that the lady beats Lord Jarret."

He was mobbed by takers; clearly no one expected Miss Lake to win.

"You're betting against me, Masters?" Jarret asked, surprised.

"You've been winning all night. Surely it's time for your streak to end."

"Your loss, then." Jarret noticed that Pinter remained as well, leaning against the post with his arms crossed over his chest. "No reason for *you* to stay, Pinter," he said irritably. "Since we annoy you so much."

"As I recall, my lord, when you came in you said there was something you wished to discuss with me later."

Damn, he'd forgotten about that.

"So I'm happy to wait." Pinter cast a glance at Miss Lake. "And watch."

"Ah yes," Gabe said, "Pinter is ever the gallant when it comes to the ladies. He wouldn't risk leaving us alone with poor Miss Lake, for fear one of us might spirit her off to our lair."

"Why?" Miss Lake asked, with a lift of her brow. "Do you three make a *habit* of spiriting women off?"

"Only on Tuesdays and Fridays," Masters said. "Seeing as how it's Wednesday, you're safe."

"Unless you're wearing a blue garter, madam," Gabe quipped. "On Wednesdays, Masters and I have a great fondness for blue garters. Are your garters blue, Miss Lake?"

"Only on Mondays and Thursdays." She dealt thirteen cards apiece to the two of them, then put the rest aside as the stock, turning the top card faceup. "Sorry, gentlemen. I guess you'll have to spirit off some other woman."

"Miss Lake's garters are none of your concern," Jarret said in a warning tone. "I suggest you remember that, or I'll show you the door myself."

He caught Masters's gaze on him and stiffened. Masters was reading too much into this, damn him, probably because Jarret was rarely seen protecting any woman but his sisters. For that matter, he was rarely seen with any respectable woman at all.

Ignoring his friend, Jarret concentrated on his hand, which was abysmal. If he didn't know better, he'd think she'd dealt from the bottom. But he could spot a cardsharp a mile away—and Miss Lake was no cardsharp.

"I wonder if this 'private wager' has anything to do with Mrs. Plumtree's ultimatum," Masters mused aloud.

"Ultimatum?" Miss Lake asked.

Jarret cursed Masters under his breath as he and Miss Lake began to play, taking cards from the stock to replace the ones played.

"Mrs. Plumtree informed her grandchildren that they must all marry before the end of next January, or she will cut them off," Masters explained. "Did you agree to marry Lord Jarret if he won, Miss Lake?"

"Certainly not," Miss Lake remarked.

She didn't have to sound so firm about it, for God's sake.

Masters's eyes gleamed with amusement. "Now *that's* a twist. Women generally fawn over our friend there. Pray tell us, what is it about Lord Jarret that you dislike?"

"I don't know him well enough to like *or* dislike him," she said primly. "Hence, marriage would be extremely premature."

"Like most women," Jarret said, "Miss Lake undoubtedly prefers a love match. She would never marry a man over a wager."

"How odd that you presume to know my opinions on the subject, sir, considering that we only just met this morning." She eyed him askance. "Perhaps *you* are the reader of minds, and not your friend there."

Cheeky wench. "You'd best hope I'm not." He laid down his jack of clubs. "Or you'll be losing this game—and this wager—in short order."

"I already know you aren't." She flashed him a smug smile as she topped his card with a king of clubs. "Because I've just won this hand."

Of course she had; no one could have won with his cards. But her luck couldn't last.

As he gathered up the cards and began to shuffle, Masters said, "Does this mean she's won everything?"

"It's the best two hands out of three, so no, she has not," Jarret said.

"And your wager really has nothing to do with Mrs. Plumtree's ultimatum?"

"If you'd given me the chance," Gabe said, "I would have told you it didn't. Jarret already talked his way out of that. Gran agreed to exempt him from it in exchange for running the brewery for a year. Then he gets to go back to being king of the tables again, without having to marry."

Jarret frowned. It suddenly sounded very irresponsible. Not that he cared. He didn't. Responsibility meant pain and loss. Better not to have it at all than to suffer with it.

"So running the brewery is just a lark for you," Miss Lake said, disapproval weighting her voice.

"Not a lark." He could feel her eyes on him as he examined his cards. "A temporary position. Getting the place in shape for when Gran returns, so to speak."

"But you have no vested interest in seeing the company succeed."

Her disparaging tone told him what she thought of *that*. His gaze locked with hers. "It's *because* I want it to succeed that your risky proposal doesn't appeal to me."

They began to play, and he took three tricks right off.

"What risky proposal?" Gabe asked.

Miss Lake arranged her cards. "My brother owns a brewery in Burton. We hope to join with your family's concern in a venture that will benefit both parties."

"Or so she claims," Jarret retorted.

"So this is a damned business wager?" Masters said. "God,

that's boring. So if Miss Lake is playing for Jarret's coopera-
tion in a venture, then what is Jarret playing for?"

"Her brother's brewery!" Gabe said. "That has to be it!"

"Don't be ridiculous," she retorted. "If I owned the brewery, I wouldn't need Lord Jarret's help. And I would certainly
never wager it in some card game. What sort of fool does
that?"

"You'd be surprised," Jarret said. "Some men will wager
anything."

"Some women, as well." Masters eyed her speculatively.

"If it's not her brother's brewery she's offering, what else
can it be?" Gabe asked. When Jarret cast him a quelling
glance, he stiffened, then shot a glance at Miss Lake.

Her cheeks were the color of poppies. The woman was trans-
parent as a sheet of glass. And Jarret loathed the idea of her character being speculated about among the men in the room.

"Miss Lake wagered her ring," Jarret lied.

She cast him a grateful glance. "It's very valuable. Worth a
lot of money."

"Ah." Masters exchanged a telling look with Gabe. "A ring.
Of course."

They both knew Jarret preferred cold, hard cash in his wagers. He never accepted jewelry as payment. And it was clear
from how they eyed Miss Lake with new interest that they'd
guessed what he was really willing to accept.

Jarret gritted his teeth. He should never have taken her
wager. After some stern words, he should have escorted her
back to wherever she was staying.

So why hadn't he?

Because he'd truly expected her to turn him down. Because
the woman had an amazing power to annoy him. And because her earthy charms roused him as no woman ever had.

It was insane and could lead to no good. But before it did, he would have her in his bed. Just see if he didn't.

Gabe shot her an assessing look. "So, Miss Lake, did you come to London alone?"

"Of course not." She took a trick. "I came with my sister-in-law and my . . . nephew."

Had he imagined it, or had she paused before the word "nephew"? The reason for that suddenly occurred to him. "How old is this nephew?"

She concentrated on her cards. "What has that to do with anything?"

"If he's supposed to be your male escort," Jarret said, "it has a great deal to do with it. What is he, five?"

She swallowed tellingly. "If you must know, he's twelve."

"Twelve!" Masters exclaimed. "My God, woman, you can't gallivant about the city with only a boy as a protector. How can your brother allow it?"

"Hugh is ill," she said. "He had no choice."

Jarret raised an eyebrow. "Did you give him any choice?"

She slapped a card on the table. "Not really."

Gabe gave a low whistle. "If you're not going to marry her, Jarret, then someone should. She needs a husband to keep her out of trouble."

"Believe me, I already suggested that," Jarret muttered.

"You did not!" Miss Lake said hotly. "You said I need a keeper. It's hardly the same thing. You're undoubtedly one of those men who believe that women are like pets, to be kept caged and only trotted out at parties."

"Honestly, Jarret," Masters chided, eyes twinkling, "you have such a poor opinion of the female sex." He leaned close to Miss Lake. "I assure you, madam, that *I* would never imply such a thing to a lady."

Even as Jarret snorted, Miss Lake arched one delicate brow at Masters. "I suspect that would only be because you hope to turn the lady up sweet."

"She's got you there, Masters," Gabe joked. "Perhaps Miss Lake is a reader of minds."

Jarret took her trick. "She can't be, or she wouldn't presume to know my opinion about women." He glanced at her. "Apparently I'm not the only one here who assumes things based on only one day's acquaintance."

"My assumption isn't based on our acquaintance, sir," she shot back, "but on what you said. If you think a woman needs a keeper, then you think her incapable of keeping herself. It's downright insulting."

"I meant no insult. I was merely pointing out that a woman must behave differently in the city than in the country. And if she doesn't, she needs someone to look after her."

"The country! I live in Burton. We have nearly seven thousand inhabitants."

Everyone laughed.

When she scowled, Gabe said, "Forgive me, madam, but London has over a million inhabitants."

"I know that. But that doesn't make Burton the country, does it?"

"Perhaps by comparison—" Jarret began.

"I assure you, sir," she said tightly, "we have our share of vice and wickedness. The difference is only a matter of scale."

The wealth of bitterness in that remark gave him pause. Had she experienced such vice firsthand? Had some scoundrel taken advantage of her? And why did that possibility spark his temper?

"In any case," she went on, "I'm perfectly aware that a woman must be careful in London." She cast him an arch glance. "I

certainly didn't set out to spend the evening with three unconscionable rogues who have the audacity to suggest that I need a
husband, apparently to protect me from the likes of *them*."

Masters laughed. "She does have a point, Jarret."

"Don't encourage her," Jarret snapped.

Masters might be an unconscionable rogue, but *he* wasn't.
He was a carefree rogue, so he didn't like being responsible
for the reputation of the tart-tongued sprite sitting across
from him. The one who'd blithely accepted the scandalous
wager he shouldn't have made.

They finished the second hand, and to his vast annoyance
it ended in a draw, both of them having won thirteen tricks.
The next one ended the same.

Grudgingly, he acknowledged that she was a better player
than he'd expected. Not that two-handed whist required
much strategy, but one did have to keep on one's toes. She'd
played some tricks expertly. He was impressed.

He was also annoyed, because he did *not* mean to lose
tonight.

Picking up the hand she'd just dealt, he glanced at the top
card of the stock to see that diamonds were trump. Ha. He'd
see how she managed when the luck was on *his* side.

"So, Lord Jarret," she asked as she led her card, "what *is*
your opinion about women?"

"Uh-oh," Masters said, eyes gleaming, "you're in for it now,
my boy."

"Why is that?" Miss Lake asked.

Gabe laughed. "Because no man can answer that question
to a woman's satisfaction. Any attempt to do so is fraught
with peril."

"Mr. Pinter," she appealed to the runner, "surely *you* have
an answer to the question."

Pinter got a panicky look on his face. "I beg to be excused from the discussion, Miss Lake. I have no opinion of women at all, I swear."

Jarret sloughed off a low card to her lead. What a lot of cowards. "I'm willing to answer." He thought of Gran and her meddling, not to mention his mother and her fateful act, and something dark welled up inside him. "Women are at their happiest when they're sowing havoc in the lives of everyone around them."

The table got very silent. Indeed, it seemed as if the entire tavern turned to stone, and every male eye in the room fixed on her.

To his surprise, she burst into laughter. "It appears that you and I have more in common than I thought. Because that is exactly my opinion of *men*."

"Is that so?" He let her win a few tricks, ridding himself of useless cards as they played their way through the stock. "And what hapless man is responsible for making you form such an opinion?"

"What makes you think it's only one man?" She raised an eyebrow at him. "What about you? Did some woman break your heart, setting your opinion about women for life?"

The stock was empty now. She played an ace, and he trumped it with a smile. He had enough diamonds in his hand to lead her out, and enough high cards to keep the lead for the rest of the tricks. This was one hand that wouldn't come to a draw. "No woman has ever broken my heart. And no woman ever will."

"That's because Jarret never lets a woman close enough even to chip off a piece of it," Gabe joked.

And why should he? They would try to change him, something he would never allow. His life had worked perfectly well for him until Gran had started her machinations. It would work well for him again once this year was up.

Granted, occasionally it was lonely, and he found himself tiring of the late nights and the sameness of the games. But he felt comfortable at the card table. It was all he knew, all he could really be sure of.

Jarret laid down one card after another, drawing out her trumps and then her other cards, enjoying how she paled as she realized she couldn't win this hand. "I should ask you the same question, Miss Lake. Did some man break *your* heart? Is that why you haven't married?"

"I haven't married, sir, because I see no benefit to it. And you and your friends aren't exactly convincing me otherwise."

"Well, you won't have to worry about us much longer." He took the last trick and smirked at her. "Because I just won this hand. We're even now, and I'm a lot closer to winning our wager."

"No closer than I." She gathered up the cards. "My turn to deal, my lord. I'll try not to be as generous to you as you were to yourself."

His eyes narrowed. "If you're insinuating that I cheat, madam—"

"Of course not." A blush touched her cheeks as she shuffled the cards. "I should have said, I'll hope for as much luck as you had."

Her peevish tone made him grin. "Do I detect a whiff of sour grapes, Miss Lake?"

"Surely even you must admit you had an extraordinarily lucky hand that time," she retorted.

He shrugged. "A bad player can make a hash of a lucky hand. Just as a good player can turn a mediocre hand into a brilliant one."

"And a mediocre player can turn a brilliant hand into a lame one," Masters interjected. "Will you two get on with it? We want to see who wins, not listen to philosophizing about card playing."

Miss Lake flashed Jarret an arch glance. "Is he always this impatient?"

"Only when he has a bet riding on something. And he's foolishly pinned all his hopes on you."

"Do trounce him soundly, will you, Miss Lake?" Masters said. "I could use the blunt. And he could use the set-down."

"Why?" Miss Lake dealt the cards. "Does he usually win?"

"He *always* wins," Gabe complained. "Though he's been off his game recently."

"But not this evening," Jarret said as he saw his hand. It wasn't as spectacular as his last one, but he could make it work.

The next game moved quickly, both of them silent, intent upon the cards. When it ended in a draw—again—the men hovering about the table let out a collective groan.

Miss Lake shoved the cards across the table at him. "We could be at this all night, you know."

"Getting tired, Miss Lake?" he taunted as he shuffled the cards.

"Certainly not. But you must admit we're evenly matched."

"Perhaps." He dealt them their hands.

"Now *I* detect a whiff of sour grapes," she teased.

"Or perhaps you just smell impending doom," he shot back.

He picked up his hand. It was one of those that could go either way. By now he'd figured out her style of playing, so he ought to be able to gauge her strategy.

But then, she could gauge his, as well.

He did enjoy the challenge of playing cards with a worthy opponent. Masters and Gabe were indifferent players; neither was willing to expend the effort necessary to figure out where all the cards lay. They were more interested in drinking and flirting with the tavern maids.

Miss Lake, on the other hand, was a serious card player. It made him wonder about her family. She had to be living with her brother and sister-in-law, since her parents were dead. That made her the maiden aunt.

It was a shame, really. She looked far too young to be a maiden aunt—she couldn't be more than twenty-five. What kind of life was that for a woman?

Of course, Minerva was twenty-eight and seemed content with *her* situation. But that was because she had her books. What did Miss Lake have? A brewery that didn't belong to her, that her brother probably kept her away from as much as possible.

Although perhaps not, given her presence here in London.

She played her first card, and he forced himself to concentrate. It would take every bit of his skill to win, or at the very least, bring this to a draw.

They played several tricks in silence and had worked through the stock into the second thirteen tricks when Masters said, "So, Gabe, since Jarret found a way out of marrying, that leaves the rest of you. Have you picked out your wife?"

Gabe scowled. "I'm waiting until the last moment."

"Wise decision," Masters said. "And . . . er . . . what about your sisters? Have they made any choices?"

Something in Masters's tone alerted Jarret. He glanced over at his friend to find Masters examining his fingernails with seeming nonchalance. But there was a telltale tightening of his jaw, and he'd gone very still.

Gabe didn't seem to notice. "Oh, Celia is still annoyed at Gran over it, and Minerva is angry as hell that Jarret got out of it. Minerva says she means to fight it, too, but I don't know what she thinks she can do. Jarret was the only one who had anything to negotiate with. Even Oliver's plan for getting around Gran failed."

"Well, if anyone can find a way around her, it's Lady Minerva," Masters said in a too careful voice.

Jarret tensed. He'd wondered if there were something between Masters and Minerva after seeing them together at the St. Valentine's Day Ball, but he'd forgotten about it after Oliver announced his engagement to Maria.

There damned well better not be. Masters might be his best friend, but he was *not* to be trusted around women. And he had a peculiar habit of disappearing to God knows where for days on end. Minerva deserved better than a sometime husband. If not for Gran's machinations, she wouldn't even have to find—

"Trumps are hearts, Lord Jarret," Miss Lake said.

He looked down to see that he'd tried to take her jack of diamonds with a five of spades, the trump suit from their last game. Confound it all to hell. The idea of Masters going after his sister had distracted him.

"Of course," he said smoothly and pushed the trick across to her.

But now he was in trouble. At least three tricks had gone by, during which he'd played without thinking. He tried to remember what had been played, but for the life of him he couldn't.

Damn, damn, *damn*! He couldn't remember where the queen of clubs or ten of hearts was. He'd had neither—he remembered that much—but which had *she* already played?

It was the last two tricks now, and they were at a draw again. He had the nine of hearts and a five of clubs—and it was his lead. He was fairly certain she had the eight of diamonds and either the queen of clubs or ten of hearts.

He did some swift calculations. If he led with the five, every possible combination ended in a draw. If he led with the nine of hearts, she could win, he could win, or it could end in a draw, depending on how she played.

He ought to lead with the five. That was the safe choice, since he couldn't lose. But he couldn't win either. What if his next hand was abysmal? At least by leading with the nine of hearts, he had a *chance* to win.

It all rested on whether she would have saved the trump or the high card. From the way she'd been playing, it was hard to be sure.

He took a long breath. It had never been in his nature to play it safe.

With his heart thundering in his chest, he laid down the nine. She shot him a quizzical glance, then played the ten of hearts.

He stared blindly at the cards. He'd guessed wrong, and now he was sunk.

The last trick was a mere formality. She'd won the bloody hand, which meant she'd won the game. And the wager.

Damn it all to hell.

# Chapter Five

Annabel gaped at the cards, hardly able to believe her eyes. Mr. Masters broke into a cheer, which triggered groans from those who had bet against him. Lord Gabriel, who'd bet on his brother, uttered a curse unfit for a lady's ears.

Lord Jarret just stared at the cards, expressionless.

That wasn't terribly surprising—he hadn't reacted to his cards the entire game, making it impossible to read his strategy. When he'd gained the lead, she'd been *certain* the game would end in a draw. She'd known exactly what cards he had left and thought for sure he knew the same for her. His friends had emphasized that he was famous for remembering every card played.

So why had he played the nine of hearts? Could he have assumed that *she* didn't remember what had been played?

No, that made no sense. Once he'd played the nine, she'd had no choice but to follow suit, which meant she'd had no choice but to win.

Had he *let* her win? That seemed the only logical explanation.

But why would he, when he'd been so opposed to helping her brother's brewery?

There was only one explanation: he'd wanted to avoid bedding her.

She thought back to their discussion. When he'd made his outrageous proposal and she'd agreed, he *had* appeared to be alarmed that his bluff had been called. And a man like that would have too much pride to back out of a wager.

Had he decided that the only way to avoid bedding her against her will was to lose? If he had, that showed him to be far less a rogue than she'd guessed. Either that, or he found her unattractive, which he hadn't seemed to do. Granted, she wasn't some fresh young thing, but she wasn't doddering on the edge of the grave either, and a true rogue wouldn't be that particular, would he?

Still, if he'd wanted to be a gentleman about it, he could simply have refused to demand payment of the debt. Or taken Mother's ring. Why hadn't he done that?

Perhaps she really *had* beaten him.

A heavy silence fell on the room. Everyone waited for her or Lord Jarret to speak.

"It looks like Plumtree Brewery will be joining up with Lake Ale, Lord Jarret," she ventured, not sure what else to say.

His eyes locked with hers, glinting green in the candlelight. "It certainly does."

Even his tone gave nothing away. It was extremely unnerving. "Thank you for agreeing to the stakes. For agreeing to play cards with me at all."

"It was my pleasure."

Ah, there it was—just a hint of irritation in his voice.

He stood abruptly. "Where in town are you staying, Miss Lake?"

She blinked, taken off guard by the question. "At the Spur Inn."

"That's in High Borough Street, right?" When she nodded, he donned the hat and greatcoat hanging from a hook on a nearby post. "I'll accompany you."

"No need for that. I can hire a hackney."

"Out of the question."

"I can take her," Mr. Pinter put in.

"No," Lord Jarret said firmly. When Mr. Pinter looked as if he might protest, Lord Jarret added, "Miss Lake and I have a few matters to discuss. Privately."

Warily, she rose. She'd assumed that their discussion would take place in the morning.

"You'll return here when you're done, won't you?" Mr. Masters asked Lord Jarret, still grinning about his win. "Now that you're on a losing streak again, I want another crack at you and Gabe."

"And you want to gloat awhile longer," Lord Jarret said dryly.

"Absolutely. You're not going to live this one down anytime soon."

"That's what I'm afraid of," Lord Jarret remarked with no trace of rancor. If he was angry, he hid it well. "Unfortunately, you'll have to have your fun another time, old boy. I'm coming back to speak with Pinter. Then I'm going home. I have to rise early if I'm to travel to Burton."

While she was still gaping at him over that, he rounded the table. "Come, Miss Lake, we'd best go."

She took the arm he offered. As soon as they got out onto the street, she asked, "What do you mean, travel to Burton? There's no need for that. Just talk to the East India Company and convince them to carry our October brew. Offer them reassurances that you'll guarantee it, or something."

He shot her a cold glance. "The wager was that I would help Lake Ale, *not* that I would turn a blind eye to anything your brother's company does. I'm not risking my family's relations with the East India Company without knowing more about your brother's brewery: its situation, the amount of ale that could reasonably be produced, the plan he has for—"

"But you *can't* come to Burton!" she cried.

His eyes narrowed on her. "Why not?"

"I-I . . . well . . ." Inspiration hit. "How will your brewery manage without you?"

The minute he saw Hugh and realized that she'd invented her brother's "illness," or that Hugh hadn't entirely approved this plan, he would back out of their agreement, wager or no wager.

He navigated her expertly around a mud puddle. "Plumtree will be fine. I'll leave instructions for my master brewer and Croft, and they'll handle things until I return. I won't be gone more than a few days." He searched her face. "Is there something you're not telling me?"

She forced herself to meet his gaze steadily. "Of course not. I merely don't want to inconvenience you."

He gave a dry laugh. "Rather late for that. You wanted my help, and now you have it. I'm happy to escort you and your family to Burton whenever you're ready to leave."

She considered that. If he traveled with them, she might be able to control the situation better than if he showed up at Lake Ale unannounced. Still, it would be altogether better if he remained in London.

"Forgive me, sir, but I can't imagine your bumping and

jostling in a mail coach with me, my sister-in-law, and my nephew," she said.

"Nor can I. Which is why we'll take the Sharpe family traveling coach."

"Oh, no, I couldn't—"

"My eldest brother is the only one who uses it, and he'll be out of the country with his new wife for another two months at least." He slanted a glance at her as they turned onto High Borough Street. "It will save you the fare to Burton."

A flush touched her cheeks. She hated to admit it, but that would be helpful. Neither she nor Sissy had dreamed that lodgings in London would be so expensive. They had precious little for the journey back, and none to stay at a coaching inn as they had coming to London.

She hadn't been looking forward to a day and a half of solid travel by mail coach with Sissy and a cranky twelve-year-old. This would enable them to stay one night at an inn, even *with* his lordship.

So she swallowed her pride. "Thank you, that is very kind of you. And of course we'll provide for your lodgings along the way."

"Nonsense. Since I'm foisting my presence on you, I'll take care of those costs. I welcome the chance to get to know the rest of your family, since I'll be working with your brother."

Panic hit her again. "What do you mean?"

"We have to hammer out the terms of this agreement. If Lake Ale is providing the brew, will he wish us to transport it? Is he planning to transport it? Does he have enough resources and good local connections for barrels, or will that be something else we provide? A venture such as this involves several variables, which must be negotiated."

She stared at him, once again surprised by his sharp

thinking. For a man running a business temporarily, he certainly had a good mind for it. That could prove dangerous.

"Do remember that my brother is unwell," she said. "He may not be able to give you the information you require."

He cast her a long, considering look that made her glance away guiltily. She wasn't exactly lying to him. Hugh *was* unwell. In a fashion.

"Just how ill *is* your brother?" he pressed as they dodged a lumbering cart.

What should she say? If she said Hugh was very ill, then he might not help them for fear of the company going under. But Hugh had to be ill enough to make it believable that he was unavailable while Lord Jarret was in Burton.

She settled for something vague. "The physician says he'll recover in good time, as long as he isn't disturbed by matters at Lake Ale. But the brewery manager and I can provide you with whatever you need to know."

"It sounds as if you spend a great deal of time there. I assumed you only brewed the ale, not helped to run the business."

"With Hugh unavailable, I have no choice."

"That's how my grandmother got into it, as well. Grandfather fell ill, and she stepped in to help. He guided her from his sickbed." Lord Jarret's voice softened. "When he died of his ailment, a family friend offered to sell the place and arrange for the proceeds to go to Gran and my mother, but Gran insisted upon taking over. By then, she knew enough to manage on her own."

"Your grandmother is a very brave woman."

"Or a mad one. Plenty of men claimed it was the latter."

"Let me guess: they were her competitors, right?"

He laughed. "They were, indeed."

There was no mistaking his grudging respect when he spoke of his grandmother. He might not approve of her tactics in trying to make his siblings marry—and Annabel could sympathize with that—but he clearly admired her.

"I understand that you and your siblings were raised by Mrs. Plumtree after . . . that is . . ."

His face hardened. "I see you've heard of the family scandal."

Oh, dear. She shouldn't have alluded to that. It made her sound so . . . gossipy. She'd heard various versions of how his parents had died. One was that his mother had killed his father by mistaking him for an intruder and shooting him, then killing herself when she realized she'd shot her husband. Another was that his older brother had shot their mother when she'd tried to come between him and his father, and then had shot his father. Both versions rang false.

What was the real story? She didn't dare ask. And clearly it wasn't something he wanted to discuss, for a heavy silence fell between them. But just as she was about to apologize for prying, he spoke again.

"Gran became our guardian when I was thirteen. But I don't think you can properly say she raised us." His voice was remote, cold. "She was too busy at the brewery for that. We raised ourselves, for the most part."

"That would explain why you're all so—"

"Wild?"

She winced. There she went again, saying things she oughtn't. "Independent."

His laugh held an edge. "That's a nice way of putting it." He eyed her closely. "So what's _your_ excuse for being 'independent'? Did your father raise you alone? Is that why you insist upon having a hand in his brewery?"

"No. My mother was an alewife. Every recipe we make was passed down for generations from mother to daughter in her family. You might say I stepped into her shoes." Her voice softened. "They were big shoes to fill."

"So you've been doing it for how long now?"

"Since before Papa died," she said. "Almost seven years."

"That's impossible. You would have been far too young."

"I was twenty-two when Mother died and I started going to the brewery."

He gaped at her. "But that would make you—"

"Nearly thirty, yes. I'm afraid I'm rather long in the tooth."

He snorted. "You're annoying as the very devil, and one of the mouthiest damned females I've ever met, but not remotely long in the tooth."

She hid a smile. Perhaps it was silly, but she was flattered that he hadn't thought her an old spinster, as many in Burton did.

They walked awhile in silence. It was easy to do with the streets so busy. High Borough Street was known for its many inns and public houses, so people were coming and going even late at night. Thank goodness he'd walked her back to the inn; his massive frame made her feel safe.

He'd been right about the difference between London and Burton, though she'd been loath to admit it to him. She moved freely about Burton, mostly because of her family's stature. She never even needed a footman—she was always quite safe as long as she stayed out of the less savory part of town.

But here . . . well, there were a number of unsavory parts in London. And though she might have been perfectly safe in a hackney, even those could be breached by a determined footpad.

They passed Plumtree Brewery, which seemed quieter with only the night staff at work, and approached Spur Inn. She'd chosen it for its proximity to the brewery and for its low cost, but she rather wished she'd chosen another. The crowd downstairs in the taproom seemed very rowdy, and she doubted she'd get much sleep tonight.

He opened the door to usher her inside. "I'll show you to your room. This is not a safe place for a woman to wander alone."

"Thank you, my lord," she said as they climbed the narrow stairs.

"Given that you offered earlier to spend a night in my bed as part of a gaming wager," he said in a husky voice, "I think you can call me something more personal than 'my lord.'"

Heat rose in her cheeks. He *would* bring that up again. It made her aware that she was practically alone with him, since everyone else in the inn seemed to be tucked away in their rooms or in the taproom below.

Why had he made that wager anyway? Simply to put her off? Or because he desired her? And if it was the latter, then why let her win?

If they were to spend the next two days closed up in a carriage together, she needed to know if he was a gentleman or a rogue. "Speaking of that, Lord Jarret—"

"Jarret," he corrected her.

"Jarret." A shiver spun down her spine. Using his Christian name seemed so intimate. "I was wondering . . ." Oh, heavens, how was she to ask this?

"Yes?"

They'd reached the next floor. It was deserted. Once again, she found herself glad he'd accompanied her, for the room she shared with Sissy and Geordie was at the unlit end of the hall. She wouldn't have wanted to be trapped alone here with some drunken fellow coming up from downstairs.

They stopped outside the door to her room. She forced herself to look him in the eye. "Did you *let* me win that game?"

"Why would I do that?"

"Because you're less of a hellion than you care to admit. Because you're a gentleman."

"I'm not *that* much of a gentleman."

She lowered her voice. "But a gentleman wouldn't want to force a woman into his bed just because of a wager."

"Then why would I make the wager in the first place?"

"To scare me. And when it didn't work, you had to find a way out of it."

His broad brow creased in a frown. "I could simply not have demanded that you honor our agreement." His voice held a trace of irritation now.

"I considered that. But that would have left me under an obligation to you, and you might have thought I'd find that intolerable. Letting me win would have been the gentlemanly thing to do."

"I did *not* let you win," he bit out.

"It's just that . . . well, there was absolutely no reason for you to lose. I watched how you played. You had to have known I had the ten of—"

"You're going to make me admit this, aren't you?" He advanced, forcing her to back up until she collided with the wall. Planting his hands on either side of her shoulders, he leaned in to growl, "You won fair and square. You beat me because of your superior playing. Happy now?"

"No! I simply cannot believe that a man of your skill with cards—"

His mouth covered hers, taking her by surprise. It was warm, fragrant with the tang of hops from the ale he'd drunk, and oh so soft. Only his lips touched her, but that was enough to bring long-suppressed urges to the fore.

It was like gulping ale on an empty stomach—the sudden rush of heat, the roiling in one's belly, the tingling that spread from her head down to the tips of her fingers and toes. The smell of wool and soap and *man* intoxicated her—she hadn't been this close to a man in years. She'd forgotten how good they could smell.

And how good they could feel, for his lips were molding hers, teasing hers. Barely conscious of what she did, she opened her mouth. He tensed against her, as if in surprise, but then his tongue sank inside and he pressed into her, his body hardening. She felt every inch of him, from the muscled chest meeting her breasts to the bulge rising between his legs.

Undaunted by that evidence of his arousal, she slid her arms about his neck and lifted up on her toes to better accept his kiss. His hands slid down to clasp her waist, pulling her between his thighs as he drank of her mouth over and over.

Time stopped. There was only this man she barely knew, taking charge of her mouth as if it were his right. His fingers dug into her waist, the thumbs caressing her ribs as his tongue tangled with hers, exploring, wreaking havoc on her senses. Wild feelings careened through her chest and belly, making her hot and achy, making her *want*. Lord, it had been so long since she'd felt the heady pulse of desire.

Suddenly a sound, like something falling in a nearby room, made him tear his mouth from hers and back away, instantly alert. For a moment they merely stood there, both panting, their gazes locked upon each other.

What had she been thinking? She'd let him kiss her, and worse, she'd kissed him back!

Though she and Rupert had made love only once, they'd come close several times before, being stupid and young and infatuated. She'd never forgotten the pleasures he'd introduced her to. Now Jarret had chipped away at thirteen years of respectable living, and she'd simply stood still and let him.

Didn't she know better by now? Encouraging such behavior never led to anything but trouble for a woman like her, especially when the man was known for his wild living. Sons of marquesses didn't marry poor spinsters from Burton. They bedded them. He'd made that quite clear.

He leaned close. "As I said, Annabel, I'm not *that* much of a gentleman." His rough rasp of her Christian name set her pulse to pounding. "I didn't let you win. I played the nine of hearts because I got distracted and failed to notice that the ten hadn't been played. I certainly wasn't trying to let you off the hook for our wager."

His eyes, glinting dangerously in the dim light, trailed down to her mouth. "If this odd conversation stems from some belief that I'm a tenderhearted fellow you can twist to your will with a pretty smile, I hope I've put that idea to rest. But in case I haven't, think twice before wagering your body in a card game with me again to save your brother's precious brewery. Because next time I'll make sure I win. And when I do, I *will* claim my prize."

Heat rose in her cheeks, though she wasn't sure if it was from shame or arousal. "Don't worry, my lord." *Show no weakness, or he'll run roughshod over you.* "There's no need for me to wager with you now that I've got you where I want you."

His gaze sharpened on her, a mirthless smile touching his

lips. "Be careful, my dear lady. Plenty of people have thought they had me where they wanted me, only to be proved wrong when I got them where *I* wanted *them*. You're playing with the big boys now. We don't roll over and play dead as easily as your brother."

He paused, as if to make certain she got the message. Then he straightened, the heat in his features cooling. "I have to speak to Gran in the morning, but I should be done before midday. We'll leave for Burton then." He tipped his hat. "Until tomorrow . . . Annabel."

Utterly incapable of a coherent response, she watched as he turned and sauntered off.

Once he disappeared into the stairwell, she collapsed against the wall, her knees shaking and her hands clammy.

Arrogant beast. *The big boys*, indeed. He was so sure of himself, so smug! It roused her temper as no man had, in all her years struggling to be accepted among the brewers.

And his other threat—to *claim* his prize . . . She wasn't the fool he took her for. *He* had been the one to make that outrageous wager in the first place, not her. She'd only accepted it because it was her last chance at saving Lake Ale. Did he really think otherwise? Did he really think she would step into that trap *again*?

Of course he did. He probably thought he could turn any woman into one of his doxies with his seductions.

Did he have doxies? Or was there a mistress stashed away somewhere whom he visited whenever he needed an outlet for his urges? The idea rankled, but only because she hated the idea of being one of many women he'd taken advantage of for . . . for *that*.

Clearly Lord Jarret was interested in women only as physical creatures with whom he could sate his lust. And she could see why women were eager to throw themselves on his pyre. The man definitely knew how to kiss. She could only imagine how skilled he must be at all the rest.

Long-forgotten images swam into her mind, of bodies intertwined, hands exploring, of driving each other to greater heights of—

A pox on him! She'd spent years tucking away all those urges and hopes and needs, and with one foolish kiss, he'd dragged them out again to plague her. She wouldn't let him do this to her!

Shaking off the unwanted heat in her belly, she fumbled in her cloak pocket for the room key and unlocked the door.

When she entered, she found the result of her youthful passion lying on a pallet near the fire, his face turned toward the hearth. Geordie had kicked off the blanket, which now lay on the floor, and his nightshirt was twisted about his skinny legs.

Annabel's heart tightened in her chest. Moving carefully to avoid waking Sissy, who was dozing in a chair, Annabel crept over to cover Geordie up. He mumbled something in his sleep and caught the blanket up to his chin.

Tears stung her eyes. Did he ever wonder why his "aunt" insisted upon coming with his mother to his room each evening to bid him good night? Or why his "aunt" was so interested in his future? Did he even care what she thought of him? Or was it only his "mother" who captured his deepest affection?

That pained her too much to dwell on. Sometimes, looking at him was like staring at a fairy-tale castle far away on a mountaintop. He was hers and yet not. Would he ever be hers? Or would telling him the truth drive him even farther away?

One of his dark brown locks lay across his cheek, and she

had to fight the impulse to smooth it back. She didn't want to wake him. He looked so sweet asleep.

"You're back," said a soft voice.

She looked up to find Sissy stirring. "Yes."

"Did you get to talk to Mrs. Plumtree?"

"Not exactly. But I did convince Lord Jarret to help the brewery."

Sissy smiled. "You did! That's wonderful!" When Geordie's even breathing broke and he turned over, she dropped her voice to a whisper. "I knew you could do it."

"But there's a catch." Swiftly she explained that Lord Jarret would be traveling with them to Burton and why.

"Oh dear," Sissy said. "What if he sees Hugh in one of his . . . well . . ."

"We'll just have to make sure he doesn't. I'm counting on you to help with that."

"Of course!"

"And we must keep Geordie from saying anything. Although I don't know what he'd say—I'm not sure he even understands the problem with Hugh. We just have to make sure he supports our contention that Hugh is ill."

"I'll speak to him in the morning. Don't worry—I won't let Hugh or Geordie ruin this. It's our only chance." Sissy settled back in her chair. "Now, tell me everything that happened. How did you change Lord Jarret's mind?"

She sighed. Sissy always had to hear the gossip, and generally Annabel was happy to recite every detail. But a more oblique version of the truth was in order tonight.

She had shamed her family once with her behavior. She wasn't about to let Sissy think she might do so again.

# Chapter Six

Jarret stalked down High Borough Street in a vain attempt to squelch the anger Annabel Lake had brought roaring to the surface. After her snide remark about having him where she wanted him, he'd been tempted to show her exactly where he wanted *her*.

But showing her he desired her had been what provoked her to make that comment in the first place. Had he lost his mind? First, he'd wagered for her very honor, then he'd besmirched it in some grimy inn hall. What if someone had come along? What if, God forbid, her sister-in-law had come out?

He'd been thinking with his cock, like some randy buck fresh on the town. The woman had a knack for fracturing his control.

Yes, she was pretty. Then again, so were plenty of women. But none of them would have braved a tavern full of men to save their family's brewery. None of them would have beaten him at cards or called his scandalous bluff.

When she'd made assumptions about the wager, it had

infuriated him. After everything that had happened, he'd hoped to at least knock some sense into her. But instead of recognizing how close she'd come to ruination, she'd accused him of letting her win.

The chit was maddening. Maddening! She had no idea how she could tempt an unscrupulous man, no sense of danger. How could she be that naïve at her age? Nearly thirty? He would never have guessed her to be that—she looked fresh and sweet as a spring bouquet. Long in the tooth, indeed.

And what was wrong with the men in Burton, that one of them hadn't made her his bride? It made no sense. Unless it was she who balked at marriage.

*I haven't married, sir, because I see no benefit to it.*

Well, she had him there. He couldn't see much benefit to marriage either, so they certainly had that in common.

But he could see plenty of benefit in taking her to bed, covering that body with his, peeling away her serviceable gown to explore the surprisingly lush breasts and the deliciously curvy waist and the—

Damn her to hell! Her obsession with her brother's brewery clearly made her take risks no innocent should take. She hadn't yet learned that risking all for some dream of success was foolish and fraught with pain. Look at him—the one time he'd broken his own rules, mixed his business with pleasure, wagering for something he had no right to wager for, it had led straight to disaster.

Of course, that was partly because he'd let himself be distracted by thoughts of Gran and her machinations. If not for her, he wouldn't be worrying over the brewery or his sibling's prospects. He'd be drifting from card game to card game, needing no one, having no one need him.

Becoming more bored with every passing day.

He scowled. Where had that come from? He wasn't bored. His life was fine.

*That is not a suitable life for a clever man like yourself.*

With a curse, he entered the tavern. Gran knew nothing about it. She'd been the one to say he should be a barrister, and every instinct in him rebelled at the idea.

"Well, well, look who's back," Gabe said with a grin.

The crowd had thinned out now that the excitement was over. Pinter sat drinking, Gabe had a tavern maid on one knee, and Masters was shuffling cards.

The minute Masters saw Jarret, he pulled out a chair. "Now that the lady's gone, you can tell us the truth about what you would have won if the cards had gone your way."

Jarret struggled to keep his temper. "I already told you. Her mother's ring."

"Right. A ring," Masters scoffed.

"Are you calling me a liar, Masters?"

Masters blinked. "Certainly not. I merely think it odd that you—"

"Think what you wish, but I'd better not hear you thinking it aloud to anyone ever again. Do you understand me?"

"God, Jarret, who put the stick up *your* arse?" Gabe asked, eliciting a giggle from the tavern maid.

"The same goes for you, Gabe," he warned. "Not one word, do you hear?"

When he turned his gaze to Pinter, the runner held up his hands. "No need to caution me, sir. I don't spread gossip about ladies."

"Pay him no mind, Pinter," Masters said dryly. "He's just sore that he lost. And to a woman, too."

Remembering *why* he'd lost, Jarret rounded on Masters. "That's another thing. Why were you asking about Minerva's prospects for marriage?"

Masters looked instantly wary. "I don't recall doing so."

"You did, actually," Gabe put in. "You asked if our sisters had chosen husbands."

"Just polite conversation, that's all," Masters said with a shrug, but the muscle ticking in his jaw put the lie to that.

Jarret walked up to loom over his friend. "Stay away from my sister."

Something dark flickered in Masters's eyes as he rose to meet Jarret's gaze. "You're behaving like an ass." He nodded his head in Gabe's direction. "Come, Gabe. Let's go to my club. Time we found more congenial company for the evening."

Gabe murmured a few words to the tavern maid, who flounced off with a pout. Then he rose, his gaze flitting from Jarret to Masters. "Lead on, old chap."

As soon as they were gone, Jarret called for tankards of Gran's best porter for him and Pinter, then dropped into a chair. He'd made a fool of himself, and for no good reason. Even if Masters did have his eye on Minerva, Minerva would have something to say about it. She didn't suffer fools—or rogues—lightly. If any woman could fend off Masters, it was his sister.

Still, he noticed that Masters hadn't responded to his admonition. He hadn't laughed it off or agreed to stay away or said anything to reassure Jarret that there was nothing between him and Minerva. And that worried Jarret.

"So you're traveling to Burton tomorrow, are you?" Pinter said conversationally.

Jarret forced his attention to the task at hand. "Yes. To take a look at Lake Ale Brewery."

"The young lady seemed surprised to hear of your plans."

"Yes, she did." And not just surprised, but panicked. She'd even tried to talk him out of it. Something was going on there, something she wasn't telling him.

He took a long pull on his tankard. Whatever it was, he would uncover it. Wager or no, he meant to go into this enterprise with his eyes fully open. Too much was at stake.

But that wasn't a matter for the runner. "Pinter, I want to hire you."

"To do what?"

He outlined his concerns about Oliver's version of their parents' deaths, which was that his quarrel with Mother had sent her off in a rage to kill Father. Oliver had said that Pinter knew everything about that night except why Oliver and Mother had quarreled, so Jarret kept that part to himself.

"So you see," Jarret finished, "I need you to track down the grooms who were there that night."

"None of them are in service at Halstead Hall any longer?"

"No. Gran took us to live with her in London after the . . . accident." He refused to call it murder. Mother would never have shot Father purposely, no matter what Oliver claimed. "Gran let most of the staff go when she closed the estate."

"But I understand that Lord Stoneville hired them back after he reached his majority and moved into your family's house in Acton."

"Not the grooms. They'd already found positions. I imagine they're scattered across England by now."

Pinter looked pensive. "Perhaps not. Servants tend to stay in the areas they're accustomed to. I doubt I'll have to look far."

"If you go out to the estate tomorrow, you can get a list of their names from Oliver's steward. He'd have the records."

Pinter squared his shoulders. "Is the family in residence at present?"

Jarret stifled a smile, knowing full well why Pinter asked. "No. The girls returned to the town house to help care for Gran after she became ill, and Gabe and I have been staying at our bachelor quarters." Jarret grinned. "So you won't have to worry about Celia and her sharp tongue."

The runner's gray eyes showed nothing. "Lady Celia is entitled to her opinions."

"Even when they concern you and your 'rigid adherence to stupid rules'?" Jarret asked, determined to get some reaction out of the impossibly stoic Pinter.

If Jarret hadn't been watching for it, he wouldn't have seen the faint tic in the man's jaw. "Lady Celia is entitled to her opinions, whatever they are," Pinter said with a deceptive nonchalance. "So, should I send my report to Burton? Will you be there long?"

Jarret took pity on the man, allowing him to change the subject. "I'm not sure. I hope not. But just in case, send a copy to me at Lake Ale Brewery. If I miss it, I can get it from you here."

"Very well." Pinter started to rise.

"One more thing." A suspicion had nagged at him ever since Oliver had made his confession. Perhaps it was time he cleared up that little matter as well, if only to ease his own mind. "I have another job for you, if you can afford the time."

Pinter sat back down. "If you can afford to pay me, I can afford the time."

As one of the most celebrated of London's Bow Street Runners, Pinter made his own hours, his own rules. He was one of the few to have an office he paid for himself, since he was widely sought after for private investigations when he wasn't working for the public good.

"Excellent. Here's what I'd like you to do . . ."

HETTY PLUMTREE WAS beginning to regret she'd ever made that cursed bargain with her grandson. Jarret would shave ten years off her life before the year was out. Entertain a proposal from some tiny brewery in Burton? Even speak to Mr. Harper about it? That boded ill.

She stared at Mr. Croft, who sat stiffly erect at her bedside, having just given her his dawn report. "You're sure he was speaking of the India market? Not the West Indies market, perchance?"

"Why would he speak of the West Indies? It's in an entirely different part of the world. I can't imagine his confusing the two. Eton's lessons in geography might be lacking, but his lordship isn't so devoid of knowledge of the world as to be—"

"Mr. Croft!" Sometimes getting information from him was like unraveling a carpet one strand at a time.

"Oh. Beg pardon. I was rambling again, wasn't I? In any case, it was definitely the India market, because I distinctly remembered your saying that you didn't intend to enter that particular area, and he told the woman something to that effect. Indeed, he seemed to agree with your assessment."

Ah, well, at least Jarret had *some* sense. The East India Company was unpredictable. Look at how its captains had turned on Hodgson's after the man had raised his prices.

"Tell me about this brewster you mentioned." She already knew that Miss Lake must be pretty, since whenever Mr. Croft mentioned her, he blushed. Mr. Croft turned into a blithering idiot around pretty women, which is probably why the female had managed to get past him.

"What do you wish to know?"

She coughed violently a moment, alarming Mr. Croft. A pox on this blasted cough of hers. When was it going to end? "How old was the woman?"

Hetty had not given up on marrying Jarret off, despite their bargain. But she wanted great-grandchildren, and the older the woman, the less likely she was as a prospect.

"Young, I would guess."

She sighed. Mr. Croft made an excellent spy in some ways, but he was not adept at judging age. "You said she pushed her way into the office. Was she a gentlewoman?"

"Most assuredly. I thought her quite genteel until she dashed around my desk."

"And my grandson did not throw her out right away?"

"No. He tasted her ale and talked with her for some time. Then he promised to speak to you last night about her proposal."

Thank God Mr. Croft excelled at listening at keyholes. "Instead he went off to play cards and drink with that scapegrace Masters." Another fit of coughing ensued, which made her even crankier. "One of these days I shall pin that lad's ears back."

"His lordship's?"

"Masters's."

A new voice sounded from the doorway. "I'll hold him down for you while you do."

She glanced up, startled. Good Lord, Jarret was here. He never came in the morning, and certainly not this early. How much had he heard?

He cast Mr. Croft a long, considering look. "Mr. Croft,

if you wish to continue in the brewery's employ, this will be your last dawn meeting with my grandmother. I won't tolerate spies."

Mr. Croft jumped to his feet. "My lord . . . I did not—"

"It's all right, Mr. Croft," Hetty put in. "You may go."

The poor man backed toward the door, keeping a wary eye on Jarret as if he thought the lad might throw a punch at him. Then he made a swift exit.

Jarret took Mr. Croft's seat, stretching his long legs out and folding his hands over his belly. "You can't trust me to run the place on my own, can you?"

She stared at him, unrepentant. "Would *you,* if you were me?"

"I suppose not." His expression hardened. "But I swear, I'll dismiss the little weasel if he ever again—"

"You will not. He supports a mother and five sisters. And he knows every inch of Plumtree Brewery from the ground up."

Jarret leaned forward. "Well then, I'll dismiss myself. Our agreement was that you would keep your hands off, and if you can't even hold to that stricture, I see no point in continuing."

"Oh, all right," she grumbled. "I will tell Mr. Croft not to come here anymore." She coughed into her handkerchief. "If you kept me informed the way you promised, I would not have to resort to such measures."

"I keep you informed well enough."

"Then why did I have to hear about this Lake Ale woman from Mr. Croft?" She erupted into another fit of coughing.

"Careful, Gran. Dr. Wright says you're not supposed to excite yourself." His unemotional tone would have hurt her feelings if not for the worry she'd seen flash across his face.

"Dr. Wright can go to hell," she retorted.

"If you don't listen to him, you'll beat him there." Now worry had filtered into his voice as well.

She shot him a sharp glance. "Are you saying I am destined for hell?"

He gave a rueful smile. "Perhaps." When she glared at him, his smile faded. "I'm saying you need to watch your health. And you're not going to do so by fretting over every little tale Mr. Croft lays at your feet."

The impudent whelp had no idea how hard it was to step back and hand over the reins at her age. "What are you doing here at this hour, anyway? I thought you played cards last night with your rascal friends."

A mild annoyance flickered in his eyes. "I see that Mr. Croft's reports are very thorough."

"They had better be. I pay him well for them." She sharpened her gaze on him. "So? What has made you rise with the chickens?"

"I'm traveling to Burton today."

She stared at him, instantly wary. "Why?"

He shrugged. "To speak to the owner of Lake Ale about our selling their October brew for them."

"To the East India Company?"

"Among others."

So the pretty Miss Lake had convinced him to consider her proposal, had she? Interesting. Now Hetty had to decide how to play this.

On the one hand, she did not wish to lose the company due to Jarret following his cock. On the other hand, Plumtree Brewery was ailing and she wasn't sure she had the strength for the battle to save it.

Jarret could do it, though. She had no intention of watching him hand the place back to her at the end of the year. She wanted him well and truly hooked. And you only hooked a fish by giving him a little line.

But could the brewery withstand such an experiment in these hard times?

It didn't matter. If she put her foot down now, she would never get Jarret near it again, and Plumtree Brewery needed someone with his intelligence to run it. She had to risk giving him his head, for the future good of the company.

Besides, this woman brewer might be the key to shifting his interest from gambling to brewing. Jarret had only the most shallow relations with women. He'd been much like his older brother in that respect. Miss Lake could change that, especially if she'd managed to interest him in a project enough to get him hieing off to Burton.

Brewing was in his blood. She had ignored that to her peril, when she had sent him off to Eton against his wishes. He had been punishing her for it ever since. So he must continue to think he was punishing her.

What he must not guess is that he was playing into her hands. And of all her grandchildren, Jarret was the most suspicious.

"I do not want Plumtree Brewery to get into the India trade," she said, feeling her way along.

With a black scowl, he sat up in his chair. "You don't have a say in it."

*Ah, that's the spirit.* "But Jarret—"

"It could bolster our profits considerably."

"It could sink us, too. It has damned near sunk Hodgson's."

He conceded that with a nod. "But Allsopp's in Burton is profiting from it. Why shouldn't we?"

"What if I forbid you from involving us?"

That stubborn look he sometimes got passed across his

face. "What if I hand you back your brewery?" He rose and headed for the door.

"Wait!" *Well played, Jarret, well played.* He would make a fine captain of industry one day. She must have been mad to think he should be a barrister.

Now came the difficult part—giving in without making it look too easy. "What am I to do about Plumtree Brewery while you are gone?"

He halted at the door to shoot her a wary glance. "Harper and Croft can handle matters for a few days. I'll make sure they know what needs to be done. I shouldn't be away long."

She scowled. "I am not giving you my blessing in this."

"Then it's a good thing I don't need your blessing." He crossed his arms over his chest. "I didn't come here to gain permission or approval. I came to keep you informed. Since I've done what I came for, I'm leaving. Is that clear?"

Insolent rascal. She managed a stiff nod.

"Good." He surprised her by coming over to kiss her on the forehead. "Listen to Dr. Wright, will you? And for God's sake, take care of yourself."

Then he was gone.

She waited until she heard the door close downstairs before calling for her slyest footman.

"Follow my grandson," she ordered him, "but do it discreetly. Eventually, he'll go to an inn. There should be a guest there named Miss Lake, whom Lord Jarret is accompanying out of town. Once he and the woman leave, find out everything you can about her from the innkeeper and report back."

With a nod, the footman hurried off to do her bidding.

Hetty collapsed against the pillow with a smile. It was already looking to be a very good day.

# Chapter Seven

nnabel watched as Sissy nervously paced the inn's common room the next morning, then halted in front of her.

"How do I look?" Sissy was wearing her best day gown of purple velvet, adorned with the amethysts she donned only for special occasions. Her cheeks were flushed, and her blue eyes bright.

"You look lovely, as usual," Annabel answered.

"And you look like a washerwoman." Sissy made a face. "I can't believe you chose to wear that brown thing. We're riding with a marquess's son, for heaven's sake!"

"We'll be traipsing in and out of inns, and it looks like rain. I'm *not* going to wear my Sunday best just because Lord Jarret happens to be a lord." And certainly not just because he'd kissed her senseless in the hall. Or made her feel things, want things . . .

She must stop thinking about that! Today he'd probably probe more into why Lake Ale was in trouble, and she had to be ready. Becoming a dreamy-eyed romantic every time he flashed his dimpled smile would not help.

With a sigh, Sissy glanced at the clock. "I do hope something dreadful hasn't happened. Shouldn't he be here by now?" Jarret had sent a note saying he would arrive at ten-thirty, and it was nearly eleven.

"I'm sure he's merely taking his sweet time," Annabel said dryly, "as lords are apt to do."

"He's coming!" Geordie shouted from the window where he'd been keeping watch for the last half hour.

The sudden leap of her pulse made Annabel scowl. "How do you know it's him?"

"There's a crest on the door and everything." Geordie puffed out his chest. "Just wait until that lout Toby Mawer sees me drive up in a marquess's coach. He'll be green with envy!"

Annabel scarcely had time to steady her nerves before Jarret strode into the common room, full of confidence and arrogance and all things lordly, from his well-tailored morning coat of Sardinian blue superfine to the highly polished sheen of his black Hussar boots. It would make any woman grow wobbly in the knees.

Not her, of course. Her knees were quite unwobbly, thank you very much.

As she rose, his gaze met hers. "Miss Lake," he said in the husky voice she remembered from last night. "Forgive my tardiness. There was an issue with the horses."

"We can hardly complain, my lord," she said as she held out her hand, "given your generosity in taking us to Burton."

He pressed her hand briefly, his gaze running over her with an easy familiarity that made her shiver. Something dark and knowing flickered in his eyes before he smoothed his features into a cordial smile.

*Now* her knees were wobbly.

Sissy cleared her throat, and Annabel started. "Lord Jarret, may I present my sister-in-law, Cecelia Lake. Sissy, this is Lord Jarret Sharpe."

As they made the requisite bows and curtsies, accompanied by murmured pleasantries, Geordie hurried to Sissy's side.

Sissy laid her hand on Geordie's arm. "And this is my son, Geordie."

"George," Geordie corrected her. He held out his hand manfully. "George Lake, at your service. Very good of you to let us use your carriage, sir. I hope it doesn't inconvenience you too much."

A lump stuck in Annabel's throat to hear Geordie sound so grown up. He must have been practicing that introduction for the past hour.

"Not at all," Jarret said with nary a trace of condescension. "Happy to help you and your family."

When Geordie fairly preened at being treated like a man, she could have kissed Jarret. For all his bluster, Geordie was sensitive, and they didn't need one of his fits of pique today.

"Shall we go, then?" Jarret offered Annabel his arm, leaving Geordie to follow suit with Sissy.

Annabel took it, fighting to quell the sudden tripling of her pulse. They had walked exactly this way last night, and it hadn't affected her so. But that was before he'd kissed her. Now she was intensely aware of the tension in his body, the flexing of his muscles beneath her hand . . . the rosemary scent of Hungary Water.

"You look well today, Miss Lake," he said.

Sissy snorted behind her.

When Jarret shot Annabel a quizzical glance, she said, "My sister-in-law wanted me to dress more extravagantly for a ride in a marquess's coach."

Amusement gleamed in his eyes. "And of course, being thoroughly unimpressed by rank, you refused."

"It looks like rain," she said defensively.

His only response was an insolent arch of his brow.

When they reached the coach and he handed her in, she caught sight of Sissy's face and groaned. Her sister-in-law wore a speculative look that showed she'd noticed how comfortable Annabel and Jarret were together.

Oh, dear. She would have to be more careful with herself around him.

Geordie paused next to Jarret before climbing in. "Would it be all right if I rode up top with the coachman?"

"Certainly not!" Sissy and Annabel said in unison from inside the carriage.

Jarret eyed them askance. "It's fine with me, ladies."

"It's too dangerous," Sissy said.

"What if there's an accident?" Annabel added. "That's no place for a boy. Get inside, Geordie. You are *not* riding up there."

Grumbling about being treated like a child, Geordie climbed in and plopped down in the seat opposite them. Even after they were settled and Jarret had ordered the coachman to drive on, he sulked, arms crossed over his chest.

But the boy couldn't stay immune to the sights of London for long. Soon he was peeking out the window at the spectacle of a barge being loaded on the river, and then he gasped as they took a corner speedily, with almost no jostling.

"This is a berline coach, isn't it, my lord?" he asked.

"Indeed it is."

"With two underperches and full underlock?"

"I have no idea," Jarret drawled.

"Geordie has an avid interest in carriages," Annabel explained.

"It has to have full underlock," Geordie went on. "It turns too neatly for anything else." He bounced on the seat. "And it's well sprung, too. It must have cost you a fortune!"

"Geordie!" Sissy chided. "Don't be rude."

"Actually, I don't know what it cost," Jarret said. "It belongs to my brother."

"Oh. Right," Geordie mumbled. "It's your brother who's the marquess." He peered up at Jarret. "Perhaps that's why you don't look like a lord."

Jarret blinked. "How is a lord supposed to look?"

"They carry quizzing glasses and fancy canes."

"Ah, yes." His lordship seemed to be trying hard not to smile. "I must have left mine in the other carriage."

Geordie's face lit up. "You have another carriage? What sort? A curricle? Or a phaeton? Oh, it has to be a phaeton—that's what all the lords drive!"

"It's a cabriolet, actually."

"A cabriolet," Geordie whispered in awe. "I've heard of them, but I've never seen one. Do you race it?"

"No. I leave that to my younger brother. Perhaps you've heard of him—Lord Gabriel Sharpe."

Now Geordie was in raptures. "Your brother is the Angel of Death?"

"Where did you hear that?" Annabel asked sharply.

"From Mother. It was in one of her gossip papers."

Sissy turned red. "My lord, please forgive my son. He has a tendency to speak without thinking."

Jarret laughed, then shot Annabel a veiled glance. "A family trait, I suppose." When she glared at him, he added, "It doesn't matter. I know what they call my brother."

They all fell silent.

After several moments, Sissy said, "We are very grateful to you for coming to the aid of Lake Ale like this, sir."

A cynical expression crossed his face. "I hope we both don't come to regret it. I've barely dipped my toe into the ale business, and this is a new area for me. Indeed, if not for our wager, I wouldn't even—"

He caught himself with a groan.

"Don't worry, my lord," Sissy said. "I know all about Annabel's beating you at two-handed whist. She tells me everything."

"Everything?" His gaze narrowed on Annabel. "Did she tell you the *terms* of our wager?"

"Certainly." Sissy patted Annabel's rigid hand. "Though she took quite a chance. Her mother's ring means a great deal to her. She should never have risked it in a card game."

When a wicked glint appeared in his eye, Annabel froze, her heart nearly failing her right there. Surely he wouldn't reveal . . . Oh, Lord, he couldn't possibly mean to . . .

"Ah, but if she hadn't, I wouldn't have accepted the bet. I needed something very tempting to convince me to take a chance on your husband's brewery." He had the audacity to wink at her. "Fortunately, Miss Lake was more than eager to provide the . . . right temptation."

Annabel scowled at him. Teasing wretch. He was enjoying dangling her reputation by one finger in front of her. Though she supposed she deserved it for agreeing to that daft wager in the first place.

"She always says it's a lucky ring, too," Sissy went on.

"Does she?" The smile playing over his lips got on Annabel's nerves.

"But I don't believe it," Sissy went on. "If it were lucky,

then Rupert wouldn't have—" She broke off suddenly, with a quick glance at Annabel. "I'm sorry, dear. After all these years, I forget that it's still very fresh to you."

At least Sissy's words wiped the smug smile from Jarret's face. Still, the stare he leveled on them was almost as disconcerting.

"Who's Rupert?" he asked.

"Aunt Annabel's fiancé," Geordie chimed in. "He died in the war right after Father and Mother married. He was a great hero, wasn't he, Mother?"

"Yes, Geordie, a fine and courageous man," Sissy said softly. "But it's painful for your aunt to talk about. I shouldn't have brought it up."

"Nonsense." Annabel forced herself to sound calm. "It was a long time ago, when I was just sixteen. And we were betrothed for only a short while. Papa said we were too young to marry and asked that we wait until I was eighteen. Then when I was seventeen Rupert's brother died in France, and in a storm of vengeful fervor, Rupert insisted on enlisting in the army. He died in the Battle of Vittoria, not long after he left England."

Although she'd stopped grieving for her youthful love, it unnerved her to speak of him to Jarret after last night's kisses. It was unsettling to expose one's life in such a pitiless recitation.

Not that Jarret would care. She was just a woman who'd tricked him into doing something he didn't want to do, an impediment to his easy life. What did it matter what she'd suffered?

Yet she could feel his gaze on her, probing, curious.

"And you never married," he said, his tone neutral. "You must have loved him very much."

"Yes." She'd loved him as any girl loves her first sweetheart, with a pure, oblivious passion that counted no cost.

She sometimes wondered if perhaps Papa had been right about their being too young. Other than proximity and the intoxication of youthful desires, what had she and Rupert had in common? She'd liked to read and play cards; he'd liked to hunt partridges and bet on the races in Burton. What if they hadn't consummated their love? Might she have found another man to love after his death, someone who shared more of her interests?

It didn't matter. What was done was done.

She forced a bright smile to her lips. "In any case, it's all in the past." She met Jarret's gaze. "So, you said you had questions about the brewery's operations. This is as good a time as any to discuss those, don't you think?"

His eyes searched her face, and he gave a small nod. "Why not?"

Although that launched them into the difficult matter of Lake Ale and its problems, she was thankful to leave the painful subject of Rupert behind. She only hoped they were done with it. It wouldn't do to have Jarret know too many of her secrets.


JARRET FOUND HIS conversation with Annabel about the brewery intriguing. She knew a great deal more than he'd have guessed. He'd had no idea that barley for the malt had become so dear or that barrel makers were demanding higher pay.

More importantly, the plan she laid out for saving her brother's company was not only sound, but it might actually work. After he'd left Gran's this morning, he'd talked to an

East India Company captain he knew from the gaming hells, and the man had confirmed everything Annabel had told him. The captain had even boasted about how much money he'd made on the first shipment of Allsopp's pale ale.

This project looked less risky by the moment. Though there was still the issue of the ill brother, and that was worrisome.

It was a pity she couldn't run the project herself. But as long as her brother owned it, no man would ever deal with her on matters of business. Women had no rights in such cases. Gran had been able to survive only because her husband had died and left the business to her, and even then she'd had to fight tooth and nail for every gain.

Annabel was certainly a fighter, but Hugh Lake was the only one who could make decisions, and from what Annabel was telling him, he continued to make them. She just performed the daily work, along with the brewery manager.

The situation seemed very odd. Worse, he couldn't shake the feeling that Annabel wasn't telling him everything. She evaded certain questions, skirted certain concerns. Was that because she didn't know the answers? Or because she didn't want to *tell* him the answers?

Then there was young George's odd behavior. Once they started talking of Lake Ale, the boy fell silent, almost as if commanded not to speak. And Mrs. Lake grew decidedly nervous whenever her husband was mentioned. It gave him pause, especially since Annabel seemed perfectly at ease.

Utterly different from when she'd discussed her fiancé.

He shot her a quick glance. Even her unfashionable day dress of muddy-colored serge didn't dim the high color in her pretty cheeks and the animation in her gold-flecked eyes as she talked about the business. It wasn't hard to believe she'd once been betrothed. Perhaps the men in Burton weren't so mad, after all.

She hadn't denied loving that Rupert fellow deeply. And clearly she had, or she wouldn't have stayed true to him even after his death. Rupert must have been a stalwart gallant, young and handsome and full of courage. Died a hero, eh? Just the sort of man that women worshipped.

He scowled. It made his own life look wasted, even though he'd had no desire to be a soldier.

And what about *her* wasted life, closing herself up in a spinster's box, keeping all men at bay because she'd lost her true love at seventeen? That was a romantic fool's path, and she was no romantic fool.

She was an attractive, vibrant woman. A sensual woman, the sort of woman who met a man's kiss with the enthusiasm it properly deserved. No missish vapors for Annabel. She seized the moment, the hour, the day, with a true lust for living. So why was she pouring her energies into looking after her brother's children and her father's brewery? She ought to be settled with some squire or wealthy merchant, gracing his table with her presence and his bed with her passion.

*That* thought didn't appeal to him, either. Why, he wasn't sure. He barely knew the woman. He had no reason to care whether she married some other chap.

Yet he did.

"I hate to interrupt you, Annabel," Mrs. Lake said, "but we're coming up on Dunstable, and his lordship might like to pause here for a little refreshment."

Annabel laughed. "You only want to stop and see your friend Mrs. Cranley at the Bear Inn." She cast Jarret a conspiratorial glance. "They knew each other as girls. The woman is a walking gossip rag, and Sissy drinks up every word."

Mrs. Lake tipped up her chin. "What's wrong with keeping up with what's going on in the world? Especially if his lordship doesn't mind. I really am hungry."

"Then let's stop there." Jarret was restless, and so was the boy. "I could use something to eat myself."

Though Annabel rolled her eyes as he gave the command to his coachman, Mrs. Lake looked very pleased, and young George finally relaxed.

After they reached the Bear Inn and Jarret helped the ladies descend, Mrs. Lake hurried George inside, leaving Jarret to accompany Annabel. Annabel fell back to put a little distance between her and her family and murmured, "Thank you for not revealing the real terms of our wager."

"I take it that your sister-in-law wouldn't approve?"

"It would most assuredly shock her."

"Not as much as it shocked me, I warrant," he said under his breath. And intrigued him. And made him want to get her into a corner for another hot kiss.

He frowned—there he went again, letting his cock think for him.

Ahead of them, a woman rushed forward to greet Mrs. Lake. "How lovely to see you again, my dear! I take it that your mission to London was successful?"

This had to be Mrs. Cranley. She looked like a typical innkeeper's wife—ruddy-cheeked, round, and ready to gossip.

"It went better than even we expected," Mrs. Lake chirped. "His lordship was kind enough to offer his brother's carriage so that we might travel in comfort to Burton."

"His lordship?" Mrs. Cranley cast him an assessing gaze. "I thought you intended to ask Mrs. Plumtree for help."

"Unfortunately she couldn't come, but her grandson has

agreed to help us instead. Lord Jarret Sharpe, may I present Mrs. Cranley? She and her husband own this inn."

As Mrs. Cranley heard his name, a palpable change came over her face. Though she curtsied stiffly and murmured a greeting, her demeanor showed that she considered Jarret one of the devil's minions. Or perhaps the devil himself. Apparently his reputation had preceded him.

As soon as she straightened, she grabbed Mrs. Lake's arm in one hand and Annabel's in the other. "Come, my dears, we must talk."

"Stay with his lordship, Geordie," Mrs. Lake admonished the lad.

Wonderful. Now he was reduced to watching the cub like some tutor on the Grand Tour.

"And make sure you visit the necessary, Geordie," Annabel added.

"Aunt Annabel!" the boy protested, his face flushing a bright red.

As she and his mother went off with the innkeeper's wife, Geordie turned to Jarret. "They always talk as if I'm in leading strings. It's damned embarrassing."

Jarret resisted the urge to point out that using words like *damned* wouldn't help the situation with his aunt and mother. "Sorry, George, but to them, you'll always be in leading strings, no matter how old you get."

The idea seemed to appall George. "Does *your* mother treat you like that?"

"No." A sudden tightness in Jarret's throat made it hard for him to speak. "She died when I was a little older than you."

"Oh, right, I forgot." George shoved his hands in his pockets. "That's awful. I wouldn't like Mother and Aunt Annabel to die, but sometimes I wish they would just leave me alone. Like when Toby Mawer is around."

"Who's Toby Mawer?"

"My archenemy. He's seventeen and bigger than me. And he's always hanging about in the field behind our house with his friends, waiting to torment me."

"Ah. I had an archenemy in school named John Pratt. Always taking my things."

"Exactly. He tried to take the watch Father gave me for Christmas, but I outran him." His words came out in a great rush. "He's always calling me Georgie-Porgie. And one time, when he saw Mother kiss me on the cheek, he called me a mama's boy. Why does she have to kiss me when the lads are watching?"

"Because women have deplorable timing for things like that. I used to cringe when Mother fussed over me while my friends were around. Although now that she's gone . . ."

He caught himself before he could reveal that he would give his right arm to have his mother fussing over him again. That watching Mrs. Lake and Annabel coddle the lad roused a ridiculous resentment in him. George had no idea how fragile such caring could be, how easily it could be snatched away—

God, he was turning maudlin. This was what came of letting people into one's life. One started to yearn for things one had no business yearning for.

He clapped George on the shoulder. "Enough about that. Why don't we get a table while the ladies are off gossiping?"

The inn wasn't crowded at this time of day, so it took them little time to find a place. Jarret ordered what George suggested the ladies might like, then decided to make good use of his time alone with the lad. "So, how long has your father been ill?"

George's face closed up. "I . . . I . . . well . . . awhile. A long while."

A long while? That didn't sound like the sort of illness Annabel had described.

"Then it's serious," he said, feeling for the boy.

"No . . . I mean . . . yes." He smiled weakly. "I'm not really sure."

Odd. "And he doesn't go to the brewery at all?"

"He goes sometimes," the lad hedged, "when he's not . . . feeling so ill."

"And when he doesn't go, your aunt goes. Do you go with her?"

"No." His expression was troubled.

Jarret well remembered the pain he'd felt at being packed off to school instead of being allowed to be useful to his family. "Why not?"

"Because everyone says it's too dangerous for me."

It seemed that several things were *too dangerous* for poor Geordie, according to his mother and aunt. "And you wonder how it can be too dangerous for you, but not too dangerous for a woman."

"I-I didn't say that."

But his lower lip quivered, and Jarret knew that he'd thought it. Jarret would have wondered much the same thing in George's place. Boys of twelve chafed at being told that a woman could do things better than they could, even if it were true.

"Father says women don't belong in the brewery," George ventured.

"Ah." No wonder Annabel was so defensive on the subject.

Yet clearly she went there anyway. Did her brother allow it because he had no choice, given his illness? Or did Annabel have to go for other reasons?

Once again, he got the feeling that there was more here than met the eye. "What do *you* think about women in the brewery?"

George blinked. Clearly no one ever asked him his opinion. "I don't rightly know, since I'm not allowed there myself. Aunt Annabel seems to like it, and Mother says she does a good job."

"And your father? What does he say about her prowess?"

Her voice answered from behind him. "He says I should get a husband and leave brewery matters to his manager." Annabel glowered at him. "But you didn't need to interrogate my nephew just to learn *that*, did you?"

Jarret met her glower with a raised eyebrow. Well, well. There was definitely more here than met the eye. Annabel was keeping secrets. The question was, what kind? And how might they affect him and this scheme of hers?

One way or the other, he would find out.

# Chapter Eight

Annabel was already cranky because of Mrs. Cranley's nonsense, and finding Jarret quizzing poor Geordie only made it worse. If Jarret found out the real reason that Plumtree Brewery was failing, there would be no more help from him.

But she didn't think he'd learned that, or he'd be angry at her. No anger showed on his face, only the sort of wariness he'd worn from the beginning.

Good. Right now they had far more pressing concerns.

"I have bad news," she went on in a low tone. "Apparently a man present at our card game in London happened to pass through here this morning. He told Mrs. Cranley that a Miss River from Wharton gambled with your lordship at a tavern last night."

A thin smile tipped up his lips. "A 'Miss River'? And your friend, Mrs. Cranley, didn't make that connection?"

"Fortunately, no. And she's no friend to me. Since her informant made . . . certain nasty insinuations about your 'scandalous conduct' toward 'Miss River,' Mrs. Cranley is full of concern about our traveling with you." Her voice turned bitter. "She says you're a notorious seducer of innocents, and we should tell you to go on while we stay here until the mail coach comes through."

His face turned stony, with only the glitter of his blue-green eyes betraying his anger. She felt a moment's pity for him. He must tire of the gossip.

Then again, the only one who would really suffer from the gossip was *her*, if anyone ever connected "Miss River of Wharton" to "Miss Lake of Burton." She wished she could give Mrs. Cranley a piece of her mind about rumormongering, but that would only focus the woman's attention in the wrong direction.

This was Annabel's punishment for having accepted Jarret's wager. She should have realized that the men in the tavern would make lurid assumptions about what a rogue like Jarret must have asked her to do in payment for the bet. Men always assumed the worst about women, and she ought to be used to that by now. Especially when their assumptions hadn't been far off the mark.

A door opened behind Jarret, and Annabel groaned. "Sissy is coming. Honestly, I think we should just leave. I don't know how much of a fuss that foolish woman will make if we stay, and you shouldn't have to put up with her nonsense."

With eyes that brooked no argument, Jarret leaned back to cross his arms over his chest. "I'm used to gossip. Besides, I've already ordered." His smile was forced. "Let her say what she will. I'm not budging until I get my roast loin of pork."

Sissy strode up, looking anxious. "I don't think my friend will say anything, my lord. I told her how kind you've been to us and how false the gossip is." She took a seat across from Jarret on the other side of Geordie. "Mrs. Cranley is no fool—I'm sure now that I've explained to her about your fine character, she'll understand."

Somehow Annabel doubted it.

Nervously, Sissy unfolded her napkin. "Though it's probably just as well that she didn't guess 'Miss River's' true identity. I swear, I can't believe the awful things people dream up. Whoever this wretched traveler was, he ought to be shot for claiming that you and Annabel were wagering for something as salacious as—"

"Sissy!" Annabel cut in, with a glance at Geordie.

Sissy colored. "Oh, right."

"What does 'salacious' mean?" Geordie asked predictably.

"Never you mind, Geordie," Sissy said. "Sit down, Annabel. I'm sure Mrs. Cranley will not be rude."

With a sigh, Annabel took the seat beside Jarret. Sissy had a tendency to think the best of people who didn't deserve it.

"If 'salacious' comes from Latin," Geordie mused aloud, "then it has to do with leaping. What is there to wager over in that?"

"It doesn't concern you," Annabel said. "You can look it up when we get home."

"But I want to know *now*!" he protested. "It could have something to do with leapfrog—"

"It means 'lustful,'" Jarret put in. When Annabel shot him a reproving glance, he added, "The lad is old enough to be told when a member of his family has been insulted."

Geordie sat up straight. "Yes, I am. Old enough to call the man out for it, too."

"Don't be silly, Geordie," Sissy said. "That traveler is long gone by now."

"And he'd be unlikely to agree to a duel with a twelve-year-old, anyway," Annabel said dryly. She raised her eyebrows at Jarret. "You see what you started?"

"If George is providing you ladies with protection," Jarret countered, "he should start thinking like a man. He can't do that when you treat him like a child."

Though Annabel bristled, Sissy flashed Jarret a strained smile. "How kind of you to take such an interest in our Geordie, my lord. Isn't it, Annabel?"

Annabel's eyes narrowed on him. "Yes. So very kind of him."

"Hardly," he remarked. "I merely remember what it was like to be twelve."

That gave her pause. What *had* Jarret been like at twelve? As feckless as he was now? Or more sober? He'd said his grandmother had raised him from the age of thirteen. Had his character changed then? No one could survive the violent deaths of their parents and be untouched by it.

Or perhaps her attraction to him was making her look for depths of character where none existed. *Careful now, missy. There's always some truth to even the vilest gossip.*

Just then, a servant approached with their food. There was no sign of Mrs. Cranley, thank goodness. Apparently the woman had contented herself with merely cautioning Annabelle and Sissy about Jarret's character.

The servant set the ale down first. Annabelle sniffed it. Leave it to Mrs. Cranley to purchase an inferior brew. She sipped some and wrinkled her nose, too engrossed in assessing its quality to notice when Sissy told the servant to take one of the plates back to the kitchen.

"The mistress insisted that I give it to his lordship," the servant countered and tried to scoot past her to put it before Jarret.

Sissy whisked it from the maid before the girl could react. "He can have the other." When the servant protested again, Sissy began to eat from it. With a shrug, the servant served Geordie.

"It's all the same food, Mother," Geordie said. "I told Lord Jarret you were fond of a good loin of pork."

"I am indeed," she said as she took another big bite. Then she made a face.

At that, Jarret's eyes narrowed. Reaching over, he snatched the plate from her and stared hard at it. "You can't eat this."

That's when Annabelle looked closer. The meat's off color and rancid smell made her gag. She glanced at the other dinners, but theirs looked fine.

"That gossipy witch Mrs. Cranley gave you bad meat, Sissy!" Annabel exclaimed. "How dare she? I shall give her a piece of my mind!"

Annabel started to stand, but Jarret pulled her down. "She didn't intend it for Mrs. Lake. She meant it for me."

"I-I'm sure it was just a mistake," Sissy said weakly.

"The only mistake was in my letting us remain here." Jarret rose to dump the plate's contents in a nearby slop bucket. Then he walked up to Sissy and held out his arm. "Come, we're leaving. We'll stop to eat at an inn in the next town."

Thankfully, she let him lead her from the table without protest.

"How much did you eat?" Annabel asked Sissy as they headed for the door.

"Not much," Sissy said.

"Too much," Jarret countered. "I'm sorry, Mrs. Lake. I didn't at first realize what you were up to." He stared grimly ahead. "Or how desperate your friend was to drag you from my wicked clutches."

"I'm certain she didn't mean—"

"Don't you dare apologize for her again," Annabel said hotly. "We don't blame you, Sissy. It's your supposed friend who ought to be shot."

When they reached the entrance to find Mrs. Cranley standing there directing a malevolent look at Jarret, he stiffened. Releasing Sissy's arm, he told Annabel in a low voice, "You three go on to the coach. I'll be there shortly."

"How was your meal, my lord?" the woman had the audacity to ask as Annabel pulled Sissy and Geordie toward the door.

"Next time you attempt to poison someone, madam," Annabel heard him say behind her, "make sure your servant is clear on her instructions. Before I could stop her, Mrs. Lake took several bites of the pork you intended for me."

Annabel glanced back in time to see the woman blanch.

Jarret's expression of righteous anger warmed her heart. "So I hope you enjoy the results of your foolish plan to 'save' your friend from my wicked influence. Because if she dies, I'll have you prosecuted for attempted murder. Do I make myself clear?"

"My lord, I didn't . . . that is . . ."

Annabel urged Sissy to the carriage. Though Sissy seemed fine now, Annabel still worried. It was so like Sissy to try to cover up her friend's behavior by taking the error upon herself. It simply wasn't right.

Annabel hadn't liked Mrs. Cranley before, and now she positively hated her. Who did such a foolish thing? And all because of some gossip! The woman was daft, if Sissy could only see it.

Jarret had seen it, though he'd taken it in stride, as if he really were used to being gossiped about. He probably was. If

Annabel had heard the stories even in Burton, then everyone had heard them.

But this particular tale had happened because of her. The thought plagued her even after he joined them and they went on to the next town. Though Sissy ate a hearty meal when they stopped, Annabel couldn't stop feeling guilty. None of this would have happened if Annabel hadn't accepted that cursed wager.

Then again, without the wager she wouldn't have convinced Jarret to come to Burton. She just wished she'd considered what could occur if people realized what the wager was about.

When they stopped near nightfall at an inn just outside Daventry that Jarret had said was recommended to him, she watched as he arranged two rooms—one for him and another for Sissy, Geordie, and her. It felt strange having a man look after her and her family. Hugh had practically abdicated his responsibility, and Rupert had never had the chance to take it.

Lately she'd always been the one to take charge, to arrange things. How wonderful to let the responsibility fall on someone else's shoulders again. And considering that she'd forced him into doing this, that he didn't even want to be here . . .

A lump caught in her throat as the four of them reached their floor, and Jarret headed for his room. "Sissy, why don't you and Geordie go on? I need to speak to his lordship a moment."

Though Sissy shot her a quizzical glance, she took Geordie down the hall.

Annabel headed the opposite direction. "Jarret!" she called out as he unlocked the door to his own room.

He paused in the doorway. "What is it?"

"I want to apologize."

He looked bemused. "For what?"

"First of all, for making you the subject of gossip yet again. Honestly, I didn't think anyone outside of London would ever learn of our card game. I certainly never thought people would guess that you and I . . . that you . . ."

She trailed off as two people passed them in the hall, shooting them curious glances. As soon as the couple had disappeared, she tugged Jarret into his room and pulled the door partly closed so they could have some privacy.

"I should never have agreed to your terms for the wager," she said bluntly.

His smile exposed his dimples. "I should never have offered them. What's done is done. No sense regretting it now."

"But it's *my* fault that Mrs. Cranley—"

"Don't be absurd. You're no more responsible than your sister-in-law. Mrs. Cranley had an ax to grind, and she used the gossip as an excuse to grind it on me. I only wish she hadn't involved your family in it. And I pray to God, Mrs. Lake suffers no adverse effects from the woman's ill-considered actions."

"Me, too. I shudder to think of what might have happened if you hadn't noticed the bad meat and stepped in. For that, I must offer you my fervent thanks."

When she went to the door, he drawled, "Aren't you forgetting something?"

She turned. "I beg your pardon?"

A wicked smile curved his lips as he approached her. "There are other things you should thank me for."

"Like what?"

"I did entertain your nephew while the two of you were off gossiping about me."

Good point. "Thank you for that, too, my lord," she said primly.

With eyes gleaming, he came to stand far too close. "Then there's the fact that I'm transporting you to Burton in the comfort of my brother's carriage."

Her pulse quickened. "The only one deserving thanks for that is your brother."

"Ah, but I made it possible for you to use it." He snagged her about the waist. "And I can think of an excellent way for you to show your gratitude."

"Writing a sonnet to your generosity?" she said sweetly, her heart racing and her knees definitely wobbly.

With a chuckle, he bent his head to brush her ear with his lips. "Try again," he said in a husky voice that made her shiver deliciously.

Her breath seemed stuck somewhere in her throat. "Brewing you a very special ale?"

"I had something more . . . personal in mind."

Then he covered her mouth with his.

# Chapter Nine

Jarret was tired of having her treat him with the cool politeness anyone showed a business partner. All her animation today had been for her brewery plans. All her soft words and smiles had been for her nephew and sister-in-law.

She acted as if last night in the hall had never happened, and it chafed him. He burned to remind her that she'd been anything but businesslike to him last night. That when he'd kissed her, she'd melted.

As she was melting now. He exulted as she arched into him, clutched at his coat, and let him delve into her silky mouth with his tongue. Groaning low in his throat, he dragged her flush against him. The hot, sweet scent of her intoxicated him. It was unlike any other woman's—no cloying flowers or perfume, just something juicy and delicious. Oranges and honey . . . something a man could sink his teeth into.

He wanted to sink his teeth into *her*. Moving his mouth along her jaw, he immersed himself in the heady scent that was Annabel. He sought the tender skin of her neck, then the tempting lobe of her ear. When he bit it lightly, she gave a full-throated gasp, though her hands tightened on his coat lapels.

"Surely I have now given you sufficient thanks for all your . . . help, my lord," she whispered.

"Then it's my turn to thank you for *your* help." He kissed his way down her neck.

"I've done nothing to deserve such extravagant thanks."

"You're kissing me." And making his blood race and his body go hard.

"Giving kisses . . . as thanks for kisses . . ." She breathed heavily against his cheek. "That could be dangerous. Where would it end up, after all?"

He knew where he'd *like* it to end up. With her in his bed, her pale thighs parting to let him in, her body pressing up against his to find its pleasure. Their mutual pleasure.

He settled for filling one hand with her breast.

She froze. "*That* is not where it should end up," she said, grabbing his hand to move it aside.

With a growl he took her mouth again, this time more roughly, sensing that despite her words, it was boldness she craved, not hesitation or tenderness. He must have guessed right, for her hand softened, then molded his to her breast.

By God, she was as eager as he, which sparked his fever higher. She might be cold to him around her family, but here, alone, she was warm and willing, driving him to madness.

He kneaded her breast until her sweet pebble of a nipple rose against his palm, palpable in its arousal even through her layers of clothes. Her low moans made him ache, until he found himself pressing her against the wall next to the half-closed door, covering her body with his, pushing between her legs—

"Aunt Annabel? Lord Jarret? Are you in there?" came a

voice from the other side of the door, inches away from them.

He barely had time to release her and move back before George came around the door and saw them.

Annabel turned red, her accusing gaze leaping to Jarret's.

Damn, damn, damn. As unobtrusively as possible, he removed his hat to hide his rampant erection.

"What's going on here?" George asked sharply.

With a forced smile, Annabel said, "His lordship and I were discussing . . . your mother."

George's lips thinned into a line. "Mother is sick. You have to come."

"Of course." Annabel touched a hand to her hopelessly mussed hair, then pushed past Jarret to go around the door. She paused in the hall to look back at her nephew. "Are you coming, Geordie?"

The lad's dark-eyed gaze never left Jarret's. "I'll be there in a moment."

Jarret stifled a curse. Was he now to be dressed down by an infant? Not bloody likely. It was none of the lad's business what he and Annabel did in private.

George closed the door and faced him. "I should like to know, my lord, what your intentions are toward my aunt."

His *intentions*? Well, that certainly put the damper on his arousal.

He tossed his hat onto a chair. "I don't know what you think you saw, lad, but—"

"I can tell when a man has just been kissing a woman," George said hotly.

If the boy hadn't looked so serious, Jarret would have laughed outright. "Oh, you can, can you?" He leveled George with a skeptical look. "You've had a great deal of experience in the matter, I suppose."

Though George flushed, he held his ground. "It doesn't take experience—I'm not blind. And you have a certain reputation with women."

"So I've heard." He stared the lad down. "But your aunt's reputation is unblemished. Surely you don't think she would allow—"

"Allow? No. That doesn't mean that you couldn't have . . . well . . ."

"Are you accusing me of *forcing* my attentions on your aunt?"

George stiffened. "I know what I saw."

"You don't know a damned thing, *boy*," Jarret shot back. "Whatever occurred between me and your aunt is our private business, and you have no say in the matter."

"*You're* the one who said I should start thinking like a man." The lad squared his shoulders. "So that's what I'm doing. If Father were here, he'd do the same thing. And if your intentions aren't honorable—"

"What if they are?" Jarret snapped.

Why the hell had he said *that*?

George stared at him, a hopeful light in his eyes. "Well then, that would be different."

When Jarret didn't reply, George eyed him warily. "So you're saying your intentions *are* honorable?"

Jarret scowled, feeling backed into a corner. Why should he have to answer to some unlicked cub, for God's sake? He'd do what he wanted, damn it, just as he always did—and use the annoying pup's suggestion to his own advantage.

"Your aunt and I have some things to work out, so I'd appreciate it if you'd keep my intentions private, George."

He couldn't have the boy running off to tell Annabel that Jarret was going to court her, for God's sake.

The boy nodded.

"Good." Jarret gestured to the door. "Now we'd better go see about your mother."

"Yes, sir." As they started toward the door, George glanced up at Jarret. "You know, if you marry my aunt, you'll be my uncle."

He stifled a groan. "Yes, I suppose I will."

God help him, there was probably a special hell reserved for a man who willfully lied to a twelve-year-old boy. And lusted after the boy's virginal aunt. And had no intention of stopping either the lying or the lusting.

As they walked to the Lakes' room, he heard sounds of violent retching inside. George hastened his steps, his face blanching. When the lad swung open the door, Annabel hurried out to meet them. She closed the door behind her, but not before Jarret glimpsed Mrs. Lake hunched over a chamber pot.

A surge of anger made him grit his teeth. If he ever saw that damned rumormongering bitch Mrs. Cranley again, there'd be hell to pay.

"How is she?" he asked Annabel.

"Not well, I'm afraid."

"Is there anything we can do?" Jarret asked.

"If you could have the innkeeper fetch a doctor—"

"Done," Jarret said.

Fear spread over George's pale cheeks. "I want to see her."

"Not now, Geordie." Annabel ruffled the lad's hair with a tenderness that made Jarret's throat tighten. "She wants to be alone with me right now. She'll be fine once the bad meat has passed through her."

But Jarret could tell from her tone that she wasn't entirely convinced.

"I tell you what, lad," he said, "why don't we go see about getting a physician for your mother, then order some dinner?" He glanced at Annabel. "Do you want anything?"

She shook her head. "I couldn't eat right now. You two go on."

The innkeeper sent promptly for a doctor, then insisted upon offering them dinner for free. They ate in silence.

When the servant brought them a currant pie, George screwed his face up, looking as if he might cry. "Mother loves currant pie."

"Then we'll make sure she gets some, as soon as she's feeling better."

George lifted his gaze to Jarret. "Isn't there anything we can do?" His expression turned fierce. "We could go back and make the constable punish Mrs. Cranley."

Jarret certainly understood *that* impulse. "And what would happen if your mother needed us while we were gone? What if your aunt has to send us on to fetch your father? We must stay here in case we're needed."

"I suppose." He stared downcast at his plate. "Aunt Annabel wouldn't send for Father, though. And he wouldn't come, even if she did."

"Why not? Is he too ill to travel?" Jarret asked.

George shot him a fierce glance. "I don't want to talk about him, blast it! Bad enough that Mama's sick, and she m-might d-die, but Father . . ."

The boy burst into tears, alarming Jarret. "Here now, she's not going to die." Not sure what else to do, he laid his arm about George's bony shoulders and squeezed. "She'll be fine. She just needs rest, and then she'll be right as rain."

All George seemed able to do was nod. Jarret could

understand George's panic over his mother, but his reaction to the mention of his father's illness seemed unreasonable, given Annabel's statement that it wasn't life-threatening.

Jarret tensed. What if *that* was the secret Annabel was hiding? If her brother were dying, it would explain the man's inability to send a letter of introduction with her and why they all got so uneasy whenever his name was brought up.

But why keep that quiet? Perhaps because she feared that Jarret might balk at an alliance with a brewery that was about to be sold? Or worried that he might try to purchase the place at a loss if he figured out how bad off Lake Ale was?

He snorted. She had nothing to fear on that score. Plumtree Brewery didn't have the liquid assets right now to buy another brewery.

But neither could he involve it in Annabel's scheme if the legal owner couldn't see the project to fruition. That would be a contractual nightmare.

He looked at George, now furtively rubbing away the remainder of his tears, and wondered if he should press the boy further.

"Why don't we play some cards, lad? It'll pass the time until your aunt or the doctor can give us a report."

"A-all right. And perhaps you could tell me about your brother? You know, the one who races horses?"

"Absolutely," Jarret said.

George flashed him a waterlogged smile, and Jarret was jolted back to those horrible first weeks after his parents' deaths, when he'd found sustenance from even the smallest kindness of a stranger.

Damn it all to hell. He couldn't torment the lad further

right now—that would be cruel. George had to be panicking, fearful of watching *both* of his parents perish, leaving him all alone in the world. Jarret would have to confront Annabel about it once the rest of this mess was done.

Five hours later, when she came down to look in on them, she seemed pleased to find him entertaining George. She managed a faint smile as she watched them playing Pope Joan, but her appearance alarmed him. Tendrils of hair straggled down her pale cheeks, and her eyes were dulled by worry.

"Aunt Annabel!" Geordie cried, leaping up from the table. "How is Mother?"

"She's sleeping right now," she said, casting Jarret a veiled glance.

That wasn't an answer, and they both knew it. He stood and held out a chair for her. "Come, sit down. You look like hell."

He winced the minute the words left his lips. It was a tribute to how frustrated this situation made him that he would say something so rude.

She arched a brow. "What flattery. You'll make me swoon."

"Sorry," he said. "I didn't mean that how it sounded. But you need to eat. Take a seat, and I'll call for something."

"Not yet. Sissy is still feverish. Perhaps later, once I'm sure she'll be fine."

"No, right now," he said firmly and pressed her into the chair. "You'll do your sister-in-law no good if you fall sick yourself."

She reluctantly acquiesced, but when the servant brought her pigeon and peas, she only picked at them. "Actually, I came down to ask a favor of you, my lord."

He wished she would stop with the "my lord" nonsense.

His hand had been cupping her breast only a few hours ago. "Whatever you need."

"Would it be all right if Geordie slept in your room tonight?"

He hesitated half a second, but he'd be a bastard to refuse. "Of course." Jarret forced a smile.

"But Aunt Annabel, I want to sleep with you and Mother!" the lad protested.

"You'll rest better if you sleep in his lordship's room," she said wearily. "And so will she."

That was probably true. Jarret wouldn't rest very well, undoubtedly, but he shouldn't complain about that under the circumstances. "Come on, lad—be a man. Men don't sleep with their mothers, do they?"

George swallowed, then squared his shoulders. "No, I suppose not."

"Don't worry about us," Jarret told Annabel. "We can entertain ourselves. We'll drain a couple of pints, gamble at vingt-et-un with the lads here, and tumble a taproom maid or two."

A laugh sputtered out of Annabel. "I suppose you think that's funny," she said, trying to regain her straight face.

"Got a laugh from you, didn't it?" he drawled.

"Only because I'm so tired that anything would make me laugh," she admitted. But she was gazing fondly at him, which did something disquieting to his insides.

"Attempt to get some sleep," he said softly, trying not to think of how fetching she would look in a filmy nightdress and bare feet. "We'll be fine, I swear."

"Thank you for looking after him." Annabel rose. "I'd best go up. The doctor gave me an elixir to administer every two hours."

She headed toward the stairs, then turned back to cast him an apologetic glance. "Oh, and I should warn you. Geordie kicks."

"Then I'll just kick him back," Jarret retorted. At Geordie's horrified gasp, he chuckled. "I'm joking, lad. I'll manage."

Still, it looked as if it would be a long damned night.

# Chapter Ten

𝒜nnabel passed the next twenty-four hours in a blur of emptying chamber pots and sponging Sissy's fevered head. At the end of their second day in the inn, Annabel dozed off in the chair beside the bed. A few hours later, she was jolted awake by the sound of a window being opened. Sissy had left the bed.

"What are you doing?" she cried as she rose to go to her sister-in-law's side.

"It's like a furnace in here," Sissy said. "We need air."

Annabel touched Sissy's head, and relief flooded her. "Your fever has broken. You don't have chills anymore!"

"I'm all clammy, though." Sissy returned to the bed and pulled the covers up to her chin, then patted the spot beside her. "Come on, you need sleep, too." Suddenly her head shot up. "Is Geordie still in his lordship's room?"

"Yes. Poor man. The last I saw him, he looked decidedly strained."

Yet he'd once again made her sit down and eat. Whenever

she'd gone down to report on Sissy's condition, he'd been downright solicitous. He'd even made sure the servants brought tea and food for her at mealtimes.

"Aren't you worried that Geordie will let something slip about Hugh that might alert his lordship to what's really going on?" Sissy asked.

With a sigh, Annabel climbed into bed. "Of course, but we had no choice. They've spent hours together now. If Geordie was going to say something, surely he would have done so already." She lay back to stare at the ceiling. "And perhaps Jarret is right. Perhaps Geordie really is getting old enough to be trusted with a few matters."

"Jarret?" Sissy said meaningfully.

A blush heated Annabel's cheeks. "We . . . that is, he . . . suggested that we needn't be so formal with each other. Under the circumstances."

"Did he, now?" Amusement threaded Sissy's voice.

"It doesn't mean anything." At Sissy's snort, Annabel added, "Seriously, you mustn't get ideas about him and me."

"Why not? It's long past time you married."

"You sound like Hugh," she chided. "You know why I don't want to marry."

"I do—but the right man won't care that you have a son. If having you means taking in Geordie, too, he'll do it."

"Wouldn't you miss him?" Annabel asked.

"Of course I would miss him. But you're as much a mother to him as I am. And he could come to visit us as often as he likes. In my mind, he's always been yours."

"But in *his* mind, he's always been *yours*." Annabel sighed. "The point is moot, anyway. I have yet to meet this 'right man.' His lordship certainly isn't it. A marquess's son take in some brewster's by-blow? Besides, he isn't the marrying kind."

He was the seducing kind. And a wanton part of her wished to find out if he was as good at that as he was at kissing.

Ever since he'd caressed her breast, restlessness had wreaked havoc on her self-control. All she could think about was how glorious it had felt to have six feet of aroused male pressing into her, caressing her, wanting her. The same way she'd wanted him. She'd ached to have him take her right there against the wall—

She groaned. This was insanity! How did he make her feel these things, when no one since Rupert had done so? And she missed it so much. She hadn't realized until this very moment how much she'd missed being touched intimately by a man.

Lord, she cringed to think how close they'd come to being caught. Had Geordie suspected what they were doing? She'd dearly love to know what their conversation had been about. She hadn't had a moment to ask Jarret, but she'd do so as soon as she could.

No doubt about it, the man was dangerous. His nature called to a wildness in her that craved escape.

But it simply wouldn't do to indulge such urges. It was fine for a man—he could take what he wanted, button up his trousers, and be done. A woman had more to fear from such an encounter, as Annabel knew only too well.

"Why are you so sure that his lordship isn't the marrying kind?" Sissy asked.

*Because he wagered with me for a night in his bed. Because every time he looks at me, I feel the heat on my skin. Because he makes me feel things no respectable man could possibly make me feel.*

"His grandmother gave him and his siblings an ultimatum:

marry or be cut off from their inheritance. But according to his brother, she agreed to exempt him if he ran Plumtree Brewery for a year. Since he accepted the bargain, I suspect he has a strong aversion to matrimony."

Sissy rolled her eyes. "All men have a strong aversion to matrimony."

"Not Rupert." Though honestly, she wasn't entirely sure of that.

"Rupert was a boy, not a man," Sissy said gently. "Boys are impetuous."

True. Why else had Rupert run off to fight the war, leaving her to fend for herself?

Jarret certainly wasn't impetuous. Except when he was holding her against a wall to kiss and fondle her . . .

Blast it, why couldn't she stop thinking about it? "Whatever the reason, Jarret is definitely not interested in marriage."

"You may not have noticed, but bachelors don't generally agree to look after children. Yet here he is, looking after Geordie to help you."

"And you."

Sissy laughed. "It's not me he follows with his eyes. It's not me he scowls at when your great love for Rupert is mentioned. It's not me he flirts with."

"You're daft," Annabel said, her heart racing. If Sissy only knew. "He's a rogue, and they flirt with anything in petticoats. Besides, he probably thinks that looking after Geordie will get us on the road faster. He wants to be done with meeting the terms of our wager."

She must tell herself that until she believed it.

"Have it your way." Sissy's eyelids drooped. "But I say you have a chance there and should seize it while you can. You're not getting any younger, you know."

"Thank you for reminding me."

"Someone should," Sissy said drowsily, and succumbed to sleep.

Annabel should as well, since there was no telling what tomorrow would bring. But her memories of Jarret's kisses made it hard. Really, it was ridiculous. She was acting like a silly girl, full of pointless romantic dreams. Nothing good could come of it. Only fools placed their hopes in rogues like him.

That was her last thought before she, too, nodded off.

The next morning, the doctor informed her and Jarret that Sissy was indeed on the mend but needed at least another day to recuperate before she started jostling her stomach in a carriage again.

Though Jarret had to be chafing at the delay, it was Geordie who received the news with ill grace. After they left Sissy and headed off for breakfast, Geordie stomped ahead of them toward the stairs. "I can't believe we have to spend *another* day here! I'll die of boredom!"

"No one dies of boredom, Geordie," Annabel said wearily.

"We'll play cards, lad," Jarret said.

Shoving his hands in his pockets, Geordie headed downstairs. "I'm *sick* of that."

"Geordie," Annabel said sharply, "don't be rude. It was very nice of his lordship to offer. None of us likes this situation, but we must adjust."

"Sorry," Geordie mumbled unconvincingly. "Can't we go for a ride? Get outdoors for a bit?"

At that moment, the innkeeper met them at the bottom of the stairs. "I hope your lordship has been comfortable these past two days."

"Perfectly so, sir," Jarret said. "Tell me, is there any sort of spectacle to be had around here that would please a young gentleman? Racing, shooting? Any chance for a sight of blood and mayhem?"

The innkeeper chuckled. "Well, now, it's market day. At the beast market, they butcher the cows and pigs."

When Annabel made a face, Jarret laughed. "I suppose they have other parts of the market?"

"Aye, my lord, booths selling all sorts of goods. And there's a man what brings an alligator around sometimes to show."

Geordie's curiosity was clearly piqued. "What's an alligator?"

"It's an exotic creature that lives in parts of America— rather like a large, scaly lizard." Jarret lowered his voice mysteriously. "They're very dangerous. I don't know if we should risk it."

"Oh, but we must! Aunt Annabel, can we go see the alligator? Please?"

"Why not?" Now that Jarret had raised the boy's hopes, there had better be one of these alligator creatures at the market, or they'd never hear the end of it.

As soon as they finished breakfast, they headed out to High Street. The weekly market there had stalls of every description—lace makers with their intricate wares, whip makers and other purveyors of fine leather, a poulterer, a farmer with fat piglets to sell.

Geordie had to stop at every booth. He never left her and Jarret alone, either, which gave her pause. He certainly was being quite the diligent little chaperone.

Meanwhile, Jarret was subdued. She caught his sharp, assessing gaze on her several times. It worried her exceedingly. What exactly *had* those two discussed yesterday?

It took them some time to find the man with the alligator,

and Annabel discovered that Jarret's description was apt. Looking like a dragon, the creature was over eight feet long and bore a nasty set of sharp teeth, though his snout was bound with a rope.

The soldier with a wooden leg, who was leading the creature about by a chain, told them that he'd acquired the unusual pet when he was fighting in the Battle of New Orleans. "It was only a wee thing, then," he said. "Lost its mother to cannon fire, so I took it home with me. Been with me for ten years."

He bent to give Geordie a toothy grin. "Would you want to pet it, lad? Cost you only a shilling."

"I'll pay you a shilling to keep it away from him," Annabel said.

"He can't hurt him, miss," the soldier said. "I fed him before we came to market, so he ain't looking to eat, and anyway, his mouth is tied real tight."

"Oh, please can I pet him, Aunt Annabel?" Geordie begged. *"Please?"*

"How about if I pet him first?" Jarret said as he handed the man a shilling. "Then your aunt can decide if she wants to take the chance."

Jarret bent to run his hand over the creature's head. When the only response he got from the alligator was a blink, Geordie turned to her. "Can I pet him? Can I, can I?"

"I suppose." The thing did look harmless, trussed as he was.

Instantly, they drew a crowd of people eager to watch. Geordie made the most of it, showing how brave he was by stroking the beast's head gingerly, then repeating it more boldly after Jarret dropped another shilling into the owner's hand.

Annabel tensed. Only three days together, and Geordie

and Jarret had become great chums. Bad enough that Geordie's "father" had turned into an unreliable and melancholy drunk. Now a charming rogue was wriggling his way into the boy's heart without a care for what would happen when he returned to London.

Jarret shot her a glance full of mischief and gave the owner another shilling. "So the lady can pet him, too."

She frowned. "You're daft if you think I'm going to touch that creature."

"Come now, where's your sense of adventure?" Jarret taunted her.

The words brought her up short. She'd said that very thing to Rupert long ago, when he'd scoffed at her suggestion that she go with him to war.

Geordie snorted. "You'll never get Aunt Annabel to pet him. Girls are too scared to do things like that."

"Nonsense," Annabel said hotly, then leaned down to place her hand on the creature's back.

To her surprise, it felt as smooth as kid leather. As she stroked, Geordie looked at her in surprise. Feeling rather pleased with herself, she smirked at him.

Then the creature turned his head, and with a squeal, both she and Geordie jumped back.

"He must like you, miss," the old soldier said, chuckling. "He don't usually pay anybody much mind when they pet him."

Several in the crowd clamored to pet it, too, so they continued through the market.

As Geordie darted ahead in search of more excitement, Jarret lowered his voice. "Do you always do that?"

"What?"

His hand covered hers, warm and firm. "Rise to any challenge a man offers you."

"I couldn't have Geordie calling me a coward, could I?"

"No, indeed," he mocked her. "To be shown up by a twelve-year-old boy—however would you hold your head up?"

She sniffed. "Shows what you know. If you don't rise to his challenges from time to time, he gets too full of himself and becomes bossy and insufferable. Rather like you, actually."

"When have I ever been bossy and insufferable?"

"In the brewery office. And at the tavern, before I accepted the wager. Admit it: if I hadn't, you would have packed me off back to the inn and told me to be a good girl and trot on home to Burton."

He frowned. "That's what I should have done."

"Then I wouldn't have gained anything I wanted."

"But you wouldn't have risked your reputation."

"Sometimes a woman has to take risks to get what she wants." She glanced to where Geordie seemed preoccupied with a saddle salesman's wares, then lowered her voice. "Speaking of risks, what did Geordie say to you after he found us?"

"It was nothing of consequence." His too-casual tone said otherwise.

"I can't believe he said *nothing*—"

"Ah, look, there's a woman selling ale by the barrel. George, come with us," he called out, bringing Geordie running back to his side. "We're going to see if that alewife makes her own ale."

Curse the rascal. Now she *knew* they'd talked about something. "Why should I care about some other brewster's ale?" Annabel grumbled.

"Because it's research. If ale is this lady's business, she'll know what sells hereabouts. Could be good information for the future."

Acknowledging the logic in that, she let Jarret lead her to the ale booth.

It turned out that the alewife not only sold her wares at Daventry's market, but traveled to the other markets in Staffordshire. As Jarret quizzed her at length about ale-buying habits in the country, Annabel could only listen in surprise. For a man who had only "dipped his toe" in the business, he knew a great deal about the marketing part, which wasn't her strong suit. It made her uneasy. What if he took stock of Lake Ale and decided that her and Hugh's plan wasn't viable?

What if he was right?

Geordie asked her for some coins and she handed them to him, distracted by the discussion with the alewife. After a few moments, however, she realized that Geordie had wandered away. She turned around just in time to see him hand the coins to a man at a table with three thimbles atop it. The man put a pea under one of the thimbles and started moving them around.

"What on earth is that boy doing?" she mused.

Jarret followed her gaze, then scowled. Before she could even react, he was striding over to the table where a small crowd had gathered. To her shock, he seemed to stumble and knock over the table.

As she hurried up, she heard him say, "Beg pardon, sir. Didn't mean to be so clumsy."

The man growled something about watching his step, as Geordie bent to help right the table.

"I was about to win, Lord Jarret!" Geordie complained.

The mention of Jarret's title made the vendor look suddenly uneasy.

"Ah well, what a shame," Jarret said. "I suppose I ruined it for you." His gaze turned to ice as he stared down at the vendor. "Give him back his money, will you, old chap? You can hardly honor his bet now."

The man who owned the table paled, then handed Geordie his coins without a word.

Geordie told the vendor, "If you'll set it up again, I can place another—"

"I don't think so, lad." Jarret grabbed his arm. "Your aunt is ready to leave. Aren't you, Miss Lake?"

Bewildered by the strange incident, Annabel stammered, "Y-Yes, of course. We should go."

Dragging a protesting Geordie from the group, Jarret walked down the lane so fast that Annabel had to run to keep up with him.

"Let *go* of me!" Geordie cried. "I can win!"

"Not at thimblerig, lad. It's a swindle meant to separate you from your money."

As Geordie stopped squirming, Annabel halted. "That's awful! We should go warn the others!"

"I wouldn't advise it," Jarret said.

"Why not?"

"Anyone running that particular cheat keeps accomplices nearby to prevent anyone from mucking with their scheme. They'll stick a knife in one's back if it serves their purpose. We're better off reporting them to those who run the market."

"Are you sure it was a cheat?" Geordie asked plaintively.

"Absolutely. They run it in the streets of London all the time. No matter how much you watch the thimble, the pea that's supposedly under it ends up wherever the man wants it to be. He palms it so he can place it where he likes."

George stared at him wide-eyed. "Like you were doing with the cards last night?"

Jarret muttered a curse under his breath. "Exactly. Let's go find a milliner's booth, shall we? I want to purchase something for Mrs. Lake."

"Wait a minute," Annabel said, "what's this about palming cards?"

"His lordship showed me how to palm cards and deal from the bottom and—"

"You taught him how to *cheat* at cards?" Annabel cried.

"Only so he could recognize a cardsharp when he played with one."

"And where is he supposed to play with one, pray tell? In a gambling hell?"

Jarret shrugged. "Card cheats are everywhere. You never know when the lad will come across one. Like with the thimblerig operator. It can't hurt George to be prepared."

The thought that Jarret was the one trying to prepare Geordie inflamed her. She knew her anger was irrational, but she couldn't help it. She'd spent twelve years trying to see that Geordie had every advantage of a genteel upbringing, yet who was Geordie turning to for advice?

"I suppose you taught him a few gambling tricks as well," she retorted as they neared the edge of the market. "So he can spend his nights in the same empty pursuits that you spend yours in."

"And what if he did?" Geordie cried, leaping to his hero's defense. "Nobody else teaches me such things. You and Mother treat me like a baby who can't do *anything*. Perhaps I *want* to know about gambling. Perhaps I'd like it if I tried it."

"Oh, God," Jarret muttered.

"See what you started?" she accused Jarret. "You made it so very attractive—"

"It appears I arrived in the nick of time," cried a voice from behind them.

They turned to see Sissy, looking markedly improved, hurrying after them.

"What are you doing here, Sissy?" Annabel asked.

Sissy shrugged. "I got tired of being cooped up in that inn room, so I thought I'd join you. I'm feeling much better now." She glanced from Annabel to Jarret. "Though it looks like I'm the only one. I could hear you arguing from three booths away."

"Aunt Annabel is being mean to Lord Jarret," Geordie complained.

Sissy smothered a smile. "Well then, we shall have to make her sit in the corner."

Annabel rolled her eyes. "His lordship seems to think that the techniques of card cheating are suitable subjects for a twelve-year-old boy."

"I'm sure he was just trying to help," Sissy said, her eyes suspiciously bright.

"Yes, trying to help Geordie follow in his dubious footsteps," Annabel snapped.

"Stop it!" Geordie cried. "If you keep being mean to him, he'll change his mind about marrying you!"

# Chapter Eleven

Jarret barely stifled an oath. But truth was, it was a miracle the lad had kept his mouth shut this long. Twelve-year-old boys weren't known for their discretion.

Mrs. Lake now regarded Jarret with that expression all matrons got when they thought they had a live one on the hook.

Annabel just looked dumbfounded.

So of course George had to make it worse. "I'm sorry, sir. I-I didn't mean to let the cat out of the bag."

Annabel's eyes narrowed on Jarret.

Damn the boy to hell.

"I was just about to look for a tea booth, Geordie," Mrs. Lake said smoothly, clamping her hand on the boy's shoulder. "Why don't you help me?"

"B-But I need to explain—"

"I think you've done quite enough. Now come along." Turning a meaningful glance on Annabel, Mrs. Lake added, "Don't stray too far, my dear. It looks like a storm is brewing."

More than one kind, unfortunately. As Mrs. Lake hurried

the boy off, Annabel planted her hands on her hips. "What was Geordie talking about?"

Faced with no good choice, Jarret decided to do what his late father had always done whenever Mother was on the rampage. Run.

"I don't know what you mean." He headed for the nearest escape route, striding off blindly down a lane.

Hitching up her skirts, she hurried to keep up with his long strides. "Answer me! How did Geordie get the idea that you wish to marry me?"

"Why don't you ask *him*?" he snapped, oddly reluctant to lie to her.

"I'm asking *you*! You said something to him, didn't you? After he found us together?"

Damn, damn, and damn. Worse yet, the sky was darkening overhead.

Time for another of Father's tactics—the counterattack. He halted to fix her with a cold glance. "I'll answer your question if you answer mine. Is your brother dying?"

That did the trick. She blanched, then hurried off down the lane ahead of him. So *she* thought to escape now, did she? Not bloody likely.

He caught up to her in a couple of easy strides. "Well?" he pressed.

"What gave you the idea that Hugh is dying?" she asked in a strained tone.

"George seemed inordinately upset about his mother's illness. And when I mentioned that his father might wish to be fetched, he said that you wouldn't do so. He said your brother wouldn't come even if you did."

She looked appalled. "I can't believe he would say that! Of course Hugh would come."

"I got the impression," he persisted, "that his father might be too ill to come. And it occurred to me that if Mr. Lake is dying—"

"He's not dying, all right? His problem is merely temporary, as I told you. He'll be up and around in no time."

Though her words held the resonance of truth, he needed more. "Then why did George seem to think otherwise?"

"I have no idea. He knows better." She frowned. "But like most boys his age, he tends to exaggerate for dramatic effect."

Well, that was certainly true. Jarret remembered those days well. "He wouldn't exaggerate so much if you and his mother would stop coddling him. It's not good for a lad that age to be coddled. They start to think they're at the center of the universe, and anything related to them becomes a matter of grand importance."

"That's ridiculous. We don't coddle him in the least."

"Really?" They'd left the market and were walking along a deserted country lane lined with pretty little cottages and barns of aging gray timbers. "He's already old enough to attend Eton, yet he doesn't even know when he's being swindled."

"*I* didn't even know he was being swindled. I've never heard of thimblerig." Her tone grew acid. "We don't have sharpers and cheats on every corner in Burton, as you apparently do in London."

"He should be in school by now, learning how the world works."

"I agree. Unfortunately, I . . . we can't afford to send him away to school. Not with the brewery struggling."

"Then tell your brother to hire him a tutor, for God's sake. And give him some room to breathe and be a boy. Stop smothering him."

She sniffed. "That's great advice, coming from a man who grew up wild because he had no one looking after him. A man who still behaves like a schoolboy because he's afraid to grow up."

He halted in the middle of the lane. She saw him as a *schoolboy?*

"I'm sorry," she went on hastily. "I shouldn't have said that."

He glared at her. "I didn't ask to play nursemaid to your damned nephew. That was *your* idea. So if you don't like how I do it, God knows I have better things to do."

Stark dismay showed on her face. "Fine. I shan't foist him on you anymore."

Trying not to dwell on how upsetting he found her reaction, he began walking again.

She followed. "Do you have any idea where you're going?"

"No," he bit out. "Nor do I care."

As if Nature were conspiring to *make* him care, the first fat drops of rain fell on his coat. Wonderful.

"Perhaps we should return to town," she ventured.

Even as she spoke, the rain began to batter them. "Too late for that," he muttered. Spotting a nearby barn, he tugged her into it. The smell of horses and fresh hay assailed him as they entered the dimly lit structure. "No one seems to be about. Everyone has probably gone to the market."

"Good," she said tartly. "Now you can answer the question you've been avoiding. What did you tell Geordie to make him think you and I are headed for marriage?"

He cursed under his breath. He should have realized his distractions wouldn't work for long. "George isn't the child you take him for. He understands a great deal."

"Oh, I'm well aware of that. So what exactly did he understand?"

"Enough to guess that you and I had been kissing."

She paled. "Oh, Lord."

"He asked me if my intentions toward you were honorable," Jarret ground out. "I had to tell him something."

"You could have tried telling him the truth," she said in that lofty tone she took whenever she felt *she* had the moral high ground.

It sent his temper rising. "The truth?" He rounded on her. "That my only intention toward his aunt is carnal: is *that* what you wanted me to say?"

She blinked. "I . . . well . . . no, I don't suppose that would have been a good idea."

He stalked toward her. "I could have said that if I'd had *my* way, you would already have spent a night in my bed."

A blush was spreading over her pretty cheeks. "No, I certainly wouldn't have wanted you to—"

"I could have told him I can't keep my hands off you." He caught her at the waist, her heightened color inflaming his senses, his need. "I could have said that all I think about is swiving you senseless. That I lie awake at night imagining how you would feel beneath me. Would *that* have satisfied your sense of truth and honor?"

"That would definitely not have been—"

The sound of voices outside the barn halted her stammering.

"Damnation," he muttered. "Just what we need—someone finding strangers here and thinking we're trying to steal their horses." He spotted the ladder leading to the loft. "Come on," he growled and dragged her toward it, then pushed her up.

Thankfully, she was a fast climber. They'd barely cleared the top before he heard the barn door open. Dragging her down into the straw, he held a finger to her lips.

The men were discussing a horse for sale, but Jarret paid the conversation no heed. He was too conscious of the fact that Annabel lay half beneath him, her face flushed in the dim light and her hair a dark swirl against the golden straw. The cold rain had turned her thin gown nearly translucent and he could see the hard tips of her nipples straining against the cloth.

Suddenly he didn't care about George or the brewery, or what she was hiding about her brother, or anything else. He cared only that she was staring at him with that warm, aware look that beckoned him to madness.

Unable to stop himself, he traced her soft mouth with his finger, his blood roaring in his veins. She was the country girl in her element, ripe for a tumble in the hay, perfectly at home in a barn. The temptation was too potent to resist. As the earthy smell of horses blended with her honey-sweet scent, he replaced his finger with his lips, exulting as she opened to him, then lifted her arms to encircle his neck.

Then he was lost to anything but her. Below them the murmur of voices continued, but he was too busy devouring her mouth to care.

God, she was wonderful to kiss. There was no hesitation, no maidenly shyness. She offered a man everything—throwing herself into it body and soul, open and giving. Nothing like he would expect from a virgin. Her blatant need mirrored his own, stoking his desire even more. He struggled to think, to breathe, to find his way through the fog of enchantment that she wrapped about him with every movement of her delectable body.

Taking advantage of the need for silence, he trailed kisses down the tender column of her neck to where a froth of lace only half hid the upper mounds of her breasts. He lifted his head to lock gazes with her and pulled loose the lace, then pushed down her damp gown and corset cups to bare her shift.

Her breathing grew ragged, yet she didn't resist—not even when he lowered his mouth to capture one breast through her shift. As he tongued her nipple, she let out a soft gasp.

But her hands clutched him close, and that was all the invitation he needed. While pleasuring one breast with his mouth, he fondled the other with his hand. Her body strained against him, her hands anchoring him to her. She wanted more. He *needed* more, wanted to give her *far* more.

When he tugged loose the ties of her shift she stared at him, her eyes as dark as the unholy lust raging in his loins. Lowering her shift, he gazed on her naked bosom, and his heart shuddered to a halt.

Damn, she was lovely. Her breasts were as full as he'd guessed, with large, rosy nipples begging to be sucked and teased. He bent his head to lick one, then the other, before caressing the damp flesh with his fingers. Her soft cry was half gasp, half moan.

It was the most erotic thing he'd ever heard. His cock stiffened to stone against her thigh. "My God, Annabel . . ." he groaned against her breast.

The voices downstairs halted, and for one panicked moment, he thought he'd been heard. Then the door opened and closed below them. The men had left the barn.

She pushed him back with an uncertain glance.

"Perhaps you should . . . let me up now . . ." she whispered, though she didn't reach to straighten her clothes.

"Not a chance," he rasped.

Her eyes widened. "Why?"

He gave a strangled laugh. "Why do you think?" Ignoring

her hands against his chest, he lowered his head to draw hard on her nipple, making her arch up against him.

"We shouldn't . . . be doing this . . ." she murmured, but her hands slipped up to clutch his shoulders.

"I want to touch you." Shifting his body off her, he inched up her skirts. "Let me touch you."

A shudder wracked her, then her eyes slid closed. "Yes . . . please . . ."

Annabel knew it was dangerous to encourage him. It could too easily get out of hand, and she could find herself in the same situation she'd been in thirteen years ago. Except this time the man who got her with child would break her heart, for Jarret was the sort to bed her and forget her.

Thus far, she'd mostly resisted his charms. But if she were intimate with him, that would be impossible. She couldn't just share a man's bed and forget about him.

Still, it had been so long since a man had touched her this way, and he was inciting her to riot. It was hard *not* to respond. Especially after the sweet things he'd said, about how he thought about her, how he desired her. Even Rupert had never courted her with such words, and she hadn't realized how badly she craved that.

Nobody knew they were here, after all. Nobody knew he was doing these things. It gave her license to be naughty.

His lips whispered over her cheek. "I promise not to ruin you."

The words startled her. How could he ruin her?

Oh, yes. He thought she was a virgin. And the truth was, she *felt* like a virgin with him. Or at least a woman who'd half forgotten how it felt to be with a man so intimately.

"All right," she murmured.

"I just want to see you reach your rapture," he said huskily, and slipped his hand inside her drawers to cup her between the legs.

Her eyes shot open. "What?"

His blindingly handsome face held a raw hunger that called to her own. "For three nights now, I've lain awake in bed imagining how you would look if I took you. I want to see if it matches my imagination." When she stiffened, he added, "I know I can't take you . . . but I can bring you pleasure."

He rubbed her most private place, and she let out a moan of pure enjoyment. With a knowing smile, he nuzzled her ear. "Let me watch you come apart in my hands, dearling."

The endearment made a dangerous thrill rise in her throat. "I suppose that would be . . . all right," she said, finishing the word on a squeak when he fingered her flesh with a particularly deft stroke.

"All right?" he said, laughter showing on his face. "I promise you, my pretty pixie, it will be far better than all right." With eyes agleam, he slid down her body.

"What are you doing?" she whispered, perplexed.

"I want to taste you."

"Where?"

In answer, he bent his head to lick the part his hand had just been caressing.

"Ohhhh . . ." she breathed. How astonishing! Who knew that a man could do such an outrageous thing?

Who knew that it would feel so good?

Holding her thighs open, he strafed her private parts with his tongue. A cry of pleasure and surprise escaped her. It was so . . . intense. She'd not felt anything that intense with Rupert.

But then, Jarret wasn't some fumbling country boy. He knew just how to inflame a woman's senses. And how could it hurt to let him? When would she get another chance like this, to be free and wild, to *desire* again?

His tongue dipped and swirled, making her ache and want. She remembered the wanting but didn't remember it being this powerful. Only half aware of what she did, she swiveled her hips up to gain more, feel more.

He chuckled. "You like that, do you?"

She blushed, but somehow managed a nod.

"And this?" He sucked on a particularly tender part of her flesh, and she nearly went insane. "Do you like this?"

"You . . . know . . . I do," she choked out as sensation flooded her, fierce and hot, making her writhe beneath his mouth.

"Just making sure," he murmured, then plundered her with his lips and tongue and teeth in more earnest.

Lord save her, what was he *doing* to her? Her memories from Rupert were of vaguely pleasurable sensations, a sense of closeness, a muted sort of enjoyment.

This was blatantly, nakedly, boldly carnal. He made her want to leap, to soar, to explode from her clothes, from her very skin.

"Jarret, please . . ." she moaned, burying her fingers in his damp hair, anchoring his head between her legs.

"Take what you will, Annabel. It's yours. You just have to grasp it."

Somehow, she understood exactly what he meant. She could feel the growth of a pleasure that lay glittering just beyond her reach. Every lash of his tongue brought it nearer . . . if she could just . . . stretch . . . farther . . . higher . . .

There!

A symphony of sensation wracked her body, dragging a keening cry from her lips. Good Lord in Heaven! Such glorious . . . amazing . . . It was beyond anything she'd ever felt. As her body shook with the force of her release, she tightened her fingers in his gorgeous tangle of silky black hair.

It took her a while to regain her breath—and her sanity. When she trusted herself to look at him, she found him watching her. Heat rose in her cheeks.

He flashed that rogue's smile that showed both his dimples. "You're so lovely when you reach the peak of your pleasure. All pink and flushed." He brushed a kiss to her inner thigh. "Here." He slid up next to her to kiss her exposed breast. "And here." He kissed her throat. "Even here."

"And you?" she whispered, embarrassed by the attention he was giving her shameless response. "What do *you* look like when you reach the peak of *your* pleasure?"

When he jerked back to stare at her, she cursed her quick tongue. A virgin wouldn't say that. Virgins were too anxious to worry if the man had enjoyment. They weren't even aware that a man could have pleasure without ruining them.

He mustn't realize she was unchaste, or he'd take full advantage. The only thing standing between her and another illegitimate child was Jarret's belief that she was a virgin.

"I-I—"

"Tell you what," he said, his eyes turning a brilliant green as he took her hand and placed it on his trousers. "Why don't you find out for yourself?"

# Chapter Twelve

Jarret held his breath, sure that she would recoil. It was one thing to be curious about a man's pleasure, but quite another to offer to bring it about.

Then again, he hadn't expected her to let him pleasure her in the first place. And he certainly hadn't expected her response to stir something dark and sweet inside him, a kind of longing he'd never felt: to possess a woman fully—not just in body, but in mind and heart and soul.

It scared him, so he beat down the feeling and concentrated on coaxing her into an illicit act.

"I'd dearly love to have your hands on me, bringing *me* to the peak of pleasure."

Her gaze grew shuttered. "I don't think that's wise."

Remembering the alligator incident, he shrugged. "Well, if you aren't certain you can manage it . . ."

"Of course I can manage it," she said stoutly. "How hard can it be?"

He laughed. "Trust me, dearling, hard enough."

When he pressed her hand to the bulge in his trousers, she went beet red. "Oh my."

The words shot straight to his cock, stiffening it even more. "Do you mean to leave me in this condition?" he asked, pushing against her hand.

"I suppose that would be . . . rude." She rubbed the length of him, and he thought he'd explode.

"Rude," he choked out. "Right." When her fingers brushed the head of his cock, he released a strangled breath. "You can take it out, you know."

A minxish smile touched her lips. She swept her hand delicately over the straining cloth. "Can I?"

"Oh, God, *touch* me," he rasped, unable to endure much more of her teasing. He began to wonder exactly how inexperienced she was. He'd lay odds that she and Rupert had done a bit more than kiss.

Poor sod, to go off to war with the memory of something like this in his head, and no hope of relief.

"Please, Annabel . . ." he rasped.

"All right."

His blood thundered in his ears. Every time she said "all right" in that understated way, it drove him mad.

She unbuttoned his trousers, then released the buttons of his drawers. As his cock sprang free, he let out a shudder of relief. With another teasing smile, she closed her fingers around him.

And then he began a slow descent into insanity as she stroked him. Somehow she made it all seem perfectly acceptable. Having this fresh-faced country lass doing what no respectable virgin would ever do was arousing as hell. If he didn't watch it, he would come too quickly. He hadn't done that since he was a lad, but she was making it damned hard to resist.

He tried not to wonder how she'd learned exactly how to please a man, but it had to be that damned fiancé of hers. And ludicrous as it was, the idea of her doing this to another man made him scowl.

She released his cock instantly. "I'm hurting you."

"God, no." She couldn't be *too* experienced, or she wouldn't look so concerned.

What was wrong with him, to care what she might have done with some stupid soldier? This was merely a dalliance.

Guiding her hand back around his flesh, he murmured, "Men are sturdier than you'd think." Their bodies were, anyway. He began to wonder about the sturdiness of their minds.

"Even there?" she asked skeptically.

"Even there." He gripped her fingers, forcing her to stroke him harder. "Yes, dearling. Like that."

It felt like heaven. He wouldn't last much longer.

She bent her head, as if concentrating on her caresses, and he brushed the mahogany waves of her hair with his lips. Her honey and orange smell filled his senses, blotting out the other scents of the barn. It was luscious, as luscious as her breast, which he couldn't help fondling, and her temple, which he couldn't stop kissing.

Had any woman ever consumed him like this?

His body galloped toward release, stampeding over anything but the urgent need for fulfillment. As the blood surged in him and he felt the little death overcoming him, he pushed her hand free so he could spend himself into the straw.

His body shook with the sheer power of it. Good God, he'd never come that fiercely in his life. He already wanted to do it again . . . inside her. That was *not* acceptable.

Lying back onto the straw, he tugged her against his chest. As he came back to earth, reality set in. He shouldn't have gone so far with her, no matter how much they'd enjoyed it. A woman like her only allowed such privileges to serious suitors, and he certainly wasn't that. He couldn't have her thinking that he was.

Never mind that he liked her. He admired her loyalty to her family, her refusal to back down . . . the utterly reckless way she came. And she was a bloody good card player, besides.

But he wasn't going to *marry* her, for God's sake. He'd already escaped Gran's plans for him. Marrying a brewster with an ailing brewery would be like sticking his head right back into Gran's noose. Gran would own him body and soul.

*Annabel* would own him body and soul . . . until the day something took her from him. And that would be far worse if he came to care for her. So he had to figure out how to explain why he couldn't marry her without hurting her feelings.

After a moment, she said, "Well, at least I got my answer."

"About what?"

"How you look when you reach the peak of your pleasure."

At the teasing note in her voice, he turned his head to stare at her. "Oh? How do I look?"

She grinned. "Like every man looks when he gets what he wants. As smug and self-satisfied as a sultan."

He lifted an eyebrow at her. "A sultan?"

"All men look like sultans in bed," she said.

Something in the way she said it arrested him. "So you've seen that many men in bed, have you?"

She glanced away, clearly embarrassed. "Certainly not. I . . . just read that somewhere."

It figured. "You have rather risqué tastes in literature."

A blush touched her cheeks. "Even a spinster can be curious, you know."

He shifted to his side so he could circle her nipple with his finger. Their discussion could wait a few more moments. "Feel free to indulge your curiosity as much as you please."

But when he bent his head toward her breast, she pushed him away. "I think I've indulged it quite enough, don't you?"

"You could never indulge it too much for me." He watched as she sat up and began to straighten her clothing. Above them the rain on the roof beat a steady counterpoint to his still pounding heart.

"You have to stop saying things like that," she warned. "And you have to stop . . . kissing me."

He plucked a piece of straw from her hair, then tickled her neck with it. "And if I don't want to stop?" Good God, what he had to stop was this deplorable habit of letting his cock speak for him.

"You must," she said firmly. "I shan't risk Geordie's catching us again. He already thinks you want to marry me, and I can't have that. And when I tell him that there's nothing between us he has to believe me. Assuming that he hasn't yet told Sissy about seeing us kiss, I can probably convince him to stay quiet. But if he finds us together again, he'll tattle for sure. And if Sissy tells my brother, he might—"

"Try to force a marriage on me."

"On *us*. And I won't be forced. Nor will I have any of them getting their hopes up about us marrying, when there's no chance of that happening under any circumstances."

The conviction in her voice irritated him. "You sound awfully sure of that."

She eyed him askance. "Come now, you know perfectly well you don't want to marry me."

Never mind that he'd had that exact thought only two

minutes before; to have her state it so casually was rather off-putting. "I suppose that's true, but—"

"And I certainly have no intention of marrying *you*."

He sat up to glare at her. "Why the hell not?"

"No offense, but you aren't what a sensible woman looks for in a husband."

"That's putting it a bit strongly." Now peeved, he rose to his knees to button his drawers and trousers. "And what exactly *does* a 'sensible woman' look for?" he asked sarcastically.

She looked bewildered. "Well, for one thing, a man who has some sense of duty. Not an irresponsible scapegrace who gambles his way through London to avoid doing anything constructive with his time. And your friends *did* say you're only helping your grandmother with Plumtree Brewery to avoid having to meet her requirement that you marry—"

"I know what they said," he snapped. He didn't know why he found her observations so annoying; everything she was telling him was true.

But *she* wasn't supposed to be saying it. *He* was. *She* was supposed to be wheedling him into marrying her, now that he'd taken liberties with her. He was a marquess's son, after all.

Granted, he was only a second son and there was a great deal of scandal attached to the family name, but why would she care? She was a brewer's daughter, for God's sake, from provincial little Burton-upon-Trent. And a spinster, too! Didn't they all want to catch a man?

"Are you saying that your friends were lying?" she asked, clearly perplexed.

"No. Just omitting a few very important details." He stuffed his shirttails into his trousers. "Like the fact that I'll inherit Plumtree Brewery one day. Gran is leaving it to me."

God, now he sounded like a pompous idiot. "That should be enough to please any 'sensible woman.'"

She blinked. "But you said that running it is temporary—"

"It is, for now. I agreed to run it for a year. Then she'll go back to running it until she dies, while I . . ."

"Go back to gambling and drinking and wenching," she said dryly. "That sounds like quite the appealing life for any prospective wife."

He bristled. How the hell had this conversation turned into an indictment of his perfectly acceptable way of living? "I'll have you know that *hundreds* of women would kill to have that life."

Amusement glinted in her eyes. "I'm sure that's true. You should definitely go find one of them to marry. Once you decide that you're ready for a wife, that is."

With a pat on his arm that was almost sisterly, she started to rise, but he pulled her down again. Anger riding him, he kissed her fiercely, deeply. Only when he had her melting in his arms did he draw back to murmur, "I daresay any 'sensible woman' would find advantages to being married to such an 'irresponsible scapegrace.'"

She brushed her thumb over his lips. "I daresay she would. But such advantages would hardly compensate for worrying about when the debt collectors would come to cart away her furniture because her husband had lost it in a card game."

"I'll have you know I'm an excellent gambler," he ground out. "I make an excellent living at it."

"When you're winning."

He had no answer for that. It was true.

With a sudden glint of remorse, she slipped from his arms and rose to brush straw from her skirts. "I'm sorry, Jarret, I wasn't trying to insult you. I only said those things because you'd made it quite clear that you have no desire to marry. I'm sure any number of women would be happy to marry you."

He rose, too. "Just not you."

She cocked her head. "Why do you care? Are you *offering* marriage?" When he glanced away, she said, "I didn't think so."

As she headed for the ladder, he caught her by the arm. "That doesn't mean we can't—"

"Have more fun in the hay?" she said, a sad look on her face. "I'm afraid it does. I shan't risk embarrassing my family just so you can have a little fun."

He stood there motionless as she climbed down from the loft. She was right. That's essentially what he was asking her to do—take enormous risks for a few wild moments of passion. Risks he wasn't willing to take himself.

He hadn't thought beyond his own pleasure. He had never needed to before. He'd cut himself off from anyone who might expect it of him.

Had she sensed that he wanted no part of being responsible for her well-being? If she had, that was galling. The only thing he hated more than being forced into dicey situations was being predictable.

He'd always seen himself as clever for not investing his heart and soul in anything, thus avoiding the pain of having things he cared about ripped away from him. But what he saw as clever, she saw as a willful selfishness that mocked the feelings of others.

It was a sobering realization—and one he wasn't sure he liked. Damn her for that.

\*　　\*　　\*

THAT EVENING IN the inn was strained for all of them, but especially Annabel. It had taken every ounce of her self-control to walk away from Jarret that afternoon. Part of her had said she should seize the chance to have a torrid love affair without any guilt.

But the sensible part of her knew that was insanity. Aside from the possibility that they could be found out, there was the even more worrisome possibility of his putting a child in her belly. She seemed to have bad luck in such matters.

She glanced over at the table across the room to where Jarret played cards with some other men in the inn. Her throat tightened. The greatest danger was that he'd make her care too much about him, that he would go back to London with a piece of her heart clutched in his fist. She didn't dare risk it.

"If you're not interested in marrying him," a small voice grumbled beside her, "you ought not to look at him that way."

Her gaze shot to Geordie. She'd thought he was asleep in the chair. Earlier, she'd taken him aside and explained that she and Jarret had decided they wouldn't suit, and that he must not tell his mother about the kiss he'd witnessed. Though Geordie had promised not to, he hadn't taken her speech well at all.

"What way am I looking at him?" she asked.

"Like he's marzipan, and you want a bite."

Geordie was slumped in the chair wearing that sullen expression he wore more and more lately. But behind the belligerence lay a little boy with hurt feelings.

"You're angry with me because I said I don't want to marry him," she said.

"It's no concern of mine," he muttered. "I just don't think

it's right of you to . . . you know . . . look at him like that and let him kiss you, if you don't mean anything by it."

"I already explained about that."

"Right. It was a moment's impulse. You were thanking him for helping us." He rolled his eyes. "*He* told me the same thing, only *he* said he wanted to marry you."

Yes, and she could kill Jarret for that. "You like his lordship, don't you?"

Geordie shrugged. "He's all right."

"You like having a man around who understands you, who pays attention to you when your father is . . ."

"Falling down drunk," Geordie bit out.

She gaped at Geordie. "You know?"

"Of course I know. I've seen him late at night, drinking in his study. Then he doesn't go to the brewery the next day, and you go instead. It's clear why: because all he does these days is drink that stupid whisky."

"Shh," she said, casting a furtive glance in Jarret's direction. "His lordship mustn't hear about that."

"I don't know why not. It's the truth." When she looked alarmed, he said, "Don't worry, Aunt Annabel, I'm not going to tell him. He tried to get it out of me our first day here, but I put him off." He glared at her. "I had to cry to do it. Like a *girl*. But at least I didn't lie." His accusing glance pricked her conscience.

"It was only a small lie," she protested. "We had no choice." She couldn't believe she was justifying herself to Geordie. "If he learns the truth, he won't help us."

Geordie stared down at his hands. "I know."

"And it's very important that he—"

"I *know*, all right? I'm not a baby."

A lump swelled in her throat. To her, he would always be a baby.

The men at the table laughed, and she glanced over to see Jarret finish off his third tumbler of whisky in an hour. She frowned. For all she knew, he spent half his time in his cups, like Hugh. He wasn't reliable. He wasn't interested in marriage. He wasn't for her.

He would *never* be for her. If anything had made that clear, it was their encounter in the barn. All he could ever want to do was give her physical pleasure. He could never give her anything of himself. She wasn't even sure if there was anything of himself to give.

Tired of thinking about it, she rose. "Come, Geordie, we'd best go to bed. His lordship means to leave early. He wants to be in Burton by noon."

Geordie followed her to the stairs. "How will you keep Father's problem secret once we get home?"

Fortunately, while most people in Burton knew that Hugh had been shirking his duties for a year now, they didn't know why. That would help. But it might not be enough. "I'll think of something."

"Well, you'd better think fast. Tomorrow night is the Brewer's Association dinner, and you know Father never misses one."

She groaned. She'd completely forgotten about the yearly dinner. She and Hugh always attended, and this year he was liable to publicly drink himself into a stupor. And if he were to meet up with Jarret while they were out . . .

That mustn't happen. Because if it did, all bets were off.

# Chapter Thirteen

Jarret woke before dawn with a headache, a dry mouth, and a disquieting sense of self-loathing.

He'd lost twenty pounds last night, even after the tempting distraction sitting across the room had left to go to bed. It used to be that nothing distracted him from a card game, and certainly not a woman, no matter how much he lusted after her. When had that changed? *Why* had it changed?

And why had he spent an entire evening drinking hard and heavy to drown out her words about gamblers and debt collectors?

That was precisely what had kept him from marrying thus far. He didn't need a woman plaguing him about how he lived his life. He didn't need to care what she thought. He didn't *want* to.

Yet he did, God help him. What had the chit done to him?

Well, no point trying to sleep now. She'd ruined even *that* for him. Besides, the sooner he rose, the sooner they could be off, and the sooner he could be done with her and her brother's brewery and the whole confounded family. Once they reached Burton, he'd talk to her brother, tour Lake Ale, then return to London, hopefully tomorrow morning. He needed to get back to Plumtree and get to work on setting things to rights.

Breakfast was a hurried affair, with young George complaining loudly about the early hour.

"George," he finally bit out as he nibbled some toast and forced coffee into his rebelling stomach, "do you think you could be a little quieter?"

Annabel cast him a glance from across her buttered crumpets and jam. "Had a late night, did you?"

"Late enough," he ground out. She had no right to pass judgment on him.

"We understand, my lord," Mrs. Lake said soothingly. "Gentlemen do like their enjoyments."

"They certainly do," Annabel muttered.

Cheeky wench.

Mrs. Lake kept up a flow of bright conversation. "I'm looking forward to seeing the children, my lord. They're staying with my mother, so I know they're safe, but one never feels quite comfortable leaving one's children with anyone else."

He could hardly comment on that, given that his mother had killed herself and left her children behind to be raised by someone else. "How many do you have?"

"A boy and two girls. In addition to Geordie." She dropped her gaze to her scone.

Four children. Good God. So Annabel had been truthful about her brother not being mortally ill. If he were, she wouldn't have been so firm about her lack of interest in marriage. *Any* marriage would be preferable to being the poor relation of a poor widow with four children. Even marriage to *an irresponsible scapegrace* like him *who gambles his way through London to avoid doing anything constructive with his time.*

He scowled. "I suppose you're eager to see your husband, too," he said to keep from thinking about how Annabel had flayed him with her tongue. "No one is quite as good a nurse as a wife, I would imagine."

Her gaze shot to his in surprise, but then she smiled and he realized he must have misread it. "Quite right, sir. I won't feel at ease until I'm sure he's well."

It was the first time she'd expressed any concern over her husband's condition, which reinforced Annabel's claim that Mr. Lake's illness wasn't that serious.

When they gathered outside the coach after the groom loaded their bags, George turned to him. "I should like to ride up top, my lord, if it's all right with you."

"Geordie," Mrs. Lake said, "we've already been through that. It's too dangerous."

Annabel said quietly, "Perhaps we should let him, Sissy." She shot Jarret a quick glance, and he could tell she was remembering their conversation yesterday. "Geordie has behaved very well these past few days, and he deserves a reward."

"Do you really think it would be all right?"

"I do."

"Well, then. Go ahead." As George let out a whoop and clambered up onto the perch, Mrs. Lake added, "But you must mind the coachman and keep your hands to yourself and stay firmly in your seat, do you hear?"

"Yes, Mother!" he cried, his young face glowing with anticipation.

Jarret couldn't help wondering why Mrs. Lake always seemed to bend to whatever Annabel said concerning young

George. Of course, Mrs. Lake wasn't the forceful sort, which might explain it.

Still, he did think Annabel was overly involved with her nephew's upbringing. She needed children of her own to manage, so she didn't feel compelled to manage her brother's.

Except for her tendency to smother a boy, she would make an excellent mother. He could imagine her dandling a babe on her knee, crooning softly to it about hot cross buns and mulberry bushes as Mother used to do.

A long-forgotten memory rose in his head—of Mother leading Celia, Gabe, and Minerva in a merry dance about the nursery to the tune of "Ride a Cock Horse to Banbury Cross." At the time, he'd thought himself far too old and mature for such silliness and had scoffed at their joy.

What an unthinking little idiot he'd been. A month later, she was dead. And he'd desperately wished he could take back every single disparaging remark he'd made that day in the nursery. The agony of that still haunted him.

He frowned. That was precisely why a man who put his trust in anyone else was a fool. Father had trusted Mother— they *all* had trusted Mother—and their lives had been torn apart for it. Jarret had trusted Gran, and what had he got for it? Nothing but grief.

A man was better off relying on himself alone.

They set off for Burton at a little after eight A.M. Mrs. Lake continued to carry the conversation, peppering him with questions about London society. He'd never met a woman so eager for the least bit of gossip, and he regretted that he knew so little.

Annabel stayed quiet, apparently fascinated by the endless landscape of spring meadows dotted with oaks and birches.

But as they neared Tamworth, their last stop to change horses before Burton, she turned to him.

"Why don't you tell your coachman to bring us to the Peacock Inn once we reach Burton? I think you'll find it a pleasant place to stay, and the innkeeper's wife is an excellent cook. Lake Ale will of course pay for your lodgings."

The tension behind her smile gave him pause. "No need for that." He wasn't going to tax their finances simply because they thought him too lofty to stay in their home. "I'll be perfectly comfortable with your family. I'm sure you have some little room I can use for the short time I'm here."

"Oh, that wouldn't do," Annabel said. "You know how it is when someone in the family is sick—the whole household suffers. You'd be far more comfortable at the inn, I assure you."

His eyes narrowed. "I thought money was tight for the brewery right now."

When Annabel blanched, Mrs. Lake said hastily, "Yes, but we have an arrangement with the Peacock Inn. Lake Ale provides them with ale, and they provide us with lodgings when we need them."

"That sounds one-sided," Jarret said. "How often could you possibly need lodgings for visitors? I hope you don't provide them with *all* the ale they require."

"No, of course not," Annabel said. "What Sissy meant is that if we need the inn for anything—lodgings or a meeting room or food—they'll take payment in ale."

"It's still a drain on your finances," he persisted. "If you give your ale away, you have none to sell."

Normally, it would be rude to insist upon staying with someone who didn't want him as a guest, but until now they'd struck him as open country folk who wouldn't mind an extra mouth at the dinner table. The fact that they wanted him to stay at an inn seemed odd.

"All the same," Annabel said firmly, "I think it will be best." There was a stubborn glint to her eye.

That's when it dawned on him why she didn't want him in the house with her. She was afraid he would try to seduce her. No doubt she had her sister-in-law worrying about it, too.

"Very well," he said. "The Peacock Inn it is. But I'll pay for my own lodgings. It's only for one night, after all."

"Only one night?" Mrs. Lake said, clearly disappointed.

Annabel looked vastly relieved, which roused his suspicions even more. She certainly was eager to rush him off. Was it because of what they'd done in the barn yesterday? Or something else?

"His lordship is a very busy man, Sissy," Annabel said. "He has a brewery to run back in London, and we mustn't keep him too long from his work."

"I suppose that's true." Mrs. Lake flashed him a kind smile. "But you should at least join us tonight, my lord, at the Brewer's Association dinner. It's the one time the brewers allow females to darken the doors, and there is always good food and dancing—"

"We won't be attending, Sissy," Annabel cut in. "How could you forget?"

"Why wouldn't we attend? Hugh always—" Mrs. Lake paled. "Of course. She's right, sir. We won't be going."

"Which means you can't go either, my lord," Annabel finished. "I'm afraid that they allow only members or family of members."

Jarret stared at her, wondering why she was reverting to formality again. She only did that when she was nervous. Something was afoot, and he had to figure out what it was.

Since she clearly didn't want him at the Brewer's Association dinner, he'd start by making sure he attended.

"It's no problem, actually. My grandmother knows Bass and Allsopp both very well." They were two of the most prominent of Burton's brewers. "I can't imagine they wouldn't be willing to wrangle an invitation for her grandson from whomever runs the association. Professional courtesy, and all that."

That struck a nerve, all right: Annabel wore a look of pure panic.

He smiled at Mrs. Lake. "Indeed, madam, I'd be happy to have you both accompany me. Since your husband can't attend."

"That would be all right," Mrs. Lake said, with clear agitation on her features. "Wouldn't it, Annabel?"

"We'll have to see how Hugh feels," Annabel said. "We'll let you know, my lord."

"You can give me your answer when I come to call on your brother this afternoon, once I'm settled at the inn."

She immediately said, "Oh, I don't think you should—"

"I have to negotiate the terms of this arrangement with him," he pointed out. "He's the one who must sign any papers we draw up, after all."

"The brewery manager, Mr. Walters, can negotiate the terms, and give the papers to Hugh to sign." Annabel's voice was decidedly unsteady. "No need to trouble Hugh with more than that."

"I don't deal with managers," he said firmly. "Unless your brother is at death's door, I wish to speak to him, even if only briefly."

She let out a sigh. "Very well."

"And afterward, I'd like to tour the brewery."

"I'm sure that can be arranged," she said dully.

"Good." He settled back against the seat. "I'm glad we understand each other."

It was time to find out exactly what the Lake family was hiding.

ANNABEL AND SISSY left Jarret at the Peacock Inn, where he ordered his coachman to carry them home before he went inside. As they pulled away, Annabel felt despair grip her. He'd be at the house in a very short time. What on earth were they to do now?

"I'm sorry I mentioned the Association dinner," Sissy said softly. "I didn't mean to make matters worse."

"What were you thinking?"

Sissy sighed. "I was thinking that the two of you could dance, and perhaps his lordship—"

"Would miraculously decide to marry me, swept away by the dulcet sounds of a quadrille?" Annabel gave a bitter laugh. "I told you, he's not the marrying sort. And if he goes tonight and Hugh goes, we're doomed!"

"Nonsense. I will simply impress upon Hugh that he mustn't drink at the dinner."

"He can't even attend! We've made too much of his supposed illness—not only with Lord Jarret, but also with the townspeople. Everyone will be suspicious if Hugh shows up there after all we said."

"But we can't talk Hugh out of going. It's the one thing he never misses. Some part of him still feels compelled to keep up appearances."

"I know," Annabel said wearily. "I don't suppose it matters anyway. Everything will go to hell the minute Lord Jarret arrives to meet him this afternoon. We barely have enough time to explain to Hugh exactly why we went to London and why Lord Jarret is here. There's no telling how he'll react, and if Lord Jarret comes in the middle of that—"

This was a nightmare. Why did Jarret have to be so stubborn and suspicious? Why was he proving to be far more competent at this business than she'd realized? And far too astute at seeing through *her*.

"Even if we can get through this afternoon somehow," she went on, "tonight will be a disaster."

"No, it won't." Sissy patted her hand. "You let me handle Hugh tonight. I can keep him away from the drink for one night. You handle Lord Jarret. Perhaps if you dance and flirt with him, he won't pay so much attention to Hugh."

"You put far too much stock in my ability to charm a man," Annabel said. "And anyway, that doesn't solve the problem of this afternoon."

They'd arrived home. Thankfully, Hugh was nowhere in sight while Jarret's coachman helped them out and directed their footmen in unloading their bags. As they entered the house, a rush of longing for a place of her own hit her, as it always did. She would never stop feeling like an intruder here.

Not that she didn't adore Sissy and Hugh and the children, but this would always be theirs alone. The pale pinks and lavenders of the wallpaper were too insipid for her taste. She longed for bright reds and golds, explosions of color to match the simmering passions that always seemed to war within her. If she ever had a home, it would hold burnished mahogany tables and richly brocaded upholsteries. With tassels. Lots of tassels. She *adored* tassels.

And it would *never* smell like old beeswax and sour wine. Not if she could help it.

As she and Sissy handed the footman their coats, the butler informed them that the master was sleeping. For one dark moment, Annabel wanted to scream. *Sleeping* was the servants' term for *passed out*. And it was barely past noon, too! He must have spent the entire night drinking. Again.

And then she realized how they could make this work. "Sissy," she said, as soon as Geordie had run off upstairs to his room and the butler had retreated, "I've got an idea. All we have to do is keep Lord Jarret from having his business meeting with Hugh until the morning."

"How does that solve anything?"

"Don't you see? Lord Jarret wants to tour the brewery this afternoon—we'll let him do that part. He'll see that the brewery is a sound one, that the men are hardworking and the brews we make are solid. And Mr. Walters will impress him with his business acumen and his knowledge of what needs to be done. Plus, Mr. Walters won't say a word against Hugh."

"I still don't—"

"While Lord Jarret tours the brewery, you and I will convince Hugh to accept our plan. We would have had to talk him into it anyway, and as long as we can keep Lord Jarret from meeting him this afternoon, we'll have time to break it to Hugh gently. Then tonight at the dinner, we can keep the conversation away from business . . . and Hugh away from the drink."

She paced the foyer, her mind working through her plan. "Hugh is always better in the morning, as long as he isn't cropsick. If we can keep him sober until morning, he'll be ready to do his part. Then Lord Jarret will be off in his coach back to London, and we can start work on getting this project off the ground! What do you think?"

"You're leaving out one important detail—how shall you

keep Lord Jarret from paying his visit to Hugh this afternoon? He seemed very determined."

"Is Dr. Paxton still sweet on our housekeeper?"

"As far as I know."

A smile curved Annabel's lips. "Then just leave this afternoon to me."

# Chapter Fourteen

*A*n hour later, when Jarret arrived, Hugh was still passed out in his bed, thank goodness. Annabel had made sure that Dr. Paxton, who'd reluctantly agreed to help her, was standing right outside Hugh's bedroom as Jarret was shown up.

She nodded faintly to the doctor, and he cleared his throat. "I gave your brother laudanum to help him sleep, Miss Lake. He should be feeling better by tonight."

"What's going on?" Jarret asked.

"Oh, you've arrived!" She made the introductions, then donned a worried frown that wasn't entirely feigned. "I'm afraid Hugh is being difficult. When we told him you were going to the dinner tonight, he insisted upon going, too. But Dr. Paxton is concerned that he can't handle it. Indeed, he is against it entirely unless Hugh rests this afternoon."

"And what about our meeting?" Jarret's voice was deep with suspicion.

She opened the door to show him Hugh's snoring form.

She and Sissy had borrowed some of Dr. Paxton's concoctions to sprinkle around the room and give it the smell of a sickroom. Now she just had to pray that Hugh didn't wake before she got Jarret out of here.

"As you can see, he's in no condition to discuss business. But he should be perfectly able to in the morning. Besides, you'll have a better sense of what you wish to do and say after you tour the brewery this afternoon, don't you think?"

He considered that. "I suppose."

"He must not be overtaxed, my lord," Dr. Paxton put in. "A business meeting followed by a business dinner would be too much for his constitution."

"Thank you, Dr. Paxton," she said, casting the older man a grateful smile. "I appreciate your help."

"Of course, Miss Lake."

She took Jarret's arm and led him downstairs. "I'm sorry to upset your plans, but Hugh was adamant about wanting to attend tonight. He felt it would be rude to let you go without him, since he feels that he's your host."

They reached the foyer. "I'll bring you down to the brewery," she went on, "and you can spend the afternoon with Mr. Walters. Then tonight we'll meet you at the dinner—if you've managed to gain an invitation?"

Jarret took her coat from the footman and helped her into it. "Bass was kind enough to include me, yes."

Of course he was, she thought sourly. Mr. Bass was probably leaping for joy at the thought of having a marquess's son attend.

As they left the house, Jarret leveled a dark glance on her. "I'm warning you, Annabel. I'm not leaving town without speaking to your brother."

"Of course not. And he wants to talk to you, too," she said calmly. He would after she and Sissy got done with him, anyway.

They walked a short way in silence. "Tell me something," he said at last. "Did you ask me to stay at the inn because you were afraid to be in the same house with me? Afraid that I might . . . try to kiss you again?"

She sucked in a breath. That certainly wasn't a question she'd expected. And how odd that he would put that inter- pretation on it. It worked well to her purpose, so she should let him keep thinking it.

Instead, she heard herself saying, "To be honest, that hadn't occurred to me. Though now that you mention it—"

"Don't worry. You made it quite clear where you stood. I don't believe in forcing women into anything."

"I never thought you did."

"Not even when I made that wager?"

"That wasn't force. I could have refused it."

"I expected you to."

She couldn't prevent a smile. "I know."

The air fairly crackled between them. She was painfully aware of the last time they'd been alone together, of how he'd brought her to heights of passion she'd never known. Of the heat on his face when he'd said he'd thought of nothing but taking her. . . .

Oh, Lord, every time he got near her, he made her wish things could be different. But they couldn't. And there was Geordie, too.

Her throat tightened. There was always Geordie to think of.

"Annabel, I—"

"We're here," she said brightly, not wishing to hear whatever lies he would tell to make himself feel better about only wanting her in his bed.

He cast her an enigmatic glance, then gazed at the brewery. "So we are."

She hurried inside, and the smell of hops and malt hit her, so sweetly familiar that it settled her nerves. It had always been that way for her. The crackle of the fires under the kilns, the rattling of the wort boiling in the coppers, and the scents of herbs soothed her. Here, she felt at home.

Here, she could be herself.

Mr. Walters was in the little office in the back of the building. When he spotted her through the glass window, he came out to greet her with a smile. She introduced Jarret, explaining why he'd come and what he wanted to see. Fortunately, Mr. Walters had approved their scheme from the beginning, so he adapted to the change in plans with nary a stumble.

"Well then," she said, "I'll leave you two to get acquainted."

"Wait," Jarret said. "Where are you going?"

"Someone has to sit with Hugh while Sissy goes to fetch the children from her mother's." She smiled. "But we'll see you tonight at the dinner."

Without giving him a chance to protest, she headed out of the brewery. Once outside, she quickened her pace. They had only a few hours to talk Hugh into doing this.

When she entered the house, she heard loud voices and groaned. Hugh was awake.

She found him and Sissy arguing in his study. Thank heaven that she and Sissy had agreed to leave the other children at Sissy's mother's house until their discussion was over, because he looked fit to be tied. He was in his dressing gown, pacing up and down the room and gesticulating wildly. With his thinning brown hair stuck out from his head like dandelion fuzz and his chin covered with a day's growth of beard, he looked like a scruffy day laborer and not the quiet, bookish man she knew and loved.

The minute she entered, he whirled on her. "This is all *your* doing, isn't it? I can't believe you went to London behind my back to talk to the Plumtrees! You said the trip was for Geordie, to get him a spot in a good school—"

"We can't afford a good school for Geordie," she shot back. "Can't you see that? Not the way things are now."

A stricken look crossed his pale face. Then he slumped into the chair behind his desk and buried his head in his hands. "I know, I know, Annie." Hugh and Papa were the only ones who'd ever called her that. "The brewery doesn't bring in enough, and I've failed the family."

"That's not what I'm saying!" This was how every conversation ended, with him bemoaning his inability to take care of his family and promising to change. Which he never did. "I'm saying that something had to be done about our difficulties."

He lifted his head to stare at her, looking like a little boy lost. "And so you stepped in as usual to do it."

"You gave me no choice," she said softly. "I saw a way to save us, and I took it." When he cast her a despairing glance, she stepped close to lay her hand on his. "Look, you've been talking about doing this for months. 'If we could only get some of the India trade,' you said. 'That India trade would get us flush,' you said. It was *your* plan."

"A stupid plan."

"No, it was a *good* plan. All I did was move it along a little."

"By making a pact with some devil of a lord—"

"He's not a devil," she said stoutly, "and we didn't make a pact." Did Hugh know about the wager? She cast a furtive glance at Sissy, who shook her head. Thank goodness. "Lord Jarret Plumtree is willing to help us with the East India captains. He's a competent brewer very familiar with the business."

Hugh snorted. "That's not what I heard."

"Well, you heard wrong. His grandmother had enough faith in him to put him in charge of her entire operation." She took his hands in hers. "And I have enough faith in *you* to believe you can make this work. If you could just—" She caught herself too late.

His eyes darkened to black. "Go ahead, say it. If I could just be more like Father."

"What? No! That is *not* what I meant to say." And she could curse Papa for everything he'd done to make Hugh this way.

"Of course it was." Jerking his hands from hers, he rose to pace. "You think I don't know what a disappointment I was to him? I know what you're thinking, you and Mr. Walters. That I can't save the brewery because I don't have the spine to deal with the likes of Bass and Allsopp, and yes, the East India captains."

She gaped at him, shocked that he even believed she felt that way. He had reasons for his feelings about Papa, but *her*? "I swear to you, I have no idea why you would—"

"Spare me, Annie." Grimly, Hugh headed for the decanter of whisky on the desk. "I see it in your eyes whenever you look at me. It bothers you that I can't be more like the great Aloysius Lake—"

"What bothers her," said a small voice from the door, "is the same thing that bothers all of us, Father."

She whirled to find Geordie standing there with a look of pure despair.

"It's the drinking." Geordie's gaze shot to Hugh's hand lifting the decanter. "It's *always* been the drinking."

Oh no, why on earth had Geordie decided to confront Hugh *now*?

Crossing his arms over his bony little chest, Geordie glared at Hugh. "I had to *lie* for you, Father. They had to tell Lord Jarret you were sick to get him to help us, so I had to lie because *they* lied."

Hugh stood frozen, his face carved in stone. Annabelle and Sissy had tried talking to him about his drinking before, but since it always sent him into an even worse retreat from the world, they'd given up.

Ignoring Geordie, Hugh shot Sissy a look of betrayal. "You told that blasted lord that I was ill?"

Geordie wouldn't be ignored. "Don't be angry at *them*. What else were they to say? That you were a drunk?" His face grew red with anger. "That you don't care about anything but that . . . that damned whisky in your hand?"

This time Hugh looked at Geordie, really looked at him, and the blood drained from his face. "Is that what they told you, boy? That I'm a drunk?"

"They didn't tell me anything. But I'm not blind. I see how you spend your nights. We all do." He dragged in a pitiful breath. "You used to do things with us children. You used to p-play cards and take us on walks and . . . You don't do anything but d-drink anymore."

Hugh set the decanter down. "Come here, boy."

Swallowing hard, Geordie approached him. "Yes, sir."

"So you went along with your aunt's and your mother's lies, did you?"

Geordie got a stubborn look on his face. "I didn't see that I had a choice. Even I know that the brewery is failing. Aunt Annabel says we've got to do something."

"And you think this Lord Jarret can help," Hugh said, half sneeringly.

"He seems a good enough fellow," Geordie said. "He treated us very well on the road. Called for a doctor when Mother was sick, and paid for it, too."

"You were sick?" Hugh said in alarm as he glanced at Sissy.

"Just a little dyspepsia," she said gently. "It passed in a day or two."

"A day!" Worry flitted over his face.

"But Annabel took good care of me, and his lordship was very kind."

"Was he?" His lips thinned. "Just stepped right in, I suppose."

"You weren't there, Hugh," Annabel put in before his temper could flare. "So he provided the service that any gentleman should."

"I'll bet he did," Hugh muttered. "I should have been the one to take care of her."

"Yes, you should have," Sissy said quietly.

The stark words seemed to affect him. He ran his fingers through his sparse hair, then cast a considering look at Geordie again. "This marquess's son. Do you think he can do any good?"

"Seems to me there's nothing to lose by asking him to help."

"I see." Hugh faced Annabel. "What exactly do you want me to do now that you've brought his lordship to Burton?"

Relieved that Hugh was going to listen, Annabel said, "For tonight, just meet him. If you don't approve of him, we'll forget the whole thing." Though she would do her best to keep that from happening. "If you do want to take a chance on him, then you can discuss business with him in the morning and figure out how he can help us sell our ale to the East India Company captains."

At his frown, she added hastily, "But for tonight, just meet him."

A long moment passed while Sissy and Annabel held their breaths. Then he said, "All right."

They released their breaths. Perhaps everything would turn out well, after all.

"But I shan't pretend to be ill, do you understand?" When she and Sissy looked panicked, he added, "I won't gainsay what you've told him, but I won't lie to him myself. Let him think what he will."

Sissy stepped close to the desk. "And you won't drink any spirits tonight?"

There was a note of steel in her voice that Annabel rarely heard. But he heard it and seemed to heed it, too. He searched her face, a softness in his eyes. "I'll do my best, love."

# Chapter Fifteen

*J*arret stood in the town hall's imposing suite of assembly rooms, surrounded by a group of brewers. Quietly sipping his wine, he tried to follow the conversation, but it was difficult when he was so distracted. He and Bass had arrived twenty minutes ago, along with Bass's wife, and so far he'd seen no sign of Annabel. Ever since her little evasion this afternoon, he'd wondered if he could trust her to appear.

Granted, she'd been right about the advantages of his viewing the brewery first. He'd been impressed. Given that Lake Ale lacked the modern equipment he took for granted at Plumtree Brewery, he was surprised by how smoothly their operation worked. And Walters was a gem among brewery managers, citing production rates and quotas off the top of his head.

But the place was clearly struggling. The hops they used weren't of the first quality, and leaks in their aging cast-iron mash tun were patched with sheets of tin. Worst of all, Walters had been so reluctant to speak about Lake himself that Jarret was back to wondering if there was more to the man's illness than Annabel had said. If Lake required constant care from a doctor and laudanum to sleep, that didn't bode well.

As the hour dragged on, he got a bad feeling in the pit of his stomach. He didn't like being played for a fool. If Annabel and her brother didn't show up here tonight . . .

"And what brings *you* to our fair town, Lord Jarret?" one of the gentlemen asked. "Trying to get a look at the competition, are you?"

He forced himself to pay attention. Earlier in the day, he'd debated whether to mention his possible investment connection to the Lakes, but in business, as in cards, it was always best to keep one's cards close to one's chest. Unfortunately, that made it difficult for him to ask questions without rousing speculation.

"Actually, I'm visiting friends," he said, using the only solution he'd hit upon. "I'm sure you know them. The Lake family?"

The men exchanged glances. He was just about to ask what they thought of the Lakes when a sound at the door made them all turn.

Speak of the devil.

He barely had time to register his relief that Annabel hadn't lied to him after all, when something else caught his attention. Not the thin, pale-looking fellow about his age who had to be Hugh Lake. No, the only person he had eyes for was the stunning beauty holding on to one of Lake's arms.

Annabel. But no version of Annabel he'd ever seen.

Her splendid chestnut hair was piled atop her head in a profusion of wild curls that enhanced her delicate features. Tonight she wasn't a pixie, but a fairy queen, adorned in sparkling gems and a silk gown that skimmed her luscious curves like a lover's caress.

At the sight of her, his blood ran hot, then cold. The gown was cut lower than those of the other ladies, harkening back to a couple of years ago, when nearly every woman in London was falling out of her dinner gown. All of Annabel's gowns were dated, and the way in which *this* one was dated set his pulse pounding. He could see way too much of the sweet swells of her breasts. So could every man here. And he didn't like that idea at all.

"Excuse me, gentlemen," he said and left them to approach the Lakes.

He couldn't take his eyes off Annabel, something that others apparently noticed—for when he did tear his gaze from her, it was to see her brother glowering at him. Damn.

As he reached the Lakes, Mrs. Lake performed the introductions, clearly nervous. And probably with good reason, given the piercing glance Lake fixed on him. Before the man could say anything, Jarret murmured, "I should warn you, sir, that I told the other brewers I was here in Burton visiting friends—you and your lovely wife, of course. I didn't think you would want our business bandied about by them."

Lake's dour look softened a fraction. "Thank you. I appreciate your discretion." A footman came by with glasses of wine. Glancing at his wife, Lake declined a glass. He looked more healthy than Jarret would have expected, given what the doctor had said this afternoon. Perhaps this illness *was* only temporary.

When Lake returned his attention to Jarret, the fierceness was back in his features. "I understand that I have you to thank for the safe return of my family to Burton."

Jarret wondered how much the women had told the man about the trip. Best to err on the side of caution. "I merely borrowed my brother's coach to transport us, sir. As I had to come this way to observe your brewery anyway, I thought we might as well travel in comfort together."

"That was generous of you, my lord," Lake said stiffly. "Though I gather that the trip wasn't without difficulties, what with Sissy's illness."

"Your wife had a bit of trouble in Daventry, yes. But your sister is an excellent nurse. I did very little. Looked after your son, mostly." He smiled. "Actually, it was mutual—he and I kept each other out of trouble. With George around, I could hardly engage in the pastimes that a bachelor generally enjoys. I figured he was a bit young for gambling until dawn and bouncing taproom maids on his knee."

The outrageous remark gained him a censuring glance from Annabel but a reluctant smile from her brother. "I daresay Geordie would disagree."

"Yes. He's more eager to be a man than his body yet allows."

Lake relaxed further. "Indeed he is. The lad has fire in him, I'll give you that."

The other brewers then joined them, obviously eager to sniff out the connection between the two men. Fortunately, the announcement that dinner was served came moments later, so he and Lake didn't have to endure questions for long.

Unfortunately, he ended up seated at the other end of the table from them. Annabel sat between her brother and some bloody fellow with an eye for her bosom. Jarret spent the next half hour torn between listening for tidbits about the brewing business and considering the possibility of poking out the eyes of Annabel's dinner companion with his oyster fork. His only consolation was that she seemed discomfited enough by the man's lecherous regard to drape her bosom with her shawl.

Only then did he relax—although he had to wonder why

the other man's attentions irritated him so. She'd made it quite clear that she could take care of herself.

She'd also set him straight on where he stood with her. He had no right to be possessive. He didn't even *want* the right.

Or he hadn't wanted it, until she showed up in that fairy queen's gown that he ached to strip from her one silky inch at a time.

Confound it all to hell. He *had* to stop thinking about her like that.

He made himself focus on what the other men were saying. The first thing he learned was that a dinner among tradesmen differed vastly from a dinner among his peers. The tradesmen actually spent it discussing . . . trade. Father would have called that vulgar.

He found it invigorating. There was an energy among these men that was lacking at the few society events he attended. And they were canny fellows, too, each trying to eke out some bit of information about his competitors without being caught. It reminded him of playing cards with a truly accomplished player. As with piquet, only the cleverest at deduction could win, and Jarret had the urge to win at this, too.

When the dancing began he was loath to leave the table, but he needn't have worried. Though the gentlemen moved to the room designated for dancing, several then congregated by the punch table to discuss the latest patents in steam boilers.

Lake soon joined the party, and Jarrett watched as the man voiced his opinions, clearly well versed in his profession, if not as enthusiastic as the other gentlemen.

When Mrs. Lake came and asked her husband to dance, Allsopp, who stood next to Jarret, said, "Miss Lake is looking very pretty tonight."

Jarret cast the man a sharp glance to find him eyeing Annabel with a more than neighborly interest. The alien feeling of possessiveness that welled up in him shook him. So did the sudden murderous rage he felt when Allsopp ran his gaze down her body.

The man had a wife, damn it! He shouldn't be looking at Annabel like that. *No* one should be looking at her like that. Only with great effort did he squelch the warning that sprang to his lips. Instead he said, "It's rather surprising that she's never married."

Allsopp downed his punch. "It's not for lack of proposals. I understand she's turned down two or three men who offered marriage."

That flummoxed him. Apparently he wasn't the only man who didn't meet Annabel's lofty standards. While that should have soothed his pride, it raised more questions, instead. Why would a woman so obviously sensual and capable of a deep love for children avoid marriage?

"Perhaps she stays at home to care for her brother," Jarret ventured.

"Well, he needs looking after, to be sure."

Something in the snide way Allsopp said it raised Jarret's suspicions. "You mean, because of his illness."

Allsopp laughed. "Is that what they're calling it these days?"

Jarret went still. Forcing himself to sound nonchalant, he said, "No, I suppose not." He held his breath, hoping the man would go on. If he asked him point-blank what he meant, Allsopp was liable to close up.

"Of course, we don't tolerate drunkenness the way you lords do. There's nothing wrong with having a tipple from time to time, but when a man neglects his business because he's drowning himself in a bottle, we can't overlook that."

A lead ball dropped into the pit of Jarret's stomach. Was *that* what Annabel had been hiding all this time?

But perhaps he shouldn't trust the word of a competitor who might have sniffed out Jarret's real reason for coming here. "I didn't realize my friend's problem had become so pronounced," he said smoothly. "The ladies said he was ill, and I assumed that was the reason for his negligence of late."

"Well, of course they aren't going to tell *you* the truth. It would be embarrassing. They've tried to hide it from everyone." Allsopp snorted. "As if that will work in a town as small as this. People talk. Servants talk. Does the man look ill to you?"

He nodded toward the dance floor, where Lake was dancing a reel quite competently for someone who'd supposedly been under the influence of laudanum only hours ago.

Then again, Lake *had* been asleep in the middle of the day. Who but an ill man did that?

*A man who's been up drinking all night.*

Confound it all to hell. Now other pieces fell into place—George's discomfort at the subject of his father's illness. Annabel's alarm when he'd said he was traveling to Burton to look at the company. Mrs. Lake's nervousness. He'd known all along they were hiding *something*. And clearly it wasn't that Mr. Lake was mortally ill.

He should have guessed. This wasn't London, and men in the provinces didn't abandon one of their own simply because he was ill. They made allowances, attempted to help the man's family, showed a neighborly concern for his condition.

But a drunk garnered no such sympathy—especially in the more conservative circles of tradesmen. He was seen as weak and unstable, which of course he was. His family was pitied, or worse, ostracized.

Anger swelled in his chest. A mortal illness could have been handled. It would have been problematic but manageable. But this was far more dicey. If Lake had lost the confidence of his fellow brewers due to a character flaw, how the hell was Jarret supposed to convince the East India captains to place orders for his pale ale?

If Lake had been on the edge of death, Jarret could have convinced the man to put Annabel in charge. Geordie would have inherited, and Annabel could have managed Geordie. But a drunk was unpredictable and untrustworthy. And anyone getting into bed with him would be deemed untrustworthy, too, or a fool.

Either way, it would be a disastrous association. Plumtree was already struggling—teaming up with a company on the brink of disaster could very well push it off the cliff. How could he have been so stupid? He'd let Annabel's talk of a quick solution to the bad market seduce him into taking a foolish risk.

No, he'd let the thought of having her in his bed seduce him. And now the company would suffer, because he could never pass up a good wager. Because he had wanted her.

*Still* wanted her, damn it all to hell. "How long has Lake been neglecting his company?" he bit out.

"A year, at least. From what I hear, he started drinking heavily after the Russian tariffs began to affect business. He began showing losses, and he couldn't handle the pressure. Or so I assume. Since then, only the efforts of Miss Lake and his brewery manager have kept the place together. Granted, Miss Lake will do just about anything to save her father's brewery, but she's a woman, after all, and she—"

"—can't effectively run a brewery that she doesn't own, can she?" said a stricken female voice behind them.

They turned to find Annabel standing there, ashen-faced, acute shame showing in every line of those beautiful features. When she glanced to him, guilt flashed in her eyes.

And he knew for sure then that everything Allsopp said was true.

A cold fury seized him, turning his heart to ice. She'd lied to him, knowing full well how it would affect his interest in the project. She'd used his sympathy for an ill man against him. For all he knew, even her kisses had been feigned to make him go along with her brother's scheme. *Her* scheme.

*Miss Lake will do just about anything to save her father's brewery.*

And he'd followed her lead blindly, like some besotted idiot. When was he going to learn? Caring about someone was the surest way to pain and loss. And the loss of the Annabel he'd thought he could trust was the cruelest blow yet.

"Miss Lake," Allsopp said after a moment's horrible silence, "I'm so sorry. I did not see you there."

"Clearly," she choked out.

Despite everything, her devastated expression tugged at his sympathies. He tamped that impulse down ruthlessly. She was a lying schemer, and he wanted no part of her.

But when he turned to walk away, she stepped forward to lay a hand on his arm. "I came to fetch his lordship for the waltz," she told Allsopp, her hand digging into Jarret's arm in a silent plea. "He asked me earlier to save it for him."

It was a bold move, and one that showed her resourcefulness, since he most decidedly had *not* asked her to dance, knowing that it would only heighten his urge to carry her off and swive her senseless.

For half a second, he considered calling her a liar to her face. But he couldn't put aside years of good breeding that easily, even for a lady who'd turned out to be a schemer. Especially when those damned soft eyes of hers quietly beseeched him.

*Lying* eyes, he reminded himself. She'd known all along that he was taking a great risk, and had willfully hidden the truth from him. She'd called *him* irresponsible? She'd railed against *him* for being a gambler? She had some nerve.

Very well. They would dance. And he would make it clear that he was done with her and Lake Ale, wager or no wager. He'd not agreed to *this*.

They walked to the dance floor in silence, both aware that others were nearby. Only when the music started and he had her in his arms did she venture to speak.

"I suppose you want the truth now."

"What a novel idea," he said coldly. "Yes, let's do have the truth. If you even know what such a thing is."

"Jarret, please don't be angry."

"All this time, you've played me for a fool—"

"No! I believed—I still believe—that investing in pale ale will save the brewery. But I knew you'd never consider helping us if you thought—"

"That your brother was incompetent? That he'd destroyed his own company by drinking himself into a stupor every day?" He cast her an icy glance, not caring one whit that half of the dancers in the assembly room were straining to see what was going on between them. "You're damned right I wouldn't have considered it."

He swung her into a turn so swiftly that she nearly stumbled, and he had to force himself to pay attention to the music, to keep his fury in check. It felt like a herculean task, which was astonishing. He'd always prided himself on being able to control his temper.

When he could speak again, he hissed, "Plumtree Brewery depends on me *not* to take unnecessary risks and *not* to drag it into the same pit your brother has dragged his company into. If you think I'll go along with your idiocy now that you've lured me up here with your sad tale of a sick brother, you're out of your mind."

"Lured you here!" Her eyes flashed at him. "*You're* the one who suggested that wager. The wager you lost. The wager you've apparently decided to renege on."

His temper ratcheted higher. "That wager was based on false pretenses, as you well know. As far as I'm concerned, that makes the whole bloody thing null and void."

They danced in silence for several moments, him going through the motions and her fixing her gaze beyond his head as they stepped and swirled and whirled in time, like two automatons turned by metal gears.

Then she shifted her gaze to lock with his. "What if we were to make the wager again—only this time, without the false pretenses?"

The steely glint in her eyes told him she was serious. And the instant response of his pulse told him he was just as swayed by the idea as he had been last time.

Angry at the way his body betrayed him, he opened his mouth to tell her to go to hell. Instead he said, "What do you mean?"

But he knew what she meant. Why was he letting her think he'd even consider it?

Because after everything, he still wanted her in his bed. And he deserved to have her, too! She'd lied to him and manipulated him. He at least ought to get something out of this damned mess.

"The exact same wager," she replied. "If I win our card

game, you help Lake Ale with the East India Company. If you win, I . . ." She cast a furtive glance around them.

He bent close to whisper, "Share my bed for a night. Say it."

She turned her head the half inch it took to whisper, "I'll share your bed for a night. Same terms as before."

He drew back to stare at her. Her cheeks were pink, but that stubborn chin of hers was set defiantly. His temper flared again at the realization of how much she was willing to sacrifice for a brewery.

*But it's no more than Gran was willing to sacrifice. Annabel has a family to save, too.*

When that thought roused unwanted sympathy, he scowled. She wouldn't give up her innocence to a *scapegrace* like him without being sure of getting something for it. This had to be some new scheme . . .

"An excellent plan, my dear. Either way, you get what you want. If you win, you gain my help with the brewery. And if I win, you go running to your brother about how I've ruined you, and next thing I know I'm wearing a leg shackle, and I'll have you and your brother's brewery on my hands for good."

She gaped at him. "What a horrible thing to say! I would never—"

"No? And why should I believe that, pray tell?"

Her gaze dropped to his cravat, the color of her cheeks deepening. "Because it's impossible to ruin what is already ruined."

She'd said it so softly he wasn't sure he'd heard her right. "What?"

"Don't make me repeat it," she told him, sotto voce. "I had a fiancé, remember? We were young and impetuous and in love. You can guess the rest." She brought her gaze up to his. "Why do you think I've never married? Because no man wants an unchaste bride."

He searched her face, but the very fact that she was telling him this lent it truth. And she'd been far too comfortable with their intimacies, too knowledgeable about things no virgin should know.

"So," he said, trying to take it in, "more lies are unmasked."

Her eyes flashed fire. "I never lied to you about that. You never asked. You merely assumed that I was . . . what you thought."

The words made him grit his teeth, but she was right. She'd never once claimed to be an innocent. And even if she had, he could hardly blame her. That wasn't something a woman revealed about herself to just anyone.

"Does your brother know?" he asked.

"Yes."

"How could he—"

"I've said all I'm going to say on that subject." Her blush had spread to the tops of her breasts—her quite exposed breasts, which he suddenly realized he could plunder to his heart's content if he accepted her proposal. *And* won the card game.

Damn, how could he be considering this? Making foolish wagers with her had already landed him in trouble once.

And yet . . .

This was his chance to extract payment for her lying to him, for scheming to bring him here in the first place. And it wasn't really a risk this time, because he would make sure the odds were stacked in his favor.

"So are you willing?" she whispered.

"I have some conditions."

Her eyes widened.

"This time we play piquet."

"Why?"

"That should be obvious. It relies far more on skill than chance." And piquet was *his* game. His eyes narrowed on her. "Do you know how to play?"

"I do," she said, but her voice quavered.

Good. It was about bloody time he got some advantage.

He tightened his grip on her waist. There was no way in hell he would lose *this* game. There'd be no distractions, no Masters and Gabe making remarks that tore his attention from the cards.

"And we play one game only," he went on. "Winner takes all. I've already wasted enough time on this scheme of yours as it is."

She lifted her chin. "All right."

There it was again—the understated "all right" that never failed to turn his blood to fire. "You agree to both conditions?"

She nodded.

They took another turn about the floor as he weighed his choices. He could throw her proposal in her face, walk out of here tonight, and not look back. But when he won, he'd finally have some compensation for her deception. And he wanted that compensation. *Christ,* how he wanted it.

What's more, he deserved it, for all the times she'd kissed him and let him caress her without its meaning *anything* to her. She'd made it quite clear he wasn't acceptable as a husband, yet she'd refused to let them continue as lovers. And with no reason, given she was unchaste. So she'd probably been trying to reel him in, to get him so besotted with her that he wouldn't care what lies she'd told him. And that possibility infuriated him.

"I do have one request before you give me your answer."

"You don't get a request," he clipped out.

"The only time that Rupert and I . . . Well, he took . . . precautions against certain eventualities. If you win the wager, I would ask that you do the same."

"I can do that," he said.

She swallowed. "Does that mean you accept the wager?"

He paused, but it was a sure thing. And he'd never been one to pass up a sure thing.

"Yes." The waltz was coming to an end, and they probably would not get another chance to speak privately. "Where and when will this game take place?"

"One A.M. at the office in the brewery. We had to let our evening staff go, so Lake Ale will be closed, but I have a key." The music stopped and they stepped back, her to curtsy, him to bow. "I'll wait for you inside."

As he took her arm to lead her from the floor, she murmured, "And I would appreciate it if you could try not to be seen on your way there."

"Don't worry. No one will ever learn of this from me."

"Thank you. I'm still considered respectable by my neighbors here."

Her tone pricked his conscience, but he frowned it away. As far as he was concerned, she'd made her bed. And now that she'd done so, *he* damned well was going to lie in it.

ANNABEL STARED OUT the window as the Lake family coach lurched homeward. She'd averted disaster, but for how long? She'd always been good at piquet, but good enough to beat Jarret? And if she lost . . .

The leap in her pulse made her scowl. He shouldn't still

have this effect on her, not after his sharp words and angry looks. But beneath his anger, desire had simmered, that ever-present desire that tugged an answering need to the surface of her very skin.

She groaned. *Admit it. You want him in your bed.*

All right, she did. Which made absolutely no sense. One of these days, she simply must learn not to crave things that were bad for her. Like certain hellions who knew exactly how to turn a woman to pudding with a dark glance.

It hadn't helped that he'd been wearing evening attire to-night for the first time since she'd met him. Seeing him so finely dressed had made something flip over inside her chest. Next to the tradesmen, with their ostentatious figured waistcoats and pompaded hair, his exquisitely tailored black tailcoat, simple white satin waistcoat, and snowy linen had fairly screamed his station as a polished man of rank, bred for greater things than socializing with the brash brewers of Burton.

Yet he'd never once showed, by word or deed, that he was aware of the difference. If not for his sophisticated bearing and his elegant clothing, no one would have guessed he wasn't just another brewer. She'd heard snippets of his conversation, and he'd held his own with the clannish brewers in a way that Hugh had never been able to. Or her.

"Lord Jarret seems a good enough sort," Hugh said, across from her. "Knew a bit more about the brewing business than I expected. He stared at me rather oddly when I said I was looking forward to our meeting in the morning, though. That *is* when we're going to meet, isn't it?"

"Yes." *But only if I beat him at piquet.*

She forced a smile for her brother's benefit. True to his word, Hugh had only had punch to drink, which technically wasn't spirits, though she suspected it had contained a dram or two of brandy.

"He seemed awfully interested in *you,* Annie," Hugh said. "Asked me about Rupert. Wanted to know what sort of man he was."

That startled her, until she realized that Jarret had probably just been trying to determine if she was telling the truth about her chastity.

Humiliation rose in her again. How could he think she would *lure* him into her bed just to trap him into getting *leg-shackled*? Beastly fellow. Though he was probably used to women doing such awful things in the city.

What had he said? *I'll have you know that there are hundreds of women who would kill to have that life.* She couldn't blame them. The idea of being his wife . . .

Ridiculous! She wouldn't want to raise a family with him, even if he did want to marry her. And he didn't. He certainly wouldn't now, after how she'd lied to him.

Remembering the fury in his eyes as they danced, she shivered. He'd been so contemptuous, so cutting. He'd arranged tonight's encounter with such ruthless determination that she feared how he would treat her if he won. She didn't know if she could bear having him bed her in anger.

"Quite frankly," Hugh went on, "I wasn't sure what to tell him about Rupert, given what happened. I finally just said he was a war hero. That much is true, anyway."

A war hero. She used to hate that phrase, knowing at what cost Rupert's heroism had come. Now it merely made her sad to think of how little being a hero meant when one lost one's chance at a life.

"I think his lordship is interested in Annabel," Sissy said, with a sly glance at her.

A bitter laugh stuck in her throat. Oh yes, he was interested. He might have lost any soft feelings for her, but he still lusted after her, thank heaven.

"Well, she could do worse, I suppose," Hugh said in a gruff voice. He tugged nervously at his shirt cuffs, then set his shoulders as if coming to a decision. "Annie, I want you to be at the meeting tomorrow."

She glanced at him in surprise. Hugh had never allowed her to attend any sort of brewery meeting. It was fine for her to keep the place running, but heaven forbid she should be in on the planning for anything. "Why?"

He shrugged. "You're the one who got him here. He might be . . . more comfortable if you're there."

Little did he know. If she won tonight, Jarret would hate her in the morning, and if she lost he would not *be* there in the morning.

"That's fine." She'd deal with that tomorrow.

For now, she had to concentrate on slipping out of the house unseen. It had been midnight when they'd left the town hall; she had little time.

Fortunately, Hugh and Sissy didn't seem inclined to linger, especially when she announced that she was exhausted and meant to retire after she fetched a book from the study. A deeply felt longing pierced her when Hugh murmured something, and Sissy giggled before they strolled up the stairs arm in arm.

She sighed and dismissed the servants, telling them she'd lock up. She waited until she was sure no one was around, then let herself out the garden door with her key.

The brewery was a short walk from the house. Fortunately, no homes lay near it, just a stables and a cooperage that was closed for the night. It was unlikely anyone would notice either her or him entering, but she did wish that Papa hadn't been so adamant about lighting the street with gas lamps. She felt very exposed.

When a large form stepped out of the shadows near the back entrance to the brewery, her heart jumped into her throat. Until she realized it was Jarret.

Then she saw his eyes, and her pulse pounded even more furiously. Because this wasn't the Jarret who'd teased her at the market, or the Jarret who'd brought her pleasure with drugging kisses, or even the Jarret who'd been furious at her tonight.

This Jarret bore an expression carved in cold stone. Between the time she'd last seen him and now, he had hardened his heart against her. He was clearly determined to revenge himself on her.

God help her if she didn't win their game. Because this Jarret was not a man she would want in her bed. Not tonight. Not ever.

# Chapter Sixteen

$\mathcal{J}$arret had spent the past hour preparing for his meeting with Annabel. While changing into attire more suitable for a clandestine meeting with a lying harpy, he'd worked hard to wall off the part of himself that she'd softened over the past few days. He'd fought to obliterate from his memory all the things that had made him admire her—her patience toward Mrs. Lake and Geordie, her obvious loyalty to her family . . . her seeming vulnerability that day in the barn.

That was the point—she'd *seemed* vulnerable, but she wasn't. Ever since dinner, he'd been going over the events of their trip, and he'd realized just how far she'd taken her subterfuge. Not only had she lied to him, but she'd convinced the rest of the family to lie, as well. She'd coaxed him into believing her scheme would work, all the while knowing that it rested on the uncertain state of her drunken brother. She'd even manufactured that little scene with the doctor at their home.

She'd made him believe in her. Worse yet, she'd made him out to be some untrustworthy rogue, when all the while she was the one who was untrustworthy. The more he'd thought about it the more his heart had frozen, until he was sure he was now immune to her smiles and half-truths.

Yet here she was, looking fragile and tired, her petite frame practically dwarfed by a wool cloak and her eyes haunted— and it threatened to destroy every wall he'd so carefully built.

Damn her to hell. Why did she affect him like this? Why had he not yet learned that everything she said and did was for the benefit of her family's cursed brewery?

"You're early," she said in a low voice as she walked past him to the door.

"I am eager for the night's festivities to begin," he clipped out. "I want to have plenty of time to enjoy my . . . winnings." He swept her with a deliberate glance to remind her of how he would take his revenge.

Instead of rousing a blush in her pale cheeks, it made anger flare in her eyes. "Assuming that you win, which is by no means certain."

She was always a fighter, and damned if that didn't arouse him.

He came up close behind her, taking petty satisfaction in the way her fingers fumbled with the keys. "It's certain enough."

Removing the key from her gloved hand, he bent past her to unlock the door. He could feel her tremble, which tugged at his conscience. With a muttered curse, he handed her the key and moved back.

"I beat you before," she said. "I can beat you again."

He snorted. "Do you know what they call me in the gaming hells of London?"

"Cocky?"

He suppressed a laugh. "The Prince of Piquet. I almost never lose."

She pushed the door open. "Then it sounds to me as if you have an unfair advantage. That's hardly gentlemanly of you."

"No, it's not," he agreed without an ounce of guilt as he entered behind her.

Shutting the door, she picked up a nearby flint and got the candle lit, then wedged it into a sconce. When she took off her wool cloak, he dragged in a harsh breath. She still wore her dinner gown, the one he'd wanted to rip off her with his teeth.

She faced him with a brittle expression, and it was all he could do not to shove her against the wall and kiss the coldness from her. But that would give her too much power over him.

"Perhaps we should choose a more level playing field." Defiance lit her features. "If you don't like two-handed whist, we can play Irish whist, as your friend Mr. Masters suggested. It can't be much different from regular whist, and if you explain the rules, I'm sure I could follow it."

A caustic laugh burst out of him. "Oh, I'm sure you could follow it very well." Giving her no warning, he caught her by the hips and hauled her close to press against his rapidly hardening cock. "*This* is Irish whist, my dear." He thrust himself suggestively against her. "Where the jack takes the ace."

If he'd hoped to embarrass her, he'd failed. She merely looked perplexed. "I don't understand. I can figure out what 'jack' refers to, but—"

"'Ace of spades' is cant for 'whore,'" he said bluntly, "because a spade resembles the triangle of dark hair between a woman's legs. Ergo, jack takes the ace."

Appalled, she shoved away from him. "Why is it called *Irish* whist?"

He shrugged. "Hell if I know. Probably because we English blame everything dirty on the Irish. 'Irish root' means a man's privates, for example, and 'Irish toothache' means a man's arousal."

A gentleman never said such things to a gently bred female, but tonight he wasn't feeling much like a gentleman. He half expected her to slap him for his crudeness, and hoped she would. He was spoiling for a fight.

"Lord, men are children," she said crisply. "Is that how you spend your time when women aren't around? Thinking up naughty terms for women's privates?"

Only Annabel would look at it that way. Forcing himself not to be charmed by that, he raked his gaze down to linger on that part of her. "When we're not thinking up ways to get *into* women's privates."

A hot rush of blood rose in her cheeks, and she whirled and headed for the coal grate. "We need some heat in here. I didn't have time to change out of my dinner gown."

"Good," he murmured as she bent to start the fire. "After I spent the entire evening imagining tearing that gown off of you, I'm looking forward to the reality."

Her back went rigid. "You're awfully sure of yourself, aren't you?"

"I always am."

When she turned her head, probably to rebuke him for his arrogance, she caught him staring at her nicely displayed arse, and she straightened to glare at him. "You think I'm a whore now, don't you?"

That brought him up short. "Why would I think that?"

"Because of what I did with Rupert."

"One night of passion with your 'true love' hardly qualifies you for status as a whore."

"Then why are you treating me differently?" she countered. "Why are you being so crude and saying such shocking things to me?"

Because he wanted her to feel the same shock he'd felt when he'd realized how she'd lied to him. Because it still gnawed at him that the fetching country lass who'd enticed him had been toying with him only to get what she wanted. "*You're* the one who brought up Irish whist."

"It's not that. You're so cold, so angry."

Hurt bled through her words, driving a stake in his righteous anger. Yet he couldn't let it go. "Can you blame me? You lied to me."

"If I hadn't, you wouldn't have come here. I did what I had to."

"Just as you're doing now," he said icily.

She folded her arms over her stomach. "Yes."

"*That's* why I'm angry. I thought you were—"

"An innocent, chaste country girl?" she said bitterly.

"Honorable."

She glared at him. "I *am* honorable, curse you."

"Is that what you call wagering your body to save your brother's brewery?"

Her eyes spit fire. "*You* suggested that wager, not I."

"But you accepted it. And you were the one to suggest this wager tonight." He stepped closer. "Which makes me wonder if all those kisses and caresses between us were ever anything but a way to reel me in."

She jerked back with a horrified expression. "You think

that I . . . You actually believe I would . . . You're daft! Surely you could tell I honestly desired you. It's not something a woman can pretend."

Satisfaction rose in him, despite his efforts to quell it. "Actually, it *is* something a woman can pretend."

Confusion spread over her face. "How?"

She was either the most accomplished actress he'd ever met, or she was inexperienced in matters of the bedchamber, despite her encounter with the heroic Rupert. He began to wonder if it might be the latter. And if it were . . . "You really don't know?"

"What I know is that *you* initiated every one of our kisses. For someone who was attempting to 'reel you in,' I was rather clumsy at it."

Her unflappable logic drove a wedge in his defenses that none of her protests had been able to do. Because in truth, she *hadn't* pursued him; he'd pursued her. And if she'd been using her body to manipulate him, she'd have been better off tempting him to bed her so she could trap him into marriage. A little pig's blood, some feigned discomfort, and he wouldn't have known she was unchaste.

Instead, she'd tried to put him off after the barn.

"As for honor," she went on, her dander now fully up, "that is a luxury some people can't afford, my lord. But you wouldn't know that, down in London where you can spend your days gambling and drinking without a thought for anyone you harm."

"Harm?" His anger surged again. "Unlike your brother, I control my appetites."

"Do you? Then why are we here?"

The words were a punch to his gut. Why *was* he here? If

he'd really thought her a coldhearted schemer, then why did he want to bed her?

Because he didn't *want* to believe that everything had been part of her scheming. Because it had mattered to him more than he cared to admit. But it hadn't mattered to her. Not enough to be truthful with him, anyway.

And that rubbed him raw.

"Touché, Annabel," he said softly. "I'm here because I want you. Because wanting you has clouded my judgment. The question is, why are *you* here?"

Her eyes went wide. "Because I want you to help us."

"And that is so important to you that you'd sell your body for it?"

She paled. "I'm not selling my body. It's a wager. I hope to win."

"Ah. And the fact that you might not?"

"Is a calculated risk."

Spoken like a worthy adversary. She found more candles and lit them from the first one. Walking over to the large desk, she placed the candles in holders, then sat down behind it, opposite the only other chair—the one with its back to the window.

He scowled. "Very clever of you, Annabel." He dragged the chair from in front of the desk around to the side. "But since that window is as good as a mirror, with no light behind it, I hope you don't mind if I alter the arrangements a bit."

She looked with bewilderment at the window. "Lord, I hadn't even noticed that."

"Right." He removed a pack of cards from his pocket and took his seat.

"I didn't! I would never cheat." As he raised an eyebrow

and began to shuffle, she grumbled, "And it's not as if I could see anything in the glass behind you, with that thick head of yours blocking your cards."

He stifled a laugh. Damn, it was hard to stay mad at her when she was being so typically . . . Annabel. And could he blame her if she really had thought to cheat? She might see it as the only way to get what she wanted. The only way to escape his bed.

That roused his anger all over again, but this time not at her. "Tell me, my dear, how long have you been doing whatever was necessary to save Lake Ale?"

She shot him a wary glance. "What do you mean?"

"Your brother inherited the company three years ago. Have you been hiding his incompetence ever since? Or did it start even before that?"

"Actually . . ." She hesitated, then steadied her shoulders. "Actually, Hugh didn't inherit the brewery three years ago. Father left Lake Ale to his bachelor brother. His will left half the proceeds to us and the other half to our uncle, but Uncle actually owned it."

Jarret stopped shuffling. Such a thing just wasn't done in England. The rule of primogeniture was nearly absolute. A man left his property to his eldest son. If he didn't, there was something very, very wrong. "Why in God's name would your father do that?"

"A number of reasons. Hugh was never like Papa—he's a quiet man who prefers gentler pursuits. They clashed over everything. Hugh has a good mind for business, but he doesn't trust his own instincts, and Papa was a . . . rather forceful personality. He was always berating Hugh for his lack of boldness. I suppose Papa thought we'd all be better off if Uncle ran the place and we reaped the benefits."

Setting the pack in front of her, Jarret asked, "Did Hugh see it that way?"

She stared down at the cards. "Hardly. He felt betrayed."

Of course he did. What would it do to a man, to know that his father couldn't even trust him with the family business?

*The same thing it did to you as a child to know that Gran didn't want you running the brewery.*

That old pain rose up to haunt him. Even now, Gran hadn't considered getting him to run the brewery until she'd fallen ill.

He scowled, angry at himself for even empathizing with Hugh Lake. The man was a drunk. Jarret was not.

No, he was a rootless gambler. So much better for running the family business.

A surge of irritation made him say flippantly, "Well, your brother clearly owns it now."

She cut the cards, showed him her card, then handed them back. "Yes, because my uncle died a bachelor, and he had made Hugh his heir. So Hugh got it anyway."

Jarret cut the cards and won the cut. He let her deal, since there was some advantage in having his opponent deal first. "Is that when he started drinking?"

"No. He managed fairly well until the Russian market dried up." With an economy of motion he seldom saw in women players, she dealt the cards. "And the more he tried to wrest Lake Ale—unsuccessfully—from financial disaster, the more he felt like a failure. *That's* when he began to drink."

Jarret had to wonder how *he* would have reacted in such a situation. And the very fact that he wondered angered him. "Are you saying all this to garner my sympathy for your brother?" *And for you?*

"I'm merely answering your question." She picked up her

cards. "Besides, I thought you should know that Hugh isn't at fault for my lies. He believed we'd gone to London to look at schools for Geordie."

That bit of information startled him. "He didn't know anything about your plan?"

"He suggested pursuing the India market, but the only time he met with the East India Company captains, it ended badly. He never pursued it again, sure that he would fail. Sissy and I hoped that if we could get Plumtree Brewery involved, it would give him the confidence to pursue it further."

"That's a great deal to hope for from a business arrangement," he pointed out.

A heavy sigh escaped her. "I know. But we had to try something." She met his gaze over her cards. "My point is, he had no idea I was telling you he was ill. He still doesn't know about the first wager, and he certainly doesn't know about the second. If he did, he would toss you out of town on your ear." Her voice sharpened. "He would certainly not try to wrangle you to the altar, as you suggested. So you needn't worry on that score."

"I'm not." He stared her down. "No one wrangles me into doing anything I don't want to do."

"Oh, I'm well aware of that," she said acidly. "You do exactly what you please, no matter what anyone else wants or needs. I surmised that from the beginning."

The fact that she was right didn't make her words any easier to stomach. "Don't fancy that you know anything about me after our short acquaintance." He picked up his cards. "You know nothing of my life except what the gossips have told you."

"And whose fault is that?" she asked in a soft voice. "What

have *you* told me about yourself? Hardly enough for me to make even a sketch of you, much less a full picture. You can't blame me for judging you based on the little you've said."

That flummoxed him. She was right. She'd told him more about her and her fiancé than he'd told her about his whole life.

But the more someone knew about you, the more they could make you care. And he didn't want to. So why was her insidious tale of woe about her brother having exactly the effect she probably intended?

Because he was an idiot. And because he understood the way her brother must have felt. How could he not?

It didn't matter. He couldn't let it matter. Her proposition had been foolish in the beginning, and it was even more so now that he knew the truth.

*Sissy and I hoped that if we could get Plumtree Brewery involved, it would give him the confidence to pursue it further.*

He cursed under his breath. Hugh Lake's lack of confidence wasn't his problem, damn it!

"Bad cards?" she asked.

"No," he said, though in truth he hardly saw the cards at all. Something else was nagging at him, something he just had to know. He set down his cards. "Why do you care so much what happens to your brother? You said he wouldn't want you to make sacrifices for him. So why are you?"

Swallowing hard, she gazed down at her hand. "Because we all depend upon him."

"You could marry," he pointed out. "The men at the dinner said you'd turned down several offers. You could have found a husband and washed your hands of your brother, forced him to fend for himself, even taken in his family if you had to."

"I couldn't marry. I'm not chaste."

The shame in her voice twisted something inside him. "A decent man wouldn't care about that, knowing the circumstances. It's not uncommon for betrothed couples to . . . get carried away before the wedding." He noted her heightened color, her shaking hands. There was something else she wasn't saying. "No, it's more than that. Why are you doing this for *him*?"

"Because what happened between him and Papa is partly my fault, all right?" Pain slashed across her face. "I owe him."

He stared at her. "How could that possibly be your fault?"

She arranged her cards with quick motions that betrayed her agitation. "I was visiting him and Sissy when Rupert and I . . . well, you know. By the time Hugh caught me sneaking back into the house, it was too late. He set out to collar Rupert and make him marry me right away, but the transport had already left for the Continent." Her voice dropped to an aching whisper. "Papa never forgave Hugh for not watching over me more carefully. It changed everything between them. Father rode Hugh so much harder after that."

"That wasn't fair to either of you," he said sharply. "Did your father really think he could have done any better? I have two sisters, and I can assure you, if they wanted to meet with a man secretly, nothing I could do would stop them, short of imprisoning them in their rooms." He thought of Masters and scowled. "Sometimes I wish I could. Your father had no right to blame your brother for that."

"I know. He should have blamed *me*."

"No, damn it! He should have blamed the man who ruined you without thinking what it would cost you."

An awareness of just how *much* it had cost her hit him like a mortal blow. She'd lived like a nun, caring for her family, unable to have a home or a family of her own. And all because of one stolen night with a man.

He lowered his voice. "You should not be taking all the burden for Rupert's sins. Or your father's. Or even your brother's."

"I'm not," she said with a wan smile. "I'm taking it for my own."

"You have no sins," he bit out.

"That's not what you said before," she reminded him.

He winced. Confound her to hell. With every new piece she revealed about her family, his image of her shifted. As did his anger. He was rapidly becoming more angry on her behalf than angry *at* her.

Was he being a fool again? Or was she really justified in her actions?

He stared at her, trying to make her out. But that was impossible with a woman like Annabel, who was a mass of contradictions—innocent and worldly, forthright and secretive. All of it fascinating.

Damn her.

Apparently growing uncomfortable with his hard stare, she gestured to the hand he'd laid on the desk. "Are we going to play piquet? Or do you plan to keep asking me questions all night?"

He tapped his cards, suddenly wishing he hadn't been so hasty to accept her wager. Short of telling her he would stay and help her, which he wasn't willing to do, he had no choice but to finish it out. And that meant he had to beat her.

But he was no longer sure he could stomach taking her to bed when she was essentially offering herself as a sacrifice for her foolish brother.

He would cross that bridge when he came to it. "Let's play," he clipped out.

And the game was on.

He had to force himself to focus. Piquet was complicated, requiring a great deal of thought. It wasn't conducive to chatting, something she clearly realized, for they spoke only during the declarations phase of the hand when the game required it.

But he couldn't quiet the muttering of his conscience.

*She is only doing what she has to in order to survive. And she deserves better than another man who will use her and leave her.*

He thrust that unsettling thought from his mind to concentrate on the cards. He'd stupidly agreed to her wager, and now he was bound as a gentleman to finish it, but he was *not* going to risk Plumtree Brewery simply because she'd told him some sad tale about her hapless brother and their godforsaken brewery.

Fortunately he'd been dealt a stellar hand, and the draw only improved it. He stared with grim satisfaction at his cards. He was not going to lose this time, thank God.

The die was cast the moment they made their respective declarations and he scored a repique, giving him ninety points. He knew that would be damned hard to beat, though she certainly tried. Her playing was good, even inspired. But no one bested him at piquet.

So it was no surprise when he won every trick, scoring him a capot and forty extra points as well. No surprise that her face paled with each successive win. No surprise that when the hand was done, securing him the win in one brutal deal, despair flickered in her eyes, though she tried to hide it with a smile.

"You won," she said with feigned nonchalance.

"I told you I would," he retorted.

"Yes, you did." She wouldn't meet his gaze. She gathered up the cards, her hands shaking, and she looked lost.

So it was also no surprise when he heard himself say, "I won't hold you to your part of the wager. As far as I'm concerned, the matter is now settled."

A strange calmness stole over him. This was the right thing to do, and they both knew it. "I only wanted to be free of this cursed deal with your brother, and now I am. So you need not share my bed. Go home."

# Chapter Seventeen

Annabel stared at him, hardly able to believe her ears. An hour ago, she would have leaped at the offer and considered herself lucky to be spared a night with a man who was so clearly furious at her.

But over the course of the evening, something had changed. *He* had changed. And after all he'd said, after how he'd softened . . .

"You don't have to do that," she said. "I pay my debts." When he flinched at the word *debts*, she added hastily, "You may not think me honorable, but—"

"It's got nothing to do with honor, Annabel." Every line of his body was tense, every feature looked carved in stone. "I'm absolving you of any responsibility for your *debts*. As the winner, I can do that, you know."

"I don't *want* you to do it!" she protested. "I chose to make that wager, and I won't have you 'absolving' me of responsibility for it simply because you pity me."

"And I won't have you sharing my bed as part of some foolish bargain." He rose to lean over the desk, his eyes stormy.

"If I ever take you to bed, it will be because you choose it—not because it was some fruitless ploy to save your family or your brother or your damned brewery."

In a flash, she understood. She'd hurt his pride. She should have realized it when he'd said those cutting words about her using kisses and caresses to "reel him in." He might not want to marry her, but clearly he didn't like thinking that she saw him only as a means to an end.

Inexplicably, that warmed her. If he cared even that much . . . "What if I'm not doing it as part of a bargain?"

He froze, and for a moment she wasn't sure if he'd understood. Then she saw the muscle ticking in his jaw. Oh yes, he understood.

"What other reason would you have?" he asked in a deceptively soft voice.

Heat rose in her cheeks. "Must you . . . make me say it?"

His expression was steady, but his eyes flared with hunger. "Yes. I'm afraid I must."

Briefly she contemplated running. He would let her go if she did—she knew that now. And the desire that his need kindled in her terrified her. She'd never felt anything like this with Rupert. The last thing she needed was this handsome, arrogant lord dragging her into the luxuriant flames with him, to be consumed by a blaze she'd avoided half her life.

But the blaze was already out of control within her; she doubted that running would extinguish it. And she *had* promised, after all.

She stood to round the desk on shaking legs. "It's been nearly thirteen years since I lay with a man, and in all that time, I told myself I didn't miss it. I told myself that I was content, that I had no need of a man's kisses or caresses. And then you came along and . . . and everything . . . changed . . ."

Her voice faltered as he shoved away from the desk to come meet her.

"Go on," he said in a husky rasp that turned her knees to jelly.

He was inches away from her now, his hand stretching up to brush her cheek, then down her neck in a slow, sensual caress that made it nearly impossible for her to think.

"I-I want you," she admitted as her gaze locked with his smoldering one. "I want you to touch me. I want you in my b—"

His lips were on hers before she could finish. He splayed his fingers across the back of her head to hold her still for a kiss that was as fiery and consuming as it was tender. His kiss ravaged like a conqueror of old, scorching the earth it left behind as he laid claim to every part of her mouth.

Curling her fingers into his coat lapels, she pulled him closer, which only made him more ravenous, until he was driving into her mouth in a frank mimicking of what they were soon going to do.

As his mouth plundered hers, he lifted his free hand to tug her sleeve down. It took little effort, since her gown had been made back when bodices barely clung to one's shoulders, and within moments, he had her breast bared for his teasing fingers.

The shock of pleasure his caress sent through her reminded her of where they were. Though she knew the brewery was empty, she didn't like the idea of his touching her in front of a window that anyone could see through. "Wait," she drew back to whisper.

"Not on your life, my pretty pixie," he growled. "You had your chance to escape, and you didn't take it."

"Who said anything about escaping?"

His gaze turned white-hot, searing her with its intensity. With her heart thundering in anticipation, she seized a candle holder and took him by the hand to lead him to a door at one end of the room. When she opened it to pull him inside, he gave a low chuckle, no doubt surprised to find himself in a small room fitted with a single bed and a writing table.

"When the brewery was running at night," she explained as she went to light a fire in the grate, "Mr. Walters used to nap in here. We haven't used it recently, but it's clean. And it has to be more comfortable than the desk."

She walked back to put the candle on the writing table, and he came up behind her to slip his arm about her waist. "No wonder you wanted to have this card game at the brewery." He pressed a kiss into her hair. "You were planning ahead, I see."

Her breath grew ragged as his mouth found the tender skin just beneath her jaw, where the pulse beat a frenzied drumming. "If you will remember . . ." she choked out, "I didn't expect you to win."

"I think you did." He skimmed his hands up to cup her breasts, making her blood run even higher. "Tell me, Miss Lake, did you *let* me win that game?"

*"What?"* She twisted in his arms to face him, a hot retort springing to her lips until she saw the dark gleam in his eyes. In a flash, she remembered what she'd said to him that day at the London inn.

Shrugging out of her sleeves, she arched one eyebrow. "Now why would I do that, my lord?"

His gaze flared hot as it fixed on her exposed corset. "Because you want the hellion in your bed more than you'll admit."

"Are you really such a hellion?" she asked seriously. "I think you're more of a gentleman than you'll admit."

He turned her around so he could loosen the fastenings of her gown. "You're the first woman to think so." He dragged her gown off of her, letting it drop to the floor.

When he brushed kisses along her bared shoulders, she shivered deliciously. "But not the first woman to . . . share your bed."

His fingers paused in the course of unlacing her corset. "No."

"How many have there been?" she asked, wanting to remind herself that this was nothing special to him. Because if she let herself believe that it was, she was sure to be hurt when she discovered it wasn't.

"Hundreds," he said sarcastically as he freed her corset and tossed it aside. "Thousands."

"That many?" she said, matching his light tone.

"Half the women in London, if one is to believe the gossips." He skimmed his hands down her sides to her hips, and his voice fell to a jagged whisper. "But none as lovely as you."

"Now *that* is a lie if ever I heard one," she said as she pivoted to face him.

But the dark intensity of his gaze as he raked it down her thinly clad body made her wish it were not. "I never lie to a woman," he said softly.

Her heart pounded in her throat. "Never?"

"There's never been a need." His expression was deadly serious. "The women I bed are most often taproom maids and ladies of easy virtue who don't expect or require promises and soft words." He caressed her cheek with the back of his hand. "It's all about the pleasure to them. Or the money."

She found it hard to breathe. "And which of those two am I? A taproom maid or a lady of easy virtue?"

"Neither." He flashed her a rueful smile. "You're in a

category all your own." He reached up to thread his fingers through her hair, tugging it loose of its pins. "Country goddesses. Goddesses of the harvest, perhaps—Ceres or Demeter."

"They're also the goddesses of fertility, so I don't think that's a good choice, given what we're about to do," she said dryly.

He laughed.

"If I must be a deity, I prefer Minerva. She's clever and beautiful, and she's the goddess of commerce."

"Sorry, but that one's not a choice," he said as he spread her hair over her shoulders.

"Because she's a virgin?" she said, disappointed.

"Because my sister is named after her." He untied her shift. "And what I'm feeling for you isn't the least bit brotherly, dearling."

*Dearling.* His use of the endearment, even after all that had happened today, made a lump catch in her throat.

He started to push her shift from her shoulders, but she caught his hands. "Not yet. Your turn."

Eyes alight, he tore off his moleskin coat and striped waistcoat, then tossed them onto the writing table. His cravat and braces swiftly followed. When he removed his shirt, she caught her breath at the sight of his naked chest with its sprinkling of dark hair, the muscles clearly defined. It wasn't the body of the indolent aristocrat that she'd expected. He was rapier-lean and fit, a Greek god in the flesh. Apollo himself could not rival his well-hewn body.

"Like what you see?" he asked roughly. He threw his shirt aside and sat down in the chair to tug off his boots.

"Perhaps," she teased.

His eyes darkened. Leaning back in the chair, he spread his legs. "Come here, you coy minx."

Her throat went dry at the sight of his rampant arousal straining against his moleskin trousers. "I thought I was a goddess," she said lightly as she did his bidding.

"Ah, but we haven't decided which one." When she got close enough, he leaned forward to pull her between his legs. "I begin to think that Venus suits you best." He teased her bare breast. "The goddess of beauty."

*And the goddess of love,* she thought, though she didn't dare say it. As his mouth closed over her breast, she didn't even dare think it. Because he was being so tender, so passionate, it made her want to weep. It made him even more dangerous to her than when he'd been angry.

Clutching his head to her breast, she prayed she could spend this night with him and not lose her heart. He wouldn't want it, and she couldn't bear to have it trampled on.

He tongued her nipple, then tugged it with his teeth, sending a jolt of pleasure from her breast to her belly. As if knowing what effect he had on her, he slipped his hand beneath her shift and into the slit in her drawers, to find where she was already liquid and eager for him.

"My God," he murmured against her breast, "you feel like hot silk, warm and ready for my touch."

She wasn't the only one ready. She brought her knee up to stroke him through his trousers. With a low moan, he pulled her to sit astride him until her tender parts lay flush against his trapped arousal. He rocked against her, and the feeling was exquisite, the silky fabric of his trousers like a caress.

He returned to sucking her breast, teasing it with teeth and tongue, then sucking the other with the same intensity. Meanwhile, he thrust against her over and over, heightening her enjoyment, making her go all fluid and hot inside.

Next thing she knew, he'd edged her back enough so he

could reach the little button of flesh between her legs that ached for his touch. His mouth and hands fondled her in tandem, rousing such intense pleasure in her belly, she thought she might scream. Soon he had her gasping and leaning into his hand, wanting more, needing more.

"Definitely Venus," he growled as he strummed her like Apollo strumming his golden lyre.

"Jarret . . ." she breathed. "Oh, heavens."

"I'll give you the heavens, my beautiful Venus. That's where a goddess belongs." He slid one finger, then another into her slick sheath. "God, you're tight. And so tempting, I don't know how much longer I can wait to be inside you."

"You don't have to wait." She reached down to fumble with the fastenings of his trousers. "There's no need."

His breath coming in great, hard gasps, he set her back and rose to shed his trousers, drawers, and stockings. Her eyes went wide at the sight of him—lean-hipped and sinewy, with a thin dusting of black hair. And between his well-wrought thighs . . .

Lord save her. She hadn't seen his member half so well in the dim light of the barn, but now she was getting quite a good look. Fully erect, his rigid flesh sprang heavy and dark from a dense thatch of curls.

Rupert had been slender, his member long but barely over an inch thick. Jarret's was easily twice that large, and beneath her gaze, it seemed to grow even more.

"Take off your shift and your drawers," he commanded in a guttural voice. "I want to look at you, too."

Though she slid out of her drawers and tossed them aside, she hesitated to remove her last piece of modesty. Would he be able to see the faint lines that her pregnancy had left on her belly? And if he did, would he realize what they meant?

It wasn't as if she had a choice. If she continued to balk at removing her shift, he would wonder why. Perhaps the dim light would hide her sins.

Before she could act, he stepped forward to tug her shift the rest of the way off. "I never thought to see you shy, dearling." He scoured her with a frank appreciation that made her breath stop in her throat. "And there's certainly no need for it. You are even more lovely than I imagined."

He slid his arm about her waist to pull her close, and his aroused flesh pressed into her below, reminding her that there was one thing she must make certain of before they went any further.

"You said you would take precautions," she whispered.

"Ah, yes." Releasing her, he went to the table and fumbled in the pocket of his coat.

"What are you doing?" she asked, bewildered.

He removed something and held it up to the light. "Taking precautions."

She stared in confusion at the long silky tube dangling from his fingers. "But that's not what Rupert . . . I mean, he . . ."

"Let me guess," Jarret remarked as he slid the tube over his erect member. "He withdrew from you before spilling his seed."

"Yes! He said that it would protect me from . . . having a child."

"It's not the best method," he told her as he tied off the tube, then came toward her. "You were lucky that it worked. It doesn't always."

She certainly knew *that* to be true. Swallowing hard, she dipped her head to indicate his strangely garbed male member. "And does *that* work?"

A smile flitted over his lips. "Cundums have always worked for me." As he reached her, he drew her into his arms. "Don't worry. I know what I'm doing."

She certainly hoped so. All his talk about the goddesses of fertility made her nervous. She didn't need any excess of fertility tonight.

Yet as he backed her toward the bed, his mouth seeking hers again, she wondered what it would be like to bear him a child as his wife. Would he stay by her side, as Hugh had done for all of Sissy's children, or would he pace the halls in a frenzy? Would he be delighted with a baby, or annoyed that his pleasures were to be curtailed by an infant's demands? She was sure he would make a good father—she had only to remember how he'd been with Geordie to realize that.

*Stop thinking such things,* she told herself as an old wives' tale rose in her head about how if one dreamed of a baby, one would conceive. God only knows what would happen if one dreamed of conceiving while bedding a man. That was surely asking for trouble.

Once he tumbled her onto the bed she had no problem putting the thought from her mind, for he was settling his body between her legs and fondling her below, his mouth scattering kisses over her breasts and shoulders and throat. "I could taste you all night, my sweet Venus," he whispered. "You taste like honey."

The reverence in his voice made tears burn the back of her throat. Would any other man be so careful with a woman he knew was unchaste? His tenderness was about to destroy her.

Not all of him was tender, though. His member lay hot and rigid against her thigh, sparking the tiniest bit of fear in her belly. She wasn't sure she could take the whole thing inside. Rupert's slender shaft had been difficult enough to manage. Though she knew that the pain she'd suffered had been a product of her innocence, would a . . . a thing as large as Jarret's hurt her?

If it did, she would bear it as best she could. That part only lasted moments anyway, thank heaven. This was what she enjoyed, the kissing, the touching, the caressing.

She was glad when he continued to stroke and caress her, to kiss and fondle her. It emboldened her to do the same to him, exploring the fine curls on his chest, the flexing muscles of his thighs, even the firm flesh of his buttocks.

When he tensed, she whispered, "Do you mind me touching you?"

"God, no. Touch whatever you like. Though it will shorten this considerably."

"Good." She wanted to have the actual act over with, so she wouldn't start fretting over the possibility of pain. So they could do more of the enjoyable part. "I want you, Jarret. I'm ready for you."

Something in her tone must have alerted him to her fears, for he drew back to stare at her. "Are you all right?"

She forced a smile. "It's just been . . . a very long time."

His gaze narrowed on her. "And you were young, and he was young, and neither of you knew what you were doing. Right?"

She nodded.

"And it hurt."

"I know it won't hurt this time," she said hastily. "I'm not afraid."

A wry smile touched his lips. "You look afraid. But there's nothing to fear, dearling. Trust me." He lowered his head to nuzzle her jaw as he rose up and pressed the tip of his aroused flesh inside her. "Trust me . . ." he murmured, sliding ever so slowly in. "Trust me . . ." he whispered and drove into her with one silken thrust.

"Ohhh," she murmured, feeling relief surge through her. The alien fullness was unexpected but certainly not painful. And the intimacy of it roused a heat in her that was almost as good as the kissing. "That's not . . . bad at all."

He chuckled against her neck. "We're only beginning, my Venus." He drew out, then thrust in. Warmth curled up from low in her belly and spread through her limbs.

Pressing his mouth to her ear, he whispered, "Before this night is over, I promise to have you begging for more."

"Cocky as always," she responded, his words sparking a thrill through her veins. "But I never beg."

"You will," he vowed, and plunged into her again. And again. And again, each stroke fiercer, harder, faster. Bracing himself up on one elbow, he reached down between them to finger her and fan the warmth in her belly to flame.

"Put your legs around me, dearling," he ordered.

When she did, he drove deeper, and wildfire scorched through her, igniting her into a mass of heat. "Oh my sweet heavens . . ." she choked out, her body singing to the cadence of his thrusts.

"Better?" he rasped.

"Yes . . . oh yes . . . Jarret, my word . . ."

His heated breath came heavily against her ear. "You're so tight, so sweet and tight and hot. I'm losing my mind . . ."

She was losing her heart. She felt it slipping away with his every word. He was taking such care with her when he had no cause to do so, and it made her heart ache and yearn as much as his body was.

"Annabel, my goddess . . ." he breathed. "Let me take you to the heavens."

"I'm already there . . ."

He gave a choked laugh. "Not yet, but you will be."

After that, he spoke with his body, pounding into her, relentlessly teasing that sensitive place between her legs. Soon the ache in her belly became a dark pleasure, and then a spiraling hunger that had her writhing against him, raking her fingers down his back. She could hardly think for the sensations rocketing through her until joy suddenly vaulted her, high and sweet, taking her right up into the heavens.

She cried out until her throat was raw with her ecstasy, as he drove into her and uttered a cry of his own. Straining against her, he threw back his head with a look of rapt satisfaction as his body reached its final release.

It was magnificent. It was terrifying. For as she clasped him close and let the shocks of pleasure wash over her, she knew she was in danger of making a great mistake.

Losing her heart to a rogue.

# Chapter Eighteen

$\mathscr{J}$arret lay wrapped in his pleasure, utterly enthralled. He hadn't dreamed lovemaking could be so piercingly sweet. He still couldn't believe how freely Annabel had given herself to him after all his harsh words. He must have been mad to think she was using her body to reel him in. He'd never seen a woman approach the act with such innocent joy.

Guiding her to her release had been a delight beyond any he'd ever experienced in the bedchamber. And now what was he to do with her? Could he really just ride away from her in the morning?

The thought made something twist in his chest. Good God, when had he become so besotted by the tart-tongued brewster? He must be mad. Or she really was a goddess come to earth to enchant him.

"Jarret . . ." she murmured softly, pressing her hands against his chest.

He must be crushing her with his weight. It wasn't like him

to forget himself so completely with a woman. He slid off as much as he could and flashed her an apologetic glance. "This bed wasn't made for two, I'm afraid."

"No," she said with a little shiver.

It dawned on him how naked they were. "You're cold." He grabbed the folded blanket lying at the foot of the bed and pulled it up over them. "Better?"

"Thank you, yes," she said, her voice shy.

He'd never seen her shy. It enchanted him even more. "Am I too heavy on you?" he asked, since half his body still covered hers. Their legs were entangled, and her arm was trapped beneath him.

"Not at the moment." She shifted from under him so she could lie on her side facing him. Her eyes looked suspiciously misty as she met his gaze.

He rubbed a tear from her cheek. "Did I hurt you?"

She shook her head. "It was just so wonderful. I never thought . . . I never dreamed . . . I-It wasn't like that before . . ."

When she trailed off, embarrassed, he said soothingly, "It usually isn't. The first time between two virgins is never comfortable, from what I understand."

"It wasn't just that. You and I . . . well, I know it was probably nothing special for *you*, but—"

"Shh," he said, brushing a kiss to her lips. "It was amazing. You're amazing."

A gratified smile touched her lips. "I rather think the prize for being amazing should go to you. I didn't really know what I was doing."

"You knew enough," he said.

Her expression at the moment of climax would stay with

him for a long time. What a thrill it had been to give her that. It made him want to crow.

It made him want answers to the questions that had been nagging him ever since she'd told him about her brother running after Rupert to get him to marry her.

He propped his head up on his hand. "Tell me about Rupert."

Her gaze dropped to his chin, but not before he glimpsed pain in it. "What do you want to know?"

Figuring he'd better start small, he said, "How did you meet?"

A relieved sigh wafted out of her. "He and his older brother were the sons of Papa's widowed brewery manager. When Rupert was fourteen and I was eleven, his father's heart gave out and he and his brother were orphaned, so Papa gave them work at the brewery. They often came to dinner at the house."

"So you saw him a great deal," Jarret asked.

She nodded. "I think I was around fourteen when I started to care for him in a different way. It took him longer. When I was fifteen, he started courting a milliner's assistant, and it made me furiously jealous, so one day I dumped a basket of fish on his head when I knew he was going to meet her. He chased me down, threatening to spank me." She smiled. "He ended up kissing me instead. And that was the end of his courtship of the milliner's assistant."

The sweet story of a village romance touched him more deeply than he liked. He could just see her at fifteen, fresh-faced and dewy-eyed, falling for a handsome lad a few years older than she. And for one shocking moment, he virulently hated the man who'd had her heart, no matter how briefly.

"When I was sixteen," she went on, "Rupert asked Papa for my hand. Papa let us become betrothed but said we had to wait to marry, since he felt I was too young. Then Rupert's brother died, and you know the rest."

"Not all of it. I gather that you sneaked out to meet him the night before he left for the war." He cupped her cheek. "But I don't understand why the two of you didn't marry after he'd deflowered you. You were already betrothed. Why not marry?"

"There wasn't time," she said in a halting whisper. "He was to leave the next day."

"Clearly, your brother thought there was time, since he ran after the man. Rupert could have obtained a special license that very night, and you could have had a hasty wedding in the morning before he left."

She shifted away to lie with her back to him. "It would have required parental approval."

"Surely your father would have been glad to give that, if he'd known Rupert had taken your innocence. I don't see—"

"He didn't *want* me, all right?"

Jarret gaped at her. "What do you mean?"

A heavy sigh shook her small frame. "It wasn't supposed to happen—the two of us making love. He'd come to the house for a farewell dinner that night, and we'd said our good-byes. Hugh had even allowed us a moment of privacy for a kiss."

Her voice dropped to a pained whisper. "But I was brokenhearted. I couldn't stand the thought of his leaving. So I packed a small bag and sneaked out. I planned to join him, you see. I begged him to take me with him. I told him we could marry, and I could go to war with him as a camp follower. He wouldn't let me."

"Of course he wouldn't." Terror burst in Jarret's chest at the thought of her near a battlefield. "No man wants to see the woman he loves in that kind of danger."

She shifted her head to glare up at him. "I'm stronger than you think, you know. I could have done it—washed for him and cooked for him, like those other women."

"Those other women are seldom sixteen-year-old, gently bred daughters of rich brewers. They've either been raised in the regiments—officer's or soldier's daughters and sisters— or they're poor women who have no choice. It's a rough life, being a camp follower. I don't blame him for not wanting that for you. Besides, enlisted men are rarely allowed to take their wives. Very likely, he would have been denied permission to do so."

"But what if he hadn't? If I'd been there, he might not have died. Who knows how long he lay in the battlefield before they found him? I would have taken care of him, bound his wounds, watched over him—"

"And he probably would have died anyway, love." He stroked her hair, his heart hammering at the thought of her blaming herself for her fiancé's death. "Five thousand men lost their lives at Vittoria. It was a brutal battle. He was right not to take you."

Her pretty eyes were dark with grief. "But he should have married me before he left. That's what you think, isn't it?"

Jarret regretted raising the subject at all. He'd figured there was a story behind it, but he'd assumed that it had something to do with her father or her own insecurities. Like a brainless fool, he hadn't considered that Rupert might just have been a bastard.

"I'm sure he wanted to," he said gently.

"I'm not. Afterwards, he said not a word about marrying

right away. He promised he'd return soon. That once the war was over, I would be old enough to wed and we would have a big church ceremony." She met his gaze with her tear-filled one. "He said he loved me. He promised we would be together. Then he ran off to fight without a care in the world. Because he didn't want me."

"I doubt that very much." Jarret suddenly found himself in the peculiar position of having to make excuses for her confounded fiancé. "But men react differently to the threat of war. He might have worried he couldn't support you on a soldier's salary. He might have been so sure he'd be coming back that he didn't consider marrying right away. Or maybe he thought you'd be better off being free to marry if he were wounded or—"

"Killed? Then I would have been a respectable widow. I could have married whom I wished, instead of having to hide . . ." She bent her head to shield her tears from his gaze.

He brushed the hair from her damp cheeks. "I was going to say, if he were permanently injured. Men sometimes return from war with scars that can't be healed—their brains damaged or their limbs gone. Perhaps he didn't want to risk you suffering that."

She gulped in air. "That's kind of you to say. But we both know that it's far more likely he just didn't . . . want to be burdened with a wife as he set out on his exciting adventure."

"If that's the case, then he was a fool. A complete and utter fool. Any man would be glad to have you waiting for him at home."

"Not any man," she said quietly.

He froze. She was right. He had no business saying such a thing when *he* would not want her waiting for him. Would he? Before he could even think of an answer, she said with forced lightness, "Anyway, it was a long time ago. Whatever his reasons, it's in the past. I acted foolishly, and now this is my life." She managed a smile. "It's not a bad life. I have nieces and nephews to love, and I can come to the brewery whenever I please."

"Annabel—" he began, feeling the need to say something, anything to make her realize her worth.

She touched a finger to his lips. "Let's just enjoy this while we can." She cuddled up against him. "Besides, there's one thing I've always wondered about you. Why did you become a gambler? You have a knack for the brewing business, and you seem to like the work. Surely your grandmother would have been delighted to take you under her wing."

He froze. The last thing he wanted to talk about with *her* was that time in his life. Letting her into his soul that deeply was the surest way to heartbreak. She would give him her soft sympathy, and he would start to care for her, and next thing he knew he'd be standing before a man of the cloth, handing his heart to her on a platter.

Not that he thought she would deliberately hurt him. He was sure she wouldn't. But he'd spent so many years keeping himself remote from anyone who might, that he wasn't about to change that now for a woman he meant to leave in the morning.

"I'm good at gambling, too, you know." He cast her a lazy grin meant to distract her. "That's how I got you into bed."

She didn't smile, her eyes huge in her face. "If you don't want to talk about it, just say so."

With a jolt, he remembered her words earlier: *What have you told me about yourself? Hardly enough for me to make even a sketch of you, much less a full picture.*

"There's nothing to talk about," he said tersely. "Gran

wanted me to become a barrister, as befitted my station. She packed me off to Eton, and I found I preferred gambling to books. You see? All this time you've being saying I'm a scapegrace, and you're right. I don't care about anyone but myself, and I'd rather have a deck of cards in my hand than do anything useful with my time."

"That's not true," she said, her eyes soft. "I know that in your heart—"

"You don't know anything," he snapped, then cursed himself when she flinched. "I'm sorry. It's just that we have only a few hours before I leave for London, and I don't want to spend it talking about my flaws." He ran his hand down her luscious curves. "I'd much rather spend it making good on my promise."

A tiny frown furrowed her brow. "What promise?"

"That I'd have you begging before the night was over."

She opened her mouth, but he cut her off with a long, hot kiss designed to drive any thought from her mind but of *this*. When at last she looped her arms about his neck and he knew he'd won, his blood poured fierce and hot through his veins.

As he tore his lips from hers to kiss his way down to her beautiful breasts, she rasped, "I told you, I never beg."

"Ah, but you will, my Venus. You will."

Then he made sure that she did. This time he pleasured her with his mouth so thoroughly that he brought her to the knife's edge of release within moments. And she did beg, for him to take her, to come inside her. He was only too happy to comply.

After they lay replete the second time, their limbs entwined, he drifted off into a doze, something he had never done with a woman. But there was something so peaceful about being with her, being held by her . . .

"Jarret!" a sharp voice said.

"Hmm?" He came slowly awake to find Annabel standing over him, already wearing her shift, drawers, and stockings.

"You have to help me dress. It's nearly four A.M., and I must return to the house before anyone discovers I'm gone."

"Of course." Wrestling himself from the fog of sleep, he sat up. "Give me a moment."

How long had he slept? A couple of hours at least, just enough to make him feel like a dead man.

She had to be feeling the same sluggishness, yet she cast him a look of such sympathy that something tightened in his chest. "Surely you can sleep a few hours at the inn before you leave, can't you?" Gathering up his clothes, she said, "Though you're probably eager to return to London. I suppose you can always sleep in your carriage."

As she handed him his clothes, then tidied up the room, all he could do was stare at her, so fragile-looking and small in that shift that left nothing to the imagination.

He was supposed to leave today. He would never see her again, never be bothered by Lake Ale's problems. He could go back and report to Gran that she'd been right—the company's pale ale had not been worth the risk to Plumtree Brewery.

The thought made his throat close up. "What will you tell your brother?" he clipped out. "About our meeting tomorrow . . . today, I mean."

"The truth, I suppose."

"Good God."

She whirled around, her cheeks reddening. "Not about you and me. I'll just tell him you changed your mind after seeing the brewery, and that you went back to London." She gave him a sad smile. "It was never very likely that you would help us anyway, was it?"

Suddenly, Jarret didn't like the idea of being a man no one could count on, and he sure as hell didn't like the idea of being yet another man in a long line who'd disappointed her—her father, her brother, her fiancé.

And if he didn't help the Lakes, where would they end up? Would she convince her brother to sell the company? It wouldn't gain them much in this market. Even if they got some money from it, they would soon sink without the income from the brewery. Especially if her brother couldn't get his head out of a bottle.

She could ask another brewer for help, he supposed. Like that damned Allsopp. *Miss Lake will do just about anything to save her father's brewery.* His blood ran cold. Not because she might want to give herself to a lecher like Allsopp, but because she might feel she had no choice. It chafed him raw to think of it.

Rising from the bed, he stalked over to the waning fire to throw the two cundums onto it and watch as they burned. Many a woman had been forced to do unconscionable things to save the people they loved. And the thought of Annabel being one of them . . .

"I'm not leaving for London today." He couldn't. Drunk or no, her brother was the key to saving Lake Ale, and if Jarret left her here alone to deal with the man, he'd be no better than that damned Rupert, with his empty words and emptier promises.

He went to the bed and tugged on his drawers. He could feel her eyes on him.

"Why not?" she asked, clearly perplexed.

He walked over to pick up her corset, then helped her into it. "I'm going to stay here and see what I can do about this scheme of yours, of course."

She froze, then pivoted to face him. "You . . . you'll speak to the East India captains? You'll contract with us for pale ale?"

The hope shimmering in her eyes fairly slew him. "That's what you want, isn't it?"

"Yes!" A brilliant smile broke over her face as she threw herself into his arms. "Yes, yes, yes!" She laughed, the dulcet tones like music, and covered his face with kisses. "But why? You don't have to. The wager—"

"I don't care about that confounded wager," he growled. "You need help, and I want to help. I can spare a few more days to see if we could make this work."

"Oh, Jarret," she whispered, "that is the nicest thing you could ever have done for me." Inexplicably, she began to cry.

Purely masculine panic rose in his chest. "Here now, dearling," he murmured as he folded her close. "I thought you'd be happy."

"I *am* happy," she gasped. "This is what I do when I'm happy."

"Then I'd hate to see what you do when you're sad."

"I cry then, too," she blubbered. "I cry a lot."

It was killing him. How many times had she cried over the man who'd left her and died? How often had her brother driven her to tears? It drove a fist in his gut even to imagine it.

"The only time I don't cry," she said as she attempted to get control of herself, "is when I'm angry. Then I yell."

"I remember." In an attempt to slow her tears, he added, "I never cry. Too messy."

She lifted a teary-eyed gaze to him. "Never?"

"Never."

"That's awful." She swiped at her tears with the back of her hand. "I can't imagine not being able to cry. I feel so much better afterward." She flashed him a watery smile. "Though I look much worse."

"You'll always look like a goddess to me." Realizing how maudlin that sounded, he turned her around so he could continue lacing up her corset . . . and avoid seeing the hope in her eyes. "So where does this meeting with your brother take place?"

"Wherever you want."

"It needs to be here," Jarret said, "and I want both you and Mr. Walters present."

"Of course."

"And I want to see Lake Ale's books."

She froze. "All of them?"

"All of them. I won't sign any contract with your company until I'm sure that one of you can keep the place going long enough to get this ale on the ships to India."

A sigh escaped her. "I don't know if Hugh will agree to that."

"He'd better, if he wants me to help him."

As he finished lacing her up, she squared her shoulders. "Then I'll make sure he does."

He couldn't prevent a smile. For all her tears, she was stalwart, ready to throw herself into any fray. "I'll need a list of your suppliers. And if you know anything about the operations of Allsopp and Bass, I'll need that information, too."

"All right."

While they dressed, he dictated other demands, mostly to make her understand that this would by no means be easy. They would have to work hard to make it happen.

When they were both ready, he said, "I'll walk you home."

"Absolutely not." Her voice was firm. "I won't chance anyone seeing us together."

"But Annabel, it's not safe."

She laughed. "I'm as safe walking Burton's streets, even at this hour, as I would be in my own home." She nodded at the door. "You leave first, and try to get into the inn without being seen. I'll follow shortly after."

He didn't like it, but he could tell she was going to be stubborn about it. "Very well." He started for the door, then paused to glance at her. "When can I see you again?"

"In a few hours, at the meeting," she retorted.

He frowned. "That's not what I mean, and you know it."

The color rose in her cheeks, but she met his gaze steadily. "Is . . . seeing me again a requirement of your staying here to help us?"

"No, damn it! That's not why I asked."

She stared at him, as if to assess his sincerity. Then a soft smile curved up her lips. "In that case, you may see me whenever you like."

His heart began to pound. "Tonight? Same time? Here?"

Mischief sparked in her eyes. "If that's what you wish, my lord."

"What I wish," he growled as he walked back to her and hauled her into his arms, "is to have you stop calling me *my lord*."

He took her mouth with his, glorying in how freely she gave herself up to it. He never tired of kissing her. Her kisses were like a drug to his senses, and he was fast becoming addicted.

She let him kiss her only a moment before pushing him away. "That's enough of that. We have a long day ahead of us."

He eyed her askance. "I can see you're going to be a stern taskmaster, Miss Lake."

"You have no idea." She reached up to smooth a lock of his hair. "Thank you."

"You're welcome."

He left then, his heart and his steps light, feeling like some knight in shining armor. Damned if it didn't feel good to be helping someone. To be helping *her*.

He could easily get used to the thought of Annabel always in his arms. If he wasn't careful, she'd have him wrapped around her little finger as thoroughly as Maria had wrapped his brother around hers.

He snorted. That was absurd. He was just doing a kindness for her. Not even a kindness—a business venture that made perfect sense, as long as he could control the variables. It was a way to boost Plumtree's flagging sales; nothing more.

By the time he reached the inn, he'd almost convinced himself that was true.

# Chapter Nineteen

Annabel practically danced through the streets of Burton. It was ridiculous, but she couldn't stop smiling. Surely the fact that Jarret had agreed to stay and help Lake Ale meant something.

Her rational mind told her it was daft to think he actually might care for her; her heart desperately wanted to believe it. Perhaps in time . . .

She mustn't torment herself with such hopes. Jarret hadn't said one word about marriage or love. The only thing he'd wanted was to ensure that they could do *that* again.

As a heady swirl of temptation rose in her body, she chided herself for being so wanton. But really, she couldn't help it. Who could have guessed that lovemaking really was so wonderful? She'd guessed that it might be, and she'd certainly liked all the parts that came before and after. But until Jarret, she hadn't realized that the act itself could be so downright glorious.

She reached the house and unlocked the door, glancing around to make sure no one had seen her. Then she slipped inside and removed her boots so she could get to her room without making any sound.

"Where have you been?" said a sonorous male voice.

She froze, her heart stampeding into triple time. Not again. Oh Lord, not again.

Then she settled her shoulders. She was not a girl of seventeen anymore, to be cowering at the voice of her brother. Schooling her expression into nonchalance, she turned toward him.

Hugh sat sprawled in a chair in the parlor. He didn't have a glass in his hand, but he looked weary, as if he'd been sitting there for quite a while. Pushing up from the chair, he came toward her with a grim expression. "Where have you been?" he repeated.

"At the brewery," she said.

That seemed to throw him off guard. "And what were you doing there?"

"I figured I'd better prepare for the meeting tomorrow. We had no time to gather information before, so I had to do it tonight." Thank heaven she'd spent a couple of hours before the dinner with Mr. Walters, pulling out files and laying out records they might need for the meeting. She could claim to have been going over those.

Lord, how she hated the lies. She hated lying to Hugh. She hated lying to Geordie. She hated lying *about* Geordie. She was sick to death of subterfuge and sneaking around. It would have to stop soon. She couldn't go on like this.

"Why?" she asked. "Where did you think I'd gone?"

Hugh dragged a heavy hand through his hair. "I'm sorry, Annie. I thought perhaps you and his lordship . . ." His shoulders slumped. "It was foolish. I ought to know better by now." He cast her a wan smile. "Don't mind me. It's been a long day, and I couldn't sleep. When I knocked on your door, and you weren't there, I got worried."

She remained silent. He was already so close to guessing the truth, she dared not let him guess any more. Or he would surely strangle Jarret with his bare hands.

"But you shouldn't be going to the brewery late at night alone," he went on. "It's not safe."

She eyed him askance. "I've been going there for years, and no one's there at night anyway."

Hugh frowned. "If a man were to follow you in there, you could be hurt." He stepped up close to her. "Annie, I know that you've had to take up the burden of the place far too much lately, but that's going to change. I want to do right by you and Sissy and the children. If even Geordie has noticed . . ." He squared his shoulders. "I'm going to look after you all better, I promise. And that means no more going to the brewery alone at night, you understand? I would never forgive myself if something happened to you."

"Now, Hugh . . ."

"I mean it. Swear to me you won't be traipsing off about town alone. It's not safe, even in Burton. Promise me."

Frustration knotted her insides. Why did Hugh have to choose *now* to remember he had a family?

She wouldn't be able to meet Jarret if Hugh was going to prowl the house late at night, watching for her. But he'd taken her in, and given her son his name. She couldn't repay that by shaming him or Sissy.

She sighed. "I promise."

"Good," he said, flashing her a hesitant smile. "Good." He held out his arm to her. "Now come, we should get a little sleep before we have to meet with Lord Jarret. Don't want to let him get the better of us in this bargain, eh?"

A hysterical laugh bubbled up in her throat that she swiftly squelched. If Hugh only knew how close they'd come to not having a bargain at all. Yet another secret she must keep.

As she slid into her bed later, it dawned on her that she'd have to tell Jarret about the change in their plans. Pressure built in her chest. What if he changed his mind about staying?

No, she mustn't think that. He'd said that being with her was not a condition for his help, and she believed him.

A shaky breath escaped her as she stared up at the ornate plaster ceiling medallion. She wanted to see him again. Wanted to feel his body meld with hers, feel his heart beat against his breast. She fell asleep remembering the touch of his hand on her cheek.

The next morning was a frantic one. She'd thought of a way to see Jarret alone for a few minutes, but other than that, she had little time to prepare for the meeting. By ten o'clock, when they all assembled at the office in Lake Ale, she was exhausted.

Jarret looked as tired as she felt. He mentioned playing cards late into the night to excuse his weariness, but she could hardly look at him for fear of giving something away.

Like how it felt to be in the same room where they'd last embraced. How it hurt to see the little door leading to their private meeting place and know that it had been their last time together.

"As I told Miss Lake at the dinner," Jarret said, "I'd like to see Lake Ale's books before we go any further. I need to be sure that you have the capacity to follow through on your proposal."

Hugh's startled gaze swung to her. "Annie, you didn't say anything about his wanting to see the books."

She feigned bewilderment. "Didn't I? I could swear I did. I'm sorry, last night is a bit of a blur. I got little sleep."

"I dare say." Hugh glanced over at Jarret, who was watching them both warily. "My fool of a sister came up here to work on gathering information for you, my lord. At night, alone. I told her it's not safe, but she doesn't listen."

She forced a smile. "My brother was waiting to chastise me when I came in the house. He's so solicitous of my welfare."

Jarret's eyes gave away none of what he was thinking. "I can see that," he said noncommittally.

"I'm not sure if I like the idea of your seeing the books, my lord," Hugh said. "You're our competitor—"

"Who is soon to be a partner of sorts. I need more information before I can make an informed decision on how we should structure this arrangement."

"I see no reason for his lordship not to look at them," Mr. Walters told Hugh. "He's offering us an opportunity we can't afford to pass up. And we have nothing to hide."

Hugh pursed his lips, then sighed. "I suppose not. Very well, we'll have to fetch them." He frowned at Annabel. "I wish you'd told me before. I would have brought them with me. Now we'll have to go back to the house, since they're in the safe."

*Exactly.* "Do you want to take Mr. Walters? He can help you carry them."

"One of the footmen will help me."

"They're both at the market with Sissy. We needed several things after having been gone so long." And she'd suggested to Sissy that this would be the perfect time for that.

Hugh's eyes narrowed as he glanced from her to Jarret. "You'd better come, too, Annie."

"Don't be absurd. I can begin discussing some of the

material with his lordship. And it's not as if he and I need a chaperone." She gestured to the window behind them. "We have at least twenty men working in the brewery who can see us at any given moment."

Her brother hesitated, then conceded the point with a faint nod. "All right, then." He rose. "Come with me, Walters. We'd best go fetch those books."

As soon as they were gone, she slid into the chair behind the desk opposite where Jarret was sitting. "We only have a few minutes," she said in a low voice.

"I wondered if you engineered this." His eyes filled with concern. "Your brother caught you sneaking in last night?"

"Yes. And he made me promise I wouldn't come here at night alone anymore."

Scowling, Jarret settled back in his chair. "I see."

"It's not what I want, either. My brother has his faults, but he and Sissy treat me well, and I can't shame them by having them think I'm . . . well . . ."

"Letting me bed you."

She nodded. "If Hugh even guessed the truth, he'd call you out. And that would do none of us any good."

"So we can't—"

"No. I don't see any way." Unless Jarret chose to court her, which he wasn't going to do. And even if he did, she couldn't marry him. What would she do about Geordie? "It's probably just as well. When you leave, it will end anyway."

"It doesn't have to," he said.

She stared at him, her pulse jumping into a staccato rhythm. "What do you mean?"

Eyes the color of the sea locked with hers. "You could come to London with me. I could find you a position at Plumtree."

Her heart sank. "A position at Plumtree? Or a position in your bed?"

His gaze grew shuttered. "Both, if you wish."

"You're offering to make me your mistress."

"No, I . . ." He glanced away, his jaw tightening. "I'm offering you a chance to get away from your family. To have your own life. You're a fine brewster—you could brew at Plumtree. And from time to time, if you wanted to . . ." He met her gaze again, his face a picture of belligerence. "You wouldn't have to be my mistress, but why not take a lover if you wish?"

She fought to hide her disappointment. Of course he would offer that. When had he ever offered more? "I don't need a lover, Jarret. And I have no desire to get away from my family or Lake Ale."

He leaned forward, then caught himself, glancing behind him at the brewery. "How much can they see from out there?"

"Why?"

"Because I want to touch you, damn it."

And she *wanted* him to touch her. How hopelessly foolish she was. "They can't see below your shoulders," she admitted.

"Good." He reached over the desk to clasp her hands in his. "You deserve better than a life as the poor relation. You're a beautiful, vibrant woman. If you're not interested in marriage, why not live your life as you please?"

"I'm already living my life as I please."

His dark gaze burned into her. "Really? Lying in your bed alone at night with only your memories for company? Watching someone else's children?"

She met his gaze steadily. "And whose children would I be watching otherwise—yours?"

That seemed to stun him. Releasing her hands, he leaned back in the chair, his face a mix of anger and uncertainty.

"You see, Jarret?" she said softly. "It can't work. We want different things. You want to follow the wind where it leads, and I want to dig my roots deep. You're a river, and I'm a tree. The tree can never follow the river, and the river can never stay with the tree."

He let out a coarse oath. "So this is the end for us. Is that really what you want?" His booted foot touched her slipper beneath the desk, and he stroked his leg along hers in a sensual caress that made her blood heat. "No more nights in each other's arms. No more trips to heaven."

"Of course that's not what I want!" she cried, frustrated by his inability to see beyond his own desires. "But I won't throw my life away on a man who shares nothing of himself with me, who has no aim beyond thwarting his grandmother's plans for him, and who thinks that spending his days in frivolous pursuits will keep him happy."

"Happiness is fickle," he growled. "Look at you—you thought you'd be happy when you gave yourself to Rupert. Instead, it ruined your life. Our only choice is to seize the pleasures of life where we can. Hoping for more is a fruitless endeavor."

"So says the river." She flashed him a sad smile. "Not only can the tree not follow the river, but if it bathes in it, it rots and dies. I won't go to London to rot, Jarret."

Striving not to show how much he'd wounded her, she rose to gather up the papers they would need for the meeting. "My brother will be back soon, and when he returns he'll need to see that we've been productive while he was gone, or he'll get suspicious. So let's review the analysis of costs that I had Mr. Walters put together."

The silence of his displeasure was a palpable pressure in the room, but she ignored it. When he was gone, she still had a life to live. She wasn't going to abandon her son or her family simply because he wanted to play with her for a while. Let him go to his London whores for that.

The thought shot a sharp pain through her breast. But this was only temporary. *He* was only temporary. And she refused to let him ensnare her so totally that she lost herself.

# Chapter Twenty

Jarret had thought for sure that Annabel would relent in the days that followed. Every day, he expected her to get him alone again to say she'd changed her mind, that she would meet him for a night of mutual pleasure. Every evening in the inn, he half expected her to show up in his room.

She never did.

The rational part of him understood why. She lived the life of a respectable woman. The community seemed to hold her in high regard, even if her neighbors sometimes didn't understand her efforts with her brother's brewery. And although Hugh Lake hadn't taken care of his family as he should, they were closely knit and clearly fond of each other.

He was the interloper. For the first time in his life, he resented that. He hated having Annabel treat him like a business acquaintance when they'd been so much more to each other.

They could still be so much more, if she weren't so stubborn. All right, so he shouldn't have offered to take her with him to London. That had been beyond the pale, asking her to lower herself when she had no cause to do so.

But damn it, he wanted to be with her again! And again, as often as he could. Worse yet, he knew she wanted to be with *him.* In unguarded moments, he saw it in the way she looked at him.

Since she made damned sure they were never alone, there was no chance of blatantly seducing her, and she cut off his more subtle efforts whenever he attempted them. If he brushed her fingers as she handed him some papers, she stopped handing him papers. If he stroked her leg under the table, she trod on his foot.

As the days wore on, he saw less and less of her, since she was busy overseeing the brewing of the pale ale. Meanwhile, he, Lake, and Walters continued to hammer out a contract that suited both companies, so he was increasingly occupied with that.

Thank God he got to see her in the evenings, which were spent with the Lakes. Their dinners had begun as strained affairs, because Lake had been resentful of his presence. But as they'd come to know each other over the negotiations, Lake had relaxed, and now treated him like an honored guest.

After dinner every night he and Lake retired to their port, but the man drank little, no doubt aware of Jarret's eyes on him. They spent only a short while away from the ladies before joining them in the parlor, where the evening generally consisted of reading or playing charades. Every night he suffered the torture of watching Annabel, knowing that he couldn't touch her.

Tonight it was even worse. He and Lake had made serious headway on their agreement. Tomorrow they had a few more details to take care of, and then there was no longer any reason for him to stay. Indeed, he'd already received one letter from Gran chiding him for neglecting the business in London. By the day after tomorrow, he could be on the road.

And he didn't want to leave.

He scowled. This was what came of letting a woman under one's skin. She tempted him to want things that were ephemeral. She made him yearn.

Tonight she was driving him slowly insane. Her gown left just enough of her creamy shoulders bare to remind him of what it had felt like to caress them. Every time she tilted her head toward one of the children, exposing the slender column of her neck, he had a fierce urge to seize her and plant a kiss on her throat, to lick the pulse there until it jumped into the wild rhythm that showed she felt more for him than she dared display.

It wasn't just that, however. Tonight the children were with them, since their nursery maid had the evening off. While he and Lake sat to one side playing loo, and Mrs. Lake embroidered a cushion, Annabel and the children gamboled about the parlor.

They adored their aunt Annabel's singing, and rightfully so, since her clear, sweet soprano was well suited to children's songs. They begged for any ditty that involved jumping about like monkeys or contorting one's body into ridiculous shapes. Even Geordie, who claimed to be too old for such nonsense, was swinging the younger ones about and lifting his little brother to ride on his shoulders.

The cozy family scene reminded Jarret painfully of his own family before his world had crumbled. He couldn't look away—their antics and her cheerful endurance of them captivated him to the point that he paid little attention to his cards. It was strange to watch a woman he desired so fiercely playing nursemaid to a handful of giggling urchins. He shouldn't find it enchanting, but he did.

Her words of a few days ago sprang into his mind: *And whose children would I be watching otherwise—yours?*

Until that moment, he hadn't even thought about having children of his own. He had no need to bear an heir, no need for a wife when there were taproom maids aplenty to tumble, and no wish to alter his way of life for some screeching harpy who didn't approve of his late evenings and reckless gambling.

But the thought of giving *Annabel* children stole the breath from his body. Any children he and Annabel might have would probably resemble the motley crew presently wreaking havoc in the parlor—bright-eyed and ruddy-cheeked, their legs akimbo and laughter spilling from their mouths. Except that they would have his eyes or his hair or his nose. And they would call him Father.

A terrifying thought. To have children dependent on him, looking to him for guidance, expecting great things of him . . . his mind boggled. How could he ever live up to such expectations?

"Enough!" Annabel dropped into a chair and flattened her hand against her chest. "I'm all sung out."

"Please, Aunt Annabel," begged the youngest, a five-year-old girl called Katie. "One more."

"It's always one more with you children," Mrs. Lake said. "Leave your aunt alone. You'll make her hoarse."

"Perhaps you can convince Lord Jarret to sing." Annabel looked mischievous. "Assuming he knows any songs that can be sung in polite company."

"I know a couple," he answered, "but you'd be better off

asking a fish to play the pianoforte. Trust me, no one would want to hear me sing."

"I can hardly believe that," Annabel protested. "You have such a lovely speaking voice."

He barely had time to register that she found his voice lovely before the children ran up to clamor for a performance. He held out as long as he could, but relented when little Katie stuck her thumb in her mouth and looked as if she might cry. "Fine," he said. "But you'll regret it."

Rising to his feet, he made a production of clearing his throat and uttering noises like the ones he'd seen professional singers make. Then he launched into the only children's song he could think of: "Hot Cross Buns."

At the first notes, the children gaped at him as if someone in the room had just farted. Even Annabel blinked, and Mrs. Lake looked downright stunned.

He plowed on with great enthusiasm anyway. It wasn't as if he hadn't warned them, and he hadn't been allowed to sing to anyone since his family had first discovered his deficit. Fortunately "Hot Cross Buns" was short, so he only had to torture them for a minute or two.

When he was done, a tense silence fell upon the room. Then Annabel said, eyes twinkling, "That has to be the worst rendition of 'Hot Cross Buns' I have ever heard."

"Annabel!" Mrs. Lake said.

"Trust me, I'm not offended," he told her with a smug smile. "I know my limitations."

"Your singing is like cats fighting," Geordie ventured.

"More like cats screaming, or so I've been told," Jarret said. "Gabe claims I sound like a fiddle that has been stomped on."

"Or a flute with a walnut in it," one of the children supplied.

"Do it again!" Katie cried. "I like it!"

Astonished, Jarret knelt to stare into her face. "You like it, moppet?" He glanced at Mrs. Lake. "You neglected to tell me, madam, that insanity runs in your family."

The others laughed, but Katie wouldn't be put off. "I don't know what 'sanity' means, sir, but your singing reminds me of the owl that screeches outside the nursery every night. I like owls. Can you sing another?"

Jarret laughed and chucked her under the chin. "Sorry, dear girl, but your parents would have me tarred and feathered."

She clapped her hands. "That sounds like fun, too!"

He cast Annabel an amused glance over Katie's head. "Your aunt would certainly enjoy it." He leaned close to whisper loudly, "She likes to make me suffer."

Annabel's blush sent the blood roaring through his veins. Then she shot him a chiding look as she held out her hands to her nieces and nephews. "Come, children, it's nearly bedtime. Let's leave his lordship and your papa in peace to finish their card game, shall we?"

"But I want to see his lordship tarred and feathered!" Katie cried. "Mama, what's 'tarred' mean?"

As the adults laughed, Annabel gathered up the children. Ignoring their whining, she and Mrs. Lake shooed them toward the stairs while Jarret rose to take his seat at the card table again. But when he picked up his cards, he noticed Lake staring at him with an assessing gaze.

"Something on your mind, sir?" he asked.

Lake set down his hand. "Forgive me for being blunt, my lord, but why did you decide to come here and help us? Even if this scheme works, there will be little benefit for Plumtree Brewery in it."

Jarret arranged his cards. "I disagree. I've seen enough of

Allsopp's success to know that it could be beneficial for us both."

"If I can sustain it," Lake said, a troubled expression crossing his brow. "Which is by no means certain."

Jarret weighed his words carefully. "Having spent a great deal of time with you this week, I've come to realize that what your sister says about you is true. You have good business instincts. You just don't trust them."

"You see how close Lake Ale is to the edge," Lake retorted. "Does that seem indicative of a man with good business instincts?"

"It's not your instincts that are the problem. It's your tendency to drown them in a bottle."

To Lake's credit, although anger flared in his face, he didn't try to deny anything. "My drinking didn't create the problems with the Russian market. My drinking didn't raise the price of barrels or hops."

"That's true. But a man's strength is measured by how he reacts to life's challenges. And until now, you haven't reacted particularly well."

"You ought to know what that's like," Lake shot back. "From what I understand, you react to 'life's challenges' by avoiding them entirely at the gaming table."

Jarret gritted his teeth, but he couldn't deny the accusation. Granted, he'd had no family to support, no reason to step in at the brewery when Gran held the reins—but he could have tried.

How would his life have been different if he'd approached Gran ten years ago and asked to be given another chance? At the time, he'd thought it foolish to invest his life in such an endeavor when all he ever got for his efforts was grief.

Now he began to wonder if that decision had been foolish.

Not trying had gained him nothing, for here he was ten years later, running the brewery anyway. If he'd started back then, he might have prevented some of the problems with the Russian market. He might even have kept Gran from getting so angry at her grandchildren that she'd felt compelled to lay down her fateful ultimatum.

That thought was sobering.

"You're right," he said. "I'm not qualified to give advice about how to deal with the hand that Fate deals us. But I'm learning from my mistakes, and one thing I'm learning is that hiding solves nothing. It just delays the inevitable. Better to make an attempt and fail, than not to make an attempt at all."

It was true. He'd found more hope, more enjoyment during this week of creating a future for their two companies than he had in years of gambling. The hand a man received might be unpredictable, but as in cards, what the man made of that hand could change everything.

The anger had faded from Lake's features, but he was still watching Jarret as warily as a fox watches the hunter. "You haven't answered my question. Why did you come here? How did Annie convince you to consider it?"

"Your sister can be very persuasive," he evaded.

Lake nodded. "She's also very pretty—something I believe you've noticed."

"A man would have to be blind not to notice that." He dared not say more until he knew where Lake was leading.

"*I* have noticed that you've stayed longer in Burton than was strictly necessary to negotiate the terms of our deal. Is there a reason for that?"

Jarret grew irritated with this cat-and-mouse game. "Whatever you wish to say to me, sir, say it."

"Very well." Giving up any pretense of continuing their game, Lake leaned back in his chair and folded his arms over his chest. "If you have honorable intentions toward my sister, you should speak up. If not, I suggest that you leave her be."

The warning was not entirely unexpected, but it rankled all the same. "What makes you think I have any intentions, honorable or otherwise, toward her?"

"For one thing, you have an uncanny ability to make her blush. I've never seen Annie blush as often as she has in the time you've been here."

Jarret forced a smile. "I make a great many women blush, Lake. I don't mean anything by it."

"That is my point exactly. I don't wish to see my sister's heart broken by a scoundrel."

Jarret's eyes narrowed. "Your sister is perfectly capable of protecting her heart from anyone."

"She had her heart broken by a rascal before."

That threw Jarret off guard. "Surely you're not referring to the heroic Rupert."

Lake snorted. "A hero doesn't court a woman above his station when he knows her family doesn't approve."

"Your father didn't approve of Rupert?"

An exasperated look crossed Lake's face. "Father knew, as did I, that Rupert was an impetuous young man with more pluck than brains. He had no money to support a wife and wasn't likely ever to get any. His father left him and his brother with nothing, and though they worked hard, they had no ambition. Given time, I suspect Annie would have seen that, and the romance would have ended of its own accord."

"So that's why your father asked them to wait to marry?"

Lake nodded. "Father knew that if he out-and-out forbade her to see Rupert, my willful sister would do the opposite. So he took a more subtle approach, hoping that if he delayed the wedding, she would eventually come to her senses."

"But the subtle approach didn't work."

"It worked better than my method, which was to try to separate them." He stared off across the room, a hint of remorse on his face. "That proved disastrous."

"How?" Jarret asked, curious to know how much Lake would reveal about what had happened between Annabel and Rupert.

Lake's sharp gaze swung to him. "The man went off to war and took her heart with him, that's how. Then he got himself killed. And she hasn't been the same since."

The thought of her pining for Rupert drove a dagger in his chest. She'd spoken of her guilt over Rupert's death, her pain that he might not have wanted her. But she'd never said if she still loved the man. That bothered him.

"Well, if her heart is still with Rupert, you needn't worry that she'll give it to me."

"Do you *want* her heart?" Lake asked.

Another blunt question. It deserved a blunt answer. "I don't know."

That didn't seem to surprise Lake. "Until you do, I suggest you leave her alone."

It was almost funny; Jarret had said something very similar to Masters not a week ago.

Lake had every reason to warn him off, and it was a mark of the man's integrity that he cared so much for his sister. Jarret admired that.

But none of it made absolutely any difference in how he

intended to treat Annabel. After days without being able to get near her, he burned even more for her than before. He *had* to see her again alone.

Making love to her should have dampened his need—it always had before with the women who flitted in and out of his life. Then again, Annabel wasn't like those women. He craved her intensely.

Unexpected noises in the foyer made him and Lake turn toward the door. Then a familiar female voice wafted to him. "I was told I might find Lord Jarret Sharpe here. Is that true?"

Jarret rose from his chair with a sigh. Confound it all to hell. He had a sneaking suspicion that his time in Burton had just come to an end.

# Chapter Twenty-one

Annabel came down the stairs slowly, her heart in her throat as she heard the interchange with the butler. The woman was here for Jarret. What did that mean? Had he lied about his associations with women? Did he have a mistress? Or even a fiancée?

The thought drove a stake through her heart.

Especially since the woman was quite beautiful. Curls of sun-kissed bronze framed a face with laughing features, and a fashionable carriage dress of rose-lavender *gros de Naples* outlined a curvaceous form that any man would desire.

Swallowing her envy, Annabel hurried the rest of the way down the stairs. "You're looking for his lordship?" she said as she reached the bottom.

A pair of green eyes that looked oddly familiar met hers. "Yes. The innkeeper at the Peacock told us he was probably here."

*Us?* "He is indeed. He dined here tonight and is playing cards with my brother."

"Then you must be Miss Lake!" the woman exclaimed,

seeming very happy to hear it. "Gabe has told me all about you." At Annabel's perplexed expression, she added, "I'm Minerva Sharpe."

"My sister," Jarret added from the doorway. "I believe I mentioned her to you a few nights ago, Miss Lake."

Remembering the context of that remark, Annabel blushed.

Clearly he remembered, too, for a roguish smile curved his lips before he turned to his sister. "What are you doing here?"

Lady Minerva frowned. "That is no way to greet your sister. At least give me a kiss."

"No kisses until you tell me what you're doing traveling alone across England."

"I'm not alone, silly. Gabe and Mr. Pinter are outside arguing over who should pay for the carriage that took us scarcely half a mile from the inn."

The look on Jarret's face was almost comical. "Pinter and Gabe are here, too? Good God, please tell me you didn't bring Gran along."

"She wanted to come, but Dr. Wright forbade it. So I've been instructed to give you a message from her." She promptly swatted Jarret's hand with her fan.

"Ow!" He rubbed his hand. "What the hell was that for?"

"I told you—a message from Gran. She wants you home."

Annabel couldn't resist a laugh, which gained her a glare from Jarret.

He then turned it on his sister. "I've got a message for *her*. Tell Gran she can damned well wait until I'm ready to return."

At that moment, Lord Gabriel and Mr. Pinter came through the front door, nearly colliding with Hugh as he emerged from the parlor. A flurry of introductions followed. Sissy, coming down from upstairs, joined the fray.

A short while later they were all ensconced in the dining room, being served ale and wine while Cook rushed to throw together a repast for their surprise visitors.

"Really, Mrs. Lake," Lady Minerva said for the third time, "we don't wish to put you to any trouble. We just came to fetch Jarret, that's all."

"Nonsense," Sissy said. "You've been traveling all day, and Lord Gabriel says you haven't even had dinner. It's no trouble at all. Any friends and family of Lord Jarret's are very welcome here."

Lady Minerva smiled her thanks, then glanced at Annabel with blatant curiosity.

Annabel tried to look nonchalant, but her heart pounded. They were here to fetch Jarret. He'd be leaving shortly. She'd known this day would come soon, but now that it was upon her, she didn't know how she could endure it.

It had been easier to barricade her heart from him that first day, with Hugh's words ringing in her ears about how worried he'd been, but it had grown increasingly harder as the week had gone on.

Sometimes Jarret gazed at her with such heat that she feared she might boil over. He followed her with his eyes, and she followed him with all of her senses, aware at every moment of how he smelled, where he stood, to whom he spoke, what he said.

Worst of all were the nights, filled with memories of their amazing evening together. In bed she touched herself, remembering the feel of his hand arousing her body . . . kneading her breasts, sliding between her legs . . . taking her to heaven over and over and . . .

"Do pour me some of that orgeat, Miss Lake," Lady Minerva said as she held out her glass. "Judging from your expression of pure bliss, it must be delicious."

Annabel started, color flooding her face. When she caught Jarret's considering gaze on her, she wanted to sink through the floor. Did he read minds? Did the entire *family* read minds, for pity's sake?

In silence, she filled Lady Minerva's glass, afraid that if she spoke, she'd say something that gave away her feelings.

After watching her a moment, Jarret settled back in his chair. "Now tell me, Minerva, what's of such dire importance that Gran sent you up here to 'fetch' me?"

"Actually," Lord Gabriel cut in, "Gran sent *me*. Minerva just came along because she's nosy."

"Not nosy," Lady Minerva protested. "Desperate. Gran is driving me mad. She keeps inviting unattached men to join the family for dinner, and if I try to get out of it, she fakes an attack."

"Are you sure she's faking?" Jarret asked with a frown.

"She recovers well enough to show up at dinner, so what do *you* think?"

Jarret chuckled. "She must be feeling better if she's up to her shenanigans again." He met Annabel's gaze from across the room. "All the more reason that I need not rush back."

"We don't want to keep you from your duties at Plumtree Brewery," Hugh said. "You and I can put the final touches on our agreement tomorrow, and you could be on your way by noon."

That twisted the knife in Annabel's heart.

A look of sheer frustration crossed Jarret's face as he stared at Annabel. "There were a few more things I wanted to discuss with you. It might take us another day at least."

"I'm happy to stay a day or two," Lady Minerva said, "but Gran's instructions were specific. We were to bring you back in time for the meeting with the maltmen."

"Confound it all—I completely forgot about that."

"If we leave by noon tomorrow, we'll just make it, but we can't leave any later than that," Lady Minerva said.

Annabel forced herself to be practical. "And the sooner you return to London, the sooner you can make our case to the East India captains," she pointed out. "Perhaps it's just as well." The thought of his leaving was killing her.

Something fierce flickered in his eyes as they met hers. "Perhaps."

The word was noncommittal. Even Lord Gabriel noticed, for he elbowed his sister, who sat next to him on the settee. "Sounds to me like old Jarret has grown rather attached to Burton, eh?"

Jarret ignored his brother, turning to the quiet Mr. Pinter. "I take it you've brought news, too?"

"Yes, sir. I've looked into those two matters you wanted me to explore. Since I wasn't sure if Lady Minerva and Lord Gabriel would be able to convince you to return, I thought it best to come consult with you on how to proceed."

"He won't say a word about these mysterious 'matters' of yours," Lady Minerva complained. "I've tried to coax it out of him for the whole trip."

"More like 'bully,'" Lord Gabriel said with a laugh. He cast Annabel a conspiratorial glance. "Our sister could strip the paint off a wall with her tongue if she had a mind to. You two would make quite a pair."

Lady Minerva flashed Annabel a dazzling smile. "So he keeps telling me, but I can't imagine what he means. You've been downright shy ever since we arrived."

"Because she can't get a word in edgewise with you," Jarret put in. "Give her a chance, and she can rival even your tongue."

"Feel free to take your brother off whenever you wish," Annabel said tartly. "We won't miss him, I'll warrant."

Everyone laughed. Except Jarret. "Not even a little?" His silky voice made shivers run along her spine.

She caught Hugh watching them and forced a light smile to her lips. "Only when we need someone to scare the townfolk from their beds with a song."

Lord Gabriel laughed. "Good God, if you heard Jarret sing, then I don't blame you for wanting to be rid of him. Never mind Minerva's tongue—Jarret's *singing* could strip the paint from the walls. It could curdle milk. It could—"

"Enough," Jarret said irritably. "They already know how bad my singing is."

"And how good your card playing is, I gather," Lady Minerva said. "Gabe told me how you and Miss Lake played two-handed whist for—"

Annabel jumped to her feet. "Forgive the interruption, Lady Minerva, but I must go check on what's happened with your dinner. Perhaps you'd come with me? We have an interesting Turner print in the hall that I'm sure you would like, since it depicts a castle much like those in Gothic novels, and I understand you write those. Is that true?"

She was babbling, but what else could she do? She didn't want Hugh to learn about the card game or the wager.

Lady Minerva looked bemused, but she stood. "I do write Gothic novels, and I happen to adore Turner."

"So do I," Jarret surprised her by saying. "I'll come with you."

But as soon as the three of them were in the hall well away

from the dining room, he told his sister, "The Turner is over there. Give it a good look, will you, while I speak to Miss Lake?"

A tinkling laugh escaped the young woman. "Whatever you say, Jarret. I'll wait here for further instructions."

Ignoring his sister's teasing tone, Jarret pulled Annabel across the hall into Hugh's study.

As soon as they were alone, he hauled her into his arms and kissed her with a fervency that sent her head spinning. She ought to resist, but how could she with the knowledge of his impending departure weighing so heavily on her chest?

She curled her fingers into his lapels and held on for dear life as he brought all his powers of seduction to bear, focusing them entirely on ravaging her mouth, making her want to swoon. Or beg.

That thought sobered her enough to make her break the kiss.

He pressed his mouth to her ear, his words heated, urgent. "I have to see you tonight."

"Why?"

"You know why."

She did. Worse, she wanted to go. Right now she didn't care about Hugh or Geordie or anything but being in Jarret's arms again. "The same place?"

He drew back with a narrowed gaze. "I thought I'd have to twist your arm a bit."

"You *are* twisting my arm," she pointed out. *And very effectively, too.*

Skimming his hands down to her behind, he dragged her into the lee of his thighs. "I'm happy to twist it some more," he said in a husky tone as he sought her mouth again.

"Not here." She wriggled free of his embrace. "Later. At the brewery."

Fire leapt in his eyes. "Are you sure you can get away? I don't want to cause trouble for you with your brother."

"I'm not sure, but I'll try."

He grabbed her hand and kissed it, then turned it over to kiss her wrist where the pulse beat a wild refrain. "Try hard," he urged her in a guttural voice. "I'm not leaving Burton until I can see you alone again."

Before she could answer, a whisper came from just outside the door. "Jarret, I hear servants approaching."

With a frustrated curse, he tugged Annabel back the way they'd come. Though he released her hand as soon as they reached the hall, she could feel his eyes on her like a caress. And when the three of them merged with the servants to head for the dining room, he took advantage of the confusion to whisper, "Until tonight, sweet Venus."

Her heart melted. She'd honestly thought she'd fortified her heart against him a little, but with every day, he'd been chipping away at those walls, and now they were nothing but piles of rubble.

The next few hours were pure torture. She could think only of what was ahead. Watching Jarret with his family was painful—they were clearly affectionate toward each other, and she envied them the chance to see him every day when she could only have him for one more night. She found she liked Lady Minerva a great deal, and Lord Gabriel kept them all laughing with tales of his racing exploits.

Once the Sharpes and Mr. Pinter left, she told her brother and Sissy that she was going to retire. When she reached her room she sent away the maid, saying that she would undress herself. Then she paced and fretted, wondering how she could leave the house without alerting Hugh that she was gone. She knew from the servants that he stayed up late every night. No doubt he was keeping an eye on *her*.

And with good reason. She shouldn't even consider this. What difference would one more night make? Her heart would be just as broken with or without it.

Still, she yearned for another night with him. It was like a sickness, this need to see him.

A sudden knock at the door made her start. Before she could jump into bed, Sissy entered. "I see you're still dressed."

Annabel's mind was a blank. She couldn't even drum up an excuse for why she hadn't donned her nightdress yet.

"I suppose you're going to the brewery to work," Sissy went on. As Annabel gaped at her, she added, "Hugh told me that you went there our first night back, and that he forbade you to go again."

"Yes. He says it's too dangerous."

"But I'm sure you must need to go tonight." Her sister-in-law searched her face. "With his lordship leaving tomorrow, you probably have a great deal to do." Her voice softened. "I understand, as your brother does not, that sometimes a woman has certain . . . needs. You *need* to go to the brewery. And I don't blame you."

Annabel stared hard at her sister-in-law. Was Sissy being particularly obtuse tonight? Or was she actually implying that she knew the real reason behind Annabel's desire to go to the brewery?

She chose her words carefully. "Hugh would disapprove."

Sissy shrugged. "You're his sister. What do you expect? But that doesn't mean it's wrong for you to . . . pursue something you think is important." She shot Annabel an earnest look. "I can take care of Hugh if you feel compelled to go to the brewery tonight."

Hope rose in Annabel's chest. "How?"

Sissy laughed. "I've been married to the man for thirteen years. I think I know how to distract him." A sly look crossed her face. "And I'll point out to him that his lordship's family will be keeping the man busy."

"Yes. Very busy, I'm sure."

"So Hugh need not worry that his lordship will require his . . . attention in the wee hours of the morning. Right?"

Her blood pounded in her veins. "Right. Exactly. No need to worry."

Sissy smiled kindly. "I never worry about you. I know you will do the right thing."

A choked laugh escaped Annabel. "I'm not sure going to the brewery tonight is the right thing."

"Sometimes you just have to make a leap of faith. And I have faith in Lord Jarret, too—especially after his conversation with Hugh this evening."

Annabel froze. "What conversation?"

"Hugh demanded to know if his intentions were honorable."

Annabel groaned. "Did he laugh in Hugh's face?" she asked bitterly.

"No. That's the point. Hugh said he seemed intrigued by the idea."

Her heart sank. "He was being polite, that's all."

"There isn't an ounce of politeness in the way Lord Jarret looks at you."

She eyed Sissy askance. "Have you forgotten his reputation?"

"Actually, no. From what I've heard, he prefers the fruit

hanging lowest on the tree: easy pickings. Forgive me, my dear, but you are *not* easy pickings. And we both know he has stayed here long past the time he should have."

"If you're helping me because you foolishly think he might marry me—"

"I'm helping you, dear heart, because you deserve a little happiness. No matter what form it comes in."

Sissy meant well. She was making it easy for her. But Annabel could never leave Geordie behind. So tonight would have to be her only night with Jarret.

# Chapter Twenty-two

$\mathcal{J}$arret was grateful that Minerva and Gabe retired once they reached the inn. His blood raced at the thought of seeing Annabel.

Before then, however, he had something else important to do. He led Pinter into the private sitting room the inn had provided upon Jarret's arrival.

"Brandy?" he asked as Pinter settled into a chair.

"Thank you, my lord."

Jarret poured. After handing Pinter his, Jarret stood sipping his own, too edgy to sit down. "So tell me what you've learned."

"I still haven't tracked down any of the grooms present in the stables when your mother rode out that night." Pinter drank from his glass. "But I thought you should hear as soon as possible what I've discovered about the other matter."

"Ah."

Desmond Plumtree, their cousin. Jarret gulped some brandy. On that fateful weekend, while coming back from the picnic, he had thought he saw his cousin in the woods.

He'd dismissed the possibility since Desmond hadn't been invited to the house party, assuming he'd mistaken some other guest for Desmond and putting it out of his mind completely. Until Oliver's tale had cast doubts on everything they'd believed about that night.

"I was right, wasn't I?" he said to Pinter. "Desmond was on the estate the night of their deaths."

"I can only prove he was in the vicinity. It took some doing, but I found a former groom from an inn in nearby Turnham who remembered cleaning Mr. Plumtree's tack the next morning."

"Astonishing that a groom should remember that after all these years."

"Not when you consider that he found blood on the stirrup."

A chill swept down Jarret's spine. His heart racing, he took a seat. "Blood?" he said in a hollow voice. "And the groom didn't mention it to anyone?"

"He said Mr. Plumtree claimed to have been hunting. That's not unusual around there, nor is it odd for a hunter to have blood on him."

"Yet he remembered it."

"He thought it odd that it was on the stirrup," Pinter said. "Who gets blood on the bottom of their boots while hunting? A man of Mr. Plumtree's position would use servants to fetch and clean his game. Still, the groom didn't connect it with the tragedy, since he'd seen Desmond drinking at the inn the night before."

"But Mother and Father might not have died at night. They possibly died earlier, in the late afternoon."

"Exactly. But most people don't know that, because of the great pains your grandmother took to cover up the truth."

Jarret nodded absently. What might have happened if Gran had told the truth, instead of trying to protect the family name? Would they have gotten to the bottom of the matter much sooner? Or would it merely have made the gossip about their family even worse?

Though how could it have been any worse than people believing Oliver had killed their parents?

"All right," Jarret said, "assuming that Desmond was there and had something to do with their deaths—a rather great assumption—what reason would he have for killing them? He wasn't the heir to anything. He'd have nothing to gain."

"Didn't you say that your grandmother has threatened to leave Plumtree Brewery to him?"

"Yes, but she said so only to torment the five of us, since she knows we hate our cousin. Besides, murdering our parents wouldn't have gained Desmond the brewery, even if he had been Gran's heir."

"But there's another way of looking at this. Perhaps your cousin expected to inherit the brewery when your grandmother's husband, his uncle, died a few years before. Or even to be allowed to take it over. I'm sure he didn't expect *her* to run it alone."

"True."

Pinter folded his hands over his waistcoat. "When he didn't gain what he might have seen as his due, he might have plotted another way to gain it. Your grandmother was already reeling from the death of her husband. Perhaps he believed that enduring the violent deaths of her only child and son-in-law—and the ensuing scandal—might push her over the edge. It might not kill her, but it could make her give up running the brewery."

Setting down his glass, Pinter rose to pace the room. "You

would have been too young yet to run it, and the young marquess too busy dealing with the estate. If your grandmother couldn't handle the brewery anymore, the logical person to run things would have been her nephew. He might even have known he was designated as heir, so if she died from the strain . . ."

"If that was his reasoning, why not just kill Gran? She would have been an easier target."

"Ah, but with your parents alive, your mother might have inherited. There was always a chance *she* would choose someone to run it. And he couldn't kill all three—that would look too suspicious."

Jarret downed his brandy in one gulp. "Still, the idea that he did it to get the brewery in his clutches is rather a stretch, don't you think?"

"But it's not implausible." Pinter halted. "Of course, there's no way to prove any of this without knowing more." He ticked things off on his fingers. "Why he was in the area. If he really was on the estate that afternoon. What the situation was with your grandmother's will at that point. We could ask her about that last—"

"No, I don't want her involved."

Pinter stared at him. "If I may be so bold as to ask, my lord, why not?"

Jarret put down his glass. "For one thing, she's still ill. For another, these are serious accusations about her own nephew, based on nothing more than some blood that a groom claims to have cleaned off his stirrup nineteen years ago and my fleeting memory of seeing him on the estate. And I wonder if Desmond even has the stomach to commit cold-blooded murder."

Then again, Desmond was a weasel. The possibility that he could have killed Mother and Father made Jarret's gut churn.

What if a viper had been in their midst all these years . . .

No, there wasn't enough proof to believe it. Not yet, anyway. "Is there no way to find out about Gran's will without alerting her?"

Pinter mused a moment. "You could give someone permission to approach Mr. Bogg with a request to view all versions of the will. Your friend Masters, the barrister, could act on your behalf and include me in the endeavor. He could say that you and your siblings want to be sure of their legal rights regarding your grandmother's ultimatum. Neither your grandmother nor Mr. Bogg would find that suspicious."

"Good idea. I'll discuss it with Masters as soon as we're back in London."

"In the meantime, I can continue to investigate. As long as I'm looking for the grooms, I can see if one of them dealt with your cousin on the estate that day. I can also question his servants about why he left town."

"Be careful with that," Jarret said. "I don't want Desmond to know that we're looking into him. If he's guilty, there's no telling what he might do."

Pinter's face darkened. "Actually, my lord, that brings me to another nasty piece of business involving your cousin. Apparently, he's been openly questioning your fitness to run Plumtree Brewery. Somehow he got wind of how this scheme with Miss Lake came about, and he's been spreading rather . . . vile rumors."

Jarret leapt to his feet. "I'll kill the son of a bitch!"

"I wouldn't advise that," Pinter said dryly. "I should hate to have to arrest you."

With an effort, Jarret jerked his anger under control. "And what would *you* advise?"

Pinter gazed at him with a somber expression. "You're not going to like it."

"Try me."

"You could marry Miss Lake."

Jarret had been resisting the idea of marriage for so long that his next words were purely instinctive. "When did you start working for my grandmother?"

Pinter chuckled. "Trust me, having met the young woman, I understand your reluctance." He sobered. "But if you want to dispel rumors, not only about Miss Lake but about Plumtree and its present difficulties, then a marriage to another brewing family would be ideal. Aside from the fact that it would give you certain advantages in the market, it would also make your recent association with Lake Ale look less the result of a questionable wager and more a clever business move. That would cut the legs right from under your cousin, and he would look a fool."

"An appealing notion," Jarret bit out, "but hardly worth marrying for." Except that he would be marrying Annabel, with her bright eyes and Venus smile. Annabel, who made him laugh and lust.

Annabel, who had the capacity to crush his heart in her capable hand if he let her that close. A shiver swept him.

The runner watched him closely. "Only you can know if marrying Miss Lake is worth it."

"I'm not even sure she'd consent. Remember what she thinks of marriage?"

A small smile touched Pinter's lips. "She was rather vocal on the subject during your card game. But surely your lordship could change her mind."

Only if he agreed to give up his reckless ways for good.

Odd, how that didn't sound as unappealing as it had a mere week ago.

"I'll take your advice under consideration, Pinter. In the meantime, I'd like you to continue your investigation. Discreetly, of course." He walked to the door and opened it. "I assume you'll be traveling back in your own equipage tomorrow?"

"Yes," Pinter said, "I'll leave first thing."

"Then I'll take my brother and sister with me in Oliver's carriage. See you in the morning."

As soon as the runner was gone, Jarret began pacing the room. Marriage to Annabel. It was the second time someone had suggested it tonight. A week ago, he would have scoffed at the idea. Because if he married Annabel, Gran would win. There was no way he could marry and still give up the brewery business. Annabel herself would practically demand that he help with her brother's company.

Besides, his gambling income was too uncertain for him to count on it to support a wife. She'd been right about that. If he married her, he might as well accept that he'd be running Plumtree Brewery—and associating with Lake Ale—for the rest of his life.

He poured himself more brandy and drank deeply. Would that be so awful? This week had challenged him in ways he hadn't been challenged in a long time. He'd found that he liked it—having a purpose, being in command, investing his energies in something greater than himself.

So what did it matter if Gran won? They could both win.

Except that at the end of the year, Gran would regain control of the company. He'd be in the same position he'd always fought to avoid: under her thumb, fighting with her over every decision, playing her lackey.

*Unless you prove yourself capable of running it alone.*

The idea arrested him. He had nearly a year. If he could wrest the company from the brink of disaster in that time he'd have leverage. He could demand that she step down. She might even do it—especially if he'd taken a wife by then. And if that wife were a brewster, that could only help.

A slow smile curved his lips. With excitement building in his chest, he downed the rest of the brandy.

He might have trouble convincing Annabel. She'd told him twice now she had no desire to marry—but he had a few tricks up his sleeve. He had tonight to convince her, and he meant to show her exactly how well it could work for them both. She was a practical female: she'd see the business advantages to such a union. He need not spout a lot of emotional nonsense he didn't mean. She wouldn't expect that, would she? After all, she'd been in love with that arse Rupert, and that hadn't turned out well. She understood that marrying for such frivolous reasons could only make a person unhappy.

Unable to wait any longer, he headed over to Lake Ale. To his delight, Annabel was already there when he arrived, stoking up the coal fire in the little room off the office.

"Jarret!" she cried as she turned to him, wearing a smile as broad as the Thames. "I was afraid you'd changed your mind."

"Not on your life," he said as he peeled off his coat and tossed it over a chair. "I had to consult with Pinter. It took longer than I expected." Perhaps he should broach the subject of marriage first. Get it out of the way.

But if she turned him down, it would make things awkward between them.

He couldn't chance that—not when he'd spent half the evening burning to bed her again. He walked up to sweep her into his embrace. "You have no idea how much I've missed you," he murmured.

"How could you miss me?" she said, eyes filled with mischief. "You've seen me every day."

"You know what I mean, you teasing wench." He bent his head to nip her ear. "I missed the taste of these tender earlobes." He speared his fingers into her coiffure to tug it loose of its pins. "The feel of your luscious hair between my hands. And this . . ."

He kissed her hot, deep, and long, with all the passion he'd kept banked during their many meetings and dinners. He kissed her until she trembled and pressed her body flush against his.

When he broke the kiss, he said in a husky whisper, "I missed this most of all—having you in my arms and holding you against me." He began to undress her, so hungry for her that he couldn't wait a moment more. "Did you miss it, too?"

"Certainly not." At his scowl, she let out a laugh. "All right, perhaps a little."

Her breath came quickly, and now that he'd stripped her down to her shift, he could see the buds of her nipples, pink and hard beneath the sheer fabric.

"More than a little, I'll warrant," he rasped. "Admit it, you minx. You thought of me at night alone in your bed. You thought of me alone in mine, aching with need for you." He slipped his hand between her legs to find her so damned wet and hot that it made him insane. "Perhaps you even touched yourself here, remembering."

"Jarret!" she cried, her cheeks going pink. "I would never—"

"Never?" he prodded. "Not once?"

Dropping her gaze from his, she removed his waistcoat,

cravat, and shirt, then went to work on his trouser buttons. "Well, perhaps . . . once or twice."

Instantly, his imagination conjured up an image of her caressing herself. His cock stiffened painfully. "Show me."

She gaped at him. "What?"

He kicked off his shoes, removed his trousers and drawers, then sat on the bed. "Show me how you touched yourself. I want to watch you touching yourself."

Her blush deepened. "That sounds . . . wicked."

"I'm a wicked man, dearling, something you've pointed out often enough. I'm a rogue, an irresponsible scapegrace, a hellion—"

"I never called you a hellion," she protested. "You called yourself that."

Grabbing the hem of her shift, he lifted it to bare her sweet, fragrant flesh. "All the same, indulge me." He stripped off her shift and tossed it aside, then settled back on the bed to enjoy the view. "Let me see you touch yourself. So I'll have something to remember during my lonely nights in bed in London."

When she paled, his pulse gave a leap. She wasn't as easy about their impending separation as she pretended. Perhaps she wouldn't be as opposed to a marriage, either.

"I doubt that you'll be lonely for long in London," she said tartly.

"Ah, but you've spoiled me for anyone else," he said. "I've become decidedly fond of a certain brewster with the body of Venus and the will of a lioness." He lowered his voice to a coaxing murmur. "Did you caress your breasts while you lay alone in your room?"

Her lashes dipped down demurely to shield her pretty eyes, and she nodded.

"Show me."

Finally, she did. She teased her nipples erect, her breath coming in throaty little gasps that set his blood afire.

"And what about your . . . ace of spades?" he said hoarsely, enthralled by the sight of her hands fondling her breasts. "Did you touch yourself there, too?"

Her gaze met his, turning coy. "Did you touch your jack?"

"God, yes."

A smile curled up her lips. "Show me."

Closing his hand around his cock, he began to work it slowly, afraid that if he did any more, he wouldn't last until he could be inside her. In response, she dropped one hand between her legs to stroke her slick and swollen flesh.

He dragged in a harsh breath. God help him. She looked so damned tempting with her hands caressing herself and her eyes glazing over with her arousal. She was the very picture of femininity—all rosy and flushed, her lips parting with her heavy breaths. His cock felt ready to explode with his need. Much more of this, and he would embarrass himself.

"Enough," he murmured, releasing his erection so he could tug her astride him. "I want to be inside you. Ride me, sweet Venus. Take me to the heavens."

Curiosity lit her face. "Ride you?"

He scooted back on the bed and pulled her knees to rest on either side of his thighs. "Rise up and take me inside you. Come down on my . . . jack. Ever since you sat astride my lap the other night, I've imagined you impaled on me, a goddess taking her pleasure."

Awareness dawned on her face, but still she hesitated. "Do you have one of those things you put on your . . . jack?"

"The cundum." He had half a mind to tell her it didn't matter, that they were going to marry, but he didn't want to ruin the mood in case she wasn't as keen on it as he hoped. So he jerked his trousers up from the floor and removed his only remaining cundum from his pocket.

He handed it to her. "Want to put it on?"

She smiled shyly, tugged the sheaf onto his rigid cock and tied it in place. Then she rose up and slid down onto him to engulf him in her silky feminine heat.

With a heartfelt moan, he thrust up into her. "That's it, dearling. Like that. Now you're in charge."

Her face lit up. "Am I?"

He groaned. She was just temptress enough to use her power over him to torment him.

She rose up and came down on him again, with slow, fluid movements that had him gasping. Her hair frothed over her shoulders like foaming porter—he'd never seen anything more erotic in his life. And her breasts, oh God, they were displayed so prettily that he couldn't resist filling his hands with them, kneading them, thumbing the nipples while she rode him.

"My sweet goddess . . ." he rasped as she increased her pace, maddening him, dragging him rapidly toward release.

Her soft gasps told him she was nearing her own release, and that triggered his, sending him over the edge into insanity just as she cried out and collapsed against him, milking him. And in that moment of intimacy, he knew he would do anything to keep her. Anything within his power.

As he held her to him, stroking her hair, brushing kisses over her brow, he whispered, "Marry me, Annabel."


ANNABEL DREW BACK to stare at him. Had he really just asked her . . . No, surely she'd imagined it. Or perhaps he'd been caught up in the moment when he said it. Lord knew they'd both been carried away. Having him watch her touch herself had roused her in ways she hadn't expected.

"Well?" he prodded. "What do you say?"

She swallowed hard. "I-I'm not sure I heard what you—"

"I asked you to marry me." Tenderly, he brushed the hair from her face. "To become my wife."

It made no sense, given what she knew of him. "As I recall, a week ago you were firmly opposed to marrying anyone."

A smile played about his lips. He wrapped her hair about his hand and kissed it so tenderly it made her heart hurt. "That was before I became so inordinately fond of you."

Well, that implied a certain amount of affection, but still . . .

He thrust up against her. "Fond of *this*."

She frowned and pulled free of him, leaving his lap to find her shift and pull it over her head. She couldn't think when he was touching her. And as long as she was naked, he would keep touching her.

When she could trust herself to speak evenly, she said, "So you want to marry me because you like bedding me."

"Because I like *you*," he said hastily. "You have a sharp mind and an even temperament. You're loyal to your family. And we suit each other."

She gaped at him. "Suit each other! You're a marquess's son, and I'm a brewer's daughter."

"I don't care about that, and you don't either. Admit it."

"Your family will care."

He arched one eyebrow. "Yes, they will. My grandmother will be so ecstatic to see me marry someone respectable, with good connections to brewing, that she'll probably dance a jig on the roofs of London." His tone held an edge. "If she doesn't hand the brewery over to you outright."

"Do be serious, Jarret."

"Sadly, I am." He rose to toss the cundum in the fire, then pulled on his drawers. "You're exactly what my grandmother would want for me."

"That bothers you, doesn't it?"

He shrugged. "A little. I hate letting Gran win."

"Then why—"

"Because there are several advantages to our marrying. For one thing, it would squelch the rumors entirely."

Her blood ran cold. "Rumors?"

A groan escaped him. "Right. I haven't told you about those yet." Sudden anger glinted in his eyes. "It seems that Gran's bastard of a nephew got wind of the gossip about our wager and is telling everyone about it, presenting it in the worst possible light."

Just what she and Lake Ale needed—more gossip. "You mean that he's telling the truth."

"What he *guesses* is the truth."

"Which just happens to *be* the truth."

"Does it matter? The point is, it won't be long before the tale reaches Burton. I don't care about it for myself, but I don't want to see you suffer more. Or your family."

She stiffened. "So you're marrying me because you pity me?"

"No, damn it! That's not—" He paced before her, clearly agitated. "I'm just pointing out the many advantages to our union." Stopping in front of her, he seized her hands. "The best way to settle this situation is for us to have a legitimate connection."

"A legitimate connection," she repeated dully. Amazing how he managed to make a marriage sound like a business arrangement.

"It would be great for Lake Ale," he said, as if he thought *that* was her only objection. "People would see our association as a family thing, which would give more weight to our new project. The East India captains would be assured that I could follow through. Or make your brother follow through."

He was right. And with every word, he drove another nail in her heart.

"As Pinter pointed out—"

She jerked her hands from his. "You're proposing marriage because Mr. *Pinter* said you should?"

"No! I mean, yes, he did suggest—" He broke off with a curse. "I'm mangling this badly, aren't I?"

"Let me put it this way. I've never heard a more cold-blooded proposal of marriage in my life. Even the butcher at least pretended he had some affection for me."

"I didn't say I had no affection for you." He rubbed the bridge of his nose, the very picture of frustrated male. "I just thought . . . I mean, you've always seemed a practical woman, and I figured that if you heard the advantages—"

"Forget the practical advantages. I need to know why *you* want to marry me. You, the person. Not you, the temporary head of Plumtree Brewery."

"It isn't temporary," he corrected her. "Not anymore. I want to run the place for good. I want to give up the gambling." He crossed his arms over his chest in a gesture of belligerence. "That was your objection to marrying me before, wasn't it? I'm quitting it. So you needn't worry about that."

That revelation nearly knocked her off her feet. Giving up the gambling? To marry her? Incredible. It almost gave her hope.

"Jarret," she said softly, "while I'm delighted beyond words that you mean to continue running your family brewery, what I want to know—what I *need* to know—is how you feel about me. Why you think we should spend a lifetime together."

The instant wariness in his gaze made her heart sink. Why couldn't he give her anything of himself? Why was it so hard for him?

"I already told you how I feel about you," he clipped out. "I like you. I like making love to you. And I should think you'd prefer a man who's honest with you, considering that you were taken advantage of by a man who claimed to love you, but ran off to the war without caring that you would suffer for his neglect."

She sucked in a breath, fighting not to show the pain his blunt words had inflicted.

A desperate look came over his face. "I'm promising to be your husband in every respect, to support you and do what I can to help your family. I'm promising to give up gambling, for God's sake. If all of that isn't enough for you, I don't know what else to offer."

*You could offer your heart.* But he clearly didn't have that in him.

While that hurt deeply, she might have been able to overlook it if she hadn't lost her heart utterly to him. She'd fallen hard for him, harder than she'd ever fallen for Rupert.

She loved how he deftly managed her brother, making Hugh think he was guiding the negotiations when it was really Jarret doing so. She loved his ridiculously bad singing. She loved that he worried about her.

But it would kill her to marry him and not have his heart. Especially since she would have to give up the only other person who had her heart. Geordie.

"You're right," she said. "I do prefer your honesty to Rupert's empty words of love. So I suppose that the least I can do is be equally honest with you."

She dragged in a heavy breath. "There's one more factor to consider in this . . . business merger you're suggesting. Something I haven't told you." She fought for calm. "Something that will probably make you think twice about marrying me."

He went on the alert, his eyes narrowing to slits. "Oh?"

There was no easy way to say it. She steadied her shoulders, looked him straight in the eye, and said, "I have a son."

# Chapter Twenty-three

Jarret could only stare at her, slack-jawed. What the hell did she mean, *I have a son?*

Out of nowhere came the memory of her words the first time they'd made love—*It's been nearly thirteen years since I lay with a man.* Nearly thirteen years.

The truth hit him like a blow to the chest. "George is your son."

She swallowed, then nodded.

"That's why you've never married."

"Yes."

"And why you were so insistent about using precautions." Things started falling into place like cards in the shuffle. "That's why your brother feels such guilt over failing you with Rupert, and why *you* feel such guilt over his guilt. And that's why you act as much like a mother to George as his own . . . as Mrs. Lake does."

"Exactly," she whispered.

The fact that she could keep so monumental a secret from him staggered him. "When were you planning to tell me? Ever?"

She narrowed her gaze on him. "Oh, I don't know—when do *you* think I should have told you? After you made it clear you had no interest in marriage, and every intention of gambling yourself into the grave?" She stalked toward him, her eyes alight. "Or perhaps after you boasted of being every bit the scapegrace I accused you of being."

"I didn't boast—"

"Oh, I know! I should have told you when you offered to take me to London where I could serve as your sometime paramour whenever you—"

"Enough," he said, suitably chastened. "You have a point."

Her anger faded rapidly, twisting into anguish. It tugged at his conscience, and something deeper: the urge to protect her, to shield her from harm. When had that urge become so much a part of him?

A troubled expression crossed her face. "I've spent Geordie's entire life protecting him from being proclaimed a bastard, of hearing his mother called a whore behind her back." Tears welled up in her eyes. "I h-have watched him call another woman 'Mother,' with my heart b-breaking a little more every time. I wasn't a-about to risk his very f-future by telling the secret to a man who won't even s-speak to me about his own life."

The tears fell freely down her cheeks now, a torment Jarret could hardly bear. "Shh, dearling," he murmured, pulling her into his arms. He'd opened the floodgates of her pain, and he didn't know how to close them.

No wonder her temper had always flared over anything regarding young George. And no wonder Mrs. Lake bowed to her decisions regarding the boy. It all made perfect sense now.

Why hadn't he seen it sooner? Because she'd had twelve years to learn how to hide it. And because he'd been too busy lusting after her to look beneath the temptress for the heart-broken mother.

He waited until her sobs had subsided a little before venturing another question. "Does George know?"

She shook her head. "I . . . I don't know how to tell him. I'm afraid he'll hate me, that he won't understand." She lifted her teary face to him. "I couldn't bear it if he shut me out of his life. I'd die if he did."

Her pain was palpable, demanding his sympathy. Demanding that he care. He didn't want to care, but he couldn't help himself. She hurt too much, and it hurt him to watch her. "How could he hate you?" he said, feeling a stab of envy for the boy who had not one, but two mothers willing to lavish all their affection on him. "You've given up your whole life for him. He has to understand what an amazing thing that is."

"I hope you're right." Her voice was an aching whisper that made him wish he could banish all the heartache from her life. "I have to tell him soon. The longer I put it off, the worse it gets."

He had no answer for that. What would he have done if his mother had come to him with the news that his entire life had been a lie? Could he have borne that without being angry at *her*?

She drew back to steady her shoulders. "At least now you understand why my marrying you is impossible."

The bleak word *impossible* arrested him. "I don't see what one has to do with the other."

"If I marry you, I either have to claim Geordie as my own and brand him a bastard, subjecting him to gossip and cruelty, or leave him with Sissy and Hugh. It's an impossible choice."

He wished she'd stop using that word. "Not as impossible as you think. He would be part of the Sharpe family, and we're used to scandal. One more would scarcely matter. We could shield him from the worst of it."

She eyed him askance. "I'm sure your grandmother would be *delighted* to open her arms to your new wife, the brewer's daughter, with her bastard son."

"My grandmother is a tavern keeper's daughter, dearling. And if I can accept your son, then she damned well better, too—or to hell with her."

"You can't afford to say 'to hell with her.' She could take the brewery away from you at a moment's notice."

He stiffened. "She and I made a bargain, and she won't go back on it. Even if she did, I'm not going to let you and George starve, so don't worry about that."

"I'm worried about hurting him. I'm worried about taking him from the only life he's ever known. And I can't leave him behind—I just can't."

"I wouldn't ask you to." He cupped her damp cheek. "But perhaps you could leave that decision up to him. Tell him the truth, then see what he would prefer—to risk some scandal by living with his natural mother, or to stay here at least until he's old enough that it doesn't matter so much to him."

"If he chooses the latter, then I can't leave. I won't leave."

He tensed. "And I can't leave London. Not while I'm running Plumtree Brewery."

"You see?" She backed away from him. "As I said—impossible."

"Stop saying that! Do you really think he'd want you to give up your *life* for him? Give up any hope of having a husband, your own household, other children—"

Her eyes went round. "You . . . you want children?"

He hadn't meant to blurt that out. The ground was shifting beneath his feet, changing with her every word. If George came to live with him, he would have a son to take care of. He would be responsible for two other people, when until now he'd only been responsible for himself. What if he disappointed them both? What if, God forbid, Plumtree Brewery went under?

"Do you?" she prodded.

"I'm sure that someday I would . . . want children."

Pity filled her face. "Jarret, admit it. This isn't what you were thinking of when you proposed. I understand; really, I do. No man wants to take on a wife and a half-grown son in one fell swoop—especially a man who only a short while ago didn't even want to marry."

Angry that she'd put her finger right on his problem, he stalked up to her. "Stop putting words in my mouth! You've had over twelve years to get used to the reality of George. You've given me five minutes. That doesn't mean I can't handle it. Or that I don't want to handle it."

"Come now, Jarret—" she began in that placating voice of hers, and it pushed him right over the edge.

"You know what the trouble with you is? You're afraid to take any risk. You take the safe way every time. You only agreed to that wager because you were sure that you could win—if you'd had any inkling you might lose, you wouldn't even have done that."

"That's not true!"

"No? *I'm* not the one who's avoiding telling my son the truth about who he is because I'm afraid it will change everything—afraid that it will force me to live for myself, instead of living for everyone else around me. You would rather embrace the devil you know than risk trusting—"

"The devil I don't know?" she said bitterly. "You're right. And that's the rub—you *are* the devil I don't know. If you ever told me anything about yourself, I might take the chance. But you haven't offered me that. You stated all the practical reasons for our marrying, yet you said nothing of your heart."

God help him, he was in trouble if she'd started talking about hearts. "I don't have a heart. Haven't you figured that out by now?"

"I know you don't *want* to have one. That's the easiest way to keep it from being broken—pretending it's not there." She stepped up to place her hand on his chest. "But I don't believe that. I couldn't possibly have fallen in love with a man with no heart."

He froze. In love? No, that couldn't be. Love was the trap that ruined a man. "Don't say that." Feeling panic rise in his chest, he pushed her hand aside. "I want you in my bed. I want to marry you. I truly believe we can have a good marriage and work out any difficulties with George. But don't ask for more than that. I don't have it to give."

The flash of pain across her face roused a similar pain in him. Damn it, he didn't want this! He didn't want to care that much!

"Who's afraid of risk now?" she said softly. "I guess I should expect a gambler to hold his cards close to his chest. But eventually you have to play them, Jarret. You have to risk losing, even in life. I'm willing to risk losing a great deal— perhaps even George—if I have your heart. But I won't settle for anything less. Neither should you."

He turned toward the bed to gather his clothes. "Then you're right. It's impossible, the two of us."

A long silence fell between them. Part of him wanted her to protest, to say that she'd changed her mind: that it wasn't impossible, that she could marry him and share his bed, even if she didn't have his heart.

Part of him knew, soul-deep, that she wouldn't. Because Annabel was like that. When she made up her mind about something, she didn't waver. He loved that about her. *Liked* that about her, he corrected himself.

God, she was infecting him with this talk of hearts and love. He wouldn't let her.

They dressed in silence. He finished first, then helped her with her corset and gown, though it pierced him to be so close to her, yet so very far away. He couldn't help thinking this would be the last time he smelled her honey-sweet scent, the last time he touched the rumpled satin of her hair, the last time he was with her, alone.

He thought about kissing her, trying to seduce her into agreeing to marry him. But how could he, when she'd said she'd fallen in love? How could he take her, knowing that it meant something so precious to her?

Swiftly finishing with her buttons, he left her side as quickly as he could. The bittersweet pleasure of being near her was too intense.

Then a worrisome thought occurred to him. He walked over to the writing table and scribbled down a few addresses. As she was pinning up her hair, that splendid mane of hair that he loved—*liked*—so much, he went back to her.

"If the rumors do reach here and you change your mind about marrying me, you can reach me at one of these places. The first is my bachelor's quarters, the second is Gran's town house, and the last is Halstead Hall. But no one's really at the estate right now." He pressed the paper into her hand.

She lifted her expressionless gaze to him. "Thank you."

"Will you be here at the brewery tomorrow?"

"There's no need."

No need for *her*, perhaps, but *he* needed to—

No, he didn't need a damned thing. Hadn't he just established that?

"Then I suppose this is good-bye," he said.

A game smile touched her lips. "I suppose it is."

He wanted to kiss her. He wanted to hold her. He did none of that. He just turned and headed for the door.

As he reached it, she called out, "Jarret?"

With a perverse hope hammering in his chest, he pivoted to look at her. "Yes?"

"Thank you."

"For what?"

"For coming here and helping my brother. For brightening my life, even if it was only for a little while. For reminding me how good it is to be a woman."

A lump lodged in his throat. "You're welcome."

But as he left the brewery and headed for the inn, he wondered if he was making a huge mistake by walking away from her. Was she right about him? *Was* he being a coward? Did he dare give her what she wanted and risk the pain that might come with it?

No, that was one thing he was certain of. He'd done the right thing. If he hurt *this* much just from leaving a woman who'd been only his lover, how much more would he hurt if he gave her his heart and something took her from him?

She'd claimed that he was afraid to take the risk. What she didn't understand is that every gambler knew that some risks were too great to take. And he was fairly sure this was one of them.

# Chapter Twenty-four

Annabel felt numb in the days that followed. Every day she replayed their conversation and reaffirmed that she'd done what she had to. Every night she reversed that opinion, wishing she'd accepted his proposal.

Did it matter that he didn't love her, that he'd conceived the idea of marriage as some way to *save* her? That was a sort of caring, wasn't it?

But always the dawn came, and she remembered again that she'd done the right thing. How could she even be sure he would quit gambling? How could she be sure he wouldn't regret taking a wife once they were married for all eternity? And she had only his word for it that his family would accept Geordie.

She sighed. Jarret had been right about one thing—she *had* to tell Geordie the truth. She *was* being a coward. The longer she put it off, the worse it would get. But she kept telling herself she should wait until after he'd finished his difficult week at their local grammar school, or until after Easter, since it was his favorite holiday or . . .

She was stalling. She knew it.

Especially since there was even less reason not to tell him these days. Everything was going well. Hugh had surprised her by taking up the reins of Lake Ale, seeming a new man. The hope Jarret had given them that they'd be able to sell their pale ale through the East India Company had bolstered Hugh's confidence, and he went to the brewery every day with an air of excitement about him.

So it was with some surprise that she peeked into his study about a week after Jarret's departure to find him sitting at his desk with a glass of whisky in his hand. It was the first time she'd seen him drinking spirits since the day they'd returned from London.

The blood froze in her veins until she realized that he wasn't actually drinking it, just staring at it, turning it this way and that in the light. He must have sensed her there, for without looking at her, he said, "Come in, Annabel. I was just about to call for you."

His tone held a deadly calm that frightened her. "What's happened?"

"I just heard an interesting bit of gossip from Allsopp. It seems that there's talk in London of my sister having made a certain unsavory wager with a certain lord."

He lifted his gaze to her just in time to see her pale. "It's true, isn't it?"

She thrust out her chin and attempted to salvage the situation. "I wagered Mother's ring in exchange for his help with Lake Ale."

"That's not what they're saying."

"I know, but—"

"And I don't for one minute believe that Lord Jarret Sharpe would take a ring as a suitable stake." His eyes searched her face. "But I'm fairly certain that Lord Jarret would jump at having you in his bed, which is what they *are* saying was the wager."

Heat rose in her cheeks. "It doesn't matter what the wager was. I won."

"So you're not denying it."

She let out a despairing breath. "Hugh, please . . ."

"I'm not surprised Lord Jarret would make such a wager, but I'm astonished that you would agree to it."

"I'm sorry to have shamed you—"

"It's not about that, blast it!" To her relief, he set the glass down. "It's the fact that your desperation to save Lake Ale made you willing to . . . You felt compelled to . . ." He crumpled, burying his head in his hands. "Oh, God, I can't believe I drove you to that."

With her heart in her throat, she walked over to lay her hand on his shoulder. "He wouldn't have gone through with it. He's a good man at heart."

His head shot up. "A good man doesn't take advantage of a desperate woman. A good man doesn't allow a woman to risk her reputation, then let her weather the gossip alone. Thanks to him, you'll be painted as a whore by half the wagging tongues in town. I ought to ride up to London and call him out just for that, damn it!"

"You can't," she said firmly.

"He deserves it!"

"No, he doesn't." She hesitated, but if he was talking about foolish things like dueling, she'd better tell him the truth. "As soon as he heard about the gossip, he offered to marry me. I turned him down."

Hugh stared at her, then rose slowly from his chair. "Why, for God's sake?"

"You know why: because of Geordie."

"You *told* him Geordie is your son?"

"I had to. He was offering for me—he deserved to know."

Hugh leaned back in his chair to scowl at her. "You never told any of those other fellows who offered for you."

"I didn't care about any of them."

"But you care about Lord Jarret."

She hesitated, then nodded.

"Aren't you worried he'll reveal the truth to someone else?"

"No, he's very discreet," she said firmly.

"I saw how discreet he was. He must have boasted to half of London about that damned wager."

"The gossip didn't come from him. He's not like that."

"Really?" Anger flooded Hugh's features. "Then why did you refuse him? I have to assume it was because he didn't react well to your revelation."

"Actually, no. He was very understanding about that."

Hugh blinked. "Now I'm confused." He stabbed his fingers through his hair. "If he had no issue with the fact that Geordie is your son, why didn't you accept his offer?"

"I won't make Geordie leave the only home he knows. And I can't bear to leave him here, so I can live in London with Lord Jarret. It's as simple as that."

"Perhaps you should let Geordie make that choice."

She snorted. "You and Lord Jarret. How can a boy his age make that choice? He has no idea how cruel people can be. If I claim him—which I'd have to do to take him to London without people finding it odd—the gossips will run wild with the tale. It will embarrass everyone, not just him. And if he chooses to stay here without me—" She broke off with a sob.

"Oh, sweetheart." Hugh took her in his arms. "You must tell the lad the truth someday."

"I know. And I-I will."

He fished out a handkerchief. "I wish I could have throttled Rupert for putting a babe in your belly when he had no intention of taking care of it. That little weasel—"

"It's all in the past now." She took the handkerchief and blew her nose. "I made a mistake, and calling Rupert names won't change that."

"Your only mistake was in trusting a young man who was too stupid to see how precious you are." He reached up to rub a tear from her cheek. "That's what worries me, Annie. That you've found another just like him. So you have to tell me the truth now. Is there any reason I should be concerned that Lord Jarret might have . . ." His ears pinkened, but he soldiered on. "Could he have put a babe in your belly, too?"

Lord, could this get any worse? "That's not possible." Jarret had made sure of it.

"I won't judge you, mind, but if there's any chance—"

"There's nothing between me and Lord Jarret but that stupid wager, I assure you," she said firmly. *Not anymore, anyway.* "And I won that wager, so you needn't worry."

He pulled her close again to rest his chin on the top of her head. "There's still the gossip. I hate to see you maligned by our friends and neighbors."

She swallowed. "Do you want me to accept his proposal? He gave me his address to write to if I changed my mind. I don't want to cause you and Sissy any more embarrassment."

"Oh, sweetheart," he said, brushing the hair from her eyes, "I don't care about that, and Sissy doesn't either. You've always been a joy to us. Besides, you'll be the one to suffer the brunt of the rumors. I only wish I could spare you that."

She pulled back and forced a smile. "It'll blow over in

time." She gazed beyond him to the glass of whisky. "You're not going to drink that, are you?"

"After all you've sacrificed because of it? No. I'm done with that."

She let out a long breath. "Thank God."

At least one good thing had come out of her encounter with Jarret. That made it almost worth the pain to her battered heart.

GEORGE STOOD FROZEN in the hall, unable to believe his ears. He was a bastard. And Aunt Annabel was his mother. His *mother*! And his real father was dead in the war. So he had no father, because the man he'd thought was his father was really his uncle.

Oh, God! How could that be? Mother treated him the same as all the other children. Surely if he weren't really her son, she would have given some hint. Surely she wouldn't have *lied* to him—

They'd *all* lied to him! Tears clogged his throat, and he choked them down with an effort. How *could* they? They'd hidden the fact that he was a . . . a bastard.

*Bastard.* The nasty word banged around in his head, making him ill. He stumbled to the stairs and hurried up to his room where he could be alone, where he could think. *A bastard.* One of those children people whispered about, like Toby Mawer. Toby's mother had never married either, just like Aunt Annabel.

No, not *Aunt* Annabel. Mother. He curled up into a ball on his bed. She was his *mother.* And she couldn't claim him as her son, because it would *embarrass everyone.* Because his very existence embarrassed everyone. Oh, God, he was going to be sick.

He ran to the chamber pot and heaved up his accounts, then dropped onto the floor and clasped his knees to his chest. His heart hurt so bad. They were all liars. All they cared about was making sure nobody knew the truth, even *him*.

Something suddenly occurred to him. Did Grandmother and Grandfather know? No, wait—they weren't even his real grandmother and grandfather, were they?

Tears stung his eyes. He didn't have grandparents, because they were all dead. Aunt Annabel's—*Mother's*—fiancé had been an orphan. And his brother and sisters weren't his, either—they were cousins. So he had no father or grandparents or brothers or sisters. He had a mother who lied to him and couldn't claim him.

Because he was a *bastard*.

It wasn't his fault! It was that horrible Rupert's fault. George didn't care if the man had been his father and a war hero. He'd put a babe in Aunt Annabel's belly—in *Mother's* belly—when he wasn't supposed to. Father had said so. No, not *Father*. He didn't *have* a father!

He buried his head between his knees, fighting back tears. He just wanted everything to go back to how it was before. When he didn't know. When he had a father and mother and grandparents and sisters and a brother . . .

His head shot up. Why couldn't it? No one knew what he'd heard. If he and Aunt Annabel never said anything, it could all be like before. He thrust out his chin. He didn't want a different mother. He wanted everything to stay the same. And it could, if he chose it. Nobody else knew the truth.

Except Lord Jarret.

He scowled. Lord Jarret, who'd made a naughty wager with Aunt Annabel and told everybody about it. Lord Jarret, who'd said he had honorable intentions toward Aunt Annabel and hadn't meant it. Aunt Annabel had told George that his lordship wasn't interested in marrying.

Sometimes she lied, too. And now she was saying that his lordship had offered for her. Was that the truth? It might not be.

For one thing, she'd told Father that there was nothing other than that wager between her and Lord Jarret, but *that* was a lie. Lord Jarret had kissed her—he was fairly certain of that. And there'd been that other time, when the two of them had come back from walking in the rain near the Daventry market and they'd looked guilty, like they'd been doing something wrong. There was the way they looked at each other, too . . . the same way Mother and Father looked at each other sometimes.

Oh God, what if Lord Jarret *had* put another babe in Aunt Annabel's belly? George wasn't quite sure how that happened, but it had to do with kissing and being in a bed. And if the wager had been that Lord Jarret would get Aunt Annabel in his bed . . .

George punched the floor. If she got a babe in her belly, the whole family would be disgraced, all because Aunt Annabel wouldn't marry on account of him. And if Lord Jarret told people about George's being a bastard, the whole family would be disgraced. Again, on account of him.

If that happened, they'd blame him and everybody would *know* he was a bastard. That couldn't happen.

There was only one way out of it. Somehow he had to *make*

Lord Jarret marry Aunt Annabel and take her away. Then everything could go back to how it was before.

Except that then there'd be no Aunt Annabel looking after him. No hot chocolate that she snuck into the nursery for him when Father was being an ass. No songs when he had a nightmare. No trips to the market to see the horses for auction.

It dawned on him that she'd done those things because she was his *mother.*

His throat felt raw. She *couldn't* be—he wouldn't let her! He would get Lord Jarret to take her away. Lord Jarret ought to do it anyway, because of the gossip. That's what Father had said. George would *make* him come back and marry her, whether she wanted it or not.

But how?

Writing to Lord Jarret wasn't good enough. He might just ignore the letter. No, George had to go in person.

The churning began in his belly again. Go to London? Alone? Even if he could do it, his parents would kill him. He scowled. He didn't really have parents, did he? Just a mother who was embarrassed by him.

*Come on, you know they would worry,* his conscience nagged him.

So what if they did? They deserved to suffer. *He* wasn't the one who'd been lying.

Or they might not even care. He blinked back tears. He was a bastard, an embarrassment. But only if he didn't fix this. If he fixed this, everything would be fine.

He imagined himself arriving with Lord Jarret to save the day. Lord Jarret would sweep Aunt Annabel off her feet and make her marry him, and George would be the hero who'd brought him back. Then everyone would forget he was a bastard. And things would go back to how they were before. That was the important part.

So how was he to get to London? He and Mother and Aunt Annabel had ridden the mail coach the first time. It left the inn at midnight, so he shouldn't have trouble sneaking out without anyone knowing he'd gone until morning. Once in London, he'd have to hire a hackney to get to the brewery, so he could find his lordship.

Now all he had to figure out was how to get on the mail coach. He was pretty sure he had enough money for a ticket from the money his grandparents gave him for Christmas. Since he'd only been to the coaching inn once, he didn't think anyone would remember him or know who he was.

But the coachman might not let a boy his age on by himself. He'd ask all sorts of questions about his parents and why he was traveling alone.

George sat on the bed to think. Perhaps he could get one of the servants to put him on the mail coach and pretend to be sending him off to his family in London. No, that wouldn't work. They'd tell on him. But who else could he get?

He sprang from the bed. Toby Mawer! He was seventeen—the coachman would listen to *him*. And ever since George had come back in a marquess's carriage, Toby and his friends had been nicer to him. Not friendly, but not as mean as before.

Besides, George had something Toby wanted—the watch Father had given him.

George pulled it out of the drawer. It was a real gold watch, with an inscription inside that said, "To George Lake, On His Twelfth Birthday, January 9, 1825." It was his first watch. A lump caught in his throat. Did he really want to give it up?

He had to. He needed all his money for London and the trip. Besides, he had nothing else that Toby would want.

Feeling a tightness in his chest, he slid it in his pocket. He'd ask Toby to help him, and they'd plan where to meet near midnight. After everyone was asleep, he'd sneak out and take the coach to London. And once it was all done, everything would be right again.

# Chapter Twenty-five

Annabel hesitated before Geordie's door. He hadn't come down for breakfast, which worried her. He'd behaved strangely last night at supper, sunk in a sullen silence. Though he fell into these moods sometimes, this seemed different, as if anger boiled just beneath the surface and he was clamping it down.

Geordie never clamped anything down. When he was angry, everyone knew it.

Probably he was just growing up, learning to control his feelings, but that made it even more imperative that she tell him the truth. It was time.

If he got wind of the gossip about her and Lord Jarret, he'd be angry at both of them, and before that happened, she wanted him to know the reasons Jarret was allowing her to endure the rumors. Why she wasn't marrying Jarret.

It had taken her all night to work up the courage.

She knocked on his door. He didn't answer. Alarm spiked in her chest. She tried the door, but it was locked. He wasn't allowed to lock his door.

"Geordie, you open this door this minute!" she cried.

No answer.

After repeating the command, she flew down the stairs to fetch Hugh, praying that he hadn't left for the brewery. Moments later they were all standing outside Geordie's door, and Hugh, his hands shaking, was unlocking it with the spare key.

They walked in to find the room empty. Empty! Where the devil could he have gone?

Then she spotted the open window and the rope attached to his bedpost, and her heart missed a beat. She flew to the window, half expecting to see him lying broken and bleeding on the ground, but there was only a set of shoe prints in the mud.

Hugh came up beside her. "Damnation, what is the boy up to?"

"He ran away. Hugh, he ran away!"

"Nonsense, there has to be some other explanation. Why would he run away?"

She rounded on him as Sissy called for the servants. "You saw how upset he was at dinner last night. Something was bothering him."

"He probably just went on some foolish midnight jaunt to set things afire in the forest or go trawling for eels at the river." Hugh was trying to sound calm, but worry lined his face. "He'll come strolling in any minute, boasting about doing something he wasn't supposed to. All boys act up at that age."

"Did you ever climb out of your window in the middle of the night?" Sissy demanded. "I daresay you didn't, Hugh Lake. You have to call the constable and get him over here right away."

"Not until we're sure he didn't just go down the road to his grandparents'."

But as the morning wore on, it became more and more clear that this was not some midnight jaunt, and he hadn't gone to his grandparents'. It was as if he'd disappeared into thin air. The servants knew nothing, and no one had seen him leave.

By noon, Annabel was frantic, Hugh was a seething mass of rage, and Sissy couldn't stop weeping. The constable had been sent for, but before he could arrive, a man came to the door with a lanky lad in tow who looked as if he'd rather be anywhere else.

"Afternoon, Mr. Lake," the man said. "Toby Mawer here tried to sell me a watch, but I saw the inscription and realized it was your boy's. I just thought I'd check with young George and make sure he really did give it to Toby."

Annabel remembered hearing Geordie complain about a boy named Toby. Fear surged up inside her. Had Toby hurt him to gain the watch?

"George is missing," Hugh said as he ushered the two inside. He trained a dark gaze on Toby. "Where is he, Toby?"

Toby effected a nonchalant manner. "Dunno, sir. He gave me the watch, is all."

"For no reason?" Annabel snapped. "He just gave it to you? I don't believe you."

Something flickered in the lad's eyes. "Think what you wish, miss. He gave it to me free and clear."

"Well then," Hugh said, "since I know the lad wouldn't part with his birthday watch, and you claim he did, we'll let the constable sort it out. He's on his way here, so we'll just hand you over to him." Hugh's voice hardened. "Of course, if George ends up dead somewhere, you'll be the one we blame. But at least you'll have that gold watch when they hang you."

"Hang me!" Toby cried, his eyes practically popping out of

his head. "Now see here, sir, I ain't done no murdering. He was alive when last I saw him, I swear!"

Hugh crossed his arms over his chest. "And where might that have been?"

Toby swallowed, then glanced nervously behind him to the door. "You won't give me to the constable, will you?"

"It depends on what you have to say."

He thrust out his lower lip. "I knew I shouldn't have helped that little mama's boy. I told him he had a fool plan, but he wouldn't listen."

"What was his plan?" Annabel prodded.

"Wanted to go see some fancy gent in London. The same one what was here last week. He had me pretend to be his older brother putting him on the coach. I told the coachman he was off to visit our uncle. George paid for the ticket himself, and gave me the watch because I helped him."

Annabel's heart faltered. Geordie had gone off to London alone?

"Why on earth would he want to see Lord Jarret?" Sissy demanded.

"I dunno, ma'am. He wouldn't say. But he kept asking me questions about what it was like to be a bastard, till I nearly changed my mind about helping him."

*A bastard.*

Annabel's gaze flew to Hugh, whose pallid color said he was thinking the same thing she was.

"Thank you, lad, for telling us the truth," Hugh said in a strained voice. "Go on with you now."

Toby frowned. "What about the watch? It's mine, fair and square."

"Just be glad we're not turning you over to the constable," Hugh snapped. "I'm not giving you that watch."

"But you can have some cake if you like," Sissy added with a wan smile. "For helping us."

Toby thrust out his chest. "Don't need any cake." He glanced sullenly at Sissy. "But if you've got some roast beef . . ."

"I'm sure we could find something you like," Sissy said kindly, herding him toward the kitchen.

Hugh thanked the shop owner and sent him on his way. As soon as the man was gone, Annabel said, "Geordie must have heard us talking about him yesterday. You know how bad he's gotten about listening at doors."

Hugh nodded grimly. "I'll get the coach ready. We'll leave for London at once. Sissy can stay here with the children, in case he comes to his senses and returns."

Annabel nodded, her heart beating a frenzied pace. Anything could happen to him on the road alone.

Hugh put his arm around her. "He'll be all right, Annie. He's a resourceful boy."

"How will he know where to find Jarret? What if he gets into trouble while he's wandering London alone? All sorts of things could happen to him in the city!"

"I know, but you can't start imagining the worst or you'll make yourself mad. We'll just have to hope he reaches Lord Jarret quickly." Hugh pressed a kiss to her forehead. "Have some faith in the lad. He has a good head on his shoulders."

That wouldn't make any difference if he came up against some of the rougher sorts. All she could see in her mind was George being accosted by footpads, robbed and beaten, and left to die in some alley. "I should have told him," she whispered. "If only I had told him—"

"What's done is done. We'll find him, even if we have to tear London apart."

The fierce determination in her brother's voice gave her little comfort, but one thing was certain. If she did find Geordie safe and unharmed, she was never going to let him go.

JARRET ENTERED THE offices of Plumtree Brewery after noon with a spring in his step. The East India captains had agreed to a contract with Plumtree Brewery to sell Lake Ale's brew. They'd been so impressed with the quality of Annabel's pale ale that they'd put in an order for two thousand barrels! That was nearly as much as had been going to the Russians. Lake Ale's cut alone would keep the small brewery going for at least another year, and Annabel would be ecstatic.

He stopped short. He should tell her firsthand; go up to Burton so they could celebrate.

So he could see her.

With a groan, he sank into his chair behind the desk. He was supposed to be putting her from his mind. Ever since he'd left Burton, he'd buried himself in work, in the project, and in setting Plumtree to rights. He'd tried to forget her.

But he couldn't. When he smelled the fragrant hops, he thought of her clean, fruity scent. When he saw the froth in the mashtun, he thought of her beautiful hair. And when the lamps were dimmed at night and the place was still, he thought of making love to her in that tiny room off Lake Ale's office, lit only by a coal fire and their passion.

Christ, he was getting maudlin again. He was starting to be maudlin all the time. He missed her. He hadn't expected to miss her so damned much.

Croft opened the door to his office. "Mr. Pinter is here, sir. Will you see him?"

"Of course." At least it would take his mind off Annabel.

As soon as Pinter took a seat, he got right to the point. "I found the groom who saddled your mother's horse that day. He says he never saw or heard anything about Desmond—had no idea he was in the vicinity. But your mother said something to the groom that might be important."

Jarret steadied himself. "Yes?"

Pinter shifted in his chair. "She . . . er . . . asked that he not mention to your father where she'd gone."

For a second, Jarret could hardly breathe. That confirmed it—Mother hadn't ridden out to confront Father. She'd wanted to avoid him. But then, how had Father known where she was headed? Why had he gone after her, when they'd barely been on speaking terms most days?

"And Desmond? Have you learned anything more about that? Masters is still trying to finagle a way to look at the earlier versions of Gran's will."

"All I know is that his mill was struggling at the time."

"Which gives him a stronger motive."

"Yes."

"Is it possible that Mother was riding out to meet *him*? Perhaps she was angry enough with Father that she wanted to plot something with her cousin. She never hated him like the rest of us did."

"It's conceivable. But once again . . ."

"I know, you need more information. Well then, keep digging."

Pinter nodded. "You should know that Desmond is still spouting his poison, but no one seems to be paying him much heed. Everyone is impressed by how you've handled the brewery. There are even rumors of a big contract with the East India captains."

"They're not rumors," Jarret said proudly.

"Ah. Then congratulations are in order. I'm sure the Lakes will be pleased."

Jarret sighed. "By the way, I did offer for Miss Lake. She turned me down."

"Did she?"

"It seems she was less than hopeful about my suitability to be a husband."

Pinter shot him a pensive glance. "Perhaps this will change her mind."

"I doubt it. I've made something of a mess of my life until now. She'd be mad to marry me."

"I've seen stranger unions. Your brother's, for one. I wouldn't give up hope just yet. In my experience, intelligent women need more time for such decisions than men think they should. You can't blame them for being skittish. After all, a woman gives up far more to marry than a man does."

After Pinter left, those words echoed in Jarret's mind. He really *had* been asking a great deal of her—to risk losing her son for him. And he'd offered nothing in return except his name and a promise that he'd be a different man, even though he'd done nothing to show that he *could* be a different man. He'd wanted her to take a leap of faith, when no other man had ever been worthy of her trust.

He wasn't even willing to let her in to the part of him he'd always kept carefully hidden, the part that was terrified of caring too much. She was right about one thing—pretending he had no heart kept him from letting it be broken. Though he began to wonder if a lifetime without her wasn't just as bad.

Somewhere in the last month, he'd gone from the Jarret who didn't care to the Jarret who cared a great deal about what happened to her. To the two of them. That terrified him. If he allowed himself to love her, and Fate ripped her away from him as it had Mother and Father . . .

He froze. Pinter's information had made it clear that Fate hadn't played any part in that. Oliver's confession had said as much, but Jarret hadn't wanted to believe it. And why? Because if Mother hadn't killed Father accidentally, if it had been a deliberate act, then he'd wasted his entire life believing a lie.

Fate might have a hand in many of life's tragedies, but many more of them were caused by people behaving foolishly or dangerously—or even, in the case of Gran, bullheadedly. If a man separated himself from people, if he refused to care, then he simply allowed those actions to continue. But the world needed people who cared enough to balance out the foolish and dangerous ones, to pick up the pieces. The world needed people like Annabel.

*He* needed people like Annabel. No, he needed *Annabel.* In his life, by his side. And no amount of burying himself in work was going to change that.

# Chapter Twenty-six

A few hours later, Jarret heard a familiar strident voice coming from the outer office. Despite everything, a smile lit his face. Seconds later, Gran bustled in with Croft on her heels.

"You really should sit down, madam," Croft told her. "You know what Dr. Wright says." He ran over to pick up the coverlet draped over the settee. "Here, this spot would be best. Then you can rest your head on the bolster and put your feet—"

"Croft, if you do not stop fluttering about me, I will put my feet up your arse!" Gran snapped. "I am fine. I *feel* fine."

"But—"

"Out!" She pointed her finger to the door. "I want to speak to my grandson."

With a wounded look, Croft carefully refolded the coverlet and placed it precisely back on the settee, then left the room.

"You really should be nicer to the man," Jarret said, biting back a smile. "He worships the ground you walk on. Every other word out of his mouth is 'Mrs. Plumtree says this' and 'Mrs. Plumtree says that.'"

"He thinks I am hovering over the grave," she grumbled as she sat down on the settee. "You all do."

"Not me. I know better; I hate having my knuckles rapped." He leaned back in his chair and folded his hands over his abdomen. "How are you feeling these days?"

"Much better," she said. "Dr. Wright thinks I am on the mend."

She certainly looked better than she had a couple of weeks ago. Jarret hadn't heard her cough in a while, and her face had good color. The very fact that she was here said quite a lot.

"You must have incredible sources if you already know about the contract."

"Contract?" she said with patently false innocence. "What contract?"

He arched an eyebrow at her. "Gran, I'm not in leading strings anymore. You've heard about the deal with the East India captains, haven't you?"

She shrugged. "There *are* rumors . . ."

"And you came to confirm them. Well, they are all true." He picked up his copy of the contract and brought it over to drop in her lap. "See for yourself."

She pounced on the contract like a profligate scenting sin. It took her several moments to scan it for the particulars, but when she got to the amount they'd contracted for, her eyes went wide. "You got them to agree to purchase two thousand barrels? However did you manage that?"

"It's a good brew at a good price. They're no fools."

"But that is almost a quarter of the market!"

"You sound surprised," he said dryly as he took a seat again. "What did you think I'd been doing up here all this time? Twiddling my thumbs?"

She must have heard the edge in his voice, for she set down the contract. "Jarret, never let it be said that I am not willing to acknowledge my mistakes. And I made a very great one when I refused to let you continue on at the brewery when you were young."

The words shouldn't have mattered so much to him, but they did. "Good of you to admit it." Somehow he managed a smile. "I wasn't cut out to be a barrister, Gran. But I realize now that you suddenly found yourself stuck with five grandchildren to raise, and you probably didn't need all of them underfoot—"

"Oh, God, it was not that." Her blue eyes deepened in sorrow. "Don't you see, my boy? I pushed my daughter to marry your father. After that ended in disaster, I realized that we had never given you a choice—your grandfather and I just dragged you to the brewery and told you that it was your future."

"It was a future I wanted."

"You were thirteen. What did you know? You had never had any other choice shown to you. I wanted you to see the world that was available to you before you entered the brewery business. I wanted you to have the same advantages as any gentleman your age—a good education, a chance for something greater."

A month ago, he would have lashed out over that. He would have told her that Eton was the last place to send a grieving boy whose family had suffered scandal and who needed familiar places and familiar people around him.

But that had been before he met Annabel. Now he understood that mothers—and grandmothers—sometimes made the wrong sacrifices for their children. Because they had limited resources or limited knowledge. Or simply because they were afraid.

That didn't mean they loved them any less. Sometimes it meant they loved them more.

"You did what you thought was right," he said softly, realizing that any resentment he'd felt for her over the past was gone. "I don't blame you for that."

She blinked back tears, then jerked the contract back into her lap and continued to read. "It is a solid agreement, with many advantages for us."

"I know."

A bark of laughter escaped her. "Cocky rascal, aren't you?"

"So I've been told." As she went on reading, he broached a subject he'd been putting off. "Gran, I intend to keep running the brewery after the year is up."

She kept reading, but her hands trembled a little. "I suppose that could be arranged."

"And you are going to retire."

*That* got her full attention. "What? You are *not* going to put me out to pasture, Jarret Sharpe."

"No, indeed. You're too valuable for that. I mean to use your expertise every chance I get." When that seemed to mollify her, he added gently, "But the brewing business is for the young. You know that, or you wouldn't have asked me to step in." He cast her an arch glance. "Besides, if your devious little plan works out and you get everyone married off, you'll soon have great-grandchildren to coddle. You'll have no time for Plumtree."

She digested that a moment. "I take it you still disapprove of my methods."

"I do. I suspect that down the road, it's going to give you grief in ways you haven't anticipated."

With a sniff, she returned to reading the contract. When she was done, she set it aside. "Do you believe Lake Ale can hold up their end?"

"I have no doubt of that. Annabel will make *sure* they hold up their end."

"Annabel?" she asked, her eyebrows lifting.

He hesitated. But he'd already decided that he had to try again with Annabel. She was everything he wanted. "You'd like her. She's a great deal like you, actually—stubborn and impudent and a plague of a woman. With a heart as big as the ocean."

"So why don't you marry her?"

"I proposed, but she turned me down."

"What?" She scowled. "Well then, I do *not* think she is right for you. Sounds like a fool to me, and you should not marry a fool."

"She's no fool, trust me. Just a bit skittish. And her life is . . . complicated."

"Well then, uncomplicate it." She stabbed a finger at the contract. "If you managed a deal like this, you can uncomplicate the life of some provincial brewster who spends her time looking after her brother's children, and has not had a man in her life since her fiancé died in the war."

He blinked. "How did you know all that?"

She tipped up her chin. "I have sources, remember?"

God help them all. No telling what other secrets she'd dredged up.

He was about to prod further when a ruckus in the outer office caught their attention. Croft let out a yelp, and a boy ran into the room, his eyes wild.

"George?" Jarret said as he leapt from the chair, his heart thundering. What was the lad doing here? And did that mean Annabel was here, too?

Croft ran in to grab the poor boy by his collar. "Forgive me, sir, but the little brat kicked me and got past me. I swear—"

"Let him go, Croft. I know him. Leave us."

Croft threw up his hands, muttered something vaguely curslike, and marched stiffly out.

George looked a bit worse for wear, with his clothes rumpled, his hair thoroughly mussed, and his shoes muddy. And were those cake crumbs on his coat?

As soon as Croft had closed the door, George said, without preamble, "You knew I was a bastard, and you didn't tell me!"

The look of betrayal on his face made Jarret's gut twist. Damn it all to hell. "I didn't know until the night before I left, when your aunt—"

"My *mother*, you mean. You can say it. She's my *mother*."

Gran cleared her throat. In horror, George looked over to see her sitting there, and his face went red.

"George, this is my grandmother, Mrs. Hester Plumtree. Gran, this is George Lake, Annabel's—"

"Son," George finished, his stance belligerent. "Her bastard son."

Gran blinked, then stood. Coming up to George, she held out her hand. "Pleased to meet you, George. I've heard a great many good things about your mother."

The lad stared at her, obviously not quite sure what to do. At last he took her hand and shook it, a trifle warily.

"Gran, would you give us a moment?" Jarret said. "George and I need to have a little talk."

"Certainly." She shot him a furtive glance. "Is this one of those complications you were talking about?"

"You could say that." And she was going to expect full details later.

As soon as she was gone, Jarret said, "It's good to see you, George, but where's your family?"

"In Burton." The lad's chin trembled, as if he were holding

himself together only with great effort. "I came to London alone. I sneaked out."

"Good God, lad, are you daft? They must be mad with worry by now."

He thrust out his lower lip. "They won't care." His voice turned bitter. "I'm just a bastard and an embarrassment to the family."

"Oh, George. I'm sure they didn't say that to you."

"No, they didn't say *anything* to me. No one *ever* tells me things. I overheard them talking about it, about how . . . Aunt Annabel refused your proposal because of me, and I came here straightaway." A look of desperation shone in his face. "You have to marry her!"

Jarret lifted an eyebrow. "I already proposed marriage, and she refused me, lad."

"That's only because she's embarrassed that people will find out about me. But they won't, because I'm not going to let her tell anyone. You're going to marry her and bring her to London, s-so everything can go back to h-how it was before."

The way the lad stood so stalwart, with his hands balled into fists and his eyes desperate, made something clutch in Jarret's chest. "I'm sorry, George, but it can never go back to how it was before. You can't un-drink the water. Even if no one else knows, *you* will. You won't be able to put that out of your head."

"Yes, I will! You have to marry her, so everything can stay the same." He steadied his bony little shoulders. "If I have to, I'll *make* you marry her."

Jarret blinked. "Oh? And how will you do that?"

"I'll call you out."

It took Jarret an immense effort to swallow his laugh. "Using what for a weapon?"

"I-I was hoping you'd have an extra dueling pistol I could borrow."

"I see. Do you even know how to shoot a pistol?"

George thrust out his chest. "I shot a fowling piece when I went hunting with Grandfather." A troubled frown touched his brow. "Well, I suppose he's not really my grandfather since he's not Aunt Annabel's father . . ."

"You see, George?" Jarret said softly. "Things can't go back to how they were. You know too much now."

"But I don't *want* to know!" he cried. "I d-don't want to h-have no father and no sisters or brother and n-no grandparents—"

Jarret was at George's side in an instant, pulling the boy into his arms. "It's all right, lad. It will be all right, I swear. Not at this moment perhaps, but in time."

"It's n-never going to be all right!" George wailed. "I'm a bastard, and there's nothing I can do about it."

"That's true." He tugged the boy over to the settee near the window and urged him down onto it, then sat beside him with his arm about his shoulders. "But it doesn't have to shape your life if you don't want it to." The way he'd let his anger and pain over his parents' deaths shape *his* life. "And I know that your mother doesn't care if you're a bastard."

"Don't call her that! She's not my mother. I won't *let* her be my mother."

"That's your choice, of course. You can continue to live the lie. But there's a chance that doing so will hurt her deeply."

His lower lip trembled. "She ought to be hurt. She lied to me. They *all* lied to me."

"Yes. And I can see how that would make you very angry. But they were trying to protect you from people who are stupid and ignorant. They weren't embarrassed by you. They just didn't want *you* to be embarrassed."

He squeezed the boy. "I know for a fact that your mother loves you very much. Most ladies, when they bear a child outside of marriage, give it away to be raised by someone else. Then they can go on to live their lives as they please, to marry where they please. But she didn't do that. She gave up the chance of marriage and having a family and home of her own so she could be near you, to see you grow up, to take care of you."

George swallowed. "I still say she should have told me. Mother and Father should have told me."

"Yes, they probably should have. But sometimes grown-ups don't know what to do any better than children. And consider this—most children only have one mother. I lost my mother when I was your age. Do you know how jealous I am of you for having *two* mothers who dote on you and brag about how clever you are? You're very lucky."

George scowled at him.

"I suppose you're not feeling very lucky right now, but that time will come."

"Does this mean you're not going to marry Aunt . . . my mother?"

Jarret smiled. "How about this? If you'll forgo the duel by fowling piece, I'll ask your mother again to marry me. But if she refuses me, there's not much I can do. You'll just have to accept her decision. Can you do that?"

"I suppose." He worried the edge of his coat with his hands. "Does that mean you're going to take me back to Burton?"

"Actually, I would imagine that your family is already on their way here."

"They don't know I came to London. I didn't leave a note or anything."

"I daresay that won't stop them," he said dryly. "If I know your mother, she has already browbeaten every citizen in Burton to find someone who could tell her where you went."

George shook his head vigorously. "Toby Mawer won't tell. I gave him a watch."

"Toby Mawer . . . isn't he the fellow you called your archenemy?"

"Yes."

"Never trust an archenemy, lad. We're better off sending an express to Burton to tell them that you're with me. I'd hate to head there and chance missing them as they came this direction." He patted the boy's shoulder. "Besides, I want you to meet my family. Just in case they become your family, too."

George's face brightened. "If you marry my . . . mother, you'd be my father, wouldn't you?"

"Stepfather, yes. And my brother Gabe, the one who races horses, would be your uncle. Indeed, you'd gain two uncles, two aunts, and a great-grandmother. Not quite as good as a brother and sisters, perhaps, but it would be something." He cast the boy a sly glance. "Of course, that's only if you choose to live in London with your mother, and let everyone know that you're a bastard. I won't blame you if you don't want that."

Leaving George to ponder that, he rose and called for Croft. As soon as the clerk entered, he gave him instructions on sending an express letter to the Lakes in Burton.

Gran strode into the room behind him. "When did you last eat, George?" No doubt she'd been listening at the door and knew everything.

George hunched his shoulders. "A lady on the coach gave me some cake this morning after I ran out of money."

A tightness gripped Jarret at the thought of Geordie on the coach alone. Anything might have happened to him.

"Why don't I go get us some pasties from the cook shop on the corner?" Gran said. "That ought to hold the lad until we can get him home for a real dinner."

"Thank you, Gran."

After she left, Jarret took a seat behind the desk. "So tell me how you managed the trip to London." After George related a tale of amazing ingenuity, Jarret shook his head. "You're quite the clever lad, George Lake. Too clever for your own good, sometimes." He cast the boy a stern glance. "You do know I'm going to have to punish you for this dangerous excursion. We can't have you taking such chances again and scaring your family to death."

"Punish me?" George squeaked.

"That's what fathers do, isn't it?"

First confusion, then anger crossed George's face, but Jarret could see a tiny bit of relief there, too. George *was* a clever boy, after all. And clever boys wanted someone to rein them in when they did something wrong.

He took George's silence for consent. "Well then, we'll have to come up with something suitable. Perhaps a day helping to muck out the brewery stables might work."

"Yes, sir," George said with a bit more enthusiasm than was warranted.

Jarrett hid a smile. George was in for a surprise if he thought he'd find any thoroughbreds in Plumtree's stables. There were only very large, very dull cart horses who produced a prodigious amount of manure. It would definitely be a punishment George would remember.

"I have a question, sir."

"Ask away."

"How do you plan to convince Aunt Annabel . . . my mother, I mean . . . to marry you?"

"I have no idea. Any suggestions?"

George frowned, clearly giving the idea serious thought. "You should start by telling her how pretty she looks. Father, I mean, my uncle, always does that when he wants to get around my . . . my . . ."

"That's an excellent idea," Jarret said gently.

"Tell her she's clever, too," Geordie offered. "She's not like other ladies, you know—she fancies herself as clever, and she gets insulted if you say otherwise."

That's because she *was* clever. Jarret loved that about her.

*Loved?*

He rolled the idea about in his mind and realized that he meant it. He'd been so busy holding on to an old way of life that didn't work—had *never* really worked—that he'd missed the truth staring him in the face.

He loved her. He didn't want to be without her. It hurt too much to be without her.

He didn't care about protecting his heart any longer. She was right—some risks *were* worth taking.

"I suppose it would help to tell her that I love her," Jarret said.

George screwed up his face. "If you *have* to. That's awfully mushy. But I guess ladies like that sort of thing."

Jarret bit back a smile. "In my experience, they pretty much expect it in a marriage proposal."

George sighed. "Women are a lot of trouble, aren't they?"

"Yes." He stared at the boy he hoped to be raising soon. Funny how the thought didn't panic him anymore. "But trust me, lad, they're worth it. They're definitely worth it."

# *Chapter Twenty-seven*

The trip to London seemed endless. They made it in seventeen hours, which was nothing short of miraculous. Hugh had spared no expense. With Geordie having several hours' start on them aboard a mail coach that could go much faster than Hugh's rig, they'd worried about the amount of time he would be left to his own devices in London.

She nearly wept with relief when their first stop, at the brewery—the only place they knew of that he might go to—yielded the information that Geordie was safe at Mrs. Plumtree's town house. Mr. Croft even accompanied them there in order to direct them, a kindness for which Annabel couldn't stop thanking him.

But as they approached the house in fashionable Mayfair, her thoughts turned to another problem. If Geordie knew the truth now, he was bound to be angry. How were they to handle that? What was she to say?

It occurred to her that Jarret might be there, too, that she might get to see him again, but she shoved that thought far down in her mind. She could handle only one looming disaster at a time.

They arrived at Mrs. Plumtree's town house shortly after ten in the morning, where they were immediately shown into an elegant dining room. There they found Geordie surrounded by Jarret's family, being pampered and coddled, fed with kippers and eggs and every delicacy the boy loved for breakfast. She recognized Lady Minerva and Lord Gabriel, and assumed that the other young woman was Lady Celia and the elderly woman was Jarret's grandmother.

Jarret sat beside Geordie, joking about something to do with horses.

Geordie spotted them, and for a moment, joy leaped into his face. Then it faded to a troubled expression that cut her to the heart. Especially when he jerked his gaze to his plate, refusing to look at her.

He knew the truth, all right. She'd lost his trust, and she didn't know how to get it back.

Jarret rose, his eyes kind as he laid a hand on Geordie's shoulder. "You see, George, it's just as I told you. They probably didn't even see the express I sent. They must have left there long before it arrived. They were worried about you."

"Terrified, more like," Annabel choked out.

Geordie just continued to stare into his plate.

She wanted to rush over and haul him into her arms for a bone-crushing hug, but she was afraid that would only make matters worse.

Jarret smoothed over the moment by making introductions. Then he turned to his grandmother and said, "I think we should let the Lakes have a moment alone."

"I want *you* to stay, Lord Jarret," Geordie protested. "If that's all right with you."

When Jarret looked to Annabel she nodded. Geordie had always idolized him, and though it hurt that her son would run to Jarret instead of her after hearing the truth, she would accept anything that might make this encounter easier.

Jarret resumed his seat while his family rose and left the room, their eyes full of curiosity as they passed her and Hugh. Hugh squeezed her arm encouragingly as they walked over to sit across from Geordie.

"How did you know I was here?" Geordie asked in a small voice, still not looking at them.

Annabel fought to remain calm. "Toby Mawer tried to sell the watch you gave him, and the shop owner saw the inscription. When Hugh threatened to have Toby arrested, he admitted that you'd gone to London to see 'some fancy gent.'"

Geordie looked up at Jarret. "You were right, sir. Never trust an archenemy."

"I don't think you realize the enormity of what you did, lad," Hugh said sharply. "You scared your mother and me to death!"

Geordie's angry gaze shot to Hugh. "Which mother? The one who pretended to be my mother while all of you lied to me? Or the one who actually gave birth to me?"

As Annabel flinched at Geordie's sharp tone, Hugh let out a low curse, but when he started to speak, she put a hand on his arm.

"Both," Annabel said. "We were all petrified with fear. I kept imagining you lying in a ditch somewhere, beaten and bleeding and all alone—"

When she broke off with a sob, Geordie looked at her for the first time. "I'm sorry. I-I shouldn't have run away."

She reached across the table for his hand, but he jerked it back. Her heart sank. "I know I've hurt you deeply by keeping the truth from you. I should have told you that I was your mother a long time ago. But I was so afraid you—"

Her breath caught in her throat, and she had to swallow before she could go on. "I was afraid you would hate me. That you'd never forgive me for lying to you. And I love you so much that I couldn't bear to have you hate me."

His chin began to tremble, and he dropped his gaze to his plate again. "You're embarrassed by me—all of you. I heard you tell Fa—your brother—that if you married Lord Jarret and took me to London, it would embarrass everyone."

She vaguely remembered saying something like that, but he was taking it all wrong. "I'm sorry, I didn't mean that how it sounded. I was thinking that I had no right to expose Hugh and Sissy to public slander by claiming you as my son." Her voice shook. "But it wasn't *you* whom I was worried would embarrass them. It was me."

Geordie lifted his gaze to her, looking truly perplexed. "Why?"

"In a situation like this, it's not the illegitimate child whom people blame; it's the mother. They see her as . . . wicked. They see her family as wicked for covering up her indiscretion. I don't mind if they call me a whore behind my back, but they would also malign Hugh and Sissy. I didn't feel I had the right to put them through that."

She took Hugh's hand. "My dear brother assures me that they don't care one whit what people say. But it wasn't just them I worried about. I worried about how you would feel, too." She lowered her voice. "I thought you might resent me. Hate me for making you the brunt of people's cruel comments."

"I don't hate you," Geordie said in a small voice. "I could never hate you."

Relief rushed through her.

"What I don't understand, boy," Hugh said, "is why you came here. What in God's name did you think Lord Jarret could do?"

Jarret met Annabel's gaze with one so kind, it made her throat close up. "He had some idea that if I married you and took you away to London, then everything could go back to how it was before. I believe young George is particularly upset about the fact that, as he sees it, he no longer has sisters and a brother or grandparents. Or a father."

Annabel's heart broke. She hadn't even considered that he might feel he'd lost most of his family in one fell swoop. Still, it hurt that he would want to be rid of her rather than lose them. It was exactly what she'd been afraid of.

"You will always be my son in my heart, boy," Hugh said fiercely. "I don't care what happens. And I know Sissy feels the same."

"Geordie," Annabel said, forcing herself to speak the words, "we can still go back to how things were." She swallowed her tears, determined not to let him see them. This was hard enough for him as it was. "You'll call me Aunt Annabel and they'll be your parents, and everything will be as it was."

"No," Geordie said firmly. His eyes misted over as he looked at her. "Lord Jarret said I can't un-drink the water, and he's right. I can't go back. *We* can't go back. We have to go on." He glanced up at Jarret. "Are you going to ask her?"

The abrupt change of subject threw Annabel off, until it dawned on her what he must be talking about.

"Yes," Jarret said, his gaze locking with hers, "but it's not something I'm prepared to do before an audience, lad." He looked at Hugh. "Mr. Lake, you and I had a discussion the night before I left Burton, and I told you I didn't know what I wanted. I do now. So if you wouldn't mind taking George for a moment, and letting me speak to Annabel alone . . ."

"Of course," Hugh said as he stood.

When Geordie came around the table to meet him, Annabel couldn't stand it any longer. She rose to grab him and hold him close.

For a moment, he remained stiff in her arms. Then his arms came around her, and he pressed his head against her shoulder. "It'll be all right, Mother," he whispered. "Really, it will."

*Mother.* Tears rolled down her cheeks. She'd waited so long to hear him call her that, and it was the most beautiful thing she'd ever heard.

She watched him until he was out the door, trying not to make an absolute cake of herself. Then she felt Jarret press something into her hand. A handkerchief.

"You're right," he said softly. "You do cry a lot."

His pity was almost as painful to her as Geordie's distance had been. She knew what was coming, after all. Drying her tears, she turned to face him. "Jarret, I know you feel sorry for me now, and probably feel obligated to——"

"Don't tell me what I feel," he said, his voice firmer. He pulled out her chair. "Sit down, dearling. I need to tell you a story."

She blinked but did as he asked. He took the chair next to hers and turned it so they were half facing each other, their knees touching.

"There was once a boy who loved going to his grandparents' brewery more than anything in the world. He liked the fragrant smell of hops and the golden color of the barley as it roasted. He would have lived there if his grandparents had let him."

He took her hands in his. "Then his parents died in a terrible accident, and his widowed grandmother suddenly had five children to raise—something she hadn't planned on while also running a brewery. She did her best with them, but the brewery had to be her first priority, since it was the source of most of the family income. The eldest—the heir to the estate—was already in school, the oldest girl had a governess, and the two young ones were still in the nursery, so they had their nursery maid. But the second son was a difficult matter."

Annabel sucked in a breath as it dawned on her what he was doing.

He gazed beyond her to the window. "He was used to spending part of each day at the brewery, but his grandmother decided it would be best to pack him off to school with his older brother. She said he ought to be a barrister or a clergyman or a soldier, something befitting his rank. And no matter how much he begged to be allowed to stay at the brewery, she refused."

"Oh, Jarret," she said softly, feeling the pain he must have felt, to lose his family and his future in one stroke.

His voice grew thick with emotion. "He didn't like school. The boys taunted him with vile rumors about the deaths of his parents, and he missed the estate that his grandmother closed up after the accident. Fortunately—or unfortunately, depending on how you look at it—he discovered he was good at gambling, that he could keep the bullies in their place with his prowess at cards. His father had taught him how to play. It was the only remnant left from his old life, and he desperately needed something to cling to from that."

A long breath escaped him. "You asked me once how I became a gambler. That's how it started. Perhaps it made sense for a boy of thirteen, who missed his family so much that he suffered physical pain every time he thought of them.

"But I let it go on long beyond the time I was old enough to know better. I fully embraced Lady Luck, and because I already knew she was a fickle mistress, I was immune to the pain she could cause. Then I set out to make myself immune to the pain people could cause. That was easy. I just made sure they never got close enough to me to hurt me."

He stared down at her hands, rubbing his thumbs gently over the knuckles. "Then I met you. You were stubborn and beautiful and clever as hell, and you entranced me from the moment you waltzed into the brewery office. I panicked, as men often do when they suddenly glimpse a future very different from the one they've imagined for themselves. I did a number of stupid things while trying to hold you at arm's length and convince myself that I couldn't care for you. That I didn't care for you."

His gaze lifted to meet hers, deepening to that color of the ocean that she always adored. "But I do." He brought her hands to his lips and kissed them. "I love you, Annabel Lake. I love the way you take care of everyone around you. I love how hard you fight for your son. And most of all, I love that when you look at me, you don't see me as I am, but me as I could be. If I could only find it in my heart."

Tears welled up and she fought them back, not wanting to spoil the moment. But it was hard, because it was when she was really, really happy that she cried the most.

He smiled his dimpled smile. "Well, I've *found* something in my heart, my love, and it's you. You fill it up so completely that I don't need anything else." His gaze turned solemn. "I don't want to be the river anymore. I want to be the earth that the tree roots in. And I believe that I can, if you'll be my tree. Will you?"

It was too much. She began to cry, though she smiled so he'd know that they were happy tears. "That proposal . . . is vastly superior . . . to your last one," she choked out between sobs. "I would very much love to be your tree."

He kissed her so tenderly, so sweetly, that her heart filled up with him, too. And it was all the more precious because she knew it wasn't just a prelude to lovemaking.

He loved her. He really loved her! And he wanted to marry her, despite—

She jerked back from him. "What about Geordie?"

He took the handkerchief from her and dried her tears. "He and I have been discussing the matter, and we think we've come up with an excellent solution to everyone's problem." He rose, tugging her to her feet. "But I want you to hear it from him. Or rather from him and Gran, since they were the ones to devise it."

His *grandmother* had been part of a solution to the problem of Geordie's bastardy? Amazing. Perhaps he was right when he'd said she wouldn't care.

Annabel let him lead her into the hall where, unsurprisingly, the entire family stood. When Lady Minerva cast her a knowing smile, Annabel blushed. Oh, Lord, they were as bad as Geordie, listening at doors.

"All right, George," Jarret said, "it's your turn. Tell Annabel your plan for where you should live."

Geordie dragged in a deep breath as he faced her. "Well, remember how you said that I should go to school? As it happens, Harrow is six miles from Ealing, and they take day pupils. Mrs. Plumtree says I could live at Halstead Hall with you and Lord Jarret, and go to school there every day."

"No one would find it odd that the boy would live with his aunt and uncle while in school," Mrs. Plumtree pointed out. "They need never know of his true relationship to either of you, if that is what he prefers."

"And frankly," Jarret put in, "he'd be better off not staying in the boarding facilities."

Given what Jarret had said about his own experience at school, she understood why he'd feel that way, although Geordie might prefer it eventually.

"For the holidays, of course, I'd go home to Burton," Geordie went on, with a furtive glance at Hugh. "If they want me there."

"Of course we want you there, boy," Hugh said. "Sissy would feel bereft if she had to do without you completely."

Geordie shoved his hands in his coat pockets. "So what do you think? No one would have me all the time, but I'd get to be with everyone some of the time."

Annabel gazed at her dear son, then at the man she loved more than life. Had she really thought she could give one of them up for the other? She must have been mad. And thank God they'd found a solution so she didn't have to.

"I think it's brilliant," she said, tears threatening again. "Absolutely brilliant."

"He's a clever boy, our George," Jarret said, sliding an arm about her waist. "But then, his mother is clever, too. Which is why she has finally consented to be my wife."

As the hall exploded with congratulations and cheers all around, Annabel didn't know whether to blush or beam or just start crying again. She was so happy, she didn't know if her heart could take it.

When the noise died down, Lady Minerva said, "Are you

pleased now, Gran? Not only is Jarret running the brewery, but you got him married off, too, and gained a new great-grandchild in the bargain. Surely that will satisfy your thirst to see us wed."

Gran thrust out her chin. "Still three to go, my girl."

"Gran!" Lord Gabriel protested. "You're being unreasonable!"

"Give it up, Gabe," Jarret remarked. "You know how Gran is when she sets her mind to something. She is not going to be moved on this." He gazed at Mrs. Plumtree. "And speaking of moving, perhaps we should move this celebration into the drawing room. Gran's been on her feet for far too long, and she's looking a little peaked right now."

"I am not!" she said, but Annabel noticed that she didn't struggle when Lady Celia and Lord Gabriel hurried to her side and each took an arm to guide her down the hall.

Lady Minerva paused beside Jarret. "Does this mean you've become a traitor like Oliver, and gone over to Gran's side?"

Jarret smiled. "No. I think she has sound reasons, but she's going about it all wrong. So if you find a way to fight her ultimatum, I'll back you every step." He cast her a considering glance. "I was thinking we should consult Giles Masters on the legal aspects of it. What do you think?"

"That ne'er-do-well?" Lady Minerva said. A blush inexplicably stained her cheeks. "I can't imagine what good *he* could do."

"He's a brilliant barrister."

"In his own mind, perhaps," she shot back, and turned to walk away. "But do as you please. He's *your* friend."

"What was that all about?" Annabel said as Jarret watched his sister walk off.

He frowned. "I'm not sure."

Hugh glanced from Annabel to Jarret. "It looks like you

and I will be having a very thorough talk about settlements and pin money, my lord."

"I'd say that's a necessity," Jarret said, "especially now that we're all going to be quite a bit richer." When Hugh looked perplexed, he added, "The East India captains have agreed to take two thousand barrels of your pale ale, along with a few hundred of some Plumtree varieties. I hope that in time, we'll have them taking even more."

Hugh just stood there, stunned. Annabel whirled toward Jarret with a little cry and showered him with kisses. "You did it! Oh, I *knew* you could do it! You're the most brilliant brewer in England!"

A broad smile split Hugh's face. "Thank you, my lord, for helping us."

He thrust his hand out to Jarret, who took it and pumped it enthusiastically. "I'll tell you all about it," Jarret said, "but first I want a moment alone with my future bride."

With a nod, Hugh put his arm about Geordie's shoulder. "Come on, son. Let's give the lovebirds a little privacy."

As soon as everyone had cleared from the hall, Jarret tugged her into the deserted dining room. He pulled her into his arms and kissed her, this time with substantially more heat than before.

After he had her quivering from head to toe, he drew back to murmur, "How soon can we be married?"

"As soon as you like."

"Gran will want a grand affair, with acres of wedding cake and a ceremony at St. Paul's. I don't want to deprive you of that if that's what you want, too."

She laughed. "As long as I have you, my love, we could get married in a barn."

His gaze smoldered. "Considering that we nearly consummated our union in one, that seems appropriate. But I'd settle for a special license and a small gathering at Halstead Hall, if you're amenable."

"That sounds perfect. Of course, if your grandmother doesn't approve—"

"Gran will approve of anything, as long as she sees me married. I daresay we could hold the wedding in the brewery next to the mashtun, and she'd agree."

"I seriously doubt that," she said with a laugh.

A sudden gleam appeared in his eye. "Care to place a wager on it, my love?"

She eyed him askance. "I thought you gave up gambling."

"Ah, but this is a private wager. Surely that can be allowed."

"What would be the stakes?" she asked archly.

"A lifetime in my bed," he said.

She bit back a smile. "And if *you* win?"

He blinked, then burst into laughter.

And as the sounds of family merrymaking drifted to them from down the hall, he showed her just what to expect from winning a hellion in her bed.

# Epilogue

$\mathcal{I}$n the end, they had a simple wedding in the Sharpe family chapel less than two weeks after Annabel's arrival in London. Though they would have preferred to wait until Jarret's brother Oliver returned to England, they had to marry swiftly. They wanted to get George into school for the next term at Harrow, and he couldn't very well live with an "aunt and uncle" who weren't married.

Now, six weeks after the wedding, Jarret headed up the main stairs at Halstead Hall. They didn't intend to live here forever—once George was done with school, they would find a place in town closer to the brewery—but he was enjoying being in his childhood home again.

If only Annabel felt better, his life would be complete. This stomach ailment of hers worried him—she'd always seemed too resilient for such things, and it was lingering too long. He shouldn't have left her to go to town with the others to meet Oliver and Maria at the docks, but she'd insisted.

He cracked open the door to find her dozing. The late afternoon sun spilled across the beautiful hair that he never tired of touching and the sweet features that always caused a clutch in his chest. It was hard to believe that she was his. Why had he ever balked at marriage? She was the joy of his life.

Not only was she an ever entertaining companion, in bed and out, but she was a wonderful partner in business, as well. Until she'd started feeling ill she'd gone to the brewery with him every day to experiment with various brews or consult with Harper about innovations Jarret wanted to try. He liked that he could talk to her about the business and she understood what he meant, what his difficulties were. She made excellent suggestions, and she knew how to put her finger on what was bothering him about any situation.

Suddenly she stirred, and his heart quickened. "How are you feeling?" he asked as he came toward the bed.

As sleep faded from her face, she shot him a daggered glance. "Awful. And it's all your fault."

"Why? I told you not to eat those pickles, since they don't seem to agree with you. But you're fond of the strangest foods—"

"There's a reason for that." She sat up, still glaring at him. "I'm not ill. I'm *enceinte*."

It took a moment for that to sink in, then relief made him so giddy, he laughed.

"It's not funny!" she cried as she rose. "You assured me that your cundum things worked. You *promised,* yet here I am, in exactly the same situation I was thirteen years ago—"

"Not *exactly* the same situation," he pointed out cheerily. "You're married."

"But what if I hadn't been? What if you'd trotted off to London and left me with child, after swearing to me that there was no chance—"

"Well, there's always a *chance,* even with cundums. There could have been a hole in it, or perhaps it wasn't tied tightly enough, or—"

She hit him with a pillow. "You told me it *always* worked! How do you know you don't have ten little by-blows running about London from all your wild living?"

He struggled to hide his smiles, but it was difficult. She was so fetchingly annoyed. And she was bearing his child. His first child!

"I assure you, my love, if I'd sired by-blows, their mothers would have come to me with their hands out by now. I'm a marquess's son, you know."

"I know only too well," she said with a sniff. "And after all those years of waltzing about town, throwing your seed wherever—"

"It wasn't so much throwing as sowing." At her glare, he laughed and drew her into his arms. "Come now, surely you're not really angry about having our baby, are you?"

The fight seemed to go right out of her. "No," she admitted. Then her features softened, and tears filled her eyes.

Jarret offered her one of the handkerchiefs he'd learned to keep always at hand. "Let me guess. You cry when you're with child, too."

"Yes, but they're tears of joy. Do you realize this will be the first time I can hold my child without worrying that people will guess the truth? I can dote on him—or her—without restraint. This baby will be truly mine."

"And mine," he protested.

She smiled at him through her tears. "Of course."

He drew her to the door. "Come, you have to meet my brother and sister-in-law."

"Now? But I look a fright!" she wailed.

"You look absolutely stunning," he said, meaning every word. "As always."

"Flatterer," she said, but a small smile played about her lips.

Still, he could tell she was nervous as they approached the drawing room. "Relax," he murmured. "I'm sure Oliver left his quizzing glass in America and broke his fancy cane while promenading at court."

That got a laugh out of her, which was why, when they entered, her eyes were sparkling and her lips sweetly curved. Jarret wanted to kiss her right then and there, and only refrained because his rapscallion brothers were watching.

Oliver must have been able to read his mind, for he shot Jarret a smug grin as he rose with his wife and came to greet them.

"Oliver, Maria," Jarret said, "may I present my wife, Annabel."

As Annabel curtsied very low, Oliver bent to take her hand and squeeze it warmly. "So you're the brewster my brother couldn't stop talking about on our way from London. I gather that you share his penchant for card playing."

She turned crimson. "Jarret, you devil, surely you didn't—"

"Gabe told him. He loves to relate the story of how my wife beat me at the tables the first time we met."

"At least she didn't try to thrust a sword through your throat," Oliver said.

Maria sniffed. "You deserved it, and you know it." She turned to Annabel with a wide smile. "I daresay you'd have done the same if Jarret had tried to have *you* arrested."

"Oh, I would have aimed somewhere lower than his throat."

Everyone burst into laughter.

"You're right, Jarret," Oliver said, clapping him on the shoulder. "She fits in with our family splendidly."

Suddenly George entered the drawing room, having just arrived home from school.

"There you are, my boy," Jarret said. "I've got some news I think you'll like." He ignored the elbow Annabel dug into his ribs. "Looks like you're going to have a brother or a sister after all."

"That's fantastic!" George cried, looking genuinely happy to hear it.

Jarret happened to glance at Minerva and saw a quick flash of envy cross her face. It confirmed for him a decision he'd been vacillating over ever since the day he proposed to Annabel—whether he should tell his siblings that they needn't worry about Gran's ultimatum anymore, because he meant to support them with the brewery.

One thing had held him back. Oliver had once said that they'd been sleepwalking since their parents' deaths, and sometimes he wondered if Oliver might be right. Minerva in particular had shut herself off from the world.

If Jarret believed for one moment that she could truly be happy alone, writing her books, he would have supported her decision and fought Gran tooth and nail for her. But he began to think that *wasn't* really what she wanted. Her books seemed as much a way of hiding from life and happiness as his gambling had been.

He wanted better for her. For all of them. Especially now that he had it himself. And though he wouldn't have chosen Gran's methods to force the issue, he was willing to let things ride and see what happened. He knew his sister would never marry without love. So if she and the others were willing to risk losing Gran's fortune to remain unmarried, then so be it: he would support them. But there was no need to tell them that yet.

"Are you sure that your wife is breeding, old boy?" Gabe asked Jarret, eyes twinkling. "You've only been married six weeks. It's rather early to know a thing like that, isn't it?"

Damn. He should have done some mathematics before he opened his mouth. Annabel was going to kill him.

"Oh, hush up, you rascal," Gran barked at Gabe as she came toward them. "This is my first great-grandchild. I don't give a damn which side of the blanket it was conceived upon."

Oliver laughed. "Actually, it's *not* your first great-grandchild. As it happens, Maria and I are also expecting a child. And I can assure you it will arrive before Jarret's."

"Oh, Lord," Maria said with a conspiratorial glance at Annabel, "now they're going to make it into some sort of competition."

"Better them than me," Gabe said.

"Your time is coming," Jarret said, meaning it for a warning to Minerva, as well. "Gran has already said she isn't relenting."

"No, I am not," Gran said. "But enough about that. This news calls for a toast."

She and Oliver wandered off, discussing which ancient wine to fetch from the cellar. Celia drew Maria into a discussion about renovations to Halstead Hall's old nursery, and George went to tell Gabe about the new rig he'd seen on his way home from school.

As Jarret gazed on his family, affection welled up to choke him. He slid his arm about Annabel's waist. "They're quite a rambunctious bunch, aren't they?"

"Yes." She shot him a minxish smile. "And I snagged the best one of the lot."

He brushed a kiss to her hair. "Sorry if I embarrassed you by announcing the baby at such an early date."

"It's all right. They would have figured it out once the child was born." She paused. "You *are* happy about the baby, aren't you?"

"*Very* happy."

It was true. He ought to be terrified. One more person relying on him, one more person he might care for, who could be taken away from him by a fickle twist of Fate.

But in the past few weeks with Annabel, he'd come to realize that he'd had everything wrong. Life wasn't for lamenting what you'd lost. It was for enjoying what you had, for however long you got to have it. While it was always terrible to lose those precious to you, it was far more terrible never to have had them at all.

So as his family laughed and toasted and shared their joy, he thanked whatever Fate had allowed him to have this moment, these people, this woman at his side. It was finally his time. And it was good.

# Author's Note

Brewing was a time-honored profession for women in England (alewives and brewsters), so I thought it might be fun to have a heroine who enjoyed that particular profession. Plumtree Brewery and Lake Ale are my inventions, but beyond that, all the details about the brewery business are taken straight out of history. India Pale Ale really did come about as a result of transporting October brews to India. And the Burton brewery business did get a huge boost from the clash between the East India Company and Hodgson's brewery over his unwise business practices and his attempts to cut out the captains of the ships. Allsopp and Bass made a fortune by taking advantage of that conflict and of the unique water of Burton, which has salts that improve the brewing process. Bass is still around today.

The alligator at the Daventry market came right out of an account I read of an English town market in this period. I embellished it a little, but I couldn't resist throwing an alligator into my story!

Turn the page
for a special look at
the next delightful romance in

The Hellions of Halstead Hall series

## *HOW TO WOO A RELUCTANT LADY*

featuring the beautiful and independent
Lady Minerva Sharpe

by *New York Times* bestselling author

## Sabrina Jeffries

Coming soon from Pocket Books

To Giles Masters's great surprise, Lady Minerva Sharpe burst into laughter. "You? As my husband? Are you out of your mind?"

He hadn't expected wild enthusiasm, but incredulity wasn't what he'd been aiming for, either. "Quite possibly."

It was the God's honest truth. He'd spent the entire journey over here rehearsing what he would say, how he would approach Minerva, how he could intimidate her into stopping this nonsense of putting him in her books. Then he'd reached the gates of Halstead Hall and seen the line of prospective suitors there in answer to her advertisement for a husband. That's when it had dawned on him that the best solution was the simplest.

Make her his wife. That way he could control her and her "fiction." She would never damage her own husband's future—she was too practical for that. And she had to marry anyway, if she and her siblings were to gain their inheritance.

A few years ago, the idea of marrying Minerva might have thrown him into a bachelor panic, but with the upturn in his career, he realized that he would have to settle down with a wife soon—especially if he became King's Counsel.

And if he must have a wife, it might as well be one he desired. Minerva certainly qualified, no matter how she tried to hide her allure. Today she wore a fashionable morning gown of printed green muslin with a number of fussy flounces about the hem, those hideous puffy sleeves that had become so popular, and a bodice that went right up to her chin.

Every feminine curve had been buried beneath furbelows and padded sleeves and lace edgings, and it didn't matter one whit. He already knew that her figure was lushly feminine. Thanks to the many evening gowns he'd seen her in, he could imagine it as clearly as if she were naked. And just the thought of taking her to bed made his blood quicken and his good sense vanish. Truth was, she did something extraordinary to him every time he saw her.

But God help him if she ever guessed it. Reading her books had offered him a peek inside her fathomless brain, so he knew she was clever enough to wrap him entirely about her finger if he ever allowed it.

"As if I would marry a scoundrel like you," she informed him with a minxish look that grated on his nerves. "Are you daft?"

"I believe we've already established that I'm halfway to being a Bedlamite. But humor me anyway." Apparently she wasn't clever enough to see that marriage to him was her only viable choice. He would have to correct that. "You ought to leap at the chance to marry a scoundrel, given how much you enjoy writing about them."

She eyed him as if he really *were* a Bedlamite. "It's not the same. You make an excellent villain in my books precisely because you would make a wretched husband. You don't fit any of my criteria for a suitable spouse."

"Criteria? Ah yes, the line of interviewees outside. You must have drummed up some questions for your prospective spouses." He glanced about the room, spotted a stack of paper atop a red lacquered table, and strode over.

When he picked up the sheaf of paper, she hurried over. "Give me that!"

He held her off with one hand while he scanned the first page. "Let me see. . . . Ah, yes. Question One: 'Have you ever been married before?' That one's easy. No."

"Because no woman would have you," she said dryly.

"That probably had something to do with it, along with the fact that I never offered for anyone. Question Two: 'Describe your ideal wife.'" His gaze trailed leisurely over Minerva. "About five foot seven, golden brown hair, green eyes, with a bosom that would make a man weep and a bottom that—"

"Giles!" she protested, hot color filling her cheeks as she crossed her arms over that bosom.

He grinned. "Suffice it to say, she's quite beautiful."

The brief satisfaction in her eyes told him that Minerva wasn't as lacking in feminine vanity as she liked to imply. "I wasn't speaking of physical appearances. I wanted a description of their ideal wife's *character*."

"I see. Well then, my ideal wife is an unpredictable hellion, with a penchant for getting into trouble and speaking her mind."

"Sounds dangerous." Her lips twitched. "And utterly unsuitable for a man who likes to keep secrets."

"Good point." Except that her unsuitability was precisely the thing that intrigued him. She was wrong for him in every way. And that only made him want her more.

Besides, he could handle Minerva. He was probably the only man in England who could.

He read on. "Question Three: 'What domestic duties will you expect your wife to perform?'" He laughed. "Are you looking for some indication of the frequency with which your applicant would wish you to share his bed? Or a description of the acts he would wish you to 'perform'?"

She blushed prettily. "Those are *not* the sort of duties I meant, and you know it."

"It's the only sort of duty that matters to those louts out there," he said coldly. "Since they intend to hire plenty of servants with your fortune, they need only focus on the essentials of having a wife. For them, those essentials are obvious."

"But not for you? You haven't answered the question, after all."

"Whatever your 'domestic duties,' I'm sure you can handle them."

She glared at him. "It's whether I *want* to that's in question."

Leaving that alone for the moment, he turned back to her list. "Question Four: 'How do you feel about having your wife write novels?'" He snorted. "Did you honestly expect anyone to answer this truthfully with you breathing down their necks?"

"Not everyone is as devious as you."

"Forgive me. I didn't realize you were expecting a procession of saints this morning."

She rolled her eyes. "Just for amusement's sake, what would be *your* honest answer?"

He shrugged. "I have no objection to my wife writing novels as long as they're not about *me.*"

"You say that now," she said with a quiet seriousness to her voice. "But you might think otherwise when you come home to find that your dinner isn't on the table because your wife was so swept up in her story that she forgot what time it was. Or when you find her sitting in her dressing gown scribbling madly, while your house goes to rack and ruin about your ears."

"I can afford servants," he countered.

"It's not just that." She gestured to the list. "Read the next question."

He glanced down at the paper. " 'What sort of wife do you require?' "

"Any respectable man requires a wife who lives an irreproachable life. Why do you think I haven't married? Because I can't live such a life without giving up writing my novels." She flashed him a sad smile. "And you in particular will require an irreproachable wife if you're to succeed as a barrister."

She had a point, but not one he would argue at present. "I've already succeeded as a barrister. In any case, I haven't lived an irreproachable life, so why should I expect my wife to do so?"

Her gaze turned cynical. "Come now, we both know that men can spend their evenings in the stews and their mornings cropsick, and other men just clap them on the back and call them fine fellows. But their wives aren't allowed to have even a hint of scandal tarnish their good names. They certainly aren't allowed to write novels for public consumption." She gave a dramatic shudder. "Why, that smacks of being in trade. Horrors!"

"I already told you—"

"Did you know that my mother was a writer, too?"

Now she'd surprised him. "What did she write?"

"Poetry for children, like that written by Ann and Jane Taylor. She used to read her verses to me, asking my opinion." A sigh escaped her. "But she stopped after she and Papa argued over her wish to have them published. He said that marchionesses did not publish books. It wasn't done." Her voice hardened. "It was fine for him to toss up the skirts of any female who took his fancy, but God forbid Mama should publish a book."

He tensed. "I am not your father, Minerva."

"You differ from him only in the fact that you're unmarried. Safer to keep it that way, don't you think?"

Damn it, sometimes his life as a scoundrel, meant to disguise his real activities, slapped him right in the face. "Or a man could change."

"For a woman? In fiction, perhaps, but rarely in life."

"Says the woman who buries herself in her books," he snapped. "Your idea of venturing out into life is to surround yourself with your siblings and hold off every eligible gentleman who might come near you."

Her eyes flashed fire. "Oh, that is *so* like a man. I'm not jumping to marry you, so I must be a spinster pining away alone in her room writing. I tried venturing out into it today, didn't I? But my brothers wouldn't let me."

"That was merely a ploy and you know it. You were never serious about interviewing gentlemen as husbands. You just wanted to provoke your grandmother into giving up her demands."

He knew he'd hit on the truth when she paled. "What makes you say that?"

"You advertised it in *The Ladies Magazine* when you could as easily have managed it privately with more discretion. And you just explained to me how no respectable man wants a woman who writes novels, yet you say you don't want *me* because I'm a scoundrel. If you don't want a scoundrel and you don't think you can have a respectable gentleman—"

"All right, drat you." She tipped up her chin. "I have no intention of marrying you or anyone else. Can you blame me?"

"No," he said sincerely. When she blinked, he added, "But your grandmother has made it perfectly clear that you must take a husband, so you have no choice. You can't touch your inheritance otherwise, and neither can your siblings. And as long as you *have* to marry, why not marry me?"

"Is that why you want me as your wife?" she shot back. "Because of the money?"

"If you mean to insult me, you'll have to try another tack. Money isn't an issue for me, Minerva."

"I doubt that. You're a second son."

"And a barrister who is widely sought after for his legal advice, and who charges exorbitant fees. I can afford to keep you in gowns and jewels perfectly well without your grandmother's money."

"That very statement shows how little you know me. I don't care about gowns and jewels—"

"But you care about Gabe and Celia," he said softly. "And they'll be left destitute if you don't marry."

A troubled expression knit her brow. "I'm working on a plan to change that."

"This interview idea?" He gave her a mocking smile. "First of all, your brothers are nipping that in the bud as we speak. They're not about to let their sister marry some stranger off the street. They're not even going to let you be *exposed* to such men. Secondly, you know perfectly well that Mrs. Plumtree won't let your antics sway her from her purpose. You'll only delay the inevitable."

"Jarret was able to sway her from her purpose," Minerva retorted.

"Because he had something to bargain with. You don't."

She turned on her heel. "Feel free to leave at any time, Mr. Masters."

"You know what I don't see in this list of bloody questions?" Giles bit out, determined to provoke her into dealing with him. "I don't see any mention of the intimate side of marriage. No questions about what your future husband would expect from you in the bedchamber. Or what *you* could expect from *him*."

She whirled on him. "That would be vulgar."

"And interviewing gentlemen for the position of husband isn't? The trouble with you, my dear, is you've looked at marriage from every angle except the one that matters." Tossing her list onto the table, he approached her with determined steps. "How you feel about a man. What he does to you whenever he comes near. Whether he makes your heart race and your body heat. And in that area, I am the perfect husband for you."

"Really?" she said, her voice deceptively sweet. "Is this the part where you sweep me into your arms and prove how you alone make my heart race and my body heat?"

"If you insist." And with that, he caught her to him.

# *True love*
### is timeless with
### historical romances from
### Pocket Books!

**A Malory novel**

## Johanna Lindsey
# NO CHOICE BUT SEDUCTION
He'd stop at nothing to make her love him.
But should she surrender to his bold charms?

## Liz Carlyle
# Tempted All Night
When deception meets desire, even the most
careful lady can be swayed by a scoundrel....

## Julia London
# HIGHLAND SCANDAL
Which is a London rakehell more likely to survive—
a hanging, or a handfasting to a spirited Highland lass?

## Jane Feather
# A HUSBAND'S WICKED WAYS
When a spymaster proposes marriage as a cover,
a lovely young woman discovers the danger—and
delight—of risking everything for love.

Available wherever books are sold or at www.simonandschuster.com